About the Author

Bonnie Woods is a Kindle-bestselling author and editor, from and based in Manchester. She also hosts the queer podcast Swords & Sapphics with her long-distance best friend, Ivy. Under the name Rachel Bowdler, she has written *Honeymoon for One* and *Summer at the Scottish Castle*.

Kindling

Kindling

BONNIE WOODS

Harper
North

HarperNorth
Windmill Green
24 Mount Street
Manchester M2 3NX

A division of
HarperCollins*Publishers*
1 London Bridge Street
London SE1 9GF

www.harpercollins.co.uk

HarperCollins*Publishers*
Macken House
39/40 Mayor Street Upper
Dublin 1
D01 C9W8

First published by HarperNorth in 2024

5 7 9 10 8 6 4

ISBN: 978-0-00-870214-4
Printed and bound in the UK using 100% renewable electricity at
CPI Group (UK) Ltd, Croydon
This novel is entirely a work of fiction.
The names, characters and incidents portrayed in it are the work
of the author's imagination. Any resemblance to actual persons,
living or dead, events or localities is entirely coincidental.

MIX
Paper | Supporting
responsible forestry
FSC™ C007454

This book contains FSC™ certified paper and other controlled
sources to ensure responsible forest management.

For more information visit: www.harpercollins.co.uk/green

1

"Okay. *Almost* worth the three-mile trek." Harper huffed out a long breath as she stopped at the bottom of the white wooden steps. They led up to a rustic modern cottage, which would be her new home for the undecided, foreseeable future. Before she could get excited, she tutted at her lilac suitcase, purchased only last week for this very trip.

Ruined. The wheels had gathered thick carpets of moss and piles of soggy leaves after she'd dragged it along a barely-there footpath, far away from the last glimpse of civilisation. Her Uber driver had kindly thrown her out on a dead-end road and left her to fend for herself in these thick, roadless woods. "I'll nae get any closer than this, love," he'd claimed. "I'm sure it's a nice walk, though. You'll be right as rain."

It was not a nice walk at all. She had decided already that she did not like Scotland.

And Scotland did not like her, it seemed, because the country had also ruined her favourite pair of burgundy ankle boots. With a groan, she used the signpost labelling the cottage Heatherley Lodge to swipe the mud from her chunky soles. When she'd booked an extended, remote holiday with her redundancy pay, the Airbnb listing hadn't specified that finding the place would add to her growing list of newly-faced inconveniences. First she had lost her job. Then her girlfriend. Now, she had lost the will to live.

Harper had already tried to call her mum (if only to cry about it) – despite turning thirty this year, she had not outgrown that habit yet. But, naturally, there was no phone signal to be found. Only tricky-to-decipher signposts had led the way.

Never mind that, though. She was here now, and "here" looked quite nice. She pulled out her phone to snap a picture of the lovely lodge. With ivy growing up the panelled walls, an autumnal wreath hooked on the arched door, and light pouring in through floor-to-ceiling windows, it was the ideal place to wallow.

No, Harper. Not wallow. You're here to write a bestselling novel, she reminded herself. Mostly, she was here to reclaim her dignity, and romanticising her sad little life on Instagram for her ex to see seemed like a wise first step.

Propping her heavy suitcase by the steps, she searched for the most flattering angle, making sure the flame-red autumn leaves surrounding the lodge were in frame as she crouched and side-stepped her way to the perfect picture. She could already imagine sitting by the window in the orange armchair she'd seen on the listing's gallery, laptop open on a sleek glass coffee table beside a steaming mug of hot chocolate placed on a quirky coaster.

"All right. *Definitely* worth the trek. I already feel like a proper author." Writing had always been something she'd left on the back burner in favour of financial stability and a steady job in the field she'd studied – marketing – but since that had fallen through, it was time to finally focus on something she cared about.

And if that didn't work, she'd surely gain a few hundred new followers while she stayed here, snapping her cosy aesthetic lifestyle like those pretty influencers she scrolled past each day. Kenzie would be jealous, probably regretful of their break-up. They'd never gone away together, minus an underwhelming caravan break in Blackpool to celebrate a friend's hen party and a spa day for Kenzie's birthday.

With a deep breath, Harper turned her back to the lodge and held her phone out to take a selfie. She sucked in her round cheeks and pouted to make her lips look kissable in that way Kenzie used to like – but she wasn't doing it for her, she told herself. *Lied* to herself.

Despite the dried tear stains on her cheeks, left behind from when she hadn't been able to contact her mum, Harper couldn't help but admire herself. With her olive-green beanie, blonde waves, and cheeks rosy from the walk, she looked almost as glossy as the view behind her – or would, at least, with a decent filter.

However, when she checked if she'd got a nice shot, one where her nose didn't look too big or her eyes weren't half-closed, her gaze snagged on something else in the photo.

On the last snap, the lodge's front door had opened… and a middle-aged man with sandy hair and a blue V-neck jumper was emerging.

She shot her head up, face warming with embarrassment when she saw the man in question hopping down the steps, keys jangling in hand.

Still, she tugged at her thick plaid "shacket" and pasted on a smile, pretending she was completely fine with being caught in the act. "Hiya! You must be the owner, Darren. Sorry I'm a bit late… You didn't say I'd have to walk so far." She played her annoyance off with a nervous laugh.

He frowned as he reached her, glancing from beneath thick brows around the woods. Up close, she saw a few strands of grey peppered his hair, which was styled in a neat side part.

"It's advertised as remote." His thick Scottish accent was music to her ears. Harper may or may not have chosen the location because she enjoyed the brogue, hoping that being surrounded by a different dialect would help her erase memories of her very Mancunian ex-girlfriend.

"Well, it doesn't matter. I'm here now. Although you might have to leave me a guide about how to do the shopping and whatnot."

Darren hummed, then glanced warily behind him to the lodge. Unease twisted in Harper's already unsettled stomach. Was something wrong? He didn't exactly look happy to see her, considering she'd shelled out a hefty deposit and already promised at least a month's rent. She hoped to stay longer, until her novel was written or she ran out of money, but she might have to reconsider if she couldn't get to Tesco on a regular basis.

"Look, I'm terribly sorry," he said, rubbing the back of his neck.

Oh, god. Harper was nauseous now. Nothing good ever started with those words. *I'm terribly sorry, but we just don't have the resources to keep you on. I'm sorry, but I don't think I love you anymore. I'm awfully sorry, but your favourite lipstick shade has been discontinued.*

"We've had a few wee maintenance issues pop up this morning, and the lodge isn't fit for guests. I'll give you the full refund, love, but I'm afraid I have to cancel your booking."

Her mouth hung open. From the outside, nothing seemed wrong with the lodge. It was perfect, exactly how it had been advertised on the website. "If it's just a faulty plug or something, that's okay. I have power packs to keep me going until it's fixed." She'd packed five just to be sure, almost as though she'd known she might get lost in the middle of the woods. It paid to be cautious, or a "worrywart", as Kenzie often called her.

Darren shook his head. "Unfortunately, it's nothing that easy. The plumbing is absolutely buggered, and the kitchen and bathroom are both flooded. I'm waiting on somebody to come out, but it'll take bloody weeks to fix the damage."

So the maintenance issues weren't "wee" at all. Harper's lungs contracted. What was she going to do?

"I... erm... So, what now?"

"Well, like I said, I'm waiting for the plumber, and then it'll be a question of repairs." He grimaced. "I don't even know if I can afford those. Hopefully, the place'll be up and running again in a couple of months."

"But what about *me*?" Her voice cracked, throat aching with the threat of tears. She shouldn't have come here. This was why she hadn't booked a long trip for over a decade. The way her spine stiffened in trepidation, her body braced for the worst whenever she was somewhere new. It wasn't worth it when she could have been tucked up in bed with Netflix, comfy at home.

But she'd been so sad in Manchester. So lost. This was supposed to be therapeutic.

Couldn't one thing in her life just… *work*?

"Oh." Darren scratched his salt and pepper stubble. He was far too tanned for this time of year, which meant he either frequented the sun beds – something Harper doubted she'd find around these parts – or had recently enjoyed the earnings of his guest properties in the sunny Mediterranean.

She waited expectantly. He must have had a backup. He couldn't just leave her here without a place to stay.

Could he?

"Well, I'll direct you to the nearest B&B, though it's a fair walk from here."

He could.

She looked at her ruined suitcase pointedly. Hadn't it been through enough? "Can't you at least drop me off in town?"

He winced as though she'd asked him to donate a kidney, glancing at his phone. "I've got to wait here for the plumber. Sorry."

If he wanted to see a grown woman cry, he was well on his way. Harper took a step back, scanning the woods in the hopes she might find a saviour. She'd settle for a walkable road or a magically appearing taxi.

There was nothing but twisted tree trunks, thin silver birches, and more of that faint, trampled footpath she'd been following. "So there's absolutely nothing you can do to make sure I don't die in the woods tonight?"

He pinched his chin, lips twitching with suppressed amusement. "It's honestly not that far. You just follow the—" His phone began to buzz, and he eyed the screen eagerly. "Hang on." Mobile to his ear, he greeted whoever was on the other end and began to give them directions. Realising Harper was still waiting for something, anything, he began pointing down the path while mumbling to the person on the line.

Shakily, Harper grabbed the handle of her suitcase, nodding as Darren held the phone to his chest and whispered, "Follow the path north."

"That would be handy advice if I had a bloody compass," she muttered under her breath. She should have listened to her mum and participated in the Duke of Edinburgh's Award as a teen, but she hadn't fancied camping with taunting high schoolers who would probably push her air mattress out onto a lake, *Parent Trap*-style.

As she wandered away, she checked if her phone had miraculously gained 4G so that she could at least use Google Maps to guide her…

But the bars were empty.

"You're getting a bad rating and review, Darren!" she shouted, and then sprinted off in case he'd heard.

Harper was officially on a holiday from hell.

2

Despair washed over Harper as she glared at the corner of her phone screen. Despite dragging her suitcase through *more* pine needles and squelching mud, plus collecting what she could only assume by the occasional waft of bad stench was fox poo on the bottom of her boots, she still hadn't stumbled across a hotspot, nor a way out of these woods.

The afternoon light waned through the trees, casting eerie shadows that stretched endlessly through the forest. She shivered both from the brisk cold and the panic jangling her nerves, her breath a visible cloud in front of her.

"This is why I wanted a nice city break, by the way!" she shouted into the deserted forest. Prague had been her first choice, if only because Kenzie was always talking about how much she wanted to go, but she'd forgotten to renew her passport last year. She was officially about to lose her mind, and nobody would ever find her. She would be destined to wander this forest for the rest of her lonely life. She would become a myth, a legend. Maybe they would call her the Wailing Witch of the Woods. Or maybe she would get attacked by wolves, or Highland cows, or *bears*. Her half-eaten carcass would be proof that there was no right answer to that "man versus bear" debate she'd seen on social media. Like most, she'd decided that to be left in the woods with a bear was the lesser evil, but that didn't mean she liked the sound of either.

A fence caught her eye, fairly new judging by the bright brick-red paintwork.

A sign of human life! Oh, thank god. She scurried over with her suitcase, then leaned against the fence to catch her breath. If she'd known how exhausting this ordeal would be, she wouldn't have quit those spin classes after the first painful, sweaty session a few months ago.

All right. That was a lie. No level of fitness was worth the chafing on her undercarriage from the cycling chair. But maybe if she ever got out of here, she'd consider getting a gym membership.

She checked her phone again, as though the fence might transmit the 4G she desperately needed. Or 3G. She'd settle for 3G. But the signal remained non-existent, and she let out a loud groan. The time on her screen read five-thirty. *Already?* Would anybody even be able to offer her a room this evening? It was October. Daylight was a thing of the past, especially this far north. It would be pitch-black soon, and then she really would be in trouble.

She massaged her throbbing temple, anger bubbling inside her where once anxiety had simmered. She should have been curled up by a lit hearth with a strong cup of tea by now, editing her photographs to post on Instagram before she opened her newly bought leather-bound notebook and got down to business. She deserved more than just a refund for this.

Exhaustion weighed on her joints as she began to inspect the fence, searching for a gap or a gate, anything that would lead her out of Mother Nature's torture chamber.

Her spirits lifted at the sight of moss-eaten eaves and wooden panels through the slats of the fence. A house! Or... a shed, maybe. But it was something! It was walls that real humans had built!

A heavy slam beat out a rhythm somewhere nearby, and she warily wondered if she was better off carrying on down the footpath. What if it was a *man*? Like most women and queer people, she barely felt safe walking through the crowded streets of Manchester. Approaching a cabin, where a loud noise was emanating, sounded like the beginning of a horror movie.

She stepped back, warming her cold hands in her jacket pockets as she considered her options. She'd been walking for over an hour and hadn't found this supposed town Darren had directed her towards. As much as she wanted to be careful, she also didn't want to die of frostbite and starvation.

She'd watched a few videos on self-defence. She could probably risk a peek at the cabin of horrors...

Harper walked further around the fence, but it was impossible to see much more through it beyond trees and shrubs. She came to a gate, finally, and breathed a sigh of relief, but when she tried to open it, she found it bolted from the inside.

Her teeth chattered as a particularly harsh wind blew through the forest. She was about to head back to her suitcase when it began to rain. Heavily.

This, she had been expecting. Living in the north meant always waiting for the next sudden change in weather.

The rain pelted, making the collar of her woollen shacket chafe uncomfortably against her neck. Her raincoat was in the suitcase, tucked deep beneath autumnal dresses and cosy jumpers that she'd spent yesterday coordinating with the right accessories and shoes.

"Oh, bollocks to it." Harper was done traipsing to a town that, for all she knew, might not even exist. Whoever was in this shed surely couldn't be any worse than the Airbnb host who had left her in this position.

She rubbed her hands together as she beheld the fence. It was at least a foot taller than her, but she could get a decent foothold. Hopefully.

She hooked the muddy toe of her boot between the slats and grabbed the sturdiest part she could find. When splinters dug into her palms, she winced, but she kept her fingers wound tight. Damp hair clinging to her face, she squinted through the droplets hanging on her lashes and stepped onto the next slat.

Immediately, she slipped and fell ass-first in the mud.

She wanted to scream.

"It's fine, Harper," she whispered to herself, remembering the TikTok tutorials she'd watched on how to *gentle parent* oneself through stressful situations. "Just get back up and try again."

She couldn't bear to look at the state of her jeans as she skidded and stumbled back to her feet. All she knew was that she was caked in muck to the point where somebody might mistake her for Bigfoot. *I hope this town has a bloody laundrette.*

This time, Harper used a low tree branch for purchase. The fence scratched her other palm as she slowly wriggled her way up it.

"Okay," she whispered between heavy breaths. "Well done, Harper. You're doing it."

And she *was*… sort of. She faltered a few more times before finally reaching the top.

Only when she got there did she wonder how on earth she would haul herself *over* it.

But she'd come too far to go back. She cocked her leg over the other side, holding on to a leafy tree branch for dear life as she shifted her weight. Somewhere, a dog began to bark, and she wondered again if she was jumping to her death. "Ohgodohgodohgod—"

"What the hell are you doing?"

The new voice made her flinch, and her grip was lost all at once. She fell to the ground with a thump and an "Oof!", the wind knocked out of her. Spotted yellow leaves rained down around her, the branch she'd used as support bending at an odd angle over the fence. Flattened spiny thistles clung to her clothes, and she groaned to discover that she'd narrowly avoided a patch of stinging nettles.

"Jesus Christ!" the man swore loudly, and then capped work boots rushed towards her sprawled figure.

Harper was certain that, if she was a cartoon character, there would have been stars haloing her head now. Dizzy, she forced herself into a seated position and sucked air back into her lungs. Her entire body smarted against the impact of the fall – and it was only made worse when a heavy lump of fur pounced on her, wet tongue swiping across her cheek.

"No! Don't attack me! I come in peace!" Harper screeched, waiting for the snarls and the pain and the blood. Had she found the man *and* the bear in one fell swoop?

But the creature just kept licking until he was shouted off by that same booming voice. "*Bernard*! Off!"

The dog – it must have been a dog, thank goodness – finally surrendered and trotted away, and the brown fur and amber eyes of a Border Collie took form.

Then her vision cleared as the man crouched over her. He was objectively gorgeous, with blue eyes framed by thick lashes and flecks of red peppering his otherwise dark stubble. His chiselled features were creased with concern, and only then did Harper remember that she was sitting in the mud, in the rain, after climbing over what must have been *his* fence.

"Shite, are you all right?" He scanned her body for injury, a firm hand finding her shoulder. "What the hell were you doing, climbing over the fence like that?"

"It's a very, very long story." She was still breathless, and also very embarrassed. He was ridiculously attractive, but had she noticed that already? A damp, coppery strand of hair fell into his eyes, and the ends curled just above his chin. His square jawline, though half-hidden by a thick promise of a beard, was sharp enough to cut paper. To make matters worse, ink curled around his muscular biceps and into the sleeves of his dirty white shirt. Tattoos guaranteed Harper's attraction to anyone, and the universe knew it. The shirt in question clung to his toned chest and abdomen, leaving absolutely nothing to the imagination. She could see more ink trying to peek through the wet, translucent fabric, and had never wanted so badly to disappear from humiliation.

He looked at her like she was mad, which she probably was. She cleared her throat and dared to look down at her ruined clothes.

She was a mess. She'd come here to reinvent herself, to become a better version of herself than the one who had lost her job and her relationship, and instead, she'd stooped to a new low. In front of a handsome stranger.

She wished she could go home. Not to her flat in the centre of Manchester, but to her parents' house just outside of it. She wished for a warm bath and to be smothered in towels and blankets, to be told, "It's okay, chicken. Everything will work out in the end." She wished to curl up on their sofa, surrounded by memories of childhood, and not have to endure this deep shame and helplessness.

But then her parents would know that she was not, in fact, a strong independent woman, rather just a lost fool who smelled of fox dung.

"I'm really sorry." She used the fence to pull herself up on shaky legs. He rose with her, arms still outstretched as though ready to catch her. He was even more good-looking when standing, if that was a thing. If it wasn't, Harper was officially dubbing it a thing. Of course, it *might* be related to the fact that he towered over her, denim jeans ragged and torn over long, stocky legs.

This was just another test, she decided. She'd survived the devastation of her cancelled booking and fought her way through the forest. Now, she just had to deal with the flutters in her stomach as she faced what might have been a literal Scottish god. She might have been pathetic and dirty, but she was still here, and that had to count for something.

If she just kept pretending, maybe she could get out of this semi-unscathed.

"Are you apologising for trespassing, for breaking a branch of one of the forest's oldest oak trees, or for crushing my saplings?" The man cocked his head and folded his arms over his chest.

"Huh?" Harper looked down. Green sprouts had been flattened beneath her boots. "Oh, gosh. For all of those things. I'm so sorry!"

His jaw remained tensed as he nodded. "Come on. Let's get out of the rain, shall we?"

She rocked on her heels nervously. "Are you going to murder me if I come with you?" On this side of the fence, she could see the cabin better. It was certainly no Heatherly Lodge, the wooden walls faded with rain and age and paint peeling from the window frames. But if he did turn out to be a psychopath, it was… adequate as a hostage prison. A weathered blue shed leaned to one side behind the cabin, fixed with a solar lantern that made it look teleported from another time.

"I'd have to catch you first. Clearly, you're skilled at fence-vaulting," he said.

When she didn't laugh, he pursed his lips and seemed to shrink just a little, taking a step back to give her space. "You're fine. Promise."

Harper supposed she couldn't do much else other than trust him.

3

Fraser tried to hide his grim annoyance as he urged the strange lass into the cabin. This was about the only place where he wasn't bothered by humans – deer and foxes and sometimes Bernard, aye, but no humans – and yet it seemed that was no longer true.

He would have to build a much taller fence.

As he shut the door behind both Bernard and the dripping woman, he couldn't help but try to gauge some impression of her that wasn't triggered by anger on behalf of his squashed juniper saplings. They'd been endangered before she got here. By the time she left, they might be extinct.

It was hard to read her at all when she was engrossed by her phone, freckled face limned by its silvery glow. She chewed the inside of her cheek, lips coming together in a plump pink rosebud as she danced around the cabin, waving the phone in mid-air.

"You'll not get signal here," he informed her, trying to quash his own amusement. Where had this woman come from?

Not these parts, that was for sure. He'd heard a northern – Mancunian? – lilt when she'd apologised to him earlier, vowels soft as melted butter. Unfortunately, that softness was nowhere to be seen now. She huffed, scrubbing a hand over her face, which only served to spread the mud from her palms across her cheeks.

"Where are we, exactly? Is this another Airbnb?" Her forest-brown eyes scanned her surroundings warily, from the workbench covered in wood shavings to the sagging couch he was no longer brave enough to sit on. Cautiously, she added, "… For lumberjacks?"

Clearly, she'd noticed his chopping block outside. Now, her attention caught on the array of saws and other tools hanging by the door in place of the old coat pegs.

"Does it *look* like an Airbnb?" Fraser couldn't help but snarl at the mention of those godforsaken rentals, popping up everywhere and ruining the Highland landscape – not to mention putting him out of bloody jobs. It was hard to tend to the forest when the trees were being chopped down to make room for guest houses, which was why he'd planted those saplings in the first place. It was his job to keep the forest a forest, keep the trees healthy and the woods populated. Sometimes, he felt like the only person here who gave a shite about any of it.

"It looks like an axe-murderer's workshop," she whispered quietly, eyes wide.

"*What*?" Fraser pinched his chin impatiently. Twice now, she had accused him of being a serial killer. He understood that women felt unsafe and that it was men's responsibility to do better, but he was trying to help her, for heaven's sake. She was the one disturbing his peace!

With Bernard trailing happily at his feet, he shifted past her, careful not to brush against her curves. Curves he was trying very, very hard not to notice.

From the box-sized bathroom, he grabbed the only towel he had. He couldn't remember if he'd used it or not, but it looked and smelled clean enough.

It was cleaner than her, at least.

He threw it to her, but since she was back to frantically wafting her phone in search of signal, it landed on top of her head.

"You were supposed to catch," he said when she yanked it down to glare at him.

"Thanks," she bit out. "You didn't answer my earlier question. Is that because you plan on kidnapping me?"

"On the contrary, I'm keen to send you on your merry way as soon as possible. Believe it or not, I have work to do." He tugged uncomfortably at his damp shirt, which clung to his body like a second skin. If he could just get her gone, reclaim his space, he could yank it off and get some work done in here.

He frowned, another question dawning on him. "How can you not know where you are, by the way?"

She sighed, rubbing the muck off her face and clothes. Beneath her rain-soaked plaid jacket, she wore a black turtleneck and ripped jeans, both of which hugged the thick crests of her body in a way that didn't make ignoring them much easier. Fraser feigned interest in patting down Bernard, who was more than happy to receive the averted attention.

18

"I can't get signal on my phone. I was supposed to be staying at Heatherly Lodge?" She said it like it was a question. It needn't have been. Fraser knew exactly where that newly built eyesore stood.

"That piece of shite," he scoffed, shoving his hands into his pockets. "It's about three miles back, although if I were you, I'd keep on walking the opposite way."

The woman's face flushed with heated surprise. "*Excuse* me?"

He shrugged. "I'm afraid I'm anti-Airbnb. They've taken too much from our town, greedy bastards."

She blinked. "Okay… Well, I'm currently anti-Airbnb, too, because the host just cancelled my booking and left me lost in the middle of the woods."

"They did *what*?" A new wave of anger rolled over him. What sort of heartless shitebag left a woman alone in the middle of the woods? No wonder she was shaken up. "They really just left you to fend for yourself?"

She sighed, wringing the towel in her hands as she nodded. "Yep. Now I don't know what to do. If you could direct me to a hotel, that would be great. But I'm not good with directions, so explain them to me like I'm ten."

"There are no Hiltons or Travel Lodges around these parts." He couldn't help but smirk. This woman truly didn't know where she was.

"There must be a B&B somewhere, though?"

There was. His friend Andy's B&B had been in the Flockhart family for generations. But thanks to godforsaken places like Heatherly Lodge, business was suffering.

"Aye, there's one in town, but…" He checked his wrist-watch, ticking away the daylight. The nights were only getting darker, and that made everyone's jobs slower than ever. Soon, there would only be a few hours of waning sun each day – and he was not looking forward to it. He always grew too restless when he couldn't keep his hands busy. "It's too late to book in tonight."

Andy would be glad for the customer tomorrow, though, especially right before they started renovating. If he could get her a place to stay tonight…

She groaned. "God, you're right. Well, it's official. I have nowhere to stay."

Wrinkling her nose, she wiped Bernard's moulted white fur from Fraser's lacklustre couch cushions before slumping on one. He raised his brows. When, exactly, had he invited her to make herself at home?

What was he supposed to do now? He couldn't get back to work, not with her in his space, disrupting his usual tran-quillity, and he certainly couldn't kick her out. That would make him as bad as the shitty lodge owner who had put her in this position.

"I knew I shouldn't have bothered with this," she mumbled into the towel. "I should've known it would all go tits up."

His mouth twitched in amusement at the expression. She might not have been Scottish, but she spoke just as plainly as any local. Something lodged into his chest like a nail tapped into splintering wood.

Shite. He was going to have to help her.

He was going to have to let her stay.

"I don't suppose you have Wi-Fi?" she murmured. Beside her, Bernard hopped onto the couch and curled up. Absently, she stroked his damp fur.

"No Wi-Fi, but…" He slapped his fist into his other palm nervously. He was absolutely going to regret this. "I have a bed."

She blushed a violent pink. "Now's not really an appropriate time for *that*, I don't think. I just got out of a long-term relationship, and—"

"Jesus Christ," he hissed, dragging a hand through his hair roughly as embarrassment pulsated through him. "I don't mean *that*!"

"Oh, god." She covered her mouth. Past her fingers, he could still see deep dimples at the corners, where her shock folded into pretty shadows.

She *was* pretty, he saw now the dirt had been wiped away. Full, rosy cheeks, long lashes, deep-set eyes, upturned nose. Her hair dried in blonde waves, curling at the ends. Something stirred in his gut, but he pushed it away quickly. He'd spent plenty of time avoiding *those* particular feelings, and wasn't about to stop for a random tourist who had no problem shelling out money to his biggest enemy.

"I meant," he said through gritted teeth, "that if you absolutely must stay here, you could. This is just where I work. I live in town. The place will be going unused tonight."

She let out several hums of varying tones, looking around once more. "Does it always smell like sawdust?"

"Aye, on account of all the sawdust," he quipped, running his finger along the workbench to demonstrate. "I'd apologise, only I don't usually rent this place out to city girls."

Without invitation, she floated up and away, through the tiny hallway that led to the one, lonely bedroom.

"Please, let me show you around," he muttered sarcastically before following her. In the doorway, she stopped, pursing her lips at the untouched single bed. He'd built it himself, his first practice project, but she didn't need to know that. Luckily, the sheets were fresh, and only slightly wrinkled from Bernard's heavy paws. "The dog sleeps on it more than I do. It's rare I stay here."

"It's not too bad," she said uncertainly. "But what about the wild animals outside? Will I wake up surrounded by wolves?"

He couldn't tell if she was joking or not. "As long as you lock the gate, you'll be okay. The wolves only come out on a full moon, anyway."

Her eyes bulged, face leaching of colour. He would have felt bad if it wasn't so funny. He leaned against the doorjamb, very aware that he was at least a foot taller than her. Defiantly, she tipped her chin to glare up at him. "You're hilarious, making jokes at my expense. If you knew the kind of day I've had – the kind of *month* I've had, even – you wouldn't be laughing!"

He rolled his eyes, not quite curious enough to ask what she meant, but still curious enough that the words lingered in his mind. "I'm offering you a place to stay. Take it or leave it."

She tilted her head, still weighing it up. He wasn't sure what there was left to weigh. Clearly, it was here or nowhere. "Is there plumbing?"

"Wouldn't recommend using the shower unless you like it cold, and you might need to double-flush the bog, but aye, it's functional."

"Great to know when I'm covered in dirt." Still, she finally dipped her head in acceptance. "All right, I'll stay. Just for the night." She rubbed her arms.

Fraser grabbed one of his wrinkled spare jumpers from the old dresser and offered it out. He took a much more worn flannel to replace his soaked T-shirt. "Gets chilly at night. Help yourself to anything you find. I'll go and chop some wood, get a fire going." He made to leave, then stopped when he realised he still didn't know her name. "I'm Fraser, by the way."

"Harper." She swallowed, looking lost in his little room with his big jumper in her hands. "Thank you so much for this. I'm really sorry, again, for… breaking and entering, I guess."

"I've had worse trespassers." With that, he clicked for Bernard to join him and headed back out into the drizzle to chop the firewood.

As he worked, he pretended not to feel her eyes trained on him from the window. Pretended that he wasn't perhaps putting more effort into his heavy-handed chops than usual.

23

4

Regret left Harper stiff and uncertain as her grumpy new host – Fraser – left the cabin. The impending silence crept over her, carrying with it all the choices that had led her here. This trip was supposed to be *good* for her. Productive. *Healing*. There was nothing healing about standing in a stranger's lacklustre bedroom clad in muddy clothes.

Before one of her usual self-pity parties could kick off – a common occurrence since being dumped – she squeezed her eyes closed and tried to soothe her nerves. *It's fine, Harper. You'll just check in to a B&B tomorrow, and everything will be fine.*

It didn't *feel* fine, but there wasn't much she could do about it. Again. She only wished she had better control over her own life. Could stop being so winded when it dragged her down an unexpected, circuitous path. She'd bet anything that Kenzie's new girlfriend, a flawless, glossy realtor with over ten thousand followers on Instagram, wouldn't spend her holiday moping. For starters, she would have had a private car waiting to whisk her away at a moment's notice, but that wasn't the point.

We're just at different stages of our lives, Kenzie had said on the day she upheaved Harper's, as though she wasn't only five years older than Harper and working practically the same job. *You're still figuring stuff out, but I know exactly what I want. I need someone I don't have to worry about all the time. Somebody with the same confidence and drive.*

Harper didn't think she'd ever be that person. Her confidence would always be a work-in-progress, boosted only when she was accomplishing something, and she'd long since hit a dead end in her marketing career. The only thing she was driven to do at present was to hide under a rock like a teensy woodlouse and never emerge.

Kenzie had apparently found that confident, driven, perfect woman not a week later in the form of a long-legged, pencil-skirt-wearing older lady with her own real estate company. Harper had at least hoped that showcasing her Scottish adventure would prompt Kenzie to reconsider her choices, but that was down the drain now. There would be no Instagram posts tonight. No homemade dinner or yummy boxes of locally baked shortbread to show off. Not even a brilliant view, since the cabin's windows were stained with moss.

"Stop it," Harper scolded herself. Finally, she peeled off her jacket and jumper, grimacing at the stench of drying muck. First things first, she needed her suitcase. As nice as Fraser was for lending her the grey sweatshirt, she would feel much more comfortable in her own clothes. Maybe later, she would even risk the cold shower to wash away the grime. It would be very daring of her. Very brave.

Very awful.

Shuddering at the cool air on her bare skin, she tugged the jumper on quickly. The thick material hung comfortably loose, which was a relief. She was often too big to borrow clothes. The jumper carried the earthy scent of the forest, but also the faint, welcome smell of deoderant and human sweat, something she had never appreciated until being deserted in the wilderness. She pressed the collar to her nose, inhaling more of it, of him, in an attempt to calm herself, as mint and sandalwood wrapped around her. She tried not to think about how she was smelling *him*, how this material had curled tightly around those tattooed muscles, but of course, not thinking about it was still thinking about it, and she had to force herself to stop.

She should have been better than this. He was just a man, for god's sake. Her taste as a bisexual woman could usually be defined as "all women and Henry Cavill provided he's sporting the right haircut", with the exception of the love interests in her favourite romance books, which didn't count, as they were almost always written by women.

Maybe it was good, though, to feel this attraction for a stranger again. She hadn't in a long time, and it would certainly keep her mind off Kenzie. Maybe it was a sign she could move on. Not with him, of course – he was far too standoffish and blunt, and she doubted she was his type – but with *someone*.

With that in mind, she dared to set foot out of the bedroom, and then the cabin, to retrieve her suitcase.

It was a mistake.

Fraser was a few feet from the cabin door, standing over the chopping block. He was working with a strength she'd never witnessed before, the hilt of the axe wrapped in his thick hands as he lifted it into the air. Her eyes were glued to the muscles of his back, rippling beneath his shirt, as he slammed hard into the wood sitting atop the block. The log split with a mighty *thwack* that ricocheted through the forest, and something unexpectedly carnal inside her pulsed in unison.

He continued cutting, turning around the block as he went, so that she saw him from all sides. His heavy knuckles, white around the wooden hilt. The way his damp T-shirt rode higher, exposing the low waistband of his jeans and the V-lines of his abdomen. The rough gasps falling from him with each movement, and the way he swore when the axe buried itself into a tough, defiant log.

She gulped. She had never imagined woodcutting would be so erotic before, but he groaned like he was—

Nope. Nope, nope, nope. Do not go there, Harper.

Still, she squeezed her thighs together at the unexpected tingle.

Bernard drew her attention away from the display in front of her, jumping up to scrape his paws down her jeans as though pleading for some love. She stroked the top of his head with a chuckle, finally alerting Fraser to her presence. At least he hadn't caught her ogling him.

"Bernard, down," he ordered with a sharp click of his fingers.

"It's okay. I had a Labrador when I was younger, so I'm used to big dogs."

Fraser nodded, his eyes lingering for a moment. She tugged at the borrowed jumper, self-conscious and unable to hide it now she was in someone else's clothes. "I'm just going to grab my suitcase. I left it around the corner."

"I'd better help." He threw the axe onto the block, kicking aside the chopped logs. "Just give me a minute to set the fire up."

"I *am* capable of getting it." Even if she couldn't quite remember where she'd abandoned it. He didn't need to know that, and he certainly didn't need to think of her the way Kenzie did: a damsel in distress, always a cause of worry.

He raised a brow and motioned her forwards. "All right, then. Just be careful of the wolves. And use the gate this time."

She glared in response to his blatantly teasing tone.

"Ha-bloody-ha." She shoved past him, but still looked both ways before opening the gate and treading back into the forest. Just in case.

A screech tore through the cabin. Beside Fraser, Bernard's ears perked into points of concern.

Fraser muttered, "Told you," into the fireplace. It didn't bring him much joy to see a woman having what was clearly an awful time, but he'd been expecting this reaction when she'd adamantly claimed she needed to take a shower to wash off the dirt. It was just a good thing he was setting up a fire for her, otherwise she'd be hypothermic come morning. He'd built this cabin himself only to provide respite from work. It wasn't well-insulated, though it warmed up better since installing the fireplace. Still, he was fairly certain a city girl hoping for a luxurious rental lodge wouldn't take to the minimalist surroundings, unless she was keen on "budget glamping", as his younger sister, Cam, had once called it.

After lighting the fresh cut logs, setting a steady amber glow flickering through the front room, he stood up on tired legs and trudged to his portable kettle set up at a counter opposite the bathroom door. As he flicked it on to boil, the sound of the shower stopped and the door abruptly swung open.

He tried to look away in time. He really, really tried. But he hadn't been expecting her to just... emerge like that in his grey towel. His gaze couldn't help but fall on her rounded shoulders, the generous swell of her breasts, the way her cleavage peeped out from the knotted towel and goosebumps dotted her pale, bare skin.

"Fuck," he muttered, turning away quickly. "A wee bit of warning would have been nice!"

"I didn't take you to be such a prude." Her bare feet padded quickly into the bedroom. "That bathroom might as well be outside. It's freezing!"

He rolled his eyes. Had she already forgotten that this wasn't actually supposed to be a bloody guest house? "Do you drink tea or coffee?" he called instead, flexing his fingers impatiently. He was supposed to be getting in his last jobs for the day, and the pressure of losing those precious hours was smothering him. He needed to be out of here and at his youngest sister Eiley's house in the next hour, otherwise he'd miss his nephew's first parent-teacher conference. As a newly single mum of three, Eiley struggled turning up to these things alone.

"Tea, please!" Harper shouted. "Wait. Is it Yorkshire Tea?"

Fraser shook his head, staring despairingly into the small tin of teabags he kept by the kettle. Most of them he'd stolen from Cam's place, not needing enough to warrant buying his own pack. She likely picked the cheapest ones she could find on the supermarket shelf.

"Aye, of course," he lied, then plopped the teabag in a mug before she could argue.

She emerged a few moments later, hair wrapped in a towel on her head as she stared down at her phone. "Still no signal. Are there any hotspots around here?"

"If you drive about an hour that way to Glasgow," he replied, pointing out the window.

She sighed, slumping onto the couch and stroking Bernard. She wore thick leggings and a chunky-knit, high-necked jumper the same shade of mustard as the leaves outside, with woolly socks on her feet. "My mum is going to start telling her Facebook friends that I'm missing soon."

Fraser hummed, not terribly interested – or at least, trying not to be. His skin prickled at the sight of her in his space, the smell of his cheap sea salt and eucalyptus soap clinging to her skin. It felt odd, having a stranger so enveloped in his cabin, his life, his bloody scent. He tried to mask the unease by bringing the mugs of tea over to the coffee table, a round redwood project he'd never had the time to varnish.

"What about food? Is there somewhere to cook here? A microwave?" she asked after thanking him, palms curling around the steaming mug.

He shook his head. "Only the kettle. Hope you like Pot Noodles." Suddenly, letting her stay felt like an even worse idea than it had originally. He couldn't just leave her here without feeding her, but he didn't have bloody time to take her into town.

He huffed, scratching his five o'clock shadow with sore, calloused fingers. "You're going to make me take you out for scran now, aren't you?"

"I only have half a packet of salt and vinegar crisps in my handbag," she admitted, wincing. "The lodge was supposed to provide a self-catering hamper."

Fraser checked his wristwatch, lips pressed tight. He needed to be at Eiley's by seven, and it was currently five-thirty. If they were quick, he could take her to the café by the loch. If he showed her the way by foot, she'd be able to manage breakfast without him, too.

"Get your shoes on," he decided finally, abandoning his tea on the table.

"I appreciate your help... even if your manners aren't great." Still, she sprang up eagerly and disappeared into the bedroom again.

If it got Fraser out of this mess sooner, he frankly didn't care about manners.

5

"You didn't tell me we'd be walking," Harper grumbled, once again trying to avoid boggy patches along the woodland footpath. Next time she looked for a place to rent, it would be a seaside cottage instead. She was sick of the sight of trees.

"Didn't I?" Fraser quipped, the corner of his mouth twitching as he slowed his pace to match hers. Clearly, he was enjoying this. "Maybe you shouldn't have assumed I'd chauffeur you about."

"You mean, like a gentleman would?"

"Those services cost extra." He shrugged, hopping over a particularly large puddle without a problem. Harper halted before it. Her legs weren't long enough to make it across without ruining her boots for good. Bernard passed seamlessly as though showing off, then barked encouragingly for her to follow.

She tested several paths forwards: either side of the puddle, but both were too muddy; around the footpath entirely, but the woods were uneven here, so she'd risk a sprained ankle.

"You're making this look like really hard work," Fraser commented, then held his hand out.

Harper stared at it for a moment. It was hard to believe he was still a stranger when she'd already worn his clothes, used his shower, and teetered over his fence, but easy when she saw the unfamiliar lines of his palm, the tattoos around his wrist creeping up into his sleeve.

She was overthinking it. But she'd watched him chop wood, got turned on, and now her stomach was all… aflutter. Like butterflies. Traitorous, confused butterflies.

"I don't mean to rush you, but I have somewhere I need to be in an hour," he prodded.

Of course. She'd disrupted his life. He was probably already exhausted by her. Probably nowhere near returning the attraction she felt for him, but certainly able to requite her annoyance. She slapped her hand into his, finding it warm and rough and steadfast as she leapt clumsily over the puddle.

"Thanks." She pulled her hand away quickly, sticking it in the pocket of the raincoat she'd hoped she wouldn't have to use. Her poor shacket was soaking in Fraser's sink. To distract herself, she checked her phone again. One bar of signal had erected itself like a tiny tower in the corner of her screen. Only two more, and she might be able to call her mum.

"So, what brings you to the Highlands? No offence, but you don't seem very outdoorsy," he said as she slipped it back into her pocket. A hint of judgement shimmered in his voice, or maybe that was just her paranoia. Either way, she narrowed her eyes to slits, taking offence, even if it was true.

She was glad when a cobbled building poked through the trees in front of her. Behind it, a band of silver water yawned out, reflecting the drab, darkening October sky. If the Airbnb listing had been at all accurate, it must have been Loch Teàrlag. If only they'd signposted it better, she could have come here first, rather than to a stranger's cabin.

She paused when she found that there *was* a signpost: a wooden one, planted squarely in her eyeline, with an arrow pointing ahead for Loch Teàrlag and the Raindrop Café. Had there been more she'd missed?

It was possible. She'd spent quite a long time with her head down, waiting for her phone signal to magically appear.

"Have you ever considered that maybe you're *too* outdoorsy?" she retorted finally.

Again, that smirk quivered on the edge of his mouth. "Did it take you all that time to come up with that?" He whistled through his teeth. "Aren't you witty?"

She batted his insult away with her hand, though inside, it stung. She wasn't witty, or outdoorsy, or adventurous. She was… *tired*. Lost. She didn't have the energy to match his taunt this time.

"Not answering the question, then?"

"I'm not here to be outdoorsy," she declared finally. "I'm here to do something for myself for a change."

"Oh, aye? Like what?" His mocking tone cleared like overhead clouds, giving way to beaming curiosity that only made her more uncomfortable. What was worse? The façade she was currently attempting, or the truth?

"To write," she said quietly.

Fraser slipped his hands into his pockets. "You're not one of those holiday house critics, are you?"

"Worried I'll give you a one-star rating?"

He chuckled, his arm brushing against hers and sending a bolt of electricity through her body. It made her entire being feel foreign, not hers. Detached from her busy brain. "Worried for my friend and their B&B, actually. If you ever make it there."

At least he was the owner's friend. That surely meant she would be able to secure a room first thing tomorrow. "Well, you don't have to. I'm not a critic. Officially, at least. I could easily critique your hospitality."

"I could easily let you find somewhere else to stay tonight, but I'm not that cruel."

They reached the café at last. The windows were wide, allowing patrons to take in the large loch, and golden fairy lights glowed inside. Finally, some sign of modern civilisation – although there weren't enough people around to make it feel quite real. A waitress was cleaning down the outdoor tables, but that was the only movement save for the gentle ripple of the water.

"They're open until half-six, and from eight in the morning, so you'll manage here. Think you can find your way back?"

He was just... leaving her here now?

Harper bit her chapped bottom lip and nodded without conviction. "Sure."

She wouldn't beg him to stay. He'd done enough for her already. On the bright side, her phone buzzed in her pocket. She had contact with the real world again.

She waited for him to leave, but he hovered, checking his watch once more. "I can stay a little longer, but I need to head back to the cabin in twenty at the latest."

"I can manage without you. I found my way through the woods, didn't I?" *Barely*.

"It's fine. I should grab something to eat before I head off anyway. Come on."

He tipped his head, holding the door open and waiting for her to enter. The warmth inside was like stepping into a hot bubble bath after a long day. The tension seeped from her bones all at once as the smell of roasted coffee beans soothed her. Perhaps she would return here to write. With the view of the loch, it might inspire her stories.

A short grey-haired woman greeted them at the counter. "Hello, stranger. You've finally been coaxed out of that cabin, eh?"

Fraser laughed politely. "Aye, something like that." When his gaze met Harper's, her knees buckled. She hadn't been charming enough to make him smile like that, and only now did she see the deep dimple softening his chiselled cheek. "Good to see you, too, Alice."

"What can I get the two of you?" She tightened the bow on her apron then turned her attention to Harper.

So did Fraser, allowing her to order first.

After perusing the menu, she said, "I'll take the halloumi burger and chips, please. And a tea."

Alice jotted it down, then waited for Fraser to add, "The same is fine. Cheers."

Harper was quick to nudge Fraser out of the way to pay on her card. "To say thanks."

"That's not necessary. I can pay." But it was too late. The transaction went through with a satisfied beep of the machine.

Alice raised an intrigued brow at both of them. Harper averted her gaze, certain she knew what this looked like, and quickly took a few napkins to a table by the window before either of them could say more.

"You're making me look ungentlemanly," Fraser commented, slipping into the seat opposite.

"You can take it off my total bill tomorrow if it makes you feel emasculated." She stretched out her tired legs, accidentally nudging his shin. Quickly, she pulled away, pretending to be interested in the view outside the window. It was pretty: the peaceful loch was a gentle, much-needed reminder of why she'd come here in the first place.

He rolled his eyes, then leaned forwards to brace his elbows on the table. His piercing blue gaze was inescapable when he was this close. "Harper, I wasn't going to charge you for one night."

"Why not?"

"Well, for starters, my cabin is not exactly the Ritz. And you needed the favour."

"I'm capable of looking after myself!" she blurted, blood pulsing in her ears. It wasn't loud enough to drown out the memory of Kenzie's patronising voice. *I need someone I don't have to worry about all the time.* Did everybody see her that way? Even strangers?

The fact her phone was currently pinging with a stream of antsy messages from Mum said yes. Harper huffed and texted that she'd arrived safely and would call her later, then returned to glowering at him.

He held his hands aloft as though in surrender. "I didn't say you weren't! I'm saying what that lodge owner did to you was shite, and I wouldn't have left you to roam the bloody woods all night. I'm not going to take money from you when you've been treated like that."

Tears pricked her eyes, but she refused to let them fall. She didn't know if it was fury at her situation or just the shock of his kindness that caused it, but she didn't like it either way. She felt so… out of control at the moment. So confused about how she would ever measure up to the person Kenzie had wanted her to be. Maybe she just wasn't built to be confident and put-together. Maybe she wasn't built to be wanted at all.

"I'm paying you for the stay," she said, lifting her chin defiantly. "Thank you for the kindness, but I refuse it."

"All right. If that's what you want." He sat back and folded his arms, the chair creaking beneath him. "So, you didn't answer my earlier question. What are you going to write?"

She hadn't ever admitted it aloud, and she was worried it would sound silly. Fidgeting with the corner of a napkin, she answered, "A book."

Surprise flashed across his features. "What sort of book?"

"I haven't thought that far ahead yet. I just needed to try something different."

"So you're not some fancy author I've embarrassed myself in front of by not recognising, then?"

"Not yet. Maybe one day."

Distracted, she snapped a photograph of the view, hoping it would be enough to convince her followers that the holiday she'd hyped up for weeks was going swimmingly. She sent it to her mum immediately, to set her mind at ease before she truly began to panic.

Fraser was yet again watching her as though she was an alien, so she opened Instagram to check her direct messages. Hours without social media had made her feel disconnected from the world – and from her life back in Manchester. From Kenzie. She'd been posting more regularly than usual since the breakup, afraid somehow that she might be forgotten otherwise.

"What did you do before?" he asked as their drinks were set down in front of them.

Harper thanked Alice, then chose to answer the question as vaguely as she could to avoid the subject of her redundancy. "I'm in marketing."

"Ah, interesting. In books, or something else?"

"For a company that sells household appliances and furniture. Nothing very exciting." She swiftly changed the topic. "What about you? What do you have to rush out for soon?"

He sipped his tea, then licked his lips. "Oh, just a parent-teacher thing at school."

Her eyes widened involuntarily. "You're a dad?"

Oh, god. What if he had a partner at home, and she'd been all jittery and flustered around him? She'd walked past him wearing nothing but a towel! She sank lower in her chair.

"Oh, no." He laughed as though the idea was funny. "It's for my nephew. My sister doesn't want to go alone, so I said I'd keep her company."

Harper released a breath she hadn't noticed she was holding.

And then she realised that this, somehow, was even worse. He wasn't just attractive and kind. He was a good uncle, and a good brother. How was she supposed to not like him?

"That's really nice," she said.

"You seem surprised," he commented wryly.

"I suppose I can't work you out. You refuse to stop helping me, but have complained about it the whole time."

"Yeah, well, you crushed my saplings and fell onto my land uninvited. I had a right to be a wee bit ticked off."

She had no response to that, mostly because he was right. Instead, she snapped a photograph of her tea.

"Why are you doing that?" he asked, forehead lining with confusion.

"To post it on Instagram while I have data."

"Does Instagram care that much about your drink?"

And just like that, not liking him became easy again. "There's nothing wrong with having an online presence. We don't all hide out in the woods with no Wi-Fi."

"Well, that's the issue. Nobody comes to take in the sights here anymore. The tourists don't come and buy from local businesses or walk around the loch. They take their pictures to make their friends jealous then go and spend a fortune on lodges like the one you booked, built by out-of-towners who are sacrificing woodland habitats so they can jet off to Malaga every year without having to work for their customers."

"You sound like my grandad," she said flatly.

"Your grandad must be a smart man."

The conversation was interrupted by the arrival of their food. Just to spite him, Harper took a picture of her burger, too, then dug in happily. She was finally enjoying her trip, and she wanted everyone to know it.

6

Harper stared at the blank document on her laptop as though the words she'd been planning to write for months might magically appear. Apparently, to write a book, she had to actually... *write*. She hadn't done that since her teens, when she'd had enough time to lose herself in fan fiction of her favourite shows. When the characters had already been living, breathing things, ready and waiting for her to mould into new, oftentimes queer, scenarios.

All the ideas she'd been ruminating over since deciding it was time to follow her literary ambitions suddenly felt silly. Had she thought this would be easy? She grunted and closed her Notes app, cursing her past self for writing nonsensical ideas down at three a.m. instead of preparing herself properly. What did "*sapphic Rapunzel retelling bit with icy skatwrs*" even mean? Had she been drunk when she'd typed this, or just asleep?

"Maybe I'll feel inspired once I've relaxed for a few days," she considered, and then cringed when she realised she was talking to herself. Again. Even when alone, she felt like she was being assessed by a scrutinising audience, which probably had something to do with the fact that she'd been dubbed weird in high school by bullies who had torn her self-esteem to shreds.

But she tried not to think about that. It was eons ago, and she was a different person now. Still weird, but awfully good at hiding it. Apparently just not in private.

A chilly draught crept into the cabin, and she pulled her cardigan tighter around her torso as she sipped her weak tea. Fraser had lied. This was definitely not her beloved Yorkshire brand, but she couldn't survive the morning without something to warm her empty stomach. She'd tried to summon the energy to head back to the café for breakfast, if only to prove that she was capable of managing the journey, but she'd eventually settled for her half-eaten packet of stale crisps.

"I give up." Harper slammed her laptop shut. Instinct had caused her to pick up her phone again, checking for messages this time, but it seemed this cabin remained in a void that no signal could reach. She'd been unable to access any since yesterday, when she'd lost connection mid-sentence on the way back from the café. She would never know whether Mum had opted for custard creams or bourbon biscuits during her weekly shop.

"This must be what prison feels like," she pondered, standing up and scanning the room for something to cure her boredom.

No, not boredom, she realised with a pang.

Loneliness.

This was the longest she'd been left with only herself for company – no contact with the outside world, no social media feeds to scroll through, no current events to keep updated on – since… well, probably ever. What was she supposed to do with all this silence?

As she stepped into the narrow hallway, a cabinet beside the bathroom caught her eye, and she found her answer. Snoop.

It was wrong, but Fraser remained a mystery, and at least some of her sleepless night had been spent wondering whether he was a decent bloke or somebody she'd better keep her distance from. Part of her wanted it to be the latter: sexual attraction was fine, but she didn't want more than that. She was still pining after Kenzie, and she certainly didn't need a repeat with a Scottish tree god who happened to be family-oriented.

Nope. She refused to like him.

But she would like to understand him.

She glanced around to make sure he hadn't secretly arrived to monitor her, because *that* would be an invasion of privacy, then opened the cabinet.

It was extremely disappointing. More tools lay on the shelves, as well as a tattered manual for woodworking. How much of the cabin's furniture had he made himself, she asked herself? None of the tables or cubbies bore the glossy charm of IKEA, and she was already sinking through the drooping couch at a rapid rate, so the answer might very well have been everything.

Her fingers stumbled across something else. It looked like a box at first, until she realised it had been decorated. Taking it out of the shadows, she saw it was a birdhouse with beige, faded paint and a pointed orange roof. The house was slightly wonky, as though it had been made by inexperienced hands – a child, maybe?

It looked too old to have been made recently, but she supposed he'd crafted it with the niblings he'd mentioned last night. She placed it back carefully, afraid of scratching it any more than it already was.

Beside that, the yellowed pages of another old book faced her. She picked it up, hoping it might be something worth reading. Something to help her escape the loneliness. Something to inspire her love of words again.

Jurassic Park. Harper hadn't even known the film was based on a book. She supposed dinosaurs were better than a murder mystery, and if Jeff Goldblum's character was equally as bisexual-coded on page, that would be a win.

The front door squeaked open without warning, and she whipped around with the book pressed to her racing heart. Fraser halted on the threshold curiously as Bernard ran past him to greet her. "Enjoying rooting through my belongings?"

"Very much," she replied honestly, then crouched down to receive sloppy licks from the bubbly Border Collie. "I thought you'd left me here forever, Wi-Fi-less and lost. I needed something to occupy my time."

"I thought you were supposed to be writing," he pointed out, stepping in and closing the door softly behind him.

"Turns out writing is a tricky business." She tucked her hair behind her ear and stood up. Bernard scurried through her legs and disappeared into the bedroom. "Besides, it's hard to concentrate in here. I think there are squirrels in the walls."

A puzzled dent burrowed between his brows, but he only shook his head. "I don't think they're in the walls, but they do scuttle over the roof sometimes. Most people like the sounds of nature."

"I'm not used to it! Don't you feel all… weird and icky this far out on your own?"

He smoothed the sides of his russet hair, deliberating. "No. It's peaceful. Or, at least, it was." He gave a crooked, pointed smirk, but it quickly vanished when Bernard bounded back in, something clattering along the floor with him. "What've you got there, Bernard?"

It looked like a red ball, only it was too hard… and too familiar.

Probably because it had come straight out of her suitcase, which lay open in the bedroom.

"Oh, no!" Harper lunged to grab her rose-shaped vibrator from the dog, but Bernard was content to keep it in his mouth as he ran around the couch and coffee table with his tail wagging. "Drop it, Bernard! That's not yours!"

"Bernard, drop!" Fraser instructed, voice hoarse with authority as he tried to catch him on the other side. Bernard slid straight through his hands and back into the bedroom.

Harper's face blazed as she ran after him. "It's fine! I'll take care of it!"

"What even is it?" Fraser questioned, nudging past her and clapping his hands together. "Bernard, drop it!" In front of the suitcase, where Harper's clothes had been strewn out in the dog's search, Bernard finally bowed his head and shamefully spat out the magenta sex toy.

Harper stuttered on her protests when Fraser reached for it, but it was too late. He picked it up, examining the curved petal-like edges and, Harper's favourite part, the tongue-like centre. Harper shrank further into her cardigan, whispering "Oh my god" under her breath.

Perfect. This was perfect. The handsome Scottish wood-cutter, who had already taken pleasure in teasing her, now held her sex toy.

"Seriously, what is this?" Fraser chuckled, and then, upon seeing her face, his eyes widened to glistening marbles of mischief. "*Oh*. I see."

She snatched it from him and placed it in the pocket of her suitcase, burying it beneath her socks and underwear before Bernard could get his teeth round it again. "As I said, I came here for a... fun holiday."

"I'm not judging."

"As you shouldn't. Any decent man would know that a woman deserves to be confident in her sexuality."

"It's really none of my business."

But Harper was used to blabbering in tense situations, and she still felt judged, even if he insisted otherwise. "Maybe you should train your dog not to snoop around women's suitcases."

She put her hands on her hips, arms feeling like jelly. She would be reliving this humiliating moment for at least another three years before she got over it. It was in her nature to endlessly wonder what impression people had of her. She'd once called her English literature teacher "Mum" in sixth form college, and often still cringed about it as she lay in bed at night.

She officially hated Scotland. She would never come back. By the end of the holiday, she might not even be *allowed* back.

"Bernard meant no harm. Besides, you can call us even now. You rooted through my cupboards, and he's rooted through your drawers." His wolfish grin was enough to make her stomach coil with a different heat altogether. Great. How would she ever be able to use that vibrator without thinking of him, now?

He sniffed, leaning against the doorjamb. "As *fun* as this has been, I've got work to be getting on with. Are you coming into town or not?"

Harper bent down to pile her clothes back into her suitcase and muttered begrudgingly, "Give me a minute."

The village of Belbarrow wasn't quite as lovely as described in the Airbnb listing. With Bernard panting in her ear from the back seat, Harper watched the crooked, cobbled shops and bright awnings grow closer, interspersed between trees scattering amber leaves across the road. A rusted waterwheel stood to the side of a tearoom adorned with black and purple Halloween decorations. Opposite was a gift shop displaying fudge and shortbread in the window, which lifted Harper's spirits. She'd promised to bring back gifts for her parents, so she would be sure to pay the shop a visit soon – for them, and for herself. Other than that, the street labelled Bridge Walk had only a few places of interest, including a pub set behind a narrow stream and a post office.

"It's very quaint," she commented for lack of anything else to say.

"What were you expecting?" Fraser replied, flicking on his indicator and turning the next corner. A bell tower loomed with stained glass windows and a heavy crown-like roof, attached to a church named St. Margaret's. A few more shops followed, including a bookstore that piqued her interest. Maybe she'd judged too harshly.

Harper shrugged, nestling into the passenger seat. His car smelled just like him, like the cabin: like fresh cut wood and rain-dampened earth. She was beginning to enjoy it, especially now she was no longer *splattered* with said earth. "Airbnb claimed there'd be plenty to do."

A candle shop and florist added fresh pastel colours further down the street, and even a couple of clothes stores were interspersed between them. Though it was certainly nowhere near as packed and lively as Manchester's Market Street, perhaps she could spend an hour or two here after all.

"There is. Didn't you see the massive loch yesterday?"

"I'm not much of a walker," she admitted.

He didn't seem surprised at this, his fingers tapping against the wheel. "Again, I have to wonder why you chose this place."

So did she. When she thought of her busy, bustling home-town, though, her innards clenched and she knew that, as much as she'd like to be in the comfort of her own home, there was presently nothing there for her. "I needed a change. A *remote* change."

"Then maybe start enjoying the *remoteness* a wee bit more," he said gently. "This place isn't so bad. I'm sure it'll give you enough quiet to work on that book of yours."

"Maybe." Perhaps he was right. She needed to give it a proper chance, even if she wasn't luxuriating in Heatherly Lodge, feet propped up on a suede pouffe, looking out at the forest without having to actually traipse through it. Truth be told, she hadn't planned to visit the town much at all, except to keep herself fed and stretch her legs when needed. She could say goodbye to that dream now.

She sighed. Fraser cast her a sidelong glance. "You okay?"

"Yeah. Of course." She pasted on a smile quickly, though it felt more like a grimace. "I'm sure I'll be fine once I settle in at the B&B."

"Well, there it is." He gestured ahead, where another narrower lane was buried beneath overgrown trees and dead leaves. A white stone cottage was the main attraction, situated on a slant where the road inclined into grassy fields and then more forest.

Harper straightened in her seat with newfound hope. It didn't look half-bad, with bay windows and red ivy decorating the outer walls. Smoke curled from the chimney and a golden plaque above the door labelled it *Flockhart's*, with a chalkboard to its right reading in white calligraphy: *where everyone is welcome*. A Pride flag rippling in the breeze splashed colour onto the scene, making her feel even more at home. She was reminded of the time she'd taken a spa break with Kenzie.

How the receptionist had looked at them both and asked if they wanted separate beds. The subtle, hostile glance when they'd answered no and reached for one another's hand. She didn't have to worry about that now, but it still warmed her to see that some places were meant for her.

"Oh, wow. This place is lovely."

"It'll be even nicer soon. Andy's putting a lot of work into it. They have to, to keep it an option when people are looking for a place to stay around here."

He parked up at the top of the road and snapped Bernard's leash to his collar. "Shall we?"

"You're coming in with me?" she blurted, caught off guard. Before, he'd seemed fairly eager to get rid of her.

"Aye. I'll help you with that naughty suitcase of yours." He smirked, and Harper swallowed hard. Of course he hadn't forgotten yet.

He tittered as he got out of the car, whistling for Bernard to follow. As he circled to the back of the pick-up truck to fetch her suitcase, Harper stepped out to drink in the brisk air. Although Belbarrow was further north than Manchester, the season's cold weather hadn't completely hit yet, and she was comfortable in her knitted layers and scarf.

"I can get it—"

"Aye, I know. You're very capable of managing by yourself," he grumbled, keeping the handle of the suitcase out of her reach. "You are allowed to accept help, y'know."

She might have been allowed, but she certainly wasn't used to it. Her steps faltered as the realisation hit her. She hated being helped. She hated having to ask for it. She hated it when people assumed she needed it. All she wanted was to be independent. Strong. More than that, she wanted other people to view her that way.

I need someone I don't have to worry about all the time.

The words sliced through her as harshly as the first time she'd heard them. She grabbed the handle determinedly, her breath catching in her throat when the cool side of her hand brushed against his warm one. He narrowed his eyes. Snatched it away. "Oi. Let me be a gentleman!"

"Let me be a strong independent woman!" she argued, yanking the suitcase back once more.

She strutted through the door to the B&B before he could stop her—

Or, at least, she tried to. She only succeeded in walking straight into the solid wood, her shoulder smarting against it. She huffed. "It's not open!"

Fraser nudged her out of the way to knock on the door.

"Hang on just a sec!" a rough voice called from inside, and the sound of feet trampling downstairs followed.

Locks twisted on the other side of the door, and finally, it opened. At the entrance stood who Harper assumed was Andy, the owner. Sporting a mussed, stylish raven mullet and burgundy dungarees over a pink knitted jumper, Andy's hazel eyes were doe-like behind round-framed glasses, their friendly smile punctuated by a lip ring. They couldn't have been older than thirty-five, though Harper supposed that made sense if the business was passed down through the generations. Still, Harper envied them. She wasn't far from that age herself, and she was nowhere near holding a steady job, never mind having her own business.

"Hiya, Fraser! What's up?" Andy slipped their hand into their pocket, blowing a feathery strand of hair from their brow.

Fraser looked just as happy to see them, that dimple returning to the corner of his mouth. "We thought you weren't in for a minute." He poked his head to look behind Andy, puzzled. "How come you're all locked up?"

"I thought I'd close early and get started on some renovations before the tourists start flocking in through December. I can't afford another quiet winter, so all the old-fashioned crap needs to go. Don't tell my mum I said that." Their shoulders heaved as they rubbed their brow glumly. "It's chaos, Fraser. I'm going to need your help. How free is your schedule this month?"

Harper's stomach sank. They were closed. As she peered at Fraser for guidance, much to her own chagrin, Andy finally seemed to notice her. "Oh, sorry. Who's your friend? More importantly, is she good at painting?"

"This is Harper…" He winced, scratching the back of his neck. "She's in a bit of a pickle, Andy. Is there any way you can offer her a room, even with the renos?"

Andy fidgeted with the ties of their dungarees, propping one foot on top of the other as they leaned against the door. "Oh, dear. What's happened?"

"Airbnb mishap," Harper explained, unable to hide her deflation.

"*Ick*." Andy wrinkled their nose in distaste. "Every Airbnb is a mishap."

"That's what I said," agreed Fraser.

"How long are you staying?" Andy asked her.

"Three months…" Harper replied warily. "I could cut it down to two. Or just until I've finished my book. How long does it take to write a book?" she pondered aloud, recognising she probably should have googled that before booking this trip on a whim, in the hopes she would "find herself" and write a bestselling novel.

Andy's face softened with sympathy, and Harper already knew she was about to get rejected. Again. The online writing community she'd recently inserted herself into would probably tell her she'd better get used to it, but that didn't help right now.

"Sorry," they said. "We can't afford to stay running for one person, especially not with all the work we're doing on the place. It's my fault. One minute, I didn't like the curtains, the next, I was ripping off wallpaper left, right, and centre."

So everybody, it seemed, was not in fact welcome. They should change the sign to "nobody welcome" instead.

Harper had never known how it felt not to have a roof over her head. She didn't like it at all. She felt… bare, somehow. Exposed. Alone.

She considered searching for the nearest train station and heading home, but her pride wouldn't allow that. She was here to become the person Kenzie had wanted her to be, to prove that she'd made a mistake in dumping her for the *Selling Salford* lady, and (as the cherry on top) to accomplish her goals. Who would she be if she gave up and went home? A pathetic failure. She refused to be that anymore.

She could look for another Airbnb, but the thought unsettled her. If they really were harming the village and woods, she didn't want to play a part.

Fraser turned to Harper, at a loss.

She pushed out her chest and tugged at the corners of her jacket. "It's fine. I'll figure something out."

"If anything changes, I can let you know," Andy said helplessly.

Harper shook her head. "I'll find something, I'm sure. Thanks, anyway. It was nice to meet you. Oh, and I am okay at painting."

"I'll message you about my schedule later," said Fraser.

Andy mouthed another "Sorry!" Fraser's way before they shut the door.

Harper scraped her wispy, windswept hair from her face, turning around to look at the village at the bottom of the hill. There had to be something down there for her. She couldn't be here just to get pushed out the same way she'd been pushed from her job, from her relationship.

Fraser sighed and pried her suitcase from her limp fingers. "C'mon. I'll buy you a pint and we'll figure this out."

"You don't have—"

He shushed her before she could finish her sentence, then said with warm sincerity: "Harper. I want to."

She supposed she couldn't argue with that.

7

Fraser set down Harper's drink in front of her, a crisp apple cider that she'd taken far too long to choose. He sat across from her with his pint of beer, feeling out of sorts. It was a tad earlier than Turloch Corner Tavern's landlord, Graeme, usually served alcohol, but he hadn't bothered to ask questions when they'd trudged in at ten-fifteen.

Besides, they weren't his first customers. Alan, the town's silver-haired, red-nosed retired postman, napped at – or rather, *on* – the bar. He emitted a belch that left Harper scowling, and she scooted her chair away from Alan as though his air was contagious.

"I can't believe this," she groused, dipping her chin behind her glass.

"It's not the end of the world," Fraser replied, sipping the froth from his own drink. "We'll find you somewhere."

He shouldn't have been drinking at all, not when he was supposed to be working, but since he was his own boss, he'd allowed himself the morning off to help Harper out. Whether she wanted that help or not, he didn't care. He'd promised her a room, and he hadn't delivered yet. Fraser never broke his promises.

"You said there aren't any other places to stay here other than the evil Airbnbs on the other end of the forest, and I'm not checking in at a Premier Inn alongside the motorway. I came here for a change of scenery. Some inspiration."

Her pink bottom lip jutted out in an endearing pout. He felt bad for her, of course, but he couldn't deny that she looked gorgeous, with an oversized terracotta jumper tucked into blue jeans rolled at the ankle, as well as a white lacy collar folded over the neckline. He didn't usually notice clothing, but he couldn't stop noticing her. She clearly took pride in being fashionable, and it suited her well.

Jesus, Fraser. Pull yourself together. Easier said than done when faced with a woman like her, fiery and bonnie and stubborn. Of course, handling her toy hadn't helped. How was he supposed to look at the roses in his garden the same, now he knew she used that little plaything to get herself off?

His knuckles whitened as he gripped the bottom of his pint glass. He absolutely could not think of her like that. Could not imagine her moans as she held the vibrating centre to her—

He cleared his throat, choking on his own line of thought. *You're a fucking shitebag*, he scolded himself, washing down the heat crawling through him with another swig. *Stop it now.* It was difficult not to tease her about it some more, just to witness that pretty blush again, but the last thing he wanted was to make her uncomfortable.

Harper soon sobered as she pulled her phone from her pocket. "I suppose I'd better weigh up my options. How do you spell Loch Whatsit again?"

"I see you did your research before arriving." He beckoned with his fingers, and she passed over her phone reluctantly. "I know the place better than you."

Fraser searched for accommodations near Loch Teàrlag, but it was as he'd suspected: most of the lodgings around the forest were rented through Airbnb. He changed the location to Belbarrow. Flockhart's appeared, but of course, it was closed.

There was a rental about six miles south, which would mean she'd be too far out to visit town without a steep taxi fare, and the view provided nothing but the grey road trailing towards the uneven landscape of the Highlands, where he doubted she would enjoy hiking. There really was nothing. Nothing, at least, that was in line with his morals.

He passed the phone back, mouth downturned. "I think we could do with another hotel out here. The choices are grim."

"Nothing at all?"

He shook his head. "Sorry."

She still scrolled for several more minutes, leg jittering under the table and causing his beer to slosh against his glass. "I can't afford to waste money on transport just to have the same problem in another town."

Her shoulders slumped, eyes flickering shut in dismay. Then she suddenly swayed forwards and shot him an intense look that was far too conspiratorial for his liking.

His stomach did that same irritating lurch, as though it was impossible not to react to her. He clenched his teeth. Said, "Whatever idea you have, the answer is no."

"You don't even know what I'm going to say!"

"I don't need to. In the last eighteen hours, you've kicked me out of my own cabin, ruined one of my oak trees, and crushed my saplings. I can't take any more of your particular brand of chaos."

"Oh, come on. You can't claim that tree. It was on the other side of your fence. The leaves were going to fall off soon anyway. I did them a favour, helping them down. Please. This could be mutually beneficial."

More stirring, this time lower than his belly. "I doubt that."

"You said yourself you only use the cabin for work! I could write by the loch, or here in town, while you hack at wood all day, and then come back in the evenings when you're gone!"

"No." The idea of his space not being his for anywhere up to three months pained him, made his skin itch with discomfort. He needed that time, that peace, and just knowing it would be disrupted by a woman who didn't know the meaning of the word would make every day that much harder.

She clasped her hands together in a plea. "I'll pay you handsomely. It would be like a second income."

"No." Despite his stubborn response, he tilted his head. It *would* be like a second income. Christmas was coming, and he could use the extra pocket money. His family seemed to be growing constantly, both of his sisters now mothers. He couldn't remember a winter where they hadn't struggled. Wouldn't it be nice to have an easier, more comfortable end to the year?

But at what cost? He loved his cabin. He loved his solitude.

"Fine." Harper opened what appeared to be a train ticket app, glumly, perhaps searching for a one-way journey back to Manchester.

"Why don't you just look for a place in Glasgow or Edinburgh?" he couldn't help but ask. "Why does it have to be here?"

She shrugged. "I needed a radical change from the city."

"A radical one, eh?"

"Yup." She avoided his gaze, her flat tone suggesting she didn't plan to elaborate.

He raised his brow, wondering what, exactly, had spurred such a desperate craving for a new life. A new career. New surroundings. What was she running from, exactly?

"There are other villages in Scotland. You can still have that break if you want it." He didn't have the heart to add that most of the other nearby towns were more expensive to stay in as they attracted double the tourists. Belbarrow was usually labelled a "hidden gem".

But Harper shook her head slowly. "I think I've had enough of this break, to be honest. I don't think I could handle another thing going wrong. Better to just be done with it." And she sounded like she believed it, detachment turning her voice steely and defeat pushing down her posture.

It didn't sit right with him. He didn't like the thought of her leaving like this, especially if it was because of his refusal to help her. He sucked air through his gritted teeth, considering his options. He could let her leave, and then lament his decision for a month. Which would mean saying goodbye now. Turning down a decent amount of money that wouldn't just help him, but his family.

He'd be another name on a long list of people who'd disappointed her.

It wasn't in his nature. If it was his sister, his mum, he'd want a stranger to help them out.

Jesus Christ, he was really doing this.

For courage, he glugged down the rest of his beer and wiped the excess from his mouth. "All right. Name your price."

Her face brightened. "Really?"

He forced a nod, convinced already that he was going to regret it.

Harper's first condition was unsurprising: Wi-Fi. "I'll pay for it myself," she told him as they wandered back to the car at a snail's pace. Fraser had soon discovered that she was like a magpie. She stopped at shiny things. They'd paused at every shop window, whether it was the pastry displayed in Pam's Pies on the corner or the charity shop beside the tearoom. He might have been annoyed if it wasn't so charming. The way her eyes widened, walk slowing as though a little person in her head was pressing down on the brakes. He'd forgotten that this village could be something other than the most familiar thing in his life. To her, it was brand new.

It made him feel a bit brand new, too.

"Well, I'll probably keep it once you're gone, so I reckon half each is fair," he replied, rolling a stone beneath his boot as they halted again. This time, it was the classic leather spines of Thorn & Thistle Books that had caught her eye. He'd noticed her attention home in on it when they drove into town, then again when they'd passed it while heading to the pub.

Her fingers tightened around the straps of her tasselled shoulder bag.

"Want to go inside?" Fraser already had his hand on the brass handle, perhaps slightly eager to keep her riveted for a little while longer. Even if he should have been back at the cabin, ankle-deep in firewood to deliver to a host of businesses and friends.

Harper dipped her head sheepishly. "I don't want to keep you for any longer."

He clucked his tongue and opened the door. A tinkling bell welcomed them inside the papery-scented shop. He didn't often frequent the place himself, only ever getting his paperbacks second-hand from the bookworm of the family, Eiley, but it was a cosy space, and a hit with tourists during the warmer months. "Come on. I know you want to."

Her lips curled with triumph. She shimmied past him through the narrow entrance, hip grazing his leg in a way that left him stirring with tight heat. He remained gormless as he watched her cross the shop and bend to browse a lower shelf, her jeans stretching over that perfect, dimpled ass, curving like a deliciously ripe peach where it met her thick thighs.

Fuck.

He swallowed, tugging at his hair. The sharp pain brought him back to reality – and to the fact that he was no longer staring at her ass, but her face.

"See something you like, Fraser?" Harper folded her arms smugly.

He pointed just beyond her, at a stack of thrillers piled on a round table. "I'm a Stephen King fan."

"Hmm. Your favourite must be *The Body*." Her eyes glittered with mischief as she slipped between the aisles, and then all he had of her was the sound of her slow footsteps, the smell of her lingering perfume.

Christ almighty. He hadn't stared at a woman's body like that since his teens. Had purposely refrained from doing it because he wasn't in the business of being a leering bastard.

But her voice calling over the shelves broke him out of his shame. "We can go halfsies on the Wi-Fi, if you think that's fair. I'll also need a heater for the bedroom."

He'd forgotten what they were talking about, and he shook his head to dispel his foolish thoughts. "Aye, I can sort that no problem."

He waved to the man at the front desk. The owner, aptly named Stephen, was a balding man with large square glasses who, judging by the entertained smirtle on his face, had been watching the whole thing.

Fraser blushed and went to search for Harper between the aisles. He found her clutching a heavy fantasy hardback.

"That'll keep you busy," he said.

She scanned the blurb on the inside cover. "I need all the inspiration I can get. Apparently, smutty fairies are a thing these days." She closed the cover with a snap. "So, we need to fix a rate for my rent."

"How much did you plan to pay for that dingy Airbnb?"

She bristled. "It wasn't dingy. Your cabin is dingy."

He reared back. "I can still kick you out if you talk badly about her!"

"Oh, she's a she?" She slid the book back onto the shelf to give him her full attention.

"Well, I built her myself. That makes her feel sort of alive."

She regarded him in surprise, blinking slowly. "You built the whole cabin, all on your own?"

He shrugged, suddenly modest. "Aye. It was a lot of trial and error, but I managed."

"Wow. That's pretty impressive."

His chest swelled with pride, a reaction he'd never experienced when complimented by his family. "Cheers."

"Now I feel like I should be paying double what I expected."

He choked on a laugh. "I think half of your Airbnb fee will suffice. You won't be getting a hot shower or a decent lie-in while you're there, after all. But I have some of my own terms and conditions."

She planted her feet. "I'm listening."

"No messing with my workspace. No touching my tools, or trampling on things that aren't yours. No rooting through my cabinets like you were this morning. And respect the wildlife. We take care of the forest here."

"And I was so looking forward to wielding your axe while hunting foxes."

"Funny." She'd be deadly brandishing any of his things. A dangerous woman with a razor-sharp tool... the image both terrified him and turned him on.

"Do you really take care of the forest, though?" Harper enquired lightly. "The way you chop into those trees... That's like saying a butcher takes care of animals."

He fought not to take offence. "I always plant a new tree to replace the old, and I never waste the timber. I didn't realise I had to run my work by you, Miss Sustainability."

"I was only saying." She lifted a shoulder, clearly satisfied – perhaps even surprised – by his answer.

"Oh, and one more house rule." He snapped his fingers. "No going in the shed!"

He must have sounded too forceful, because she frowned. "What's in the shed?"

"More tools," he lied.

She cast him a doubtful look but said no more. "Okay. I accept those terms."

"Good." He held out his hand. "Let's shake on it."

She did, her palm warm and soft, grip just tight enough to make his heart pound against his ribs. He would have to get these feelings in check if he was going to be running into her every day.

He pulled away and they continued perusing the aisles, Harper running her finger across the spines. "So, what will you spend the extra cash on? A new boiler, I hope."

He deliberated the possibilities. The extra money would do wonders for his family. Plus, there were all sorts of problems that needed fixing in town. The cost of living was affecting everyone, and it would only get worse once winter hit.

"I'll look into the boiler," he decided. "I could do without you catching hypothermia."

"Me too. Though after the month I've had, it would be the icing on the cake." She sighed, flicking through another book. Again, he wanted to ask what she meant, but her expression shuttered as though she already regretted sharing so much.

They'd reached the children's section, which struck him as odd, but maybe she had children in her family, too. He crouched to peer at the lower shelves, looking for something his oldest nephew, Brook, would like for his upcoming sixth birthday. He spotted an illustrated book about an astronaut that seemed perfect.

Meanwhile, Harper stuck to young adult and middle-grade titles, opting for one that looked Medieval-inspired, featuring a sword and a dragon on the cover.

"I've changed my mind about the fairy romance. I'll be back." She dashed off, leaving him at the front of the shop alone. Fraser picked up another book about a little girl and an alien travelling through the solar system together for good measure, and then put them on the counter.

"Morning, Stephen."

"Nice t'see ye, Fraser." Stephen's accent was so thick that even Fraser struggled to understand it sometimes. He typed in the prices of the two books at the till manually, then glanced suspiciously in Harper's direction. "New lady friend, eh?"

Fraser shook his head, snorting. "Not like that. She's staying in my cabin."

"Aye, I bet she is." He winked, placing the books in a paper bag. "Where'd you find her?"

Fraser shifted on his feet. He didn't like the way Stephen spoke about her as though she was a trinket he'd collected. Maybe that was why Stephen was a perpetual bachelor who resorted to flirting with anybody he could find in the tavern each weekend. "In the woods, actually. Long story."

"One that we probably shouldn't tell people." Harper reappeared, bumping her hip against him as she placed a tall pile of books on the counter. When Fraser whistled at the tower of pages, she shrugged. "I got carried away."

"A common occurrence, it seems."

Harper rolled her eyes at him, then shifted her gaze to the nook by the window. Shelves filled the walls, and a reading space had been set up with a homely green couch for adults and a colourful kids' chair with giant crayons for legs. "How's the Wi-Fi in here? Would I ever be able to come in here to work?" she asked Stephen.

"Oh, aye, that's no problem with me," Stephen said. "One of those freelancers, are you?"

"You could say that." Harper rocked on her heels as though uncomfortable with her own version of the truth. She paid for her mountain of books, and Fraser swapped bags with her to shoulder the heavier stack before she could protest.

She pursed her lips, then quietly said, "Thanks."

"Don't mention it."

Bernard pulled Fraser impatiently outside and immediately cocked his leg on a lamppost, leaving them to simmer in an awkward silence. Their first one, he realised, since he'd met her.

"Did he think we were a couple?" Harper questioned finally.

Fraser chuckled. "Aye, I think so. He's harmless, but he's a nosy parker. I once visited with my mum and he thought we were together. Then when I set him right, he started hitting on her in front of me."

"Yikes." She wrinkled her nose. "Maybe I *won't* be working in there much, then."

"He'll leave you be if you ask him."

"Fraser…" Harper gnawed at her lip hesitantly.

"Aye?"

She sighed. "I just wanted to thank you for helping me out. I know it's a pain for you, but I appreciate it."

He softened, unsure how to reply. Was it so surprising that somebody would support her in such a situation?

What company did she usually keep?

"It's no bother, Harper," he replied. "Well, it's a wee bit of a bother, but I'm actually doing it for the literature of tomorrow. Who am I to stand in the way of an author writing their first book? I hope I'll be mentioned in the acknowledgements."

She burst into laughter and pulled out her phone. "We'll see. Okay, let me take some pictures while I have data, and then we can head back."

Fraser left her to it. He could put up with plenty, but an addiction to social media was a little too much for a man who didn't even have Facebook.

8

Harper woke to the sound of a piercing, mechanical, constant whir. She groaned into her pillow and tussled with the thick duvet, unaccustomed to the new weight and strange smell. It took her a moment to remember where she was. A cabin in the middle of nowhere.

And her alarm was one hell of a racket.

"*No!*" she shouted at nobody in particular. She checked the time on her phone, which was charging on the nightstand. "No, no, *no!*" she repeated when she saw the time. Seven-forty. So early that the sun was barely up, the cabin shrouded in dusky shadows.

Angrily, she rose from the bed and stumbled her way to the door. Her brain was still foggy from sleep, but she could guess where the noise was coming from. She opened the door and bellowed: "*NO!*"

The whirring stopped. At the workbench, Fraser lifted his head from his power saw, his eyes filling with mirth behind a pair of goggles. "Aren't you a ray of sunshine in the morning?"

She wanted to take that saw and use it on him. They'd agreed that Harper would not disrupt Fraser's work schedule, but that was when Harper had assumed he would give her ample time to leave the cabin before he began hacking away at his wood. "It's not even eight!"

Bernard dashed towards her, sniffing around her feet before jumping up for cuddles she was too tired to give.

Meanwhile, Fraser's gaze scraped over her from head to toe, and back up to her head again, and only then did she realise what a mess she was. She looked down, finding her pyjama shirt rumpled at her waist, which gave him an excellent view of her shortest pair of shorts and her bare legs. She let out a disgruntled sound and yanked the shirt down to at least cover the most immodest parts.

"Don't look at me like that!"

He flashed a set of white teeth as he grinned. The front ones overlapped just slightly, only adding to his rugged charm, but Harper was not focusing on that today. She was focusing first on the ungodly hour he had intruded upon, and then, after she had stewed in her own consciousness for a while, the book she planned to write.

"Like what?" he asked innocently.

"Like… *that*!" She flapped her hands, flustered and annoyed. "Why are you here so early?"

"Well, *someone* kept me busy all day yesterday, so I've got work to catch up on."

She glowered. Admittedly, she *had* kept him busy. He'd dropped her off at the cabin, and then gone out to buy her a heater and order Wi-Fi installation. Still, that didn't warrant such an early, raucous alarm.

A cold breeze bit into her bare arms, and she tucked them around her midriff quickly. "You're a terrible host."

"You're a terrible guest." He powered up his saw before she could reply. Lucky for him, because it drowned out her expletives as she stormed back into the house, slamming the door behind her.

She was certain she heard him laughing the next time he turned it off.

Harper was still muttering irritably to herself as she pulled on her corduroy pinafore dress. Bernard watched from the bed, eyes slowly falling closed before popping back open again defiantly. At least she had some company here.

Once she'd peeled on her tights, she huffed and plopped down on the corner of the thin mattress, playing with the ring on her finger. Today would be the first real day of writing, and she didn't feel ready. It was daft, really. All she had to do was open her laptop.

What if she found herself staring at a blank Word document all day? What if she found out she was no good at writing, and all of this had been a silly idea?

"Pull yourself together, Harper," she whispered to herself. Bernard's ears pricked, the point of one slumping crookedly.

Then, she gritted her teeth. After a short intermission, the power saw was back to polluting the peace. Scared or not, she had to get out of here before the noise drove her mad.

She packed up everything she'd need for the day, including the books she'd purchased yesterday and the grey leather-bound notebook with gold, celestial etchings. She even had a pink fluffy glitter pen and an array of pastel sticky notes. Maybe if she bought enough stationery, the universe would be fooled into believing she was a real author and all would turn out okay.

With a deep breath, she drained the last of her morning tea and shrugged on her long camel coat before stepping into her chunky black boots. She commemorated both the moment and her chic autumnal look with a selfie to post once she reached the café, then gathered her satchel and umbrella and ventured out into the damp morning.

It took Fraser a moment to notice her, protected by goggles and ear defenders. He removed both, balancing them around his neck and over his beanie while tugging up the waistband of his jeans. Rain dusted his shoulders and droplets fell from the curling ends of his hair; it was difficult not to follow their uneven path down towards his collarbones.

"You look nice," he said, breaking her out of her reverie. "Is there a party I don't know about?"

"I'm just heading to the café." She brushed some invisible lint from the front of her dress. "What time is the Wi-Fi being installed?"

He checked his watch. "In about forty-eight hours."

"Ugh." She'd hoped it would be today. Evenings without Netflix here were interminable. "This must be how Bear Grylls lives."

"It's terrible, the trauma you're facing," he quipped. "You should start a blog about it. Inspire people in similar situations."

"That's not a bad idea, actually." Blogs were booming in popularity these days. "Or a podcast. But then, you need Wi-Fi to actually post those things. It's a vicious cycle."

He pinched the bridge of his nose as though at a loss, which she couldn't help but enjoy. Leaving him speechless was fast becoming a favourite hobby of hers. "I'll stop by the café around noon if you want," he said. "Give you a lift into town. The tearoom has free Wi-Fi, although I'm sure Alice won't mind sharing her password with you, either."

"You think?" She perked up at that. Her measly phone data plan wouldn't survive for over a month on its own. She could do with some alternative options. Luckily, writing didn't require a connection, but procrastinating probably would, and she had a feeling she'd be doing an awful lot of that. TED Talks on YouTube and cute TikTok videos of domesticated racoons would likely be needed to boost morale at some point.

He nodded. "At least I'll always know where to find you. I'll just follow the Wi-Fi signal."

Her chest fluttered. "Be careful. I might start thinking you like having me around."

His lips twisted with amusement. "Aye, well we wouldn't want that, *sunshine*."

"Is that nickname really going to stick?"

"It suits you," he teased, then slipped his goggles and ear defenders back on before he returned to sawing.

She grimaced. She really did hate that noise, although the nickname she could live with. The sight wasn't so bad, either: Fraser hunched over his workbench, jaw clenched with focus, biceps rippling beneath his shirtsleeves. His top clung to the muscles around his shoulders as the rain picked up.

Just like that, she was ogling him again. Opening her flimsy black umbrella, she stumbled down the steps and towards the gate, shooing Bernard away – and any impure thoughts about his owner, too.

Harper was glad to be out of the drizzle. She shook out her umbrella before stepping into the Raindrop Café, surprised to find a woman much younger than Alice standing behind the counter today. Her dark auburn hair was tucked back into a floral headband, a choppy fringe swept out of her bright eyes, and tattoos ran along her arms and crept over her collar-bones. She must have been just slightly younger than Harper, but far prettier. She was intimidating and queer-presenting enough to give her bisexual panic, but then, it didn't take much.

"Hello, there!" the woman greeted kindly between wiping down the counters, her voice gravelly with the Scottish brogue Harper loved. "You're a new face."

"As are you," Harper joked, making her way up to the counter. "No Alice today?"

"She's off sick today, so you've got me instead. Just visiting, I take it? You don't sound local."

Harper nodded. "I'm taking a sort of 'sabbatical'."

"Oh, aye? To do what?"

"Write. Rest. Make a fool of myself somewhere else for a change." She dipped her head with a self-deprecating smile, glad when the woman laughed. The name badge pinned to her navy T-shirt flashed with the movement, reading *Cam*.

"Well, you won't have much of an audience for that here," Cam said. "The village is fairly quiet this time of year, and the hikers keep to themselves."

"I've noticed." Harper tucked her hair behind her ear and scanned the menu written on the chalkboard behind Cam, her stomach growling at the options. "Can I get a full English—" She paused, realising she wasn't actually in England anymore. The menu only had the option for a Scottish breakfast. Harper hoped there wouldn't be much difference – it wasn't as though she was in a completely foreign country, was it? "Sorry. Habit. I'll get a full Scottish breakfast, please. And a pot of tea. I think I'll be here for a while."

"Well, I could do with the company. It's my first day back from my maternity leave, and I'm already falling asleep." Cam yawned as she input the prices into the till. "But god, I miss my wee baba already."

"Oh, congratulations!" Harper chirped and clapped her hands. She loved babies, even the screaming, pooping ones. One of her ex-colleagues, Michael, had brought his newborn into the office once and she'd cried more than the infant.

"Cheers!" Cam turned around to grab a fresh teapot. It was a pretty sky-blue colour painted with bright daisies, adding to the breezy décor of the café. "Feel free to take a seat."

Harper went to the same table as yesterday, offering the best window view of Loch Teàrlag. She couldn't see much with the thick spray of rain coating the woods, but she could make out a single boat cutting through the gloom on the water. She opened her laptop and snapped a photograph of her empty Word document with the atmospheric landscape behind, uploading it straight to her Instagram stories while she had a few bars of signal.

And then she waited, watching anxiously as the views came in. Her mum was the first to reply, writing **Living the dream!** with ten heart emojis and a thumbs-up. Harper responded with an update about her day, already missing their chats over tea and biscuits.

But you're living the dream, Harper, she scolded herself. She was tired of her brain plucking out all the negatives to focus on.

Cam set the tray of tea down on the table. "There you go."

Harper startled. She hadn't even noticed her approach, too busy dwelling on her existential problems. "Thank you!"

Cam nodded and disappeared behind the counter again.

After pouring her tea into a delicate, daffodil-patterned cup and adding a generous splash of milk, Harper took a picture of her new setup. She viewed her stats again, just to see if perhaps Kenzie had seen her posts yet, but… nothing.

She sighed, unable to suppress the instinct to look at Kenzie's profile. Her last post was a simple shot of the Manchester skyline at golden hour, taken from one of the rooftop bars she used to drag Harper to as soon as a little bit of sun came out. Underneath was the caption: **Life's not half bad when you're with the right person.** She'd posted it only yesterday.

Ouch. Harper's skin prickled all over, and she quickly locked her phone to prevent stumbling across anything else she might find painful.

The right person. Who wasn't her, apparently. Because Harper had never, not once, been the right person for anybody. Not Kenzie. Not Will, either, her ex-boyfriend she'd dated through university, who had been texting other women to keep his options open after graduation. From her very first "relationship" in primary school at the age of eleven, with her once best friend Sophie, she'd always been dumped for somebody better. In Sophie's case, because another tween had proposed with a blade of grass shaped like a ring in the playground.

She laid her phone face down and set to writing.

Or not. After five minutes of staring some more, she used the hotspot on her phone to Google "*How to write a bestselling book.*"

She thanked the internet gods when she found that somebody had laid out a five-step plan.

Step one: Meet your characters.

That was what she needed: characters! She hadn't even thought about who her book might be about.

Pinterest was swiftly opened but loaded slowly. She scrolled through hundreds of images and boards, searching for an aesthetic that called out to her.

She had no luck. All of the Pinterest models were slim and pretty, flawless. Harper was bored of seeing perfect characters, both in books and in film. She wanted to see more women like her, chubby and awkward and a little bit lost but beautiful in their own right.

"Writing is harder than it looks." She blew her hair out of her eyes and leaned back in her chair.

"I bet." Cam smirked as she approached with a laden plate in hand. She set it down in front of Harper with a knife and fork. "Enjoy!"

Harper wanted to, but one look at it suggested she might not. Something that resembled grey mince sat next to her scrambled eggs.

"Erm, what's that there?" She sniffed it curiously. It smelled like seasoned meat, but not any she was used to.

"Haggis!" Cam said cheerfully. "It's not a traditional Scottish brekkie without it!"

"Oh…" Harper swallowed the bile rising in her throat. She might have liked the sound of it if she didn't know what, exactly, haggis was. She'd always thought the dish was a cliché that most Scots didn't truly enjoy. Clearly here, she would get the full Highland experience. "Thank you," she forced out, taking her cutlery.

"Not a problem. Let me know if I can help with anything else."

As soon as Cam disappeared into the back room behind the counter, Harper nudged the rest of the food away from the haggis, wishing Bernard was here to eat it for her. She didn't want to seem rude or… anti-Scottish. If somebody came to Manchester and didn't eat gravy or curry on their cheesy chips, she would find it very offensive, but there was a difference between chip shop sauces and sheep's organs.

Thankfully, the rest of the meal was delicious, from the creamy scrambled eggs sprinkled with ground pepper to toast with lashings of butter. She continued scrolling through Pinterest as she chewed her crispy bacon.

How was she going to do this?

She must have been staring at the document for a while, because Cam eventually returned to hover over her. "Struggling?"

Harper grimaced. "I've come to realise that I don't actually know what to write about."

"Maybe you just need some inspiration. You'll find plenty round these parts. Here." She plucked a pamphlet from the otherwise bare cork board by the door and stuck it in front of her. It was titled *Things to Do in Belbarrow and Beyond* and displayed the forest in all of its autumnal glory. After her nightmarish trek through it, Harper was no longer fooled by the aesthetic. "Angus offers boat trips around the loch, so you could start there. There's some gorgeous scenery, and I know there are a few hiking groups around the village. Also, some castle ruins are not far from here, but you'd have to go by car."

Boats. Hiking. Castle ruins. All things that were decidedly outdoors.

But she wasn't getting any inspiration from sitting inside, eating foods she'd tasted before and avoiding anything unknown.

"Write what you know" was advice she'd heard often. Harper knew nothing at the moment, not about the big wide world. She knew how to design a website for a client. How to hook customers in with a social media campaign.

She did *not* know how to be an author. Not yet.

Harper stabbed her fork into her haggis and decided that it was time for change.

9

Fraser frowned as he stepped into the café, just a fraction later than most would consider lunchtime. Harper was not there…

But his sister was.

"Cam?" He marched over to the counter, baffled. "I thought you weren't coming back 'till next week."

Cam looked perfectly comfortable, albeit exhausted, behind the display of cakes and sandwiches. The café was completely empty, but worry gnawed at him all the same. It only felt like a few days ago when she'd been in the hospital, recovering from her emergency C-section with a newborn latched onto her. Why hadn't she told him she was coming back to work?

"Oh, no. You've got that look," Cam said, chewing on the end of her pen.

"What look?"

"The 'I'm about to be insufferably overprotective' look." She leaned over the counter and poked his chest. "Alice came down with the flu, and I was getting cabin fever anyway, so Sorcha and I agreed it was time."

He ignored her first comment. It wouldn't be the first or last time his sisters had accused him of being too protective, but someone had to be. After their dad abandoned them, he'd shouldered the responsibility as best a thirteen-year-old boy could. Sought to protect them from any more hurt. And the scare Cam had experienced, with a heavy bleed during the surgery, had only made him worse. Things could go wrong so quickly. If Cam wasn't ready to come back to work—

"Ow!" Fraser exclaimed when Cam flicked his forehead roughly.

"You're still doing it! Stop!" Cam ordered. "I'm fine!"

He huffed, glaring as he rubbed away the sting of her long nails. "Well, I'm glad you are. Who's watching Isla and Archie?" Sorcha was already back working long hours as a home care nurse. Fraser didn't know how they did it between them.

"Nobody," Cam deadpanned. "Left them at home all alone."

"Hilarious."

"They're with Mum, you tube. Probably having the time of their life."

That put him at ease. It was lucky Mum loved being a granny. With five grandchildren, she never got a moment's peace, but even when her arthritis was affecting her mobility, she claimed she far preferred it that way to living alone.

He looked back at the tables, just to check Harper hadn't suddenly materialised. "I assume you met my new tenant."

"Eh?" Cam's blue eyes, identical to his own save for her smoky black liner, widened. "What d'you mean, your new tenant? You mean the hot blonde author girl?"

He slumped against the counter, pretending to be interested in a custard tart. "Some might describe her as that, aye. She's staying in the cabin. Couldn't find her anywhere else when her Airbnb reservation fell through."

"*What?*" She gawped at him, a slow smile creeping across her forever mischievous face. "Oh, this is good. I like this. A gorgeous woman living in your cabin… The possibilities are endless."

"Oi!" He snapped his fingers, desperate to put an end to *that* train of thought. He didn't need his sister putting ideas in his head – or Harper's. Mostly because the ideas were already there for him, and he was trying desperately to get them *out*. He'd got here late because he hadn't been able to. Because instead of doing his job, he'd been daydreaming about her. About her laugh and her curves and that bloody vibrator in her suitcase. "Stop. It's not like that."

"But why shouldn't it be? You need some fun."

"I don't have time for 'fun', or any of the other nonsense that comes with it."

Cam scoffed, crossing her arms over her apron. "Sometimes I wonder how you got to be so boring. I bet Grandad has more sex than you."

"Jesus, Cam. Don't say 'Grandad' and 'sex' in the same sentence." He clenched his jaw, resenting her words. Why did people have to fuck around and date and get married and have kids to be considered "fun" or "normal" these days? He wasn't boring. He kept himself plenty entertained. Besides, he'd seen how messy relationships could get, first with his parents and then with Eiley. He was quite happy to remain alone with Bernard and save himself the hassle. "Do you know where she is or not?"

"Why? So you can stand five feet away from her in fear of catching feelings?"

Before he could think of a rebuttal, the door jangled open and Harper spilled through, dripping from the rain. She battled with her umbrella, which was twisted inside out and, by the looks of the protruding metal, broken beyond repair. "Blooming 'eck, it's wild out there." She closed the door, then noticed Fraser and stopped. "Oh, hello. Finally remembered your guest, did you?"

"It's been a busy morning," he lied. "Where've you been?" He didn't like to think of her outside alone in this weather after how lost she'd been upon arrival, and the image in front of him didn't make sense. They'd established she wasn't outdoorsy, so why had she been out in this torrent?

Happily, Harper sashayed in and petted Bernard, who licked the rainwater off her boots. "I've been making plans."

"Oh, aye?" He cocked his head. "What sort of plans?"

"Inspirational plans," Cam answered for her.

"That's right. I need to live a little if I'm going to write a decent book. Explore my surroundings. So I'm starting with a boat trip across the loch tomorrow."

Oh, this was definitely the work of Cam. She'd been hired by Alice three years ago mainly because she was the village's unofficial tourist information point. She'd worked briefly at the B&B before Andy had taken over from their parents, then the tavern. If anything interesting was happening in Belbarrow, Cam knew about it, just as she knew which tourists would enjoy a sunrise hike through the woods and which would prefer a day trip to Oban. It was how she'd met Sorcha, in fact: offering an impromptu tour of the place had been Cam's way of flirting.

"Now, I need more ideas. Hang on." Harper riffled through her handbag, retrieving an elegant leather-bound notebook and a pink, fluffy pen. At the counter, she left it open between them, so Fraser could see what she'd written in an impressively neat cursive: *"Harper's Guide to Inspiration"* under a lengthy step-by-step plan of how to become a bestselling novelist.

She wrote down the number *1* and circled it. "Book a boat trip," she announced. "Check. What else would you recommend?"

Harper's eyes sparkled as she looked at Cam. Fraser didn't like it. Admittedly, his sister was charismatic… but was she deserving of *all* of Harper's attention?

"There's the Fairy Trail," Fraser butted in, and felt foolish for it. What was he doing?

"Perhaps you should take her there, Fraser." Cam winked, causing his palms to sweat.

Harper glanced between them. "Are you two friends?"

"Worse," Fraser said. "Siblings."

"Oh!" She hopped back as though she'd seen a ghost, scrutinising each of them in turn. "So it runs in the family…"

"What does?" Cam asked, amused.

"Nothing," Harper murmured, but she blinked rapidly all the same, which only made Fraser want to know more. "You didn't tell me your sister worked here, Fraser!"

"Well, that's because she wasn't supposed to be back for another week," he replied pointedly.

"It's okay. Fraser doesn't tell me things either, like how he has a gorgeous woman living in his cabin. Aren't you shivering away in that thing?"

Harper was the colour of a beetroot now, and Fraser wasn't far behind. He cleared his throat uncomfortably. "I bought her a heater."

"I bet you did." Cam bit her lower lip suggestively.

Now, it was Fraser's turn to flick her, right in the middle of the forehead. "You're like a kid!"

"That's because you're like a grandad. Show the lass a good time, for goodness' sake."

"I can have a good time all on my own," Harper said, lifting her chin.

"Oh, so I've seen." Fraser grinned crookedly, and he saw the realisation dawn on her. Yes, he was thinking of her toy again.

Clearly, so was she, because she jabbed a finger in his face. "Do not!"

Cam gasped. "What? What? I want to know!"

"Nope. No, you don't. If you'll excuse me, I have a list to write." Harper sauntered back to the table, notebook and fluffy pen in hand. She gestured two fingers to Fraser in an "I'm watching you" motion.

He could feel Cam's eyes scorching the back of his neck, and he whipped around quickly. "I'll have a tea. And one of those special paninis you make just for me. I miss those."

"I made you one last week when you came round."

"Alice's panini maker is better." With that, he slid his cash across the counter – more than she would have charged him – and then walked over to the table with Bernard. Harper didn't look up from jotting her notes as he sat down.

"The Fairy Trail is beautiful," he said, raking a hand through his sopping hair. "Hard to find, though. I could take you there at the weekend. If you like."

He didn't know why he was asking. Or, rather, he did and wished he didn't.

He wanted to make her trip a good one, since she clearly needed it, but he'd already decided to give her nothing more than that. Even if he kept wondering what it would feel like to put his hands on her thighs, her hips, her cheeks. Even if he knew the colour of her sleep shorts and just how high they could ride in the night.

Harper stopped writing, slowly lifting her head. "Can I admit something?"

"Aye?"

She pressed her palms into her eyes. "I don't know what I'm doing. I planned to start writing this morning. Then I realised I don't even have a main character. And I don't even know what the story would be about. I just came here expecting everything to fall into place, because absolutely nothing was in place at home. But it isn't working out like that."

Fraser was taken aback by the confession. For the first time, he saw the uncertainty behind it all. How lost she was, not just because she'd stumbled through the woods, but because she was trying to figure something out, like most people were.

He couldn't help but lean forwards so that she knew he was listening. "You must have wanted to write something before this."

She glanced down at her fidgeting hands. "Yeah, but it used to be easier. Now I know I want to create a story that matters, that could *be* something, there's all this pressure."

"Okay…" Fraser pursed his lips as he spoke softly. "So, what if you put the phone and the laptop down for a minute? It sounds to me like you're used to working too hard. What if you stopped?"

Her forehead creased. "Then I wouldn't get anywhere."

"What's wrong with that?"

"I'd go home the same as I left."

"Would you?"

She hesitated, tracing the edges of her notebook. "I need something to show for all this."

Like Instagram pictures? he wondered. He didn't get it. Couldn't pretend to. He felt like perhaps he was verging too close to an edge, and wanted to retreat before he said something that might upset her. Something that might make him sound like he thought she was shallow. He was certain there was more to her obsession with social media than that, but he couldn't know what.

Maybe she had the right idea in making a list of places to visit, things to do. If she needed to step out of herself, Belbarrow could help with that. The village may have been quiet, but there was always something to keep you busy. Somebody in need of help.

"You're here for, what, two months at the very least?" he asked.

She nodded.

"So let the first week be about whatever this is." He pointed at her list. "Inspiration. If nothing else, you'll get some decent pictures out of it."

"That's true. But… mud. Cold. Rain," she argued wryly.

"You'll get used to that soon enough."

She tapped her cheek with the fluffy end of the pen and then, finally, straightened up. "Okay. I shall take you up on your offer for the Fairy Trail, whatever that is. Thank you."

He beamed, jittery at the prospect of spending more time with her. "Not a problem, sunshine."

10

Harper's Guide to Inspiration

Books, books, books
Boat trip
Fairy Trail (?)
Yoga (?????)
Hiking (why does inspiration involve so much exercise?)
Castle ruins

Harper examined her new list, compiled with the help of Cam and Fraser, and also the internet. She wasn't sure how, exactly, all of these things were supposed to open up her brain enough to transform her into a competent novelist, but the logic seemed sound.

"Why is there a question mark next to 'Fairy Trail'?" Fraser's voice behind her made her jump. He'd arrived to grab some tools bright and early this morning, and she'd stationed herself on the couch with a cup of strong tea while waiting for him to leave. Apparently, he had firewood to deliver around town.

Bernard nestled beside her, his chin balanced on his crossed front paws.

She twisted around with a glare. "And you say I'm the snoop."

He feigned being hurt, holding a hand to his chest. "Don't you trust me and my tour guide expertise?"

"I'm just very surprised that at your big age, you believe in fairies." Harper shrugged, propping her socked feet up on the coffee table.

He swatted them off quickly with an "Oi", then perched on the opposite arm of the couch. That explained why one side was so much lower. "You'll understand when you see the trail. It's gorgeous. Why is yoga on the list now?"

"According to my mother, who thinks she is a seasoned yogi after one class last week, I need to meditate and 'reconcile my body and mind'. Also, I bought yoga pants in a sale last month and need an excuse to wear them."

He cast her a sideways glance. "Interesting."

Unconvinced, Harper could only hum. She'd tried yoga, and pilates, and spin classes, and tai chi, and meditation, all with Kenzie, but she wasn't known for her fitness and her instructors usually shouted at her for doing it wrong. Exercise had been tainted for her since high school P.E. classes, when she'd been teased for jiggling as she ran. She'd long since stopped caring about her shape and weight, but the rest of the world hadn't caught up with her fight for body positivity. Now, she preferred to focus on things that made her feel confident, like dancing in the shower and doing handstands in the garden after a few too many glasses of wine.

But perhaps she could find a peaceful spot in the woods to do yoga, all on her own. There were plenty of instructors on YouTube, including her favourite plus-size one, Meditate With Melanie. If she could stay within range of the newly installed Wi-Fi, she might manage.

"I'm just trying to take the pressure off," she decided eventually, "like you said. Find inspiration from the world around me."

He clasped his hands between his thighs, which were spread wide across the couch's arm. It was impossible not to notice those long legs, with their hard planes of muscle clearly defined through his jeans. It surprised her, really, how... decent he was. Most attractive straight men in Manchester strutted around like peacocks, vying for women's attention only to mess them around. Fraser was the most gorgeous man she'd ever laid eyes on, and he just... minded his own business. Looked after his sisters. Chopped wood. Occasionally stared at her ass, then got flustered when she caught him, which she didn't mind one bit as long as he wasn't judging her. As long as he liked what he saw, which he seemed to.

There had to be more to him. Nobody was this... together. This perfect. Why was he single? Why did he keep to himself in the middle of the woods when he could be dazzling the world with his good looks and decent sense of humour? It made no sense. Maybe the forest should have come with a warning. *Caution: sinfully handsome woodcutter resides here. May induce heart palpitations.*

When she broke out of her thigh-induced haze, she found him smirking at her with those piercing eyes. It was easy to believe that he knew exactly where her thoughts had taken her.

"There are other ways to take the pressure off," he said finally, voice raspy as gravel scraping under heavy boots.

Her thoughts immediately descended into chaos. Images of his lips on hers, hands all over her, raised goosebumps on her skin, and she gulped as her breath came out jagged. "What…" Her voice cracked, and she cleared her tight throat quickly. "What do you mean?"

His eyes dipped to her lips. They only lingered a moment, but she felt them there like hot coals.

Quickly, he tore away from her, standing up and finding a slab of wood on his workbench to sand down. "Have you ever been wild swimming?"

She shook her head, then realised he couldn't see her with his back turned. "No, but it sounds like a quick way of catching some exotic infection. I've watched too much *Grey's Anatomy* to like the sound of that. If a worm crawled into my hoo-ha and made a home in my digestive tract, I'm not sure I'd ever recover."

He snorted, turning back around and perching on the bench to face her. "Do you always jump to the absolute worst-case scenario?"

"Yes. It keeps me safe," she replied bluntly. "And parasite-free."

He pursed his lips. "I know something about that. The safety thing. Not the parasite. The good news is our loch is probably cleaner than your public pool. People have been swimming in Teàrlag longer than either of us have been alive."

"Wouldn't it be freezing this time of year?"

He grinned wickedly, making Harper's pulse stutter a new rhythm. "It's not for the faint of heart. Depends if you're daring enough."

"I knew it. You really are trying to kill me. You just want to make it look like an accident." She shuddered at the thought of dipping into icy, open water teeming with god only knew what. Bacteria and rotten fish and duck poo. The boat trip was daring enough for her.

But Fraser chuckled. "I'm just saying, when I want to sort my head out, the loch does the trick. It's like a natural reset button for the body."

That gave her pause for thought. *I need a reset button for my entire life*, she thought. "I will tentatively put it at number seven on the list." She scribbled it down with ten more question marks and then, in brackets: "*(probably not)*".

"Well, I shall leave you to your wood," she decided, closing her notebook firmly. "*Chopping* your wood," she hurried to clarify as he lifted his brows. "As you are a woodchopper. Cutter. Your tree wood, I mean."

She shook her head, shrinking as she backed into the bedroom. Nobody in all of history had ever been as terrible at talking to people as her.

But Fraser seemed to like it nonetheless, the sound of his laughter following her through the walls.

The cabin was quiet when Harper returned that afternoon, and she hated the disappointment that welled inside her at the fact. She'd wanted to tell Fraser that she'd Done the Thing, crossed off the first item from her slowly growing list – and all by herself, no less. She never used to book things alone, always asking if Kenzie or Mum would fancy accompanying her. If the answer was no, she would cancel.

The boat trip itself had been fairly boring, mind. The loch was beautiful, no question, but the woods looked the same no matter which side of the water they were facing and she'd been the only passenger. The old silver-haired captain had offered her a sixty-minute lecture on the many different species of trees they could see. She'd waved at Cam on her way past the café, then popped in for lunch after escaping Angus's monologue. Now she was back and lost once again. More so because the person she was quickly growing accustomed to bouncing her ideas off wasn't here.

Or maybe he was.

The sound of banging and clattering emerged not from the cabin, but from the shed around the back. The shed that was off-limits because, apparently, the dozens of saws and axes visible from here weren't enough tools and he still had more to store.

Harper hesitated. She shouldn't interrupt him…

But she wanted to.

"Oh, Fraser!" Harper called into the slatted old wood, then grimaced when she spotted a cobweb across one of the hinges. *Ick*.

The bangs ebbed to thumps, and then a predictable, disgruntled sigh muffled through the grotty door. "I'm not home."

"Don't you want to hear about my riveting boat trip with Captain Angus?"

"Nope. *Don't* come in."

Well, that was weirdly insistent. Harper had joked before about how strange this whole thing was, but was he hiding something in there? Or maybe he was just working in the nude... A mental image that – to her utter mortification – made her breathe audibly. *Don't be a pervert, Harper.*

"Will you ever feck off?" Fraser shouted. "I'm trying to work in here!"

She took a step back, feeling bruised. She knew she'd promised not to interrupt him. She'd just thought…

They'd been getting along so well that she'd thought perhaps they were friends.

"Okay. Sorry." She trudged away, the sound of Bernard's whines on the other side of the door doing nothing to lift her spirits. She knew when she wasn't wanted. She would just have to spend the rest of the day following her list, and since she didn't feel like being too adventurous today, an afternoon of reading sounded just fine.

Or, so she told herself.

11

When Fraser emerged from his cave to mottled blue twilight, he knew he would have to apologise for brushing Harper off earlier. Only, when he knocked on the cabin door, nobody answered, and the place was still plunged in darkness.

"Must be at the café, eh, Bernard?" he muttered, clipping on Bernard's tartan leash and getting into his truck. He rubbed his cold hands together before turning on the radio, finding the skin sore and dry as ever.

The rain began to spit across his shoulders as he made the quick walk to the café. He couldn't wait to find out how Harper had liked her boat trip.

His chest squeezed tight as he realised he couldn't remember the last time he'd looked forward to spending time with someone who wasn't family.

There was nothing wrong with it. He had no reason to be wary or feel nervous. But he did, still, just like the last time he'd tried to date, or when a girl in the tavern had tried to flirt with him and he'd shut her down without meaning to. He was fairly certain he was allergic to intimacy, and he didn't fancy finding out the hard way.

When they entered the café, Cam blinked at him, startled.

"Someone's in a rush," muttered the older woman at the table closest to the counter, over her frothy cappuccino. Her name was Mrs. Boyle and, since retiring from her teaching job at the local primary school last year, she could often be found here with a plate of shortbread and a puzzle book. Cam routinely complained about how she chewed her ear off for hours on end.

The other non-stop talker, the one Fraser had come here for, was nowhere to be seen.

"Hmm," Cam agreed, mouth curling with amusement. "I wonder who he might be looking for, Mrs. Boyle."

Fraser paid no attention and marched up to the counter with Bernard in tow. Mrs. Boyle tutted. "That dog of yours should be outside. People are eating in here, lad."

"Dog-friendly café, remember, Mrs. Boyle?" Cam asked, her perky tone barely concealing the annoyance beneath.

"Aye, and what's next? Have them climbing all over the tables?" the older woman groused, then went back to munching her shortbread.

Cam gritted her teeth and leaned in close. "I will pay you to get rid of her."

"Just be glad she didn't teach you," Fraser replied quietly. Only Fraser had experienced the pleasure of being nagged by her as a child. "Have you seen Harper today?"

"Aye, she came in for lunch after her boat trip." Cam scrutinised her brother. "Honestly, Frase, I hope you're going to show that woman a good time while she's here. If I wasn't married, I certainly would."

He narrowed his eyes. "I'll tell Sorcha you said that."

"Sorcha would say the same thing. She's fucking hilarious and not to mention ridiculously hot. I know you're not usually into blondes, but come *on*."

"That's no way to speak about a lady!" Mrs. Boyle chimed in.

"I've told her the same thing," Fraser said, shaking his head at his sister disappointedly. "Lesbians these days, eh? No manners, Mrs. Boyle."

Cam batted him with a damp tea towel, and continued in a lower voice: "I'm just saying, you have chemistry. Why aren't you taking her out? Wining and dining her? Why was she on that boat alone today?"

"Well, for starters, I have work," he replied. She didn't need to know that he'd taken a rare day off today – she'd only demand to know why, and he was not ready for *that* conversation. Not even close. "And just because a pretty lass turns up, it doesn't mean I have to woo her. The world doesn't just stop when a woman appears."

Cam scrunched her nose. "'Woo'? Dear lord. Are you ninety-four?"

His patience was quickly fraying, and he shifted from foot to foot in annoyance. "Just stop, will you? I'm not looking for anything."

"You never are."

"And?" He bristled, fists clenching. "Not everybody needs a wife and kids to be happy."

"Not everyone does," she agreed. "But you? You love family. You love coddling people. You love being needed. So make her need you, if you catch my drift." Cam winked, leaving him to scoff.

Sometimes, he didn't like his sister at all, even if he loved her enough to hypothetically run into a burning building for her. He was glad at least one person in his family was willing to pursue what they wanted so boldly, but it meant he was also subjected to advice he simply didn't want to follow.

"Do you know where she is or not?" It was dark out, and if she wasn't here, that probably meant she'd gone into town – on foot, since there were few taxi services around these parts. She could easily get lost, especially if she returned in the dark.

"Not," Cam confirmed. "But Eiley has been trying to get hold of you today. She said you have dinner plans."

He pinched the bridge of his nose. He'd forgotten about those. In an effort to cheer Eiley up and give her some time away from the kids, he'd promised to take her for a pint and a decent meal at the tavern. She was still getting back on her feet after the break-up, and he wanted to make sure she knew she wasn't alone.

But she would be if he didn't bloody meet her soon.

"Do you want to come with?" he asked, already pulling out his phone to text Eiley he'd be there ASAP.

Cam shook her head. "I'm knackered. Sorcha promised a takeaway in our pyjamas. Let me know how she is, though. I've been rubbish at asking, mostly because I don't want to upset her."

"She's going to be fine. But I'll let you know."

"Cheers."

Fraser made to leave with Bernard, but Cam called him when he reached the door.

"Oh, and Frase?"

He turned around, already knowing what was coming.

It still pissed him off, though, when Cam said in that teasing, singsong voice: "Hope you find Harper."

A din of clinking glasses and conversation welcomed Fraser as he stepped into Turloch Corner Tavern, hands in his pockets and hair mussed with stress. After he dropped Bernard off at home, he still hadn't been able to find Harper, and the phone number she'd given him when they'd made their little deal was of no use. She was probably ignoring him, but he'd still at least like to know if she could make it back to the cabin safely.

He was ready to apologise to Eiley, who he soon found sitting on her own in the corner booth, far quieter than most of Graeme's patrons at this hour. She was the complete opposite of Cam – her hunched posture always made her look as though she was trying to shrink into the furniture, trying not to take up even an atom of space, and Fraser hated it.

He threw her a wave, and then froze when something gold caught his eye. On the other side of the pub, a familiar blonde was just visible behind a gilded hardback.

Harper.

She had come to the pub… to read?

Not just to read. She lowered her book to take a healthy swig of something red. Cider, or vodka cranberry if he'd had to guess, though he clearly didn't know enough about her to make that sort of assumption, considering he hadn't even thought to look for her here. He'd tried the bookshop, which was about to close, and had even knocked on Andy's door to make sure Harper hadn't been angry enough at him to move out and find emergency accommodation elsewhere.

But here she was. Lost in a book, with no idea he was currently standing like a fool in a stale puddle of beer, watching her.

He signalled a finger to his sister and mouthed, "One minute." She nodded patiently, her curious gaze following his journey to Harper's table.

"I've been looking everywhere for you. You can't just disappear like that!" Relief sank through him as he sat on the chair opposite.

She lowered her book, revealing a cool glower. "What?"

"I didn't know if you even knew the way to town on foot," he explained, doing his best to keep his composure despite his thrumming heart, "and you certainly shouldn't be walking back to the cabin in the dark!"

She went back to reading as though he had nothing of interest to say, gaze slipping over the pages nonchalantly. "You told me to 'feck off', so I did."

"Harper…" He shouldn't have been so short before. He'd just thought she understood his need for peace, or at least would be respectful enough not to interrupt him when he was busy. That had been the deal, after all. He'd more than kept up his end.

"I only meant that I was tied up, not that you should get yourself lost in the woods to prove some kind of point."

She sighed, closing her book and putting it on the table. It was forest green and titled *Emily Wilde's Encyclopaedia of Faeries*. "I'm not lost in the woods. I'm in a pub, enjoying my holiday. Contrary to popular belief, I *am* actually able to get myself from one place to another. It's signposted from the loch."

He opened his mouth to say that, although he knew that, she was still new to the area – but she lifted a finger to stop him.

"And I wasn't trying to prove anything. I'm minding my own business, as I was told to. Maybe you should do the same."

God, she was infuriating. He gritted his teeth, scraping a hand through his beard. "I know I was rude earlier. I didn't mean to be. That shed is just…" He would sound ridiculous if he completed that sentence. "I was distracted. That's all. I didn't mean to make you feel… however that glare means you're feeling."

"I'm not glaring," she lied, eyes narrowed to slits.

He tried to suppress his amusement. Failed. She was just too fucking adorable, with her sass and that little dent between her brows and the fact that she'd come here, of all places, to read books about fairies. The huge stack ranging from children's titles to familiar classics was piled next to her on the bench, along with her open notebook, whose pages looked fuller now than they had this morning.

"Look, my sister is waiting for me over there—"

Harper's gaze followed the jab of his thumb over his shoulder. "That's not your sister. She doesn't even have tattoos."

"My *other* sister, Little Miss Know-it-all. Come and eat with us. She hasn't many friends around here, and I'm sure she'd be happy to meet you."

"I don't think she'd be happy about you telling strangers that she has no friends."

He couldn't help but nudge her shin under the table playfully, relishing in the rosy glow it left on her cheeks. She shoved him back, harder, and he laughed. "I can take you back to the cabin when we're done."

"And save me from the big bad forest? You're my knight in shining armour." Sarcasm dripped from her words. It must have been made of gasoline, because it lit a flame in his chest, a burning sensation he shouldn't have liked so much.

"You're a pain in the neck," he muttered.

"Yup," she chirped proudly. "But you don't have to invite me to a family meal under the pretence that *she's* the one with no friends. We both know that's me. And I don't need a pity tea. It's fine."

"Harper—"

"We agreed I wouldn't interrupt your work, and I did. That's on me. I didn't mean to piss you off," she said, quieter now. Instead of looking at him, she stared at her drink. "It won't happen again."

He didn't like this side of her. Not at all. He'd rather she keep teasing him than sag further into her seat – just like his sister did – like she didn't want him to look at her anymore. Like she thought maybe he wanted her to disappear.

He sighed, shifting from his chair to the bench beside her. The wood creaked with his weight as he took her hand – beneath the table so that Eiley wouldn't see if she was watching. He didn't need another meddling sister on his case.

"It will happen again, because you're living in my cabin. And I'll get short with you, because I forget how to talk like a normal person when I'm lost in work. That's just how it is. I can promise to try to be less of a dick if you try to give me my privacy when I'm in the shed."

"That seems like a fair deal. Easier for me to keep to than you, though. Being less of a dick? Are you sure you're capable of it?" Her eyes glimmered with mirth.

He wanted to kiss away her smugness. Stop her front teeth from sinking so seductively into that bottom lip, until she was gasping and speechless. He supposed that meant he was not yet keeping his promise. He was still as dickish as ever, because he wanted her. Every second spent with her only made him hungrier.

Her eyes fell to his lips as though she could read his thoughts clear as day.

He snapped out of a momentary trance, aware of his sister watching them from across the room. Too aware of the twitch between his legs, a promise that it wasn't just going to be fantasies making this hard for him, but his body, too. Literally.

"What are you drinking, sunshine?" He stood up, motioning to her glass. "I'll order you another one."

"Vodka cranberry. Thanks," she replied hoarsely, then cleared her throat and crossed her legs. *Fuck,* did she feel it, too?

He went to the bar and tried – failed – to shake himself out of whatever was making him like this.

The problem was that *she* couldn't be shaken out of him. She was already deep under his skin.

12

Harper was nervous as she followed Fraser over to his sister's table. She'd already met one of his siblings, but this felt oddly... formal. He was introducing her. He could have just left her in the corner with her books, but instead, he'd insisted she eat with them. *And* he kept calling her sunshine with that unexpected fondness.

Weird was what it was. Sweet, but weird. Or maybe she was just making it weird because she was the weird one, with weird, weird feelings spreading through her like a wildfire through the forest.

"I hope you don't mind a third wheel," Fraser joked as he set down the drinks in front of his sister. "Eiley, this is Harper. She's a..." His eyes flashed over to Harper uncertainly. She was a what? A friend? A disaster? A charity case?

"New in town," he decided. "Staying in the cabin."

"Oh, this is the girl Cam was talking about!" Eiley scrunched up her features, much the same way Fraser did when he was scrutinising Harper. Her hair was styled in a flat, strawberry blonde bob and her features weren't as immediately disarming as Cam's, but softer, a little like a porcelain doll. She too was gorgeous, with a heart-shaped face and blue-grey eyes, but she didn't seem to care if other people thought so the way Harper did. She wore little makeup and a comfortable, old-fashioned patchwork jumper with a raincoat and leggings.

"Aye. Cam just loves to talk about my business." Fraser sat beside his sister, nudging her lightly. Like with Cam, warmth was radiating from him, which felt contagious as Harper took the chair opposite them both.

Her pulse pounded in her ears. Cam had been talking about her? *Saying what?* she wondered. Did she even want to know?

"It's nice to meet you," she said to Eiley. "I hope I'm not making a complete pain of myself or intruding on some brother-sister bonding."

Eiley shook her head. "Not at all, although I'm not the best company. Fraser can corroborate that."

"Fraser can*not*," he protested. "Besides, Harper is the worst company ever."

"Oi!" Harper kicked him under the table as his face broke into a wide grin.

"I'm sure that's not true." Eiley ducked her head shyly as she sipped her drink. "I have to say, I'm surprised Fraser is letting you stay. He's like me: keeps to himself. Prefers his own space, too. His eye starts twitching whenever I bring my kids to mess up his house."

"I can believe that." Harper giggled, resting her chin on her palm. "How many kids do you have?"

Eiley brightened at the question. "Three. Two boys and a girl. My eldest, Brook, is about to turn six; Sky is three, and wee Saffron is just seven months."

"Fraser is lucky to have so many niblings. I'm an only child. I used to ask Father Christmas for a bigger family when I was young," she confessed.

"I do love those gobshites," Fraser agreed, fondness softening his tone. "They're a lot of work, though."

"Tell me about it." Eiley's curiosity fell suddenly on Harper's pile of books, and she straightened in her chair. "Oh, look. *Peter Pan*! I've been reading lots of classic retellings to the preschool kids recently. They loved this one."

"Are you a teacher?" Harper asked eagerly. For a while, she'd wanted to become one herself, but the idea of going back to school, the place where so many of her insecurities stemmed, hadn't been all that pleasant.

Eiley shook her head. "Unfortunately not. I just volunteer at Sky's playgroup at St. Margaret's. They need all the help they can get. The bairns love spending time with new people, so if you ever fancy reading to them, feel free to drop in."

"It can be mayhem, though," Fraser added. "Be warned."

Harper was quite tempted to find out for herself, despite the slow shake of his head.

"I'm just going to nip to the loo," Eiley said, sliding out of her chair then disappearing behind a door beside the crowded bar.

The air changed immediately, returning to that usual stifling atmosphere that plagued the two of them. Fraser's blue eyes glittered as he edged closer so she could better hear him.

She felt her stomach fizzing, as if she'd just gulped several mouthfuls of his coke. "Just so you know, my sister is the most introverted introvert out there. You should feel extremely special to be invited into her life."

Harper was taken aback by his sincerity – especially when his attention drifted towards the bathroom door. She hadn't missed the way he'd gone quiet through their conversation, silently observing as though he hadn't wanted to interrupt. "I do feel very welcomed."

"Good." He brushed the beer mat across his knuckles, a faint frown appearing between his brows. "She's having a tough time."

"Is she a single mum?" Harper enquired gently, then added: "If it's okay to ask, of course."

"Aye. She moved back into our mum's house when Saffron was born in early spring, but her relationship with Finlay was rocky for a long time."

A strained sigh racked through him, and she had the urge to reach out, take his hand, tell him that Eiley was okay – she had to be, because she had someone like him looking out for her. Though Harper hadn't known him long, she knew that much. He'd seen him interact with his sisters. Saw the way he cared for them, the way he put them first. It wasn't like any sibling relationship she'd seen before. Her own mum hadn't talked to her brother in ten years, since a falling out when Nanna was moved into a care home. Kenzie's siblings had been more typical, taunting one another, unable to ever be earnest enough to show that love lay behind their insults.

What Fraser had, the way he acted… It was lovely.

After a moment's pause, Harper couldn't help herself. She laid her hand over his. Her palms tingled as though his skin was made of tiny needles, and the sensation shot up her arm until it was difficult not to lose her breath. "I'm sure she'll be all right. She has you and Cam, and from what I've seen, that's a wonderful thing. You're a good brother."

"Thank you." He chewed on his bottom lip, some of that darkness dissipating as he leaned closer. "That means more than you know."

"I might not be a single mum, but I know a bit about being left in the lurch. If she ever wants to talk, I'm here as well."

"I'm sure she'd appreciate that." He paused. "Who left you in the lurch?"

She shrugged. "My ex-girlfriend. I don't really want to talk about it now."

"Hmm. That's why I tend to steer clear of relationships."

Harper said nothing, and he hastily changed the subject. "Well, maybe you should take her up on that offer to read to the kids. It could help you with your writing. Cam's daughter, Isla, is very creative already."

"I'll think about it. Add it to my list."

"You never did tell me how the boat trip went."

"It was wet and dreary, and I've never met a man with so much hair coming out of his ears."

His laugh cut through the burble of music and conversation surrounding them, the only reminder that it had ever been there at all.

She was closing the gap between them, but so was he. Like every sentence was tugging them into one another. If she was smart, she would have let go. Getting involved with her new landlord, a man who was very clearly anti-relationships, was a recipe for disaster, especially so soon after her break-up.

But he edged closer still. "Captain Angus is an interesting character, isn't he?"

"He can name every tree within a five-mile radius, and not just by species. I didn't even know that was a thing. The tall redwood outside Raindrop Café? It's called Janet."

Another laugh, this one thundering with its intensity. She couldn't help but join in, electricity sparking through her when he twined his fingers with hers. "Oh, aye. He's very serious about giving them all names. What was the fir opposite the ferry dock called, again?"

"Douglas, obviously."

"*Obviously*." He shook his head, glancing down at their tangled hands. "She's a wee bampot, by the way."

"Who, Janet? That's not very nice."

"No…" He licked his lips, jaw ticking with tension. "Your ex. She's out of her mind if she thinks she can find a woman like you somewhere else."

White-hot flames seared through her veins, from the crown of her head to the tip of her toes. She didn't know what to say. Was afraid that saying anything would drive him away and all of this would turn out to be a delusion. Something she'd dreamed up in the loneliness of the cabin.

She wanted to kiss him. Wanted to show him just what sort of woman she could be when the right person set her alight.

And that's what he was doing. She hadn't expected to feel like this so soon after the break-up, but she wasn't complaining. Maybe she'd needed the reminder that she *could* feel like this for someone other than Kenzie.

Reality came back to her in a harsh, icy draught. He pulled away as Eiley returned to the table none the wiser with menus in hand. It was like watching a roller shutter door slam down. One minute, he had been hers. The next, he was nobody's. Unreadable, unreachable.

Harper tried to shake it off, pretending to listen as he and Eiley began to talk about something else, but inside, those flames that burned a moment ago turned to ashes.

What was she doing, catching feelings for a near-stranger in the middle of nowhere?

More importantly, what was *he* doing letting her?

13

In the end, Harper was grateful for the lift back. She absolutely would have got lost in the woods – again – without any light to guide her way. As they pulled up outside the cabin, she snuggled deeper into the passenger seat, feeling too comfortable in the earthy warmth of Fraser's truck to want to face the cold. Still, a gentle buzz hummed inside her. It had been a good day. Her first good day in a long time. She may not have written a bestseller yet, but she'd kept her promises to herself, without beating herself up, and she'd even received more than eighty likes on her latest Instagram post – a rain-spotted, windswept selfie on the boat.

"Tired?" he asked as he shut off the engine, leaving them in a thick quiet, broken only by the chirping of birds in the trees.

She nodded, unable to keep from smiling. "It wasn't a bad day, in the end."

"See? Belbarrow isn't all rain and mud after all."

"No, it isn't." Certainly not with him around. He was one great big surprise. She hadn't prepared for it, for him, but here he was beside her, hands resting on the steering wheel and eyes settled firmly on her... like they belonged there.

She still couldn't work out if he wanted her the way she wanted him, but now, just sitting in his presence, her atoms buzzed, from the hairs on her arms to her tightly wound core. She would need her vibrator tonight, that was for sure – and she didn't care if it made her think of him. She was already thinking of him. Constantly.

He rubbed his lower lip with his thumb as though deliberating something. "You know, I, er..."

"Yeah?" she murmured, unwilling to let him trail off and leave the unspoken words hanging in the air between them.

He offered a half-grimace, half-smile. "I enjoy your company, is all."

"I thought I was a pain in your neck," she accused, unable to reign in her smugness.

He snorted. "You are. Somehow, I enjoy your company *despite* that."

"Hmm." Her body felt like it was on the edge of something. A precipice, with a rope bound around her waist to keep her from falling. Only, she *wanted* to fall.

She wanted to feel his skin touch hers again, like it had in the tavern. She wanted to be devoured by his wolfish grin, wanted him to whisper in her ear how much he hated to ache for her. Wanted to feel his breath graze her jaw, her neck, fanning over her like embers ready to catch fire.

She'd forgotten what this sort of desire had felt like. Forgotten she was even capable of it. She often held it at bay, too afraid it might not be reciprocated. She used to leave Kenzie to initiate every moment of intimacy, just in case she read it all wrong and made a fool of herself.

He was staring at her, she realised. Waiting for something more.

When she met his eyes, he let out a long puff of breath and shook his head. "Shite, Harper."

"What?" she asked, not confident enough to believe she might already know.

"You are… not what I was expecting."

"No?"

His Adam's apple bobbed as he leaned forwards, clicking loose both his seatbelt and then hers. "Are you teasing me on purpose?"

"I don't know what you mean," she lied.

His nose brushed hers, and the jagged breath that left her betrayed her waning resolve. It was easier to let it show in the darkness of the truck, with shadows all around. Part of her hoped he wouldn't see her blush. The other part hoped he would, so that she wouldn't have to say it, either.

So that they could just let it happen, whatever *it* was. Clearly, he didn't do relationships, and she was in no position to start one, either, but there was something between them she couldn't ignore.

His thumb brushed her lips as he whispered, "Do you need me to say it?"

Slowly, she dragged her finger across his chest, up to the space between his collarbones. He shuddered beneath her, telling her all she needed to know. "Why say it when you can just... do it?"

His mouth was on hers in an instant.

He felt like she'd imagined he would, in her bed last night. Rough stubble, rougher kisses, with fingers hungry to explore the shape of her jaw, her neck, her shoulders. He was a sculptor and she was his clay, moulding into something new with every touch.

"We just need to get it out of our system," she convinced herself between rasps and kisses. It didn't feel like this would ever leave, though. She was a live wire, suddenly aware of every minute sensation in her body. Aware of places she hadn't known existed until now.

"Yep. That's all it is." His hand slid up her thigh, stopping just before it reached the place where she wanted him most. "Can I touch you?" He was leaning over the gearstick now. It couldn't have been comfortable, but he didn't seem to care.

She groaned and shoved his hand further up her legs until it landed below her zipper. "Please."

But he didn't start there, instead shifting up her jumper, mouth roving the rolls of her stomach with reckless abandon. She shimmied over to wrap her legs around him, elbows and knees crashing into a thousand different things as she tried to get comfortable on his lap. If they were calmer, more sensible, they could have been doing this inside the cabin, but she wanted him more than she wanted to move away. Couldn't risk that one of them might change their mind given the chance.

"I've been thinking about you for fucking days, sunshine," he growled against her, and then her breasts were in his hands and he was drawing noises she'd never made before out of her. "That fucking vibrator. Your fucking shorts. Your curves, your thighs, your fucking mouth." He moved back up to kiss her lips, sucking on her lower one until she squirmed. God, she'd never been touched like this. Like he might not survive if he didn't coax out every hint of her pleasure.

She arched her back, yelping when her head slammed against the window. "There isn't enough room in this bloody truck!"

He laughed, and it rumbled through every part of her like thunder. *That*. She wanted that against her, wanted it to run through her again and again. She raked her fingers through the thick waves of his red hair, tugging roughly until he kissed her again.

"We can move—"

"Don't stop," she pleaded. She wasn't sure she could take his absence. Needed his weight against her body like she needed air.

So he didn't, instead his eyes darkening at her command. One of his hands slid across her stomach, the other roughly palming her through her jeans. Stiff fabric rubbed against her clit, and she rocked her hips to feel more of it until she couldn't bear it anymore. Until she was unzipping them, pushing them down her thighs in an awkward battle.

Fraser yanked her closer to him, eliciting another whimper of surprise from her. "There isn't enough time to do everything

I want to do with you," he muttered. "All the ways I want to touch you, feel you."

I'm here for months, she wanted to say, but she didn't dare presume he might want her come tomorrow. Or the day after. Maybe they would wake up and feel satiated enough to brush aside their chemistry for good. Maybe he would regret it, regret her, and she would hate herself for letting him have her.

She wanted to recoil at that thought, but she'd come too far to go back now. So she tightened her legs around him. He looked up like he'd never seen anything like her, lips parted, arched neck flushed. She ran her fingers through his short beard, and he hummed with pleasure.

"I can trust you, can't I?" she whispered, feeling suddenly, achingly vulnerable. "Whatever this is… you won't make it weird? We'll still be sort-of-friends? I'll still stay in your cabin, and you'll still take me to the Fairy Trail or whatever?"

His eyes softened to pools of blue. "Of course, love."

"Okay. You can trust me, too. Probably." She barely had time to laugh at her own joke. One moment, his fingers were curled into the soft cushion of her hips. The next, they were somewhere else entirely – massaging her through the damp fabric of her underwear.

She shivered, tensing against him until he kissed her neck. She fumbled for his belt buckle, then gasped as her thumb grazed the taut bulge beneath. "You're so hard," she breathed, kneading his cock through his jeans, relishing in the way he twitched against her.

"Fuck, Harper."

His eyes fluttered shut. When they opened again, they were blazing with defiance. He crooked his finger inside her as though beckoning, and it didn't take long for her to move with him, thrusting desperately as he swapped one finger for two, two for three. He didn't have to fill her up: she was already a writhing, moaning mess, melting into him as her clit sought friction against his palm. Her hips luxuriating against his crotch must have teased him more, because he swore again, voice cracking.

"Use me," he begged. She did, rolling her hips onto his hard thighs while he played with her. It was hard to believe she could feel this good when she was still covered, still mostly dressed, but his touch, his deep urgent voice, his deft fingers, kept her building towards delirium.

When she was close, she unzipped his jeans and took him in both hands at last, fingers curling around his impressive length. His hair-dusted belly shuddered against her touch, and she was certain she couldn't take much more—

His fingers sank back into her, and there was no more holding on. She was falling all at once, orgasm rolling through her body. Fraser groaned, voice hitching as he came in her hands. Slowing, she rested her damp forehead against his, closing her eyes as he teased out the last of her climax in gentle circles.

"Well," she said, "that was fun."

"Aye." He smirked, twirling his fingers through her dishevelled hair. His lips were swollen, neck red and bearing the crescent indentations of her nails.

Oops.

Something changed a moment later. Anyone else might not have noticed it, but Harper lived on high alert, always waiting for somebody's interest to fade.

His didn't, but it ebbed, his grip turning slack.

She drew off his lap, rolling her jeans back up and fastening them before she could feel too bare. He reached across her, pulling wipes from the glovebox so that they could both clean up. "So, is it out of your system?"

"You could say that," he muttered, adjusting himself and zipping up his fly. "You?"

"Yup. Definitely," she lied. Naturally, all she could think about was feeling the length of him again, seating herself on it, and riding him until she was seeing stars.

But that wasn't what he wanted, and she was fine with that. Of course she was. A one-time hook-up was what *she'd* suggested, after all.

"It is alllll the way out," she continued, because she was prone to rambling at the best of times, never mind when she didn't know where she stood with someone. "Way, way out. You could probably find it in Glasgow. Or Carlisle, even."

"Then I know where to go next time." He ran a subdued hand over his cheek. "Will there be a next time?"

She tried not to show her excitement as she admitted, "I wouldn't complain if there was."

"We're adults. We can have fun if we want to, can't we?" He asked her like he wasn't sure of the answer.

"I do believe those are the rules of adulthood, yeah. But if you're not keen…"

"Oh, I'm keen," he insisted quickly. "It's just… Like I said earlier, I don't do relationships."

She looked down at her wrinkled clothing to avoid the intensity of his gaze. "Me neither. Not right now, at least. Then… We'll see what happens, I guess? Keep things casual?"

He nodded. "Aye. Okay. Good."

They shared a final, knowing smile that sent another zap through her body, and then she escaped the silence of the truck before she could pounce on him a second time. And a third. She wouldn't have minded a third. She was known to be a bit greedy when she wanted.

And she very much wanted.

"Goodnight, then." She cast him a wave, only then realising her fingers were shaking.

He returned it with a lopsided grin. "Night, Harper."

14

It felt strange for Fraser to knock on his own door – not just one he owned, but one he'd made and fitted himself. Harper had made him a guest in his own cabin, but he couldn't find it in him to mind. Not after the other night.

He flexed his fingers, trying to calm the jitters. This was supposed to be casual, yet he felt anything but when he was around her. Still, he wouldn't ruin their newfound fun with whatever was happening inside him. It had been too long since he'd been touched the way she touched him, kissed the way she kissed him, and he needed more. He'd been starved. He hadn't realised just how hollow and hungry he'd felt before her. Now, no amount of her would feel like enough.

When nobody answered, he looked down at Bernard as though the dog might know where Harper was. "What d'you think she's up to today, bud?"

Bernard wagged his tail, just happy to be privy to thoughts that probably wouldn't have been voiced aloud by any sane owner.

His breath caught in his throat. What if she'd left? Or perhaps she was avoiding him. They'd both been fine, normal, *casual,* since their heated collision in the truck two nights ago, but... Harper had just got out of a serious relationship, one that had clearly left her hurt. Maybe this had all got too overwhelming for her. It had happened so quickly, and neither of them had stopped to talk about it yet.

"Harper?" he called, knocking louder this time.

Maybe she's gone for breakfast before our walk, a more rational part of him reasoned. *Or into town. Didn't she say—*

"Ow! Bloody hell." Harper's grunts drifted from somewhere behind the cabin and were followed by a bizarre, heavy shuffling.

"I dread to think what she's doing," he muttered, and then followed the sounds around the cabin and shed, to the back garden-in-progress, where he had first met Harper.

Whatever possibilities his brain conjured were nothing compared to the scene in front of him. Harper was sprawled on a Barbie-pink yoga mat in neon purple leggings, jumper tied in a knot just beneath the curve of her breasts. If she was aiming for a pose, it would have been called something along the lines of "three-legged frog", because her rear end jutted into the air while the rest of her squatting limbs flailed at interesting angles. One of her legs was tucked under her hips, her torso collapsing in on itself as she gasped for breath.

"I don't bend that way, Melanie!" she screamed at the ant-sized yoga instructor on her phone, propped against one of Fraser's taller, sturdier saplings.

Fraser stayed back, amusement and desire rolling through him in equal measure. She was ridiculous. He loved it. Of course, the bright nylon hugging her curves, accentuating all of her softer parts, helped. Heat uncoiled within him as she shifted, revealing the exposed, glorious, pale skin of her middle.

"Tuck your left foot further under your hips to really get that stretch in," Melanie the instructor was saying in a syrupy Californian accent. "Breathe through it, relax into it. Just like that."

"I hate you," Harper muttered, then let out several deep breaths all the same.

"Good job. Now, slowly push up on your arms and let your breaths guide you back into downward dog."

Oh, this, Fraser looked forward to seeing. Harper didn't mirror the movements quite as elegantly as the instructor, kicking her leg back with a loud, "Fuck me!", but the result was the same. A perfect view of her perfectly round bum.

Through her parted legs, Harper finally noticed him and her upside-down eyes widened. "Ah!" she shrieked, collapsing into a heap on the mat.

"Good morning to you, too," he drawled, releasing Bernard from his lead. He bounded over to her limp body, covering her in sloppy kisses as she squirmed beneath him.

Fraser's chest and cheeks ached with laughter as he watched their battle. "I think it's fair to say that we're both *very* impressed with your moves."

"Bernard. Remove your tongue from my ear canal, please." Harper's voice was muffled through her hands. She sat up slowly as Bernard continued to sniff, tail wagging so quickly that it was a blur of brown and white.

Fraser was kind enough to finally guide him away with a click of his fingers and a stern utterance of his name. Bernard wandered off, cocking his leg on one of the saplings to do his business.

Slowly, Harper removed her hands. Her face was flushed, eyes narrowed. "You were spying on me."

He shrugged. "I'm only human. I must say, your downward dog had me all flustered. The frog thing before that, not so much."

"It was supposed to be lizard pose." She reached for her phone and turned off the video. "Melanie seems to think that we all have superhuman flexibility."

"Well, you're certainly one of a kind." He offered out his hands, helping her rise to her feet as he met her gaze. "Will you be capable of walking after that?"

"Remains undecided," she muttered, shaking out her legs with a huff. "I didn't think you'd be here this early."

He checked the scuffed watch on his wrist. "It's almost twelve in the afternoon."

"It's a Saturday. That basically makes it seven in the morning."

"Well, we're on the cusp of winter in Scotland, so you have about four hours of daylight left. Figured you wouldn't want to waste them." He couldn't help but brush an errant curl from her eyes, tucking it behind the pink-tinged arch of her ear. Her skin was cool to the touch, but when she shivered he was sure it wasn't because of the weather. "We don't have to go today if you'd rather spend some more time with Melanie."

"Melanie is not my favourite person at the moment," Harper said, locking her phone. "Which is good news for you, because I'm all yours."

That was music to his ears. He tugged her closer, hands sneaking down to her lower back and tracing along the thick band of her leggings. He didn't know if he was allowed to touch her like this, and yet it was instinct. "Is that right?"

"Well, actually, it depends." Her forehead scrunched suddenly. "We haven't really talked about what's happening here. Properly, I mean."

And there it was. The conversation he hadn't been much looking forward to, mostly because he didn't have any answers. He wasn't interested in starting up something serious, not with anyone, but especially not with a woman who wouldn't be here come January.

Then again, he wasn't usually interested in casual sex, either. He'd thrown his reservations out of the window for her.

"What do you want to be happening?" he asked, hoping she didn't hear the faint quiver in his voice.

"I don't know. I guess I need some clarification on what 'casual' means. We don't know each other that well, after all…"

"We know each other enough that I consider you a friend," he replied. "A friend I may or may not be very attracted to, mind."

Her lips twitched with the trace of a smile. "So, we'll be doing it again?"

"If you'd like." His stomach stirred at the thought.

"Which makes it a friends-with-benefits thing."

"If that's what you want to call it. Like I said. We're two adults having fun."

She nodded zealously. "And there won't be any catching romantic feelings, right? We agree? Because I don't think this needs to be overcomplicated, and I don't think it would be wise to start something. I have to focus on my book. You have to focus on...wood."

"I have other interests than wood, sunshine." But still, he agreed, "No catching feelings. No complications."

Satisfied, she stood on her tiptoes to peck the corner of his mouth, her lips silky against his rough stubble. "Then we have a deal. Let's go and see some fairies — casually. As friends. But first, I have to change."

He pressed his lips together, wondering how many times she planned to specify *just* how casual they were. Did she think he needed the reminder, or was it for her own benefit?

Still, he followed her into the cabin, Bernard at their ankles, and tried not to let it irk him. Tried not to wonder *why* it did.

"Would you take a picture of me on this tree stump?" Harper asked, shoving her phone into Fraser's hands before he could object. They'd only just begun their walk along the Fairy Trail footpath, and it had taken close to an hour to reach the trailhead.

Mostly, it had been because Harper refused to continue without a cup of a cinnamon and hazelnut hot chocolate from the coffee truck stationed in the car park. Then, she'd needed a wee. Then, she'd had to video herself for an Instagram story to inform her followers that she was about to meet fairies she didn't even believe in. Delving further into the world of Harper was certainly an experience, and one that tested his patience. At least she'd kept his grumpy face out of the shot.

He sipped his own latte, then propped the cup next to his feet so he could give his subpar photography skills his full attention. Harper climbed onto the wide, growth-ringed tree stump, which stood among an assortment of whimsical garden gnomes, plucked wildflowers, and, weirdly, a single pack of sliced cheese – soggy offerings that people had left for the fairies in exchange for good luck. This place had been part of local seelie and pixie lore for hundreds of years. Though most people no longer believed that little winged creatures lived in the wildflowers surrounding the woodland walk, people still brought gifts and allowed themselves, for a moment, to believe in magic.

It was his favourite place to take his nieces and nephews for that reason.

"Okay. Smile."

Harper didn't, instead angling her body sideways and sweeping her hair back, her gaze landing on the forest floor.

Fraser waited. Cleared his throat. Wondered if maybe she'd seen a spider and was paralysed by fear, as he secretly would be. "Erm… Are you alright?"

"Are you taking them or not?" She huffed, still frozen in position.

"Oh. I thought you were distracted."

"I am trying to look natural! Candid!"

His brows lifted, but he tried his best to school his features into sober understanding. "Ah. I see that now. Sorry." The phone clicked incessantly as he captured her, still staring downwards, still looking like she was trying not to step on a flower with one heel lifted off the ground.

She looked beautiful, of course, in a cream turtleneck and dark green tartan trousers beneath her duster coat. She always did. But he didn't really get it. This wasn't her. Her followers wouldn't see her smile, or her bright eyes, or the way her entire body changed with every expression she made, every emotion she felt.

Selfishly, he was glad. He wanted to keep those parts for himself. Let him be the only one who really saw her, if only while she was here.

But that would be doing the rest of the world, or at least the virtual one, a disservice. If this social media shite was important to her, the least she could do was showcase herself properly.

He decided that, if she wasn't going to do that, he would wrestle it out of her. He gasped, pointing to the nearest tree. "Is that a wee pixie?"

She hopped up on her toes and shouted, "*Where*?" just as the camera shuttered. He beamed. Perfect. The last image showed the real Harper, mouth parted in a half-smile, face illuminated as she searched the foliage for something that didn't exist.

Chuckling, he said, "I thought you didn't believe in fairies."

Her pout was nothing short of adorable, so he snapped that, too, until she covered her face. "Stop! I need a *nice* picture! You're not taking your duties seriously."

"Oh, shut it. I got plenty of nice pictures, see?" Just as he reached out to hand the phone back, the squeak of rubber soles against wet wood sliced between them.

It happened in slow motion. Her arms windmilled through the air as she stumbled back—

Phone still clenched in his hand, Fraser caught her, bearing her weight before she could topple off the stump entirely. "I've got you," he whispered.

And he had. All of her. She looped her arms around his neck, breaths serrated enough to convey her surprise, as well as that split moment of terror that must have jolted through her before he'd steadied her.

"That was close," she said, the smell of cocoa and spice lacing her breath. She was so near he could feel its heat fanning across his face, teasing him with how she might taste if he kissed her.

Would that be casual enough?

Did he care?

"And you wonder why I don't want you walking in the woods alone," he groused, gaze snagging on the soft pink of her cold nose, the depthless molten brown of her irises.

She giggled, using him as a crutch as she landed on solid ground again. The last dregs of her drink sloshed around in her cup, and she drained them as though unfazed. "You just wanted an excuse to feel me up."

"Oh, aye. That's what it was."

His grin was unwavering as she snatched her phone and skipped away. Would he ever be able to catch up to her, or would she always be one step ahead of him? She was wittier than him. More complicated, yet somehow easier to read.

She was more than he could ever prepare himself for, and when she walked away, he could do nothing but follow.

So he did.

15

"Oh, wow. Look at these." Harper bent down to admire the little wooden carvings scattered along the winding trail. Somebody had crafted a fairy house out of tree bark and moss, with a roof made of pinecones and tiny painted toadstools flanking either side of the grass-green door. "This is gorgeous. I wonder who made them!"

Whoever it was, they were talented. Wooden fairy figurines guarded the miniature house, with silver wings and bright clothes. One of them wore a green dress with blonde, shorn hair and rosy skin like an androgynous version of Tinkerbell. Another had a gorgeous brown complexion and wore an iridescent rainbow sari. On the other side of the trail, more guided the way, diverse in their styles. A pixie sitting in a moss-covered wheelchair made of twigs. A boy with silver piercings in his ears talking to a carved squirrel.

It only occurred to her then that all of the fairy ornaments she'd admired in antique shops had looked the same. White, slim women with long, flowing hair. She saw her own body type here, among so many others. Somebody had taken time to make these figurines look like real people.

Harper leaned back on her haunches, a flutter rising in her. She'd been wrong to dismiss this place. It was beautiful. Magical.

"The kids love playing with this stuff." A sweet smile graced Fraser's lips, as it did every time he talked about his family. Harper could very easily swoon over it, but she wouldn't. It shouldn't have been so groundbreaking, to see a big, strong man with a gentle heart. Her standards, it seemed, were lower than the ground her boots sank into.

"Shouldn't they be kept out of reach? What if someone breaks them?" Harper snapped photographs, then twisted to take a selfie with the fairies for good measure.

Fraser evidently suppressed a smirk. "I think whoever made them wanted them to be enjoyed. New ones appear all the time. The artist is local."

"You know them?"

"No. They stay anonymous. But this is the only place where they appear, so everybody reckons they must live close by."

She whistled, and then indulged herself by opening the arched door of the fairy house. Inside, miniscule lights twinkled against the darkening afternoon. "I want to live here. It's almost as big as your cabin."

"And it matches your height perfectly," he quipped, causing her to stick her tongue out at him. She wasn't *that* short at five foot four, but his tall stature made her feel it.

"Good things come in small packages."

His eyes grazed across her ass. "Aye. That they do."

Harper's collar felt tight. She stood up, brushing the wrinkles from her jeans and continuing along the trail. She sensed that same fire burn a hole in her back and knew he was still admiring her, which almost made her forget how to walk.

As they wandered over swirling paths and meandered through heather-dappled woods, the beginnings of a story began to take shape in her mind. It was only a glimmer, a couple of words here and there, but the images flashed in front of her like scenes from a movie. Taffeta whispering across pine needles. Heavy boots trailing behind. Maybe even gossamer wings of the mythical beings she'd mocked not so long ago. She'd been very much enjoying her journey into fairy literature, after all.

Hastily, she riffled through her suede shoulder bag, pulling out the contents in a wild panic to find her stationery. "We need to stop. My brain is finally working like an author's and I need to write before I forget everything."

Fraser caught her belongings, bewildered. A pile of all sorts of rubbish she'd forgotten to clear out of her bag since last autumn grew in his hands, then spilled into his arms. An old makeup bag with brushes and loose powder. A hairbrush with bent bristles. A bag of Haribo sweets – "You can have them, if you want," she offered. "Haribos don't expire, do they?"

"The gummy bears' faces have melted," he replied, scrutinising the colourful sweets before catching another round of rubbish, including several receipts and a bar of chocolate melted into the shape of her house keys.

Of course, her notebook had fallen to the very bottom as the heaviest thing inside. She shifted from foot to foot impatiently as she finally dragged it out along with her pen. "Okay—"

"Give that here," he interrupted, gently tugging the strap of her purse over her head so he could begin putting her things back inside. He opened the sweets, throwing a cola bottle up in the air and catching it in his mouth.

She arched an eyebrow. "Impressive." Secretly, she also found it strangely attractive, but right now, she had other things to worry about – such as the bestseller coming to life in her head.

"Turn around," she demanded. "I need a flat surface."

Fraser appeared amused. "Or we could go and sit on that bench by the loch." He pointed beyond the trees, and she followed the direction to find they had, in fact, circled back around to the other side of Loch Teàrlag. The water lapped like the tide onto the silty shore, and benches decorated with wilting flowers looked upon the vast view.

She ran between the trees, through overgrown, wet blades of grass and wilting heather, and seated herself on the first bench she came to, wincing when the damp seeped into her trousers. But she couldn't care about that now. She opened a fresh page in her notebook, jotting down the new, fictional world yawning open in her mind. She'd thought about starting with a children's book, assuming, probably incorrectly, that it would be easier for her to write a shorter work without all the complications of adult life, but the characters she was envisioning now were her age. Two people colliding in a timeless, far-off place. They didn't have names or faces yet, but she saw their lives weaving through the forest. She saw fairy friends and a shelter among the trees.

She was only vaguely aware of Fraser's presence warming her side, and worked hard to tune out the sounds of him chewing on her melted sweets. "So, what are you writing? Will it be inspired by your trip?"

"Shh!" she hissed sharply, hand aching as she kept writing. When he tried to peer over her shoulder, she shimmied down to the end of the bench. "You've distracted me enough this week."

"Oh, so I'm distracting?" He kicked out his legs, wearing a self-satisfied expression that made her own lip curl. His cockiness was all for show. She'd seen beyond it already, seen him act kind and loving and humble. He just liked to tease her.

"You're annoying," she muttered.

"You love it."

That, she couldn't deny. Her mouth tugged up at the corner, proving it, but she kept her eyes trained on her page.

Fraser stayed quiet as she worked, growing still as he surveyed the view. He relaxed finally, pressing himself into the bench and resting an arm behind her back. Across the water, the lights of the Raindrop Café twinkled, and Captain Angus's tall, beloved trees reflected in the bleak grey surface of the loch.

The quiet that had fallen upon them was disarming once she crawled out of her busy brain for long enough to become aware of it. Harper couldn't remember the last time she'd felt so at ease.

It wasn't just being here. His presence offered peace, like he was an anchor grounding her into the here and now. Before, she'd forgotten that the here and now existed. She was too busy trying to perform all the time. Too busy thinking of the next interesting or funny thing to say, or filling the silence by posting online. Too busy trying to predict a future that remained terrifyingly uncertain.

Harper's pen hovered over the page, as she found herself suddenly relieved that she wasn't currently wallowing in the flat she and Kenzie had shared in Salford. Had she ever felt so comfortable there, with her?

"Finished?" Fraser asked, yanking her out of her thoughts so quickly that she flinched.

"Um…" She looked down at her page and could no longer remember what she wanted to write next. She'd been so certain that she'd found her story, but all at once, it was gone. Her brain was white noise, a million questions buzzing like static until they blurred into one. "The inspiration has passed, I think."

"Well, you got something down. That's progress, eh?"

It didn't feel like it. It felt like, by letting Kenzie intrude on her thoughts again, she'd fallen back five steps after walking forwards only six. She sighed, closing the book and setting it aside to take in the view.

"Your magical Fairy Trail worked," she admitted, wrapping her jacket tighter. "I can tick it off my list."

Fraser scanned the area, then smirked mischievously. "We could cross something else off, if you wanted."

She frowned. "What d'you mean?"

"It's perfect weather for a swim, don't you think?"

"No," she replied immediately. "Absolutely not."

"Oh, c'mon. Where's your sense of adventure?" He was already standing up, unzipping his coat as though they weren't on the cusp of winter. In the north of the UK. On an overcast day. Granted, it wasn't as cold as Harper had prepared for with her autumnal layers, but still…

But still, you're a coward, that little judgemental voice in the back of her mind chimed.

It was right. It could have been summer, and she still wouldn't have felt particularly ready to strip off and wade into the water. She usually only planned things she could predict the outcome for, like buying a succulent, knowing the worst thing that could happen was it might (would) die, or applying for a job while already expecting the rejection.

If she went into the loch, she could drown, or catch a disease, or have to walk back to the car damp and uncomfortable.

"I like to prioritise my health over adventure," she murmured, folding her arms.

"Well, I fancy a nice, cool swim…" He peeled off his jumper and T-shirt without warning, and Harper's entire world pivoted too quickly for her to hold on.

He was glorious. Toned and broad, with a pouch of softness around his stomach. Tattoos swirled up his arms and across his chest, some of them interweaving patterns and others gorgeous artwork: a wolf on the thickest part of his bicep, an eerie copse of trees beneath his collarbone, a compass on his sternum.

He was beautiful, and that was only more reason *not* to join him. She wasn't brave enough to be so bare. So exposed. Not in front of him.

He kicked off his boots and tugged off his socks, leaving them neatly by the foot of the bench before heading out to the shore. She watched feathered, inky wings flap across his shoulder blades as he moved and let out a quiet groan. Did she really want to hold back from this, from him? Would she regret it?

The wind blew open her notebook, and she seized this serendipitous moment to flip through to her *Guide to Inspiration*.

7. Wild swimming?????????? (probably not)

Maybe it was time she started keeping promises to herself.

Fraser waded into the loch in his black briefs, his gruff laughter bounding over the surface like a skipping stone. "Fuck, that feels good!"

Harper gulped, the sight of his jeans abandoned on the shore a tantalising temptation. His strong, muscular frame tensed against the small waves lapping his waist.

She couldn't resist him.

"Fuck's sake," she muttered as she toed off her boots, then triple-checked there was no one watching as she made her way down to the water. She took a deep, trembling breath – and then shucked off her clothes slowly, waiting for instinct to kick in and knock some sense into her.

It might have, only Fraser's mouth fell open a fraction as he watched her undress, and he dipped his chin below the surface of the water with shadows in his eyes. Goose-bumps left her skin sensitive and coarse, her nipples firm and aching against her bra. She closed her eyes, trying not to wonder if he liked her body, or liked her in spite of it.

She hated to think of herself like that, but she knew that people – albeit weak people she tried to avoid at all costs – often preferred women who didn't take up too much space. Women whose skin was smooth and whose stomachs were flat.

"Is it casual enough for me to tell you that you're fucking beautiful?"

Fraser's words took her aback. She fluttered her lids open, finding his gaze dark and lustful. Beads of water dripped from his beard, and he licked his lips in a way that made her toes curl into the gritty sand.

Desire warmed her freezing skin, driving her forwards. "I'll never say no to a compliment."

"Well then, you'll like plenty of what I have to say."

Harper's legs trembled as she stepped out of her trousers leaving them beside his. She wasn't brave enough to take off her underwear, but was certainly thankful she'd chosen her more expensive pair, a matching mint-green set with a rose lace trim, just in case they accidentally fell into another unplanned state of undress.

Just when she felt *sort of* sexy enough, though, she dipped her toe in the water – and screamed. It was freezing. "Are you *kidding*?"

"Oh, come on. It's not that bad. Easier if you just get in."

"Not that *bad*?" she repeated incredulously, teeth chattering. "I was right. You do want me dead."

He splashed her, causing her to squeal again. "Stop!"

"Come on, sunshine. Get in here. You've teased me enough, don't you think?"

She narrowed her eyes, half-tempted to *keep* teasing him from the comfort of her current body temperature. But he beckoned her towards him, daring her, and she refused to admit defeat.

She inched further, wincing as the cold penetrated her skin, straight into her bones. She held her breath, relieved when it became bearable.

The water rippled between them as she reached him. She uttered another shriek as she lost her footing on the silt loch bed, but he was there to catch her. Again. Wispy laughter passed between them as he steadied her, his hands squeezing the dips of her hips. His skin was a current of warmth in a sea of ice.

"You're a liar," she mumbled, lowering herself so that her hair floated on the surface like tendrils of light. The chill crawled up her neck, or perhaps that was just the anticipation buzzing between them. She could no longer decide which her body was reacting to, the feelings too intense to pinpoint where one started and the other began. "It's not easier."

"If you were still up there, getting in one toe at a time, you'd never make it."

"I think…" She shuddered, teeth clacking without her control, "…that this is the most ridiculous thing I've ever done."

"Vaulting over my fence is the most ridiculous thing you've ever done."

She stumbled closer, their knees colliding. "You're never going to let me live that down, are you?"

Fraser shook his head resolutely. "Nope." He brushed a stray hair from her eyes, tucking it behind her ear. "I've never seen anything like it. Never seen anything like you."

"Is that an insult or a compliment?" she asked, although she thought she knew the answer. His expression was affectionate enough to make her gut swirl.

"It's a compliment, Harper," he whispered, leaning closer. "How could it be anything else? Look at you."

His firm hand found her ass; squeezed as though in promise.

Suddenly, she wasn't thinking of the cold at all. Only he existed, and she preferred it that way.

She leaned in and kissed him. He pulled her close with effortless determination, her body moving through the water as compliantly as if it were his. Her breath escaped her lungs in a gasp at the feeling of such weightlessness. He could do anything with her. She would let him.

Heat bloomed between them as her hands roved his bare torso, from the smooth path of his spine to the hair dusting his chest. His tongue travelled along the seam of her lips, begging for access. She granted it freely, fingers curling into his sinewy shoulders when he hoisted her legs around his waist. When he cupped her ass again, a guttural sound fell from his throat, which made her shudder.

Kissing her neck, he waded with her into a shadowed cove, where the water was so deep that only their shoulders remained above the surface. He tasted like mint and moss, and it made her dizzy. Control fell away as she began to rock against him, her searing core driving against his erection until she felt him twitch.

"What if someone catches us?" she whispered. His answer wouldn't stop her: she was already reaching to pump him in her palm, feasting on his small moan when she traced the shape of his tip. Anticipation was a living thing inside her, rushing through her blood.

"Nobody can see us here. Too far from the path." He nuzzled his cold nose against the crook of her neck, carrying her shoreward until a smooth rock met her back. "Fuck, Harper. Let me taste you. All I want is to taste you."

"Here?" At least if they were in the water, nobody could see their bodies intertwining. As much as she wanted his mouth on her, lapping against her like the waves – and god, she wanted that so much – she was afraid, not just of others seeing them, but of him seeing her. She'd always felt so exposed with other partners when they were pleasuring her, sometimes so much that she was too preoccupied to climax. It had taken months to feel comfortable with Kenzie.

Fraser lifted her onto the flat, sturdy rock behind her back, looking up at her. Droplets fell from his lashes, his hair, and he licked his lips hungrily. "Here. If you want it."

She looked beyond him. The loch stretched out in a sheet of endless silver, the café barely a red dot on the other side. He was right: there was no one here to see, the path hidden behind the trees and the cove shielding their cosy corner of the world. He wouldn't let her do this if it was dangerous – she was certain of that.

She nodded, nipples hardening with desire. "I want it."

Carefully, he peeled her underwear down her thighs, her calves, kissing her cool, wet skin along the way. He rose back to her inner thighs, following the white stretch marks she'd always hated before but now, suddenly, adored. She would adore anything he could kiss, anything he could touch, when it made her feel this good.

As he got closer to the place where she needed him most, she tilted back on her elbows, one hand knotting in his damp hair as she restlessly shimmied her hips closer to his mouth. His broad shoulders tensed, his muscular arms surrounding her in a ring of safety on the surface of the loch.

His laughter rumbled through her like a tight string plucked deep in her core.

"Eager," he muttered. Water dripped from the curling ends of his hair and onto her lower abdomen, only teasing her more. Wetness pooled between her legs, and it had nothing to do with the swim.

"So get on with it," she begged.

He did, tongue parting her slick folds without warning. He kissed her clit until she was shaking, writhing, a sob of pleasure wracking her when he finally slipped a finger inside her. His beard scraped against her thighs so that she could feel him everywhere, and it was almost too much, but still, somehow, not enough.

"Fraser," she rasped, tugging on his hair as her vision blurred. He didn't stop, not even when her thighs grew tight around him, instead holding her hips down with a heavy hand while he toyed with her.

She needed more. She lay back, the cool stone sending a zap of awareness through her. Her jolt only caused more friction between her clit and his rough, desperate mouth, and the water washed over her floating ankles as she squirmed once more.

"So…" he whispered between sucking her, "fucking…"

She cried out, her body tightening with the promise of release.

"Beautiful…" He dragged her hips beneath the surface, his head disappearing with them. The contrast between the cool water and his hot, relentless tongue left her soaked in a bliss she'd never felt before.

Her orgasm roiled through her, yanking her arched spine off the rock and then throwing her back down. As he rose to the surface, he kept her steady, safe, while he savoured her. Until she was so sensitive she could no longer feel her legs.

Fraser kissed her thighs with a new, tamed tenderness, then pulled away, as breathless as her. His hair covered his brow, eyes hooded as his tongue slipped across his lips. Tasting her, she realised. He was still tasting her.

She found the strength to tear herself from the rock and look at him hazily. "Your turn."

16

Fraser was barely able to take his eyes off Harper as he delivered a mug of tea to her designated place on the cabin floor, as close to the lit fire as she could get without singeing her hair. She was too busy typing away to return his gaze as she thanked him in a low mumble, blanket slipping off her shoulders. He joined her cross-legged on the tatty old rug, still chilly from their swim. Of course, his temperature mattered little compared to the satiation she'd given him in that loch. Her mouth around him had felt so insanely good that he'd been sure he was about to ignite, trembling as he came. The way she had flicked her tongue against him, taken him past pleasure and to something completely uncharted...

He was fucked. Literally and figuratively. They weren't "getting it out of their systems" – or, at least, he wasn't. She was etched too deep inside his, and tunnelled deeper every moment they spent in the same room, the same space. Now that he'd tasted her, and she him, he only wanted to know what it would feel like to sink inside of her in every way.

She was dangerous and he was completely *not* casual about it. A casual man wouldn't roar her name as he orgasmed.

A casual man would not be getting a semi just from smelling her damp hair and remembering how it had looked splayed across the rocks. A casual man would not be staring at her right now, and she must have known it, too, because she slowed her typing to peer up at him.

"What?"

He shook his head, settling into the couch as he sipped his tea. "Nothing. Just admiring the view."

She rolled her eyes. Scoffed. "You're a bit of a cheeseball, deep down."

And she didn't know how to take a compliment. That much he was realising. He scratched at his wiry beard, glad for a distraction from his worries. "So, can I know what you're writing yet?"

She smirked. "Let's just say, I got some fresh inspiration."

"Oh, so it's a naughty book, is it?"

"It wasn't supposed to be." She nudged the laptop away to stroke Bernard, nestled beside her on the rug. "I guess I didn't know what it was supposed to be. I'm beginning to find out, though."

"*Harper's Guide to Inspiration* works."

"I'll be publishing a self-help book in no time," she joked. "But today really did help. Thank you for taking me. Literally."

He chuckled, nudging her with his toe. "You're very welcome on both accounts."

"I think I'm going to carry on... with the 'trying new things' thing."

"Aye?"

She nodded as she crawled up the rug to sit closer. "Yeah. I've spent too long doing the same stuff every day and expecting things to change. No wonder Kenzie wanted someone new." She wrinkled her nose. "I was boring before I came here. All I did was go to work and come home."

"Oi!" He jabbed her deep in the ribs, causing her to squirm and slap his hand away. This ex of hers had clearly done some damage. As far as he was concerned, she could fuck right off. "You could never be boring."

"Well, I'm no fancy realtor," she muttered bitterly. "And I definitely don't own my own business."

"What's that got to do with anything?"

"That's what Kenzie's new girlfriend is. She owns one of the most successful real estate companies in the northwest. So she's rich *and* hot – perfect, in other words, just like the mansions she sells. Whereas I'm just the fixer-upper Kenzie couldn't fix."

"You don't need fixing," he said through gritted teeth.

Harper just picked at the frayed ends of her cardigan, shadows dancing across her face, with bursts of orange reflected from the fire. "I shouldn't even be talking about Kenzie."

"You can talk about her as much as you want," he replied. "What you shouldn't be doing is talking about yourself like that."

The sadness dragging down the corners of her mouth left his fingers curling into his palms. His chest ached as he realised she didn't see it. Didn't see herself, not really. Not the way he did.

He wasn't sure how it was possible. Harper was loud and confident and hilarious. She never seemed too afraid to take up space, and those around her were grateful for it. Fuck, she'd even pulled Eiley out of her shell, and *she'd* been shy since the day she was born. How could she be that amazing and not know about it?

His hand found hers, hard and cold as stone on her warm thigh. She frowned at their intertwining fingers as though she didn't understand them. "You're a pain in the neck, Harper, but I think you're perfect."

"Does it bother you that I'm bisexual?"

"Why would that bother me?"

"It bothers some men. Makes them all insecure, like I'm going to go and snog the first woman I come across. Or they ask if that means we can have a threesome, which would be fine if they weren't being misogynistic perverts about it."

He choked on nothing, half-amused and half-alarmed. Was that really what it was like for her? Cam was a lesbian, so he'd seen the occasional judgemental glance thrown her way when she held hands with Sorcha in the street. Not in this town, thank goodness, but it happened.

He hadn't really considered that Harper might have faced her own problems. The way he saw it, someone else's sexuality wasn't something for him to judge. People deserved to define themselves and love however and whoever they wanted, and the idea of that being used as a weapon in any capacity made his blood boil. For his sister, for Andy, for Harper, for every other queer person he'd met, and those he hadn't.

"Jesus. You've come across some serious bastards," he uttered sourly. "No, it doesn't bother me in the slightest."

She finally met his eye, surprise widening her own. Why did she always expect something else? Something worse? Was it because she thought he was a wee bawbag, or was it just that she really had been accustomed to awful people who tore her down?

He cleared his throat, feeling overwhelmed by the intensity of her eye contact. Instead, he looked down and brushed the pad of his thumb around the rim of his mug. "So, this Kenzie… Are you trying to get her back or something? Is that why you're posting all those pictures on Instagram and writing a book and whatnot?"

He tried to keep his tone nonchalant, but he couldn't ignore the waver of dread, the one that whispered it might be true. That she might just be here to transform her image into one that outranked the realtor girlfriend, or at least get revenge by achieving more than Kenzie and this new girl combined. It was natural to want to prove something after being hurt.

Was it natural to have really, really good foreplay with a random bloke in the process?

Thankfully, Harper said, "No. I think maybe I'm better off without her. Although… I wish I could go back and shove it all in her face with a nice six-figure book deal and a glow-up." She chewed on the inside of her cheek. "No, actually.

Scratch that. I wish I could stop caring enough to *want* to shove it in her face."

He sagged against the couch, relieved. He didn't want to be the rebound, even if he still technically was. Even if this was just for fun.

She sighed, grabbing her phone from the wobbly coffee table and beginning to scroll. "I keep checking to see if she's viewing my posts. How sad is that?"

"Well, it's not that easy to let go of someone who's been in your life for a long time." Not that he'd know. He never kept people around for long enough to. Maybe because he'd already experienced enough abandonment to last a lifetime. Even as a thirty-three-year-old, twenty years after his dad left, he still felt it deep inside. That question: *why*? Why hadn't he and his sisters been reason enough to stick around? The arguments with Mum had been relentless, but that wasn't supposed to be their burden, too. Why hadn't Dad ever tried to make it right?

That, he supposed, was proof enough. People lingered, whether you wanted them to or not.

She hummed. "Anyway, enough about her. Let's see if you got any Insta-worthy pictures of me."

"I think you'll be impressed. I am very good at pressing the capture button."

She clicked through the images he'd taken, the posed ones that didn't look like her. "Not bad," she mused.

Unable to help himself, he pried the phone from her hands and flicked to the last few, where she'd been attempting to scope out fairies, and then laughing when she realised she'd fallen for his trick. "These ones are perfect."

Her face contorted with disdain. "I look drunk. And look at my double chin."

He rubbed the nape of his neck. "You look like a real person, having a good time instead of just pouting at the trees. You look like you."

"Oh, Fraser. You are so naive." She tapped his shoulder. "You're not supposed to look like yourself on social media. You're supposed to look like the person everybody else wants to be."

He let out a sharp tut. "Look at this one. You're smiling. Happy. Gorgeous. Isn't that what everyone wants to be?"

She paused, mouth parted in surprise. He could see her scrutinising the picture. Looking for a flaw. As far as he was concerned, there were none.

"There's a leaf on my head," she said finally.

"I know. You walked around the whole trail with it. It was very funny."

She slapped him playfully. "You're awful."

"Yup."

Her eyes snagged back on the picture. "You can see my teeth," she said.

"Breaking news: Manchester woman has incisors."

"I don't like my teeth," she explained. "They don't fit in my mouth properly."

"That's not how teeth work."

"That's what my orthodontist said!"

"You need a new orthodontist."

She huffed, glaring at him like he'd been the one to plant such silly ideas in her head.

It was adorable. It was devastating. He wanted her to see what he saw.

Slowly, he traced figure eights on her thigh. "When you smile, your eyes sparkle," he said. "And you get a little dimple just here." He tapped the side of her mouth. "And here." The side of her chin. "And your cheeks turn round and pink, and I want to kiss them over" – he kissed that ghost of a dimple – "and over again." Another, across her nose and into her Cupid's bow. "I think everybody deserves to know that."

She smiled against his lips. "You always know the right thing to say. It's irritating."

"Aye, I know. I'm terrible," he teased.

She slung her legs across his hips, straddling him – and left her phone abandoned on the floor beside them as she kissed him over and over again.

17

Harper stepped into St. Margaret's the following Monday to a cacophony of song and squeals echoing through the church. It was as lovely inside as it was out, with stained glass windows casting colourful prisms across the pews and the children's artwork scattered on the walls.

She followed the unsynchronised chorus of "The Wheels on the Bus Go Round and Round" towards an oak door, where a laminated sheet of paper was fixed, reading *Community Room and Playgroup* in jazzy WordArt.

She stopped in front of it and took a deep breath. Was this strange? She wasn't part of the community. She didn't have a child. She was only beginning to get to know Fraser, let alone his sisters...

But she'd been invited. Fraser had promised Eiley that she'd be here after talking her into it between slurps of their Pot Noodles yesterday.

So she would be.

She opened the door and stepped inside, barely noticed by the circle of parents, children, and volunteers singing nursery rhymes. Halloween garlands with paper pumpkins and ghosts were draped on every wall, fake cobwebs shrouding every corner in preparation for the coming weekend. A toddler wearing galaxy-patterned ear defenders and a T-shirt reading "Boo!" waddled over to her, a rusk biscuit melting to goo in each fist.

"Hello," Harper knelt down to greet them. The kid was adorable, with wide blue eyes and fine, strawberry blonde hair down to their shoulders. They smiled widely at Harper, displaying two gapped front teeth.

"Sky!" called a soft, familiar voice. Giggling, Eiley tiptoed between toys and children before picking up the toddler and planting kisses on his cherubic cheeks. She looked at Harper and exclaimed, "You came!"

"I did…" Harper straightened up and pouted fondly at Sky, tickling his soft tummy. He looked just like his mum, fair and kind. "Hello there. You're gorgeous!"

Sky let out a stream of giggles, then kicked to get down. As soon as his feet touched the ground, he was off again, seeking out a xylophone to play with.

"Wow, you're lucky you got a smile! He doesn't always pay attention to new faces."

Harper's spirits lifted. She was just glad to receive any welcome at all. "Thank you again for inviting me."

"Of course. Thank you for coming." Eiley tugged at the hem of her jumper nervously. "Would you like to meet my youngest?"

"Yes!" Harper said quickly. They crossed the room to a pram, where an alert baby played with a stuffed lamb. Like Sky, they had bright eyes and wisps of golden hair.

Eiley unfastened them from the seat and tucked them into her chest. "This is Saffron," she said proudly. "Would you like to hold her?"

"Is that okay?" Harper's voice turned frail. She really did love babies.

Eiley tucked Saffron into her arms. Harper wasn't quite sure how to hold her. She adjusted her carefully, letting her jittery, tiny body rest on her arms.

"Oh…" Harper breathed. "She's so precious."

"She's Sky's partner in crime," Eiley replied, smoothing Saffron's hair down. "She's getting big now. She'll be one in spring."

She smiled down at Saffron, holding her attention with silly faces and whispered words.

"She likes you," Eiley said. "Her eyes are usually wandering all over the place, desperate to take everything in."

"Well, I like her, too," Harper said. "I might keep her."

"I might let you. She keeps me up all night long. And my poor mum."

"I bet that's tiring. If you ever need a babysitter, I'm more than happy to steal them away. Did you say you had another?"

She nodded. "Brook is in primary school." She waved someone over, calling, "Sorcha!"

A dark-haired, plump lady who looked not much older than Harper appeared. Her loose jumper was slightly patchy with what Harper feared was regurgitated milk from the heavy baby she burped in her arms.

"All right? You must be Harper!" Sorcha greeted, her inky eyes brimming with warmth. "My Cam's been telling me all about you and Fraser." She cast Harper a knowing look. "How's her matchmaking going?"

Harper's cheeks warmed. *Better than planned*, she wanted to say, but thought it wise not to mention their… *casual* activities in the middle of a preschool gathering.

Still, Sorcha grinned. "Ah, that well, eh?" Her accent was both thicker and huskier than Fraser's and his family's – Glaswegian, Harper suspected. She wore a golden nose ring that twinkled when it hit the light, and her smile was the kind that made Harper want to smile, too, all apple cheeks and crooked lines. She wondered which of them had fallen first: Cam or Sorcha. They were both easy to adore.

"It's… erm, we're just friends."

"Ah, okay." Sorcha's nod was drenched in sarcasm, but she was kind enough to change the subject. "Either way, it's nice to meet you. And this here is Archie."

Archie was much bigger than Eiley's daughter, with chubby arms and legs and bubbles blowing out of his small mouth. Like Cam, his hair was a tuft of auburn curls. It wasn't fair to be surrounded by so many cute babies. Harper was going to melt.

"And over there" – Sorcha continued as Harper shook her hand, and then feared she might never get her index finger back when Archie's fist curled around it – "is his big sister, Isla."

Isla was playing with Sky, kindly passing him toys when he reached for them and showing him how to use them. She must have been one of the oldest children here, with a long black plait down her back, and calmness radiating from her cross-legged position. She was all joy, just like her mothers, and bore more of Sorcha's dark features.

"So," Harper asked, "how can I make myself useful?"

Eiley grinned, and beckoned. "If you're up for some reading, we have the perfect audience for story time. Come with me."

On his lunch break, Fraser found Eiley pacing outside St. Margaret's. Her phone was pressed to her ear, and she murmured responses to whoever was on the other side.

Fraser had a feeling he already knew, and he didn't like it.

She toed the overgrown grass creeping over the footpath, one arm around her middle as though she was trying to hold herself together.

He didn't make himself known until she put the phone away, and then she turned and her shoulders sagged when she saw him waiting. Ready. Her eyes were watery. Only one person could break her resolve like that. He wanted to block Finlay's bloody number from her phone and never let her think about the radge bastard again.

"What was it this time?" he asked quietly. "Did you tell him I have a chainsaw?"

She scoffed at that, but her bottom lip wobbled. "It's fine. It was nothing. Aren't you supposed to be working?"

He shrugged. "I'm on lunch. Jack and I are working at Flockhart's today. Andy went a bit mad with their renovation ideas, so I'll be there for a few weeks." Even with the short notice, he was glad Andy had enrolled him. Jobs grew scarcer this time of year, even with Jack sometimes calling him in to help with carpentry jobs. "But never mind that. What did the bawbag say?"

Eiley massaged her temples wearily, looking out onto the high street. He knew that meant it was nothing good. She didn't look at him when she didn't want to tell him something – because she knew he'd get angrier about it than her. Where she took blow after blow, he was ready to ruin Finlay's life for hurting his sister. It had been years since the problems had started, just after Sky was born, and he hated it. Their mum hated it. Cam hated it, though she was much better at hiding it. They could all do nothing but worry that Eiley wouldn't be able to manage on her own with three kids forever, not when Finlay was still causing problems. Calling her drunk in the middle of the night, claiming that he wanted to see the kids and then not showing up when she allowed him. Somehow, Fraser thought it was worse than what their own dad had done. At least he hadn't bothered to come back and keep upsetting them.

"We've been trying to organise a time for him to see the kids," she said finally, gnawing on her thumbnail.

"Again," Fraser muttered.

"He was supposed to come this afternoon, but he's finding it hard to make time in his busy schedule to get down here."

"Again."

She shook her head, welling up. "Saffron barely even knows who he is."

He pulled her into a hug, resting his chin on the crown of her head. She smelled like Mum's house, like home, but it didn't bring the comfort it once would. It was just another sign that she was struggling. She'd done everything she could to avoid moving back in, and constantly worried she was too much of a burden, but there'd been no other option. She couldn't work when her kids needed her. Saffron was still so tiny. With Sky being autistic and non-verbal, he'd need all of her attention and care until they could find him a school that suited his needs. Fraser tried. So hard. But there was only so much he could do, and he hated it.

"I just don't understand why he doesn't care," she whispered. "Three kids, and he barely sees them. Never thinks to give me any money towards their food and clothes."

"If you're struggling—"

"That's not what I'm saying, Fraser." She pulled away, glassy-eyed and taut with pain. "I know you like to fix things, but it isn't your job this time."

He wouldn't accept that. Couldn't. "I can give you some money, anyway. You know that. I have more coming in with Harper's rent. And if you need me to babysit more, I'm always here."

Eiley sighed, brushing her tousled fringe from her eyes. "I know. Thank you."

"I'll come round later. See if there's anything I can do. Didn't you say Brook's bed is falling apart?"

She nodded glumly. "Everything's falling apart."

It broke his heart. Eiley had always struggled, but he'd once been able to solve every problem with a silly joke or a long, tranquil drive around the woodlands. He wished it was that easy now.

Still, he rubbed warmth into her arms and promised, "I'll fix it."

"You should be spending time with Harper, anyway," Eiley said. "She's just inside, helping out with Dot and Sorcha. The kids adore her, and so do the rest of us. So do you, I bet."

He let out a *pfft* that he hoped sounded natural. "We're just mates."

"Didn't say you weren't," she said with a sly glance, clearly seeing right through him. She always had been able to.

So, he didn't bother hiding it anymore, instead dipping his head.

"Sky's taken a shine to her," she continued. "You know how long it usually takes him to warm up to people. That's proof she has a good nature if you ask me."

That was true. Sky didn't like being cuddled the way Saffron and Brook did. He rarely made eye contact with any of them and was usually lost in his own little bubble. Eiley and the local support workers were doing an amazing job, and he progressed every day, but it was still difficult for him to adjust to certain people and changes. If he was comfortable with Harper, that could only be a good thing.

Or a bad one. What if he got too attached, and then one day Harper was gone?

Sky, that was. Not Fraser.

Not Fraser.

When he said nothing, she elbowed him lightly. "You're allowed to admit you like her. It's not like you aren't making it obvious."

"I *do* like her. Very much…" He fidgeted with his collar, a weight pressing in on him. "Too much, maybe. It's not a good time for either of us to be getting into something, and we agreed to keep things casual."

"*Casual.*" Eiley rolled her eyes. "Finlay and I were casual once. Now we have three kids."

"That's different."

"Yeah, because I fell in love with a selfish prat. You have a bonnie wee girl in there who cares about kids and family and makes everybody around her happy. Don't be a plonker and shut down a relationship because it's out of your comfort zone."

He whistled, rocking on his heels. "Ouch. When did you get so blunt?"

"When I realised that my kids and I are getting walked all over." She winced, running a palm over her tired face. "Sorry. I'm low on patience these days."

"You're exhausted. How about I babysit this weekend? You can have some time to decompress. Watch those sitcoms you like with Mum."

"Are you sure?" she asked, straightening up.

"Certain. Come on. Let's head in." He nudged her into the church, watching her from the corner of his eye as they walked into the preschool room.

This was why he couldn't let things get serious with Harper. People depended on him. His *family* depended on him.

He couldn't afford to be distracted.

18

Harper smiled at her phone screen. After posting a selfie with her laptop in the bookshop this morning, announcing that she was, in fact, writing her first novel, her notifications were full of excited comments from friends, acquaintances, and strangers alike. As she sat with Bernard on the top step of the cabin's porch, though, scrolling through her feed, her good mood soon soured.

Kenzie had posted another picture with her new girlfriend, this one of them in a fancy restaurant, with white wine and tapas on the table as Kenzie nestled into the brunette's ear.

Yuck. Nobody needed to see that. "It should come with an explicit content warning," she said under her breath.

Of course, Harper had felt cute when *she* had taken a similar shot with Kenzie, and her followers had certainly agreed at the time.

She closed her phone before she could start obsessing, finding that it was much easier than it once had been. She wondered for a brief moment whether Kenzie was as happy as the photographs made her look, then brushed the thought away.

She didn't care, she realised. She *really* didn't care. The pain of rejection still lingered, like a barely-scabbed-over wound. Once, she would have wondered what Kenzie was doing right this second, what she was wearing, who she was talking to, whether she'd visited her mum recently, whether she had any holidays booked, what she'd had for lunch. But it had been a while since she'd really wondered what Kenzie's life was like now, detached from their history together. Her only thoughts were bitter and fleeting, like shots of cheap tequila. They burned her throat briefly, but she was moving on.

She leaned against the railing, glad when she heard the squeak of the shed door opening and closing to her right. She'd barely seen Fraser since he'd popped into preschool yesterday. She knew he was busy with Eiley's problems and his own work, but… she'd missed him.

He strolled into view, heading for his chopping block and stilling only for a moment when he realised she was home. "You're back early."

"I wrote four chapters today!" she gushed, but her smile faltered. He wasn't… *looking* at her properly, not the way he usually did. Not with lust and desire, or even with curiosity.

"Nice. Well done. If you were planning to work on it some more, I'm about to be chopping some wood, so…"

Well, that felt like a polite way to tell her to buzz off. She frowned, propping her elbows on her knees. "I'm happy to watch. Maybe you'll serve as some inspiration for the spicier scenes."

He tore the axe from the block, assessing it as though he'd never seen it before. "Oh, aye? It *is* that sort of book, then?"

"Maybe." Her voice lilted with seductive mischief, but whatever she'd hoped to summon from him never came. He turned away, focused on his tool.

Had she misread something? They hadn't been able to keep their hands off one another, and now he would rather gaze longingly at his axe. He positioned the first humongous log with a heavy grunt, muscles taut beneath his shirt. With repetitive, dogged swings that left beads of sweat shining on his brow, he hammered the blade into the wood until it finally cracked open.

"Are you okay?" Harper asked.

He didn't hear her, instead kicking half of the split log away. Then, he kept chopping through the first, biting his bottom lip. His nostrils flared with the force of his determined breaths, every ounce of energy used to splinter through the wood.

Something was wrong. She tried to remind herself that she *always* felt like something was wrong. Secretly, she'd been waiting for Kenzie to dump her since the moment they'd got together, because nothing good lasted and she couldn't imagine somebody wanting her long-term. It hadn't been a surprise when Kenzie had confirmed that insecurity.

But this isn't the same thing. This is casual, she reminded herself. She decided to go inside and make some tea – one for him, in case he decided to pay attention to her.

On the sofa, she opened her laptop, glad when Bernard curled up beside her so she didn't feel so alone. She should write while she had the time.

But her attention kept returning to the man outside. She was tempted to Google "*how to know if a man is giving you the cold shoulder or just really interested in wood*", but that felt silly. She was not doing this. She was easy breezy!

Of course, she tried to write, but no words came, despite them having flowed out of her in torrents this morning. Her hands still ached from all the typing. So, she spent what felt like hours staring at her document until the sky darkened and Fraser finally came inside.

"You really… went to town on those logs," Harper said quietly.

"Yeah, well, it's getting cold. People need firewood."

"How much do you charge, if you don't mind me asking? I should probably start paying for mine. I always have the fire lit!" She let out an awkward laugh, glad when he perched on the arm of the couch beside her. A good sign.

"I don't charge the locals for firewood. If people are able to donate a bit of cash to keep me going, they're welcome to, but with the cost of living going up, I'd rather make sure everybody's keeping warm for free. It's the least I can do."

Her insides turned to hot syrup. He was such a good person, and he said it as though he didn't even realise it. She tilted her head to look up at him. "That's a really kind thing to do for people."

He shrugged. "We're a community. We all do what we can for each other."

It wasn't like that in the city. Her mum's neighbours were fine enough, although they didn't like to talk much and their garden was so overgrown that Mum was always complaining about their tree creeping over the fence. Then Harper had spent much of her twenties in dank and crumbling apartments, with vampiric landlords and elusive flatmates who each survived on microwave meals for one.

"Well, it's lovely. You're very lovely."

His tight-lipped smile was bashful. Hesitant. He got up suddenly. "I have to go, anyway."

"Oh. I was going to ask if you fancied grabbing dinner or something."

He was already tugging on his coat, whistling for Bernard to stop snoozing. "I promised Eiley I'd babysit for her. She's got a lot going on."

"Fair enough." Harper stood up, slowly rounding the couch to face him. "Tomorrow, then? I'm going on a hike with Dot in the morning, but my afternoon is free."

The preschool organiser had been eager to drag Harper along with her hiking group, and made it difficult to say no. Strangely, Harper was looking forward to it. She was enjoying her little adventures more and more each day. Apparently, many authors had made the trek up to Macaskill Ridge, taking inspiration from the vast Highland view.

But Fraser's wariness soon knocked the wind from her sails. "You're going on a *hike*?" he repeated.

She put her hands on her hips. "Yes! And?"

"Are you sure that's safe for anyone involved?" His eyes glinted with devilment.

She nudged him roughly in the arm. "Stop making fun of me! I am finding my outdoorsy side, whether you believe in me or not. Dot said it's beginner-friendly, anyway."

She made to slump begrudgingly back onto the arm of the couch, but he caught her hand lightly, offering an apologetic grimace.

"Oi. Don't be like that. You know I think you're capable of anything." Still, his compliment wasn't delivered nearly as gently as usual, and he soon let go of her.

Her head pounded as she took a step back, schooling her features to hide her hurt. "Is everything all right, Fraser?"

"Why wouldn't it be?"

She played with the edge of the couch nervously. "We just haven't spent much time together this week. You don't seem interested."

"Well, we said this was casual, and I've been swamped with work…"

"I didn't think 'casual' was synonymous with 'hot and cold'." She cleared her throat. "But that's fine. I get it."

"Harper." He stepped towards her again. Finally, some of the warmth she recognised flickered across his features. "I am interested. Of course I am. I'd be mad not to be." His voice was earnest.

Relief left her breathless, limbs going slack, but she tried to mask it with a self-conscious laugh. "Okay. Good."

He traced her jawline with calloused fingers. A shiver went down her spine. She'd missed his touch. Too much. Maybe he was right to back away. She most certainly didn't feel casual tonight. Was she scaring him off?

He didn't seem scared when he kissed her. His tongue pushed into her mouth without warning, fingers tightening across the small of her back.

He pulled away too quickly, leaving her cold, and she fought the urge to complain.

"I'll see you tomorrow," he promised. "Good luck with the hike, eh?"

She nodded, though she wasn't sure if she could keep expecting the things he'd given to her just a few days ago.

Maybe it was over before it had really begun.

"Are you all right back there, Harper? You sound to be breathing quite heavily…" Dot called out from somewhere far, far above Harper. Pausing on the craggy incline of Macaskill Ridge, Harper sucked in as deep a breath as she could manage and looked up, only for cold rain to pelt against her face and blur her vision. She stood in the dreary mid-morning shadow of Dot's hiking group, who waited for her at least twenty paces away in drenched raincoats. All of them middle-aged or older, all of them fitter than Harper and unbothered about the dire weather, all of them smiling like maniacs. Did they really enjoy being beaten up by Mother Nature this much?

God, this was embarrassing. Almost as embarrassing as fancying a bloke who clearly didn't want to take things any further.

Harper wiped the sweat-mingled rain from her clammy skin and rested against a slimy slab of rock, which had an arrow carved into it, pointing up. She hoped that meant she was nearly at the top. "I'm all right. Just a bit out of shape after Christmas."

One of the silver-haired men frowned. "Christmas was ten months ago."

She wasn't sure what his point was. It took Harper a full year to recover from all the cheese boards her mother brought out each year, and by then, it was time to stuff her face all over again.

"Well, maybe it's the altitude. I've never been this high before." She loosened her scarf, fanning her flushed face. If there was any cool air, she could no longer feel it. "What are the symptoms of altitude sickness?"

A few chuckled. Others gawked at her like she'd gone mad, which she probably had.

"Come on. I'll help you up." Dot weaved her way back over the cobbled footpath and offered out her hand with a kind smile. Her curly ginger bob whipped around her face in the harsh wind.

Harper hesitated. She felt ridiculous. If Kenzie were here, she'd be muttering something disparaging: *Breathe through your nose so nobody hears you struggling.*

Come on, slowcoach. Keep up.

Maybe you'd better stay at home next time.

"Maybe I should call it quits. I was never cut out for hiking," she decided finally, voice crackling with pain she was trying very hard to stamp out.

"Well, you could, but that would be very silly…"

She dipped her head, waiting for the criticism to come.

Until Dot continued, "Seeing as you're about thirty steps from the peak."

Surprise struck Harper, and she snapped her head up. "Really?"

Dot squeezed her arm. "You've already made it to the top, and you didn't even know it. You're a wee trooper."

A rattling laugh escaped Harper, and she covered her mouth quickly. Dot motioned for the others to go on ahead, as she linked her arm through Harper's. "It took me years to hush up that voice at the back of my head telling me I couldn't do it. That I was just embarrassing myself. I walked up this hill dozens of times before it felt any easier. But of course, it wasn't my voice at all."

"Whose voice was it?" Harper asked, and barely even noticed when Dot began leading her into a stride again. The soles of her boots slipped against the muddy ground, but she dug her heels in. Persevered.

Dot puckered her mouth like she was sucking on a sour lemon. "That miserable ex-husband of mine. He was always telling me I was incapable of things."

Harper faltered. Dot kept her upright. "Careful. This part's the worst."

But it wasn't the uneven path that had left her stumbling. Was it her own voice claiming she couldn't climb this hill, or was it Kenzie's?

No. That voice had been there before she'd met her.

It had existed for years, growing louder after the bullying at school began. It morphed into a different pitch, a different

173

tone, each time she stumbled across a new person who put her down.

It might have been Kenzie's now, but it hadn't always been. Sometimes, it was her boss, Chris, telling her she was slacking off for taking so much as an afternoon off for a doctor's appointment. Before that, it had been ex-boyfriends, ex-colleagues, teachers, schoolmates.

Maybe that's why she'd put up with it for so long. She was used to it. That voice thrived on other people's doubt, collecting insults like seeds and then planting them back into Harper, as though always waiting for proof that she wasn't enough.

Harper was struggling, but that didn't mean she couldn't do it. Newfound determination surged through her. She pushed her aching muscles up, up, up, with Dot providing support. And just like that, Loch Teàrlag appeared over the ridge. A moment later, the full view spilled out around her, the water a smooth, silver disc at the foot of the hill.

She'd reached the summit.

"See? Not so bad, after all." Dot patted her arm.

Harper would disagree. She was sore from her ribs to her calves, and her side still cramped with a stitch.

But it was worth it to feel this elation. She'd proved her own evil inner critic wrong, and everybody else who wouldn't have believed her capable.

Her reward was a howling gale slapping her hood against her ear and cold, wet mud seeping into her socks, but... she'd done it.

She lifted her hands in the air triumphantly, throwing her head back to feel the rain on her face, and bellowed, "I did it!"

The hikers offered applause, some snorting in amusement, but she didn't mind. Suddenly, embarrassment was not something she had any interest in feeling anymore. All it did was hinder her. If they were laughing at her, let them laugh. She'd accomplished something, and she didn't care what anybody else thought about it.

She took out her phone and captured the view, from the rolling hills dipping into thick forest around them, to the loch she was growing to love. She zoomed in on Raindrop Café, just so she could show Cam later. Maybe she would post the pictures on Instagram, or maybe she would keep them for herself, because this little summit was serene and made her feel tall, and she didn't need likes or comments or views to bring her back to earth just yet.

Her book awakened in her head, her heroine's large silhouette taking form on a mountain much higher than this, where clouds haloed the crags and a quest awaited. Harper wished she had her notebook to jot it down, though it would have turned to soggy mush in this weather.

"So, tell me about these writers you mentioned," Harper asked Dot, shouting to be heard over the downpour.

"Oh, well… I forget who it was. Robert Someone-or-other. He apparently wrote his poems on that bench over there." She pointed to a faded old bench by a plaque engraved with the words "*Macaskill Ridge: where stories begin*." Dying heather and wilting wildflowers surrounded the weathered bronze.

"You sounded much more knowledgeable about it when you were trying to convince me to join the hike," Harper teased.

"And it worked! You're welcome!" Dot gave her a playful nudge, then wandered to chat with two older ladies who were dressed in much more practical gear. Would they let Harper use those sticks to help her balance on the way down? Her legs were starting to feel like jelly.

She edged away from the group, sitting on the bench despite the rain seeping through her thermal leggings. Even if she didn't know which author had sat here, or even if any had at all, it didn't matter. She hoped that, maybe here, she would see the world through a real writer's eyes. Here, maybe more of her book would unfold.

She fell quiet, waiting for it to happen, half-hoping the ghost of this Robert fella might whisper the answers to her.

"Any tips on writing a bestselling book?" she whispered into the wind.

If he replied, she didn't hear it. Maybe he was just shy. Or maybe she was relying too much on external forces to do the hard part for her.

She stood up. Just then, another gust whooshed into her with a force she wasn't expecting, dragging her into the small crowd of hikers. "Ah!"

One of the older women caught her swiftly. "Blimey," a disembodied voice muttered from somewhere inside the lady's big hood. "That's a bloody strong gale!"

Dot grimaced, tightening the strings of her raincoat. "I think we'd better head back before we get blown away!"

But Harper wasn't ready to leave. She tightened her scarf again, eyes never leaving the view. Like the plaque said, her story had just begun. She'd come here for inspiration, after all. "I think I'm going to stay for a while."

19

The weather was miserable, and so was Fraser. What was he trying to prove by keeping Harper at arm's length, other than that he was an eejit? He'd mastered the art of caring for people from a young age, looking after his sisters when he could barely look after himself. Yet now his problem was that he cared too much about a woman who was destined to leave soon enough.

He was a walking paradox. He hated it.

He huffed his way into the tearoom, boots squelching against the glossy wood floors as he approached the counter. His sour mood hadn't been improved by Andy. He loved supporting his friends, but Andy was stressed, and taking it out on everyone. Today, Andy had yelled at Fraser for making too much noise when drilling, then for not working fast enough when he'd quietened down. Jack had suffered a ten-minute rant simply for asking if he could use the bathroom. "I'm losing money every minute we spend closed," Andy had reminded everyone – which made Fraser wonder if they regretted not letting a room to Harper when they had the chance.

Andy's uncharacteristically high-maintenance behaviour *might* have had something to do with their parents being back in town after a summer spent travelling. No doubt, Andy wanted to make the retired owners proud after the management had been passed down just last year, and Fraser understood that completely. He just hadn't known that, beneath Andy's nonchalant exterior, was a grizzly tyrant he was quite afraid of.

Either way, they were on a time crunch. Fraser had volunteered to grab lunch just to be free from all the pressure for a few moments, but the knots didn't leave his shoulders even when he was two streets away from Flockhart's. The miserable weather didn't help. By the time he reached the tearoom, he was soaked through and dripping rainwater all over the polished tiles. He picked up enough sandwiches from the fridge to feed a small army, then ordered a coffee and two teas to go.

As he leaned against the counter, exhausted, he caught Dot waving at him. She sat at a table by the window with the rest of the hiking group, who always finished their Friday morning walk with a natter here. He wasn't much in the mood to socialise, but he went over so as not to be rude, tearing his hood off his head. "Afternoon, Dot. Did you brave the weather this morning?"

They all looked drenched enough to confirm the answer was yes. Their commitment to hiking was something even he couldn't understand, but it was nice to see that the community was so unwavering. Rain or shine, nothing ever really changed in Belbarrow. He wouldn't have it any other way.

"Aye, not even a tornado could stop us!" Dot chortled as her friends agreed jovially. "And we had a new member today. Your Harper!"

"She's, uh, not *my* Harper, Dot." He surveyed the café as though he might find her sitting somewhere nearby. He was sure that if she heard anybody calling her *theirs*, she'd blow a fuse.

"Well, she's *our* Harper now, and she loved it. She even stayed behind to enjoy the wee view! It's ever so nice up on Macaskill. I told her all about Robert Whatshisname writing there."

Fraser blinked. He had no clue who Robert Whatshisname was. Still, the ground swayed beneath him as realisation struck him.

She'd stayed behind. On Macaskill Ridge, of all places.

"She... She's up there in this weather?" He worked to keep his tone light.

"It wasn't so bad," Morag, the tearoom's owner, chimed in beside Dot. "We only got swept around a wee bit."

Her bedraggled grey curls, sitting on her head at all angles, said otherwise.

Ice-cold dread chilled the nape of his neck. "Does she know the way back?"

"Oh, aye. Keith stayed too so he could help her down." Dot patted Fraser's arm. "Besides, she texted me when they were on their way back. She's a big girl. She's fine!"

Was she, though? He wouldn't like it if Cam or Eiley walked to the bus stop in this weather, never mind down Macaskill Ridge.

He wrung his hands as he stared out of the window. It was chaos out there. Howling winds and pouring rain. So dark it might as well have been evening already.

"When did she text you that?" he asked.

Dot squinted. "Well, about… forty minutes ago?"

He shook his head. How could they just leave a tourist out in this? He knew Keith was an experienced hiker – Fraser had met him a few times while delivering firewood to his elderly mother – but *still*…

Whirling on his heels, he pulled out his phone and called Harper. The sight of his thumb trembling against the screen was a shock to his system.

Why did he care this much? Should he? Did he want to?

He told himself he would have reacted the same no matter who it was. He remembered not too many years ago, an air ambulance had been called at that same ridge because a hiker had slipped in severe weather conditions. It could happen easily, and he…

He couldn't finish that sentence. Not when Harper didn't pick up. His call went to voicemail without even ringing.

"Shit," he whispered. Then, to Morag's son at the counter: "Could I grab this order when I come back?"

"Okay." He frowned but put the sandwiches aside. Fraser thanked him then rushed out, away from the chatter of the hiking group and into the relentless torrent. He slipped into his truck quickly and tried to call Harper again.

"Pick up, Harper," he hissed.

She didn't.

There was no way he was going to leave her out there, not knowing if she was all right.

He set off towards Macaskill Ridge and prayed he would find her in one piece.

The rain smudged his view of the cabin, turning the walls and surrounding forest into a grim smear of drab brown and grey. Fraser drummed his fingers against the steering wheel, windshield wipers squeaking through the tense silence as he slumped back in his seat. There was no sign of her near Macaskill, nor inside.

There weren't many places left to look. After a few more moments swimming in panic, he forced himself out of the truck and followed the trail to the café on foot. His last hope. His body bristled with dread, his strides heavy. To anyone else, he would seem ridiculous. Paranoid. Overbearing, just like Cam accused. But he considered it his job to keep Harper safe, just as it was to keep his family afloat. She was his guest. She *trusted* him. If something had happened…

The lights of the café glittered into view, their reflections roiling in the restless loch like yellow watercolours. He marched straight inside, glad to find his sister at the counter, though she appeared alarmed by his dramatic entrance.

"Have you seen her?" His tone bordered on desperate.

Cam smirked. *Smirked.*

His fingers curled into his palms, car keys digging into his flesh – until she gestured over the counter to something behind him.

Slowly, he turned around – and his heart stuttered into its usual rhythm again.

Harper hadn't even noticed him come in. She had her earphones in and typed furiously on her laptop, lost in whatever universe she'd been creating ever since their visit to the Fairy Trail.

He collapsed against the counter, relief searing his skin like scalding water spilled from a kettle. Now he just felt silly. He'd been imagining her in all sorts of states, and she was here. Warm, healthy, safe.

"Something the matter, Frase?" Cam questioned, mirth dancing in her voice. "You look a bit on edge."

"She didn't come back with her hiking group," he muttered. "You could have texted me."

She twirled a strand of hair around her finger, feigning nonchalance. "To save you from having to confront your obvious infatuation? That doesn't sound like me."

"I was worried sick!" he snapped, and then recoiled, an ache building behind his eyes. He wished he didn't always imagine the worst. He might have been thirty-three, but he felt like a kid lost in the supermarket far too often.

Cam's face morphed into worry, the mirth quickly wiped from her features. "Fraser…"

"What's wrong?" Harper's voice echoed in the otherwise empty café, calm and oblivious to the storm raging inside him.

"What's wrong is that I thought you were lost, or hurt." He paced towards her, anger replacing his anxiety without warning. "You didn't come back with Dot."

She regarded him with bewilderment. "I wanted to stay a while longer. There was a nice view."

"In this weather?" He jabbed a finger at the rivulets running down the windows. The loch heaved outside, leaves whistling through the wind as though pulled along by strings. "You could have slipped up there!"

"I wasn't on my own."

"Jesus." Fraser shook his head, nausea bubbling inside him. Of all the strange, unwelcome feelings he'd had for Harper, this was the one he hated most. This was why he'd put distance between them. This was why he didn't do relationships.

"Fraser…" Harper stood up. Took a tentative step towards him.

"Why didn't you pick up your phone?"

She pulled it from her pocket and checked the screen. "No signal. The Wi-Fi must be down. Sorry. I didn't know. But I was fine. I *can* manage a day without you, you know." Her own words were barbed now.

He was in no mood to fight with her. If anything, he wanted to drag her home and kiss her until the tempest inside him settled. Until there were no more doubts that she was safe. Until he could feel her blood pumping, heart beating, and this close encounter with his worst fears became nothing more than a distant memory.

He tore off his coat and draped it over the back of the nearest chair before sagging into the one at her table. He glared at the back of her rose-gold laptop until she sat down opposite, clearly unsettled.

"You're still drenched," he pointed out, pinching one of her damp curls between his fingers.

She shrugged. "I was too cold for a shower in the cabin, and I couldn't find any firewood. Thought I'd dry off here. It's warmer."

"I bought you a heater," he prompted.

She clucked her tongue. "Okay, fine. I was scared the flimsy walls were going to come down in this wind, but that doesn't make me a damsel in distress!"

He wanted to laugh but couldn't find it in him. Now the fear was gone, the anger subdued, he felt hollowed out. His insides were a shipwreck.

Why? Why had this – *she* – affected him so much? *Because she's my guest*, he tried to reason with himself, but that didn't feel like a good enough explanation for such a ridiculous reaction.

"The walls aren't flimsy." When he took her hand, she shivered. "I have a perfectly functioning hot shower in my house."

"Well, I know you're upset, but there's no need to brag." She shut her laptop abruptly.

He scoffed. "You are an eejit, Harper. That was an *offer*, not a brag."

Narrowing her eyes, she leaned forwards. He hated that, even now, in all her stubbornness, she was perfect, baby hairs sticking to her temples and her cheeks an endearing rosy pink. A beauty spot kissed her jaw, just under her double-pierced right earlobe. Why hadn't he noticed it before? Why hadn't he already kissed it?

"An offer," she repeated as though suspicious of some hidden clause. "Does this come as a perk for all your cabin guests?"

"Only the obnoxious ones."

She rolled her eyes and stood up, burying her laptop and notebook in her oversized shoulder bag. "You didn't even ask me how my hike was."

"I know how it was. Wet, windy, and dangerous."

"Cam, your brother is a wrongun," she called over his head.

Cam chuckled. "Only when he cares, believe it or not. That means you have to forgive him."

He couldn't help but admire his sister for recognising this truth. For better or worse.

"I'll think about it," Harper said.

But then she smiled at him and he was certain that, for just a moment, the rain stopped pouring.

20

"I'm in trouble because of you," Fraser said as he fetched a rattling set of keys from his jeans.

Harper fiddled with the sleeve of her jumper, feeling coy as she waited for him to open the white front door. She hadn't known what to expect when he'd offered to take her to his house: it was hard to imagine he lived anywhere that wasn't made from the trees he spent all day caring for. But they'd meandered back through Belbarrow, passing quiet avenues of terraced houses and, at the very end, a crooked collection of narrow cottages set beside an empty playground on a marshy football field.

He'd halted at the end of a street named Farmview Way. His house was set back behind a withering garden and a row of neat hedges. Beside her, a drain gushed rainwater, and she sidled under the portico to keep dry. There, she noticed a black cat hiding behind the dustbins, tail wafting as its alert green eyes watched Fraser open the door.

"Why are you in trouble? But more importantly, is that your cat?"

He mumbled something nondescript, no doubt about her short attention span. "The neighbour's. She's Bernard's buddy. She's always waiting for him to come out."

Speaking of whom, the dog's barks echoed behind the door. Once it opened, a blur of white and brown raced towards them. Harper giggled, bending down to greet Bernard properly.

"Come on. Let's get dry." Fraser ushered them all inside, then kicked off his boots. He disappeared down a narrow corridor into what looked to be a kitchen and opened the back door, commanding Bernard to do his business.

Harper hovered on the welcome mat, feeling suddenly out of her comfort zone. It had been easy to convince herself she didn't know Fraser well enough to fall for him, when she'd only seen half of his life.

But here was the other half. Pictures of his sisters, nieces, and nephews on the walls. The fragrance of spiced apples and fresh laundry in the air. While he refilled Bernard's food and water bowls, she crept forwards and peeked into the living room. A cream throw was draped across the back of a grey couch. Toys and books were cluttered haphazardly in one corner, and in another, a shelf was piled with a jumble of DVDs, CDs, and books. A fireplace spanned one wall, a TV mounted above it. It was nice. Cosy. A perfect mixture of chaos and stability.

Bernard came in and shook the water from his fur, leaving paw prints on his way to the food bowl.

"You don't have to wait there," Fraser said, closing the door on the rain before returning to her. "I'll grab you a clean towel, and you can take that shower."

Harper really was looking forward to a hot shower, even more than she'd like to admit. Still, Fraser wasn't looking at her properly, and she wasn't sure she wanted to take her clothes off in a place where she didn't feel completely safe.

"You didn't answer my question. Why are you in trouble because of me?" Her heart hammered against her ribs as he drew closer.

He barely seemed to be listening, his gaze roaming her features, slow and intent, as though seeing her for the first time. That familiar tension throbbed between them, and it was an effort to remain still beneath its weight. "I was supposed to be working with Andy at the B&B," he explained. "They aren't happy that I disappeared on them."

"I'm sure they'll forgive you – but you can't blame *me* for it. I was minding my own business. It isn't my fault you're devastatingly obsessed with me."

The ghost of a smirk crossed his face. But it wasn't enough to reassure her.

"Why have you fallen out with me, Fraser?" She nudged him, hoping he didn't hear the crack of vulnerability in her voice.

Fraser frowned as he swiped a damp ringlet from her eyes and tucked it behind her ear, rough fingertips grazing her skin. "I haven't fallen out with you, sunshine. What are you on about?"

"You've been… off. And you made a scene in the café, in front of your sister. You were angry."

He scraped his hair back and huffed. "Aye, because I drove around all afternoon, wondering if you were dead in a ditch somewhere."

"Again, *why*?" Harper asked. "I was fine, and I'm not your responsibility."

"The authorities might disagree if they find out a woman living under my roof went missing."

Ah. So that's what it was. It wasn't that he cared, not really.

She turned away. "Lucky you got off easy this time, then." She made to brush past him, assuming the shower he'd promised would be up the carpeted stairs, but he reached out and drew her close, so close that her breath caught in her throat.

"And I was worried about you," he muttered. "Obviously."

"*Obviously*," she repeated with a hint of snark, though lust and something far hotter, far rawer, bloomed within her.

He kissed her lightly, his mouth feathering across her cheek. "Sorry for being a bastard."

"At least something about you is consistent," she taunted, resting her hand against his chest.

He clasped it with tender care. "You're freezing."

"So warm me up." It was a dare, one she hoped he'd accept. She hated to be so transparent, but it felt like eons since he'd last touched her like this, and she *needed* him. Her entire body fluttered with desire and, god, she wished she could read him half as well as he could her. She wished she knew why he pushed her away only to pull her back closer than ever. Did he only want her when it suited him? Was she falling into a dangerous pattern?

Her worries must have been etched across her face, because he paused with his lips only a hair from hers. "What's wrong?"

"I just wish I knew what you were thinking," she admitted.

"I'm thinking" – he kissed her slowly, hungrily – "that you drive me mad. All the time. I could barely work this morning thinking of you."

"Keep talking," she whispered, softening into him finally.

He kissed her again, tongue heavy and slow in her mouth. "I'm thinking that I don't feel very casual anymore, and that's a problem."

"Is it?"

His hands roved the back of her thighs, encouraging her to rise. She hitched herself onto him, legs wrapping around his hips. His features were sombre as he nodded. "In case you haven't noticed, I lost my mind today."

"I'm good with you losing your mind over me."

He sighed. "Harper. You're not going to be here forever."

That was true, though it was hard to remember what her life had looked like before coming here. Meeting him. She'd been looking forward to going home and bragging about her wonderful trip. How productive she'd been. How excited she was to pursue a new career. Now, the thought of leaving at all made her deflated and numb.

She pushed it all away, cupping his jaw in her hands. "So why can't we just make the most of it? We have time."

He hesitated as though there was so much more he wanted to say. She understood. She was afraid, too, to give too much of herself and end up regretting it when it was time to say goodbye. Kenzie had already stolen so many pieces of her. Would there be any of her to salvage if she left more with him?

But with Fraser it was different, she convinced herself. She already knew that this was going to end, which meant she could prepare for it. He couldn't break her heart. He could only crack it, and cracks healed. It was worth it to feel what she felt now. Alive, desired, confident in her own skin for the first time in her life.

Fraser flashed her a ravenous grin. "Making the most of it sounds like a decent idea."

She expected him to put her down – surely his arms ached by now – but he was unwavering as he carried her towards the stairs, and then up them. His strength left her tingling all over. It had been a long time since anybody had made her feel dainty, and she couldn't pretend she didn't enjoy it.

They fell into a bedroom with exposed brick walls and forest-green accents. She was glad for the mess around them, the abandoned jeans pooled in a corner and the dresser top scattered with toiletries. It was good to know he wasn't *completely* perfect, even if he felt terribly close to it in this moment.

She giggled as he laid her on the bed, and his smile grew wide. Unbridled. Her fingers dug into his jumper to keep him there, keep him close, and he parted her legs with a nudge of his knee.

"You still want me to warm you up?" he asked huskily.

Harper's core pulsed with anticipation, and it was an effort not to clench her thighs against him. "Yes."

"And how, d'you think, should I do it?" Gently, he traced up the seam of her thermal leggings. Suddenly, she hated being so covered. She needed to feel him properly. Needed to get rid of all the things keeping them apart.

"Use your imagination." She slipped her hands beneath his jumper.

He jerked back from the cold, chuckling as he grabbed her hands and locked them above her head. "I'm not sure I want you touching me with those blocks of ice."

When his fingers inched towards his belt, she gulped. Was he going to…?

He unfastened the buckle with one swift swipe, yanking the leather from the loops of his jeans one-handed while the other kept her wrists pinned on the bed. It might have been the sexiest thing she'd ever seen. Sexier when he asked, "Is this okay?"

She pouted, fighting against his grip with a squirm, though secretly, she wanted nothing more than to let him take the reins. "What if I *want* to touch you?"

Fraser nudged the waistband of her leggings down, brushing the cool leather belt against her stomach. She bucked her hips, letting him unveil the rest of her. Her leggings were thrown behind him, rendered useless.

"There'll be plenty of time for that later." Ducking, he peppered kisses along the fabric of her underwear. "Fuck, Harper, do you know how many times I've wondered what it would feel like to be inside you? Nobody's ever done this to me before."

"Nobody?" she asked, surprised. She'd assumed he'd had a long line of lucky women in his past. With that face, that body, that charm, he could have anybody he wanted.

But he nuzzled between her breasts hopelessly, drawing up her jumper at a torturously slow pace as though they had all the time in the world before finally ridding her of it. "Nobody like you. I never want to let you go."

"Then make sure I don't," she said, and realised that she meant it. Usually, she loved feeling in control, but right now, lying in his bed in just her sports bra and thong… She wanted to cede all control to him. Give everything over to him. "Tie me up."

Surprise, wild desire, and a hint of trepidation danced in Fraser's eyes. But before he could respond, something behind him stole Harper's attention, and she gave an awkward laugh. "Please can you distract Bernard? He's at the door."

Fraser snapped his head up, snorting at the sight of the dog standing there with one ear cocked. "Jesus. Sorry." He rushed over, nudging Bernard out into the hall. "Bernard, this is not for your eyes, I'm afraid."

The door clicked shut, and Bernard's disgruntled whimper gusted from the hallway.

Fraser returned, both of them chuckling again as he bent over her once more. "He's not used to me having company."

The interruption was soon forgotten as Fraser roved her body with his hands and mouth. It was difficult not to respond in kind, but her hands were still cold, and part of her was content to lie back and let him map her body. She relaxed into his mattress, skin throbbing from the lightest of touches.

"I fucking love these curves," he murmured gruffly, caressing the soft lines of her hips, her waist, the cups of her sports bra. His thumb ghosted across her nipple, and a small keen escaped her. If this was surrendering, maybe she should do it more often. It felt good. *Right.* "Tell me they're mine, Harp. Just for tonight, I want all of you to be mine."

"It's all yours." She arched her back, showing him that she meant it. "*I'm* yours. What do you want to do to me?"

Wonder and lust melded in his stare again, but he shook his head. "I won't be doing anything *to* you. I'll be doing it *for* you. Everything for you." And then, finally, he unhooked her bra, and peeled off his own jumper. She admired his form, dizzy with awe. At the loch, it had all been a blur, but she had time to drink in every stunning inch of him now. His shoulders were sturdy enough to bear anything, but the hard lines of his torso softened beneath his belly button, where a strip of dark hair disappeared into his underwear. His legs were as delicious as she'd imagined, freckled and muscular and adorned here and there with more tattoos.

He looped his belt around her wrists, the brush of the leather leaving her breathless. He tied it just tight enough for her to feel the pressure, then kissed the skin beneath to make sure there was give.

To make sure she still felt safe, she realised.

"Tell me if you don't like it," he said. "I'll take it off."

"I like it," she whispered, surprising even herself. She let her legs fall open – she was wet and desperate now.

Her whole body was his to take, but it had never felt so much like hers before, either. Finally, she controlled it, decided whether it was beautiful or not. Her wide thighs only meant more kisses from him as he made his way around her body, only meant she felt more places where his stubble brushed her skin. Her round stomach and large breasts offered more valleys for him to explore. And when he said, "You're so fucking beautiful, Harp," with sheer reverence shimmering like moonlight in his glossy eyes, she believed him.

"I want you," she begged when she could take no more teasing. When he'd removed her underwear, and taken his time working between her nipples and her clit with more confidence than last time, now he knew what she liked.

Fraser stood from the bed, the tautness of his black briefs accentuating his size. She watched him with anticipation as he went to the nightstand, opened the bottom drawer, and pulled out a silver foil.

They were really doing this. Her legs kicked in an eager search for friction. He watched her splayed form hungrily as he returned to the end of the bed. Finally, he took off his briefs and opened the packet with his teeth. A shudder crawled through her body when he sheathed his cock with the condom, her bottom lip tucked away behind nervous teeth.

"You sure?" he questioned.

"I'm sure."

Once Fraser had buried himself in her, he never wanted to emerge. The way his body sank into hers, it was like he'd been made just for this. Harper released a gasp, fingers clenched in their binding as she wrapped her legs around him and arched her back. He couldn't move, couldn't breathe. Nothing had ever felt this good before.

He squeezed his eyes closed, twirling one finger around her swollen, pink nipple while the other hand kept her bound wrists pinned to the bed. They squirmed against his belt now: impatient, restless.

"Still okay?" he whispered against her neck.

She nodded frantically, then rocked her hips. "More. No need to be gentle."

But she'd said he was in charge tonight, so he was taking his time. He pushed into her slowly, luxuriating in her whimpers. Her lips parted with the pleasure of his movements, then more impatience left her rutting against his tip.

"Fraser," she whispered. Pleaded. He'd never particularly liked his name until now. Until she uttered it like the words of her favourite song.

He thrust into her again, pleasure burning bright inside. He grabbed her hips, angling her so that he could go deeper, quickening his rhythm, so that her keens would turn to moans.

"I want to touch you," she growled, eyes blazing and wild now.

"You want me to take it off?" he replied, breathless.

But she shook her head, back rising from the mattress as he moved quicker. "Don't. Don't stop."

So he didn't, because he would give her anything she asked for. His climax felt dangerously close already, but he needed her to come first. He dragged a finger around the slick base of his cock, then up to slide over her clit. "God, I love your perfect pussy. So wet for me. Is this mine, too?"

"Oh, god," she cried out. "Now. Untie me."

"You didn't answer my question, Harp," he teased, smirking down at her as he slowed his pace, one hand brushing the belt buckle. "Whose. Perfect. Pussy. Is. This?"

"I'll. Say. It," she taunted, "when I'm on top."

He swore, more than willing to comply. She broke free in a frenzy, hands journeying across his chest, his back, his ass, then they landed in his hair, tight and unforgiving.

"This is mine?" she murmured as she nipped at his bottom lip, then again as she closed one of her pretty hands around his neck.

"*All* yours." He rolled onto his back, filling his palms with her perfect thighs as she straddled him.

"Does this still feel okay?" she asked, wide-eyed, lowering herself until she was taking all of him. *Okay* was an understatement. He felt like the luckiest man on the fucking planet.

"Fuck, yes," he muttered roughly.

Still looking straight into his eyes, she sought purchase on his chest and began to circle her hips, slowly at first, telling him what she'd promised to and more – saying things that made him gasp in rapturous shock. Then, when he began grazing her most sensitive parts with deliberately light pressure, she dissolved into wordless abandon. God, she was beautiful when she did that. Watching her use him, fuck him, was an image he wanted seared into his brain forever. Wanted it in an oil painting on his fucking wall.

Her head fell back, jerking as a whimper escaped her. "Are you close?"

He'd been close since they'd started, but he could feel the haze creeping over, the pleasure getting tighter. "So close."

Her answering cry bounced off his ceiling, and he forced his eyes open to watch her fall apart as she clenched around him. They came together, tangled and writhing until at last she fell forwards and melted against his chest.

"Well," she panted, "that was… liberating."

"Aye." He laughed thickly, kissing her forehead. "*Making the most of it* really was a very, very good idea."

21

"Nobody else knows about this," Fraser warned as they approached his shed door.

Harper's eyes widened. She hadn't been very impressed when Fraser led them back to the cabin on the morning of Halloween, claiming he had a surprise for her. The place was growing on her, sure, but the only surprising thing she'd found there so far involved the big hairy spiders in the bathroom and what temperature the shower might be each day. She'd have much preferred staying at Fraser's, having almost forgotten what sleeping in a real house felt like.

But excitement and nervousness stirred within her now. What was Fraser hiding in the shed that he'd been so tetchy about? "It isn't a secret sex room or something, is it? I don't know if I'm ready for that."

He laughed, and took out a rusty key. At their feet, Bernard let out a bark before running off to chase the squirrels. "No sex room. I don't think we need one after last night."

She flushed at the memory.

"But it is personal," he said, "so please don't make too much fun of me."

"I would never do that."

"You always do that," he reminded.

She pursed her lips. Making fun was in her northern blood as much as her obsession for cheesy chips and gravy was, but she schooled her features to show her sincerity. "Only about silly things. If you're trusting me with something... well, I won't make you regret it. Promise."

She took his hand, squeezing gently, and he relaxed. Still, his jaw ticked as he nudged the door open, and she realised he might truly be showing her something real. Something he cared about.

Fraser opened the door and they stepped inside. The air hung thick with the scent of gloss and wood shavings, chalky paint and glue. He flicked a switch, and the shed was bathed in dull light.

Harper gasped. The small outhouse hadn't looked big enough to contain so much. The dusty space was filled with elegant furniture that was not at all the same shabby-chic style as the cabin's. Gilded storage chests carved with swirling cartouches, wall cabinets etched with elaborate vines and flowers, tables and chairs with ornate legs and paint-speckled surfaces. Standing against the wall to her left was a sky-blue bookcase that would look perfect in a child's room. Fluffy painted clouds billowed over the frame, which rose to a roof-like point at the top, and a colourful hot air balloon drifted above the top shelf.

"What do you mean nobody knows about this?" She whispered it as though she was in some sacred space. This wasn't just furniture. This was art, and the style was more beautiful than any she'd seen before. "*Why?*" she added as an afterthought, lost for words.

His shrug was too nonchalant for her liking. "I've been wanting to gift some of these pieces for years, but…"

"But?"

"I'm worried it would stop being a hobby. It would stop being *mine*, if other people knew about it." He avoided her gaze, swiping a finger along a dusty worktop surface, and she couldn't help but wonder if there was more to it. More he wasn't saying. His reasons were valid, but they sounded robotic, rehearsed. Like something he didn't believe was true.

And if it *wasn't* true, hiding all this would be such a shame. This furniture was extraordinary. He'd even collected patches of fabric, and some of them were laid out on the worktops, in the process of being sewn together to make seat cushions. A week ago, she wouldn't have believed such heavy hands could handle a needle and thread, but she'd since learned that his deft fingers were capable of *anything*.

And that wasn't all. On the bench against the back wall was a host of smaller, delicate pieces. She edged closer, taking care not to disturb the treasures towering on either side of her. They looked like figurines—

She paused mid-bend, coming face to face with a dark-eyed fairy with platinum hair and a dress made of dried, layered autumn leaves.

She recognised this style.

"Oh my god," she breathed. "*You* made those ornaments on the Fairy Trail!"

Fraser scuffed his feet and shoved his hands in his pockets as though trying to protect himself from something. Embarrassment?

She had never wanted to kiss him more than she did now. All that work, that beauty, kept anonymous because he'd just wanted to make people happy while keeping himself happy, too. Those calloused hands that had roamed every inch of her skin last night were capable of whittling wood into something else, something alive.

"Fraser..." She could see his heart all over this shed and it was beautiful. Gleaming. Gentle.

And he was showing it to her. How could she be the only one he'd allowed in here?

"Not even your sisters—?"

"No one," he said. "They were only meant to be studies, so I could practise carving and painting. It's silly, but I loved making them. One day, I left one on the trail. I thought people might like them. People like silly things sometimes."

Harper shook her head. "They're not silly. They're brilliant."

She held one to her chest, her breast swelling with a strange feeling of fullness.

He smiled wryly. "You can keep that one if you want. You inspired it."

Curious, she peeked at the fairy again.

She saw it now. The dark eyes. The blonde hair. The round pink cheeks and faint smattering of freckles. She didn't know what to say. She felt lightheaded, and wasn't sure if it was the dust, the chemicals, or something she was afraid to name.

"I made something else for you, too." He beckoned her across the shed, to the back left corner. She followed him, fairy still cradled in one hand, to a handsome pale pink desk with blue drawers and lilac shelves. She didn't understand at first, not until she saw the wooden plaque stationed above the top shelf. *Harper's Writing Corner* was painted on it in gold.

A writing desk.

She looked closer, and saw that he'd used the same gold tint to pattern the desktop with little suns. *Sunshine.* "Are you kidding?"

"I haven't varnished it yet, and I didn't know if you liked these colours or…"

"I mean, they are bisexual colours in *pastel*!" she gushed, running her trembling finger along the smooth surface.

He nodded. "I saw the flag on your phone case and figured…."

"I'm going to cry," she admitted shakily. He'd noticed her *phone case*? She'd almost forgotten that she still used the one she'd bought from Manchester Pride last year.

And he'd noticed. He'd really noticed.

He sucked in a sharp breath. "It's that bad?"

"It's that *good*! Nobody has ever done something this thoughtful for me before!"

He finally smiled, though it was lopsided with what she now recognised as self-doubt. She'd been so certain that they were polar opposites, from where they lived right down to their interests. But maybe they weren't so different underneath.

She dabbed her damp eyes, launching into his arms. "I love it so much, Fraser. Thank you."

He pressed a kiss into her hair. "I'm glad you do, Harp. I figured it would look well enough in the cabin. I'll get the crappy workbench out of there, give you some more space to write. I know it's not ideal when I'm working outside, but I still want you to feel like it's yours."

"Watching you chop wood while you work is more than ideal. I just need some noise-cancelling headphones. Can you make those from wood, too?"

He seesawed his hand, pretending to take this request seriously. "I don't think they'd be very comfy, but I'll see what I can do."

"Hmm." She let out a long, content sigh, placing her fairy figurine on the top shelf of the desk. "This makes me feel like a proper author. And a proper fairy."

His fingers drew slow circles on her lower back. "Well, you are both those things in my eyes – and a lot more."

Harper gazed up at him, spellbound and speechless. In that moment, she was a little bit in love with him, but he didn't have to know that. "That time you caught me snooping in your things… I found a birdhouse in the cabinet. Is that why you didn't want me looking? Did you make that, too?" It wasn't nearly as polished as the furniture in here, but every artist started somewhere.

Fraser sniffed and looked away. She narrowed her eyes, worried she'd stepped too far – but why? He'd shown her his work. Why did he still seem… *ashamed* of it? If she had this sort of skill, she'd be flaunting it for everyone to see.

"I did make that," he admitted quietly, "when I was a kid."

"Wow. So, you've been doing this for a really long time!"

He shook his head, turning his back to her as he leaned against the workbench. "No. I stopped for a while, after that. I only really got back into this after I built the cabin a few years ago."

"Oh." Harper frowned. This wasn't the first time he'd been difficult to read, but it was the first time she'd felt as though she was treading on eggshells around him.

Fraser cleared his throat and explained. "My dad was – is? – a carpenter, so working with wood was always something I was interested in."

She risked a few steps closer, if only to let him know she was listening. She couldn't remember him talking about his dad before, and his voice sounded tender and sore.

"He gave me my first tool set for my eleventh birthday, and I wanted to make him something nice. Something he'd want to keep. So, I made the birdhouse." A humourless chuckle fell from him. "He didn't like it."

Anger rose in Harper. "*Why*?"

"Those tools weren't supposed to be for 'artsy fartsy shite', as he called it. I was supposed to be the man of the house, learning how to fix up things so I could be a carpenter like him one day, not wasting wood and paint on silly wee gifts."

Harper didn't know what to say. She put her hand on Fraser's shoulder, giving it a gentle squeeze. No child should have been dismissed like that, but especially not him.

He turned to Harper slowly. "I still think about how disgusted he was that day. He left us a couple of years later, but it took me over a decade to even think about trying again, never mind showing my work to people. It's daft, but part of me still thinks he's right. I *am* the man of the house, especially now, and this work is my weakness. It's the complete opposite of everything I'm supposed to be. Nobody else needs to know about it."

She blew out a breath. "Your dad was wrong. You're not *supposed* to be anything, Fraser. What, because you're a labourer, you can't make art? That's ridiculous!"

"I know that, deep down." Fraser smiled, but it was shaky. Sad. "But you never forget your first rejection. I never want to feel that again. My sisters rely on me to be what he wasn't, and my work feels like my armour, somehow. If I keep labouring, keep getting jobs, then I'm sturdy and reliable. I can be strong for them. I was wary to even get a job in forestry. Planting trees, keeping them healthy... God, he'd hate that." He tapped his temple. "His wee voice is always there, in the back of my head, telling me I'm doing everything all wrong, even though I haven't seen him since the day he walked out. How mad is that?"

Tears pricked her eyes. He'd deserved so much better. It was his dad that was the problem, not him. She wished there was a way to make him see that, to take away all those years of damage.

"It isn't mad at all. He's your father, and you depended on him to show you the way. Instead, he planted insecurity. The only thing that's mad is him and the ways he failed you." She took his hands. "You're strong, and you're a good man, and none of those things are dependent on where you work, or what you work on. Whether it's a hammer or a chisel, a paintbrush, a knitting needle, or even a—"

"Aye, I get the message." He smiled, shaking his head.

She rolled her eyes. "Do you mind? I was going somewhere with that."

"Carry on, then. I'm listening."

She took a deep breath and said, with a sense of finality she hoped he wouldn't argue with, "You're strong because you're you." She stood on her tiptoes to cup his jaw. "Your work is beautiful. There isn't a person in this village who wouldn't agree. There's nothing, absolutely *nothing*, to be ashamed of. You should only be proud."

Finally, he relaxed, his fingers tangled in her hair and his gaze swimming with tenderness. He offered a light kiss on the tip of her nose. "Thank you, sunshine. Really. That means more than you know."

"I should be thanking you, for showing me all this. It really is wonderful. I hope you know that."

He let out an uncertain hum, his hands drifting over her clothes. She usually hated wearing leggings unless she was lounging in the house, but today, she'd felt comfortable enough to forget about looking stylish. It made her feel free, especially when he squeezed her curves more tightly. "Tell me a few more times and I might start believing you."

She played with the buttons of his shirt, feeling triumphant when his body responded, already hardening against her. "I can tell you plenty," she whispered against his neck. "And I can show you, too."

His groan was all disappointment as he tugged her close. "As nice as that sounds, I owe Andy a visit. I didn't finish my work yesterday. Then I have to check up on Mum and Eiley. *Then* I promised I'd take the kiddos trick-or-treating."

"Oh." She perched on one of his handcrafted chairs, trying not to look put out.

"You could come with me to the B&B," he suggested. "I wouldn't recommend it, mind. Andy is a tyrant when we're working."

"If I help out, do you think they'll give me a discount when they reopen?"

He tssked. "Just like that, you turn your back on my cabin, where your new writing desk will soon be."

"I will take my writing desk with me, but… normal showers. Quicker Wi-Fi. No owls keeping me awake all night."

"Did you hear that, Bernard?" He called over to the mutt, who had curled up on a tattered blanket by the door. "She prefers hot water and superfast broadband to us."

"Don't bring Bernard into this!" she chided, and then, to Bernard: "Don't listen to him, Bernard. I would take a thousand freezing showers for that boopable face."

Fraser laughed as he kissed her, a soft finger tilting her chin so she couldn't look away. Not that she wanted to.

She huffed dramatically. "I suppose I can *pretend* to work with you. Only if I'm rewarded for it tomorrow, though."

Fraser nipped her ear lobe playfully. "I'm sure that can be arranged, sunshine."

Harper stepped into the B&B and couldn't help but gawp at the mess. Stairs had been torn out, doorways went without doors, and the wallpaper had been ripped from the walls. It might have been nice before, but Harper couldn't see much beyond the dust sheets and, well, dust. Apparently, this was normal, because Fraser didn't falter as he called out, "Help has arrived!"

"A whole twenty-four hours late!" Andy's voice drifted from somewhere nearby. They appeared in the hallway wearing an expression of thunder, tapping their Converse-clad foot impatiently. Their dark hair was covered by a black beanie today, choppy ends feathering around their elfin face. "What's your excuse? Did your dog eat your tools?"

"I left my tools here, smart ass," Fraser said. "Since your tongue is so sharp today, perhaps it's you who's eaten them."

He stepped aside so that Harper was in view. She waved nervously, suddenly unsure if she'd be welcome here after all. She wasn't very good at... well, *any* kind of DIY, let alone DIY that would be judged by someone whose personality was the love child of Gordon Ramsay and Scary Spice.

But Andy's scowl lifted when it fell on Harper, their hazel eyes lightening as they uncrossed their arms. "Oh, hi, Harper! I didn't know Fraser had brought company! You'll have to excuse the state of this place. I am being very calm about it, as you can probably tell."

Fraser let out a *Ha!* so sardonic he almost choked on it, and Harper nodded sagely. "Well, *I* am sort of renovating my entire life at the moment, and I, too, am very calm about all the chaos it's brought. I'm absolutely not having a crisis."

"Good. No crises here, then. Or is it 'crises'?" Andy rubbed their pointed chin with a wry smirk, displaying chipped black polish on their bitten-down nails.

"How come you're nice to her but not me?" Fraser asked incredulously.

Andy slapped his chest as they passed him to fling their arm over Harper's shoulder. "Because Harper is pretty."

"*I'm* pretty," Fraser grumbled.

"He is very pretty," defended Harper, her resolve melting due to the compliment nonetheless. Having felt on the edge of the queer community for most of her early twenties as a femme who had dated mostly men, such validation felt like a rare, special thing. That was probably why she'd been so crazy about Kenzie in those years. A confident, attractive lesbian with experience? It had taken Harper at least a year to believe such a woman might actually like little old her – and about five seconds to realise she no longer did, in the end.

"Besides," Fraser said to Andy, rocking on his heels. "It was Harper's fault I didn't come back yesterday."

"No, actually, that's not the truth, Fraser." She turned to Andy. "He just doesn't trust me to walk on my own."

Andy's head snapped between them as though they were watching a tennis match. They scratched their paint-smeared cheek in bewilderment. "I am ever so sorry, but I actually don't care about any of *this*." They narrowed their eyes, wafting a hand through the air between Harper and Fraser. "I care that my parents are coming back to town for the autumn festival next weekend, and the beloved B&B they entrusted me to take care of is *fucked*!"

"It's not fucked." Fraser leaned against a closed door and almost tumbled through it. He caught both the door and himself from falling just in time, inspecting the wood as he propped it against the frame. "Okay. It might be a little bit fucked."

"Jack said he fixed that yesterday!" Andy groused.

"I'll sort it. Don't worry." Fraser reached out and rubbed Andy's arms. Andy glowered before letting Fraser soothe them.

"And I will pretend to look busy with this." Harper picked up a hammer from the floor, waving it around like she was wielding Thor's great weapon – and nearly crashed into Fraser when the heavy weight sent her teetering back.

He let Andy go, and his fingers curled around Harper's so that he could snatch the hammer away. "Let's not play with heavy objects, please."

She huffed, but didn't try and grab the tool back, instead picking up an abandoned paint roller from the floor. "This?"

"That would actually be a big help." Andy swiped their shaggy fringe from their eyes, patting Harper's shoulder appreciatively. "I'll give you a hefty discount as soon as we reopen. How's that?"

Harper couldn't help but raise her hand, waiting until Fraser begrudgingly high-fived her. "Great! I was totally not expecting that! Thank you!"

"She totally was, and that's why she's here." But Fraser's mutter was distracted, his brows furrowed as he examined the non-door he'd just fallen through. "Jack's usually great at this stuff."

Andy tugged the ties of their black hoodie tighter. "And *you're* usually great at not abandoning people in need. When

Jack realised you weren't coming back with our lunch, he decided to call it a day as well."

Fraser cast Andy a grave look, and Harper took a wary step back. Suddenly, it didn't feel like they were joking anymore, and she was certain that the rough edge of Fraser's grimace was laced with pure guilt.

"I'm sorry, Andy. Truly," Fraser said, his eyes shining with sincerity. "I let you down, but I'll make up for it."

Andy's face remained stony as they shoved their hands into their pockets. "I can't do this without you and Jack."

"And you won't," he promised.

Harper didn't know what to do. She felt like she should have been apologising, too, but what for? She hadn't asked Fraser to search for her yesterday. She hadn't known that her going on a hike would lead to *this*.

Wasn't this just part of life? People let each other down sometimes. People got busy and dropped the ball. Harper couldn't count all the meetings she'd cancelled, friends she'd forgotten to reply to over the years.

But it seemed like nobody expected that of Fraser.

Nobody expected him to be human.

She cleared her throat, picking up the tin of orchid white paint. "So, where do you want me?"

"Erm… There." Andy looked around before choosing a patch on the faded blue back wall.

Wordlessly, Harper walked over and stationed the paint beside her feet on a large towel. She grabbed a tray and poured some out into it, then stilled for a moment as an image flickered in her mind.

If Fraser ever revealed his secret hobby, his furniture could go here. People would see it and ask about it, generating more interest, more business. In a town *full* of small businesses, such unique furniture would add lots of rustic charm – the kind of charm she'd come here for. Charm many tourists would want to see, too. She glanced over her shoulder at Fraser, surprised at how familiar his sturdy presence and chiselled features felt to her now. He didn't notice her attention, didn't look up from correcting the hinges on the door. Just like when he was chopping wood, he remained completely focused, a bead of sweat already glistening in his hairline.

Harper's stomach swooped. It hurt to imagine that he would always be embarrassed of his art because of his father. She wanted more for him than just helping people out. His work was noble, but he had so much passion to give, and nobody knew but her.

He was sort of magnificent.

She was sort of falling for him.

That thought made her feel like she was slipping into a deep, dark hole, so she turned around quickly and got to work. She found a relaxing rhythm with each stroke of paint, though her arm quickly began to ache. Andy paced, watching them like a hawk between nailing down a chair rail on one of the already painted walls. Soon, the broken door was secured, and Harper saw relief seep from Fraser. He began applying primer to the next door, veins snaking beneath sinewy, tattooed forearms.

Yep. She was definitely falling. She knew because, in the time it had taken him to fix a door, she'd barely covered half a wall.

Andy sidled up beside her, and she quickly returned to looking busy. Still, she knew she'd been caught, and her face burned.

"I won't hold it against you. You wouldn't be the first woman to swoon over Fraser and his mega muscles." Andy nudged her in the ribs with a sharp elbow, a sly grin curling beneath their lip ring.

"I'm not swooning. I don't swoon," she lied, suddenly showing a lot of interest in her paint roller.

"Good. You shouldn't. You're hotter than him."

"Well, that's blatantly not true," she murmured, surprised the pale paint wasn't reflecting the beetroot-red of her face now. "But thanks."

"No, you really are. Anyway, sorry I'm a bit awful today. I know he's being very generous, helping me out, and I don't mean to get so…" Andy shuddered. "I think I'm turning into my mother."

"Happens to us all." She paused. "Do your parents expect a lot from you, managing the B&B, or…?"

Andy tugged their earlobe. "It's just important to them, and I practically begged for them to retire so that I could run the place independently. I've never found my own calling, so I just wanted to prove that I'm not a waste of space. I don't want to be a failure." They sighed, planting their hands on their hips as their eyes scoured their unfinished surroundings. "I sort of see this place as a mirror. If it looks bad, I must look bad, too."

That, Harper could relate to. Through school, she hadn't been liked very much, so she'd chased academic accomplishments instead and had never really stopped. When she'd been unemployed after graduation, she'd sunk into a pit of despair for months. Lounged on Mum's couch in her pyjamas, feeling horrible and useless. She'd wanted to avoid falling back to that place after losing her job this time, and thank goodness she'd been able to.

Although…

What if she felt that way when she got home? What if her book was rejected and her relationship with Fraser was over, and she had nothing, absolutely nothing, to show for her life again?

"It isn't bad. It's a work in progress," she said finally. "And you're not a waste of space. Not in the slightest."

Andy hummed. "Thanks. I just didn't think it would be this hard to run things on my own."

Harper wondered if there was more Andy could do to reel guests in. "You know, when I Googled places to stay in Belbarrow, nothing but the Airbnbs came up. Do you have a website?"

"Aye, but I always forget to update it. My dad set it up, and he never really got it running. It was easier to rely on word of mouth back in the day. We have a Facebook page."

"Facebook is good." Harper nodded slowly. "I work – worked – in marketing. I could take a look, if you'd like? See if there might be any quick fixes to get more eyes on this place?"

Andy brightened. "Would you?"

"I'm already thinking that you should hold a little reopening party once it's ready. Maybe find a few bloggers or travel vloggers willing to come and take a look? If you offer them a free night's stay, they might give you a nice review, get some of their followers interested."

Andy wrapped their hands tightly around Harper's arm like an overexcited child. "I hadn't even thought of that!" They tugged Harper away from the paint, beneath the arched doorway that led into the dining room. "Fraser, I'm stealing your girl!"

Fraser grinned, making Harper feel giddy. "Aye, I've noticed. Just make sure to bring her back soon."

22

By the end of the afternoon, Fraser was relieved. The B&B didn't look half as bad now. The doors were in place, and he'd already made a start on varnishing the stairs.

He wiped the sweat from his forehead with the back of his arm, straightening and slapping the dust off his sore hands before checking the time on his phone.

His stomach lurched when he found a chain of texts from his mum, starting from over an hour ago. After Andy had glared at him for reading an email earlier, he'd put it on silent.

```
Eiley's in a bad way. Can you come earlier?
Finlay's upset her all over again.
He came round the house!!!!! Bloody useless
nitwit. Come soon please.
Fraser????? Hello????
```

He tried to remain calm, but his chest soon turned to ice that froze through his ribs, threatening to crack everything around and within them. Finlay visiting could mean nothing good. He couldn't remember the last time Eiley had talked to him without crying.

"Shite." He texted Mum that he'd be round soon, then went to search for Harper and Andy. He found them perched on a couch covered in dust sheets in the dining room, a laptop open in front of them as Harper typed away.

"How's it going in here?" he asked stiffly.

Andy perked up, excited. "Harper is fixing the B&B's website for me and helping me out with social media stuff. This might actually work! She thinks I should collaborate with Graeme and Captain Angus to offer package deals – that way, we all get more business come tourist season."

"That sounds good." Fraser wanted to ask more, but the walls were pressing in on him, and they would be until he went to see that Eiley was all right. "I'm really sorry, but I have to get going. Eiley's struggling again."

"Ugh, that little shithead. What's he done now?" Andy stood up and braced their shoulders, intimidating despite their short stature. He wouldn't mind pushing Finlay into the same room as Andy just to see how much damage they'd inflict on him.

"I don't know."

"Is she okay?" Harper asked, also standing, concern etched in the lines on her forehead.

Fraser shook his head. "Don't know that, either. I need to go and see her."

"Of course. Don't worry about me. I'll just walk back or something." She wiped her palms on her leggings, making to sit back down.

He didn't want her to, he realised. Then again, he wouldn't ask her to come with him. She didn't need to be dragged into all the drama, not when she was supposed to be here on holiday.

"Unless…" His heart lightened as she rose to full height again. "I can come with you, if you want? Maybe Eiley needs a friend? I don't want to intrude, though, so just tell me if I'm overstepping."

He breathed a sigh of relief, car keys already in his hand. "Are you sure? It might be messy."

"I'm very good with messy. Haven't you noticed?"

He smiled, though it felt stiff and achy on his face. "I'll have to pick up Bernard on the way," he decided, beckoning with his head towards the door. "Are you sure? Final chance to keep your Saturday peaceful."

"Your definition of peaceful is frightening," Andy said, closing their laptop and leaning back in their chair. "Just take her, Fraser. We all know you're joined at the hip."

He tssked at this, though it was starting to feel quite true. Maybe he shouldn't be taking her home, shouldn't let her become a friend to Eiley when she was fragile, and Harper was due to leave. Maybe—

Harper bumped his hip with hers, drawing him out of his sudden panic. "Come on, then." She met his gaze. "Don't worry, Fraser. I'm sure she's going to be fine. She's a single mum. She can handle anything. Besides, she has you."

He nodded, swallowing down his fear, then took her hand. After saying goodbye to Andy, they headed to the truck parked out front, buried now among fallen leaves and syca-more seeds.

He opened her door first, then his own, taking a deep breath once the keys were in the ignition.

Harper squeezed his knee. "I'm here, too, okay?"

Emotion took hold of him like an iron vice, then. He couldn't remember the last time someone had said that to him. He pinched the bridge of his nose, pressing his thumbs where tears burned at the corner of his eyes. "Thank you, Harp. Really."

"Take a minute. Take as long as you need," she whispered.

He nodded, feeling silly. Feeling unstable. He didn't know why. He'd done this plenty of times by now. It wasn't the first time Eiley had been hurt. It wouldn't be the last. He was called to the house almost on a weekly basis, if not because of her selfish ex, then because one of the kids was sick, or Sky needed extra support, or Mum had a hospital appointment, or the hot water had stopped working again.

He was always needed. He always would be, and he was used to that.

But today, it weighed heavier. Maybe because of how he'd let Andy down yesterday. Maybe because Harper was here, and she saw him, and that made him vulnerable. Maybe because there was always something, and the thought of this happening over and over again suddenly felt more draining than he could put into words.

"I just… I don't know how to fix this."

"Of course you don't. It isn't your situation to fix." She said it as though it was a simple fact. "You can only be there for her. That's all. And I can be there for you."

He scraped back his hair, bracing his wrists against the steering wheel as he looked out onto the village. It was a busy Saturday afternoon, most likely because the weather was dry for a change. People milled in and out of shops, taking photographs of St. Margaret's spire and browsing the books in Thorn & Thistle as the sky turned the colour of a dark bruise against the setting sun. Harper should be among them, enjoying herself, not supporting him through a minor melt-down. If she was coming with him, the least he could do is stop grumbling about his problems.

Jaw clenched, he turned on the engine. She leaned back in her chair, but still watched him carefully. As they idled through the shopping streets, he tapped the steering wheel impatiently. "So, you're helping Andy with marketing. I thought you didn't like it so much anymore."

"I like it when it feels important. A local B&B run by one person? I'm sure Andy works hard, but that won't be enough unless they get the name out there. People need to be able to find it. Everybody relies on technology for that." Harper tucked her chin into the thick roll neck of her knitted mustard jumper. As much as he admired her usual fashionable get-up, he liked her best the way she was today, makeup-free. Unmasked. At ease.

"Who'd have thought that just a few weeks ago, you were an Airbnber with no small-town values," he mused, shooting her a dry, shaky grin.

She nudged him in response, tutting. "Clearly, people change."

"Clearly, they do." And she had changed him. Too much.

"I could help you, too, you know. With your forestry and handyman stuff, but also… if you decided to start selling your handcrafted work. I could come up with a whole plan, make sure it would take off enough so you can keep at it. I was thinking, if you gave Andy some of the furniture, have it front and centre inside the B&B—"

"I told you, I don't want that," he murmured, though something bitter bubbled inside him, making his words taste acrid. Like a lie. He didn't have the capacity to consider why that might be now, his focus still on Eiley.

"I know, but I was thinking if you had support – you know, the way you support others – then maybe it wouldn't be so daunting," she continued. "Your work is beautiful, Fraser. Please don't keep it in the dark forever."

"I'll decide what to do with it when I'm ready." His knuckles turned white over the wheel. He didn't want this, not now. It wasn't the time to be making a show of himself. Who knows what people would think when they found out the fairies came from the local handyman. Plus, his family would only demand to know why he'd been so secretive, and… They had enough to deal with already.

She tapped her thigh, deliberating before she finally admitted defeat. "Will you at least think about it?"

He tensed at the idea, but one look at her and he knew he couldn't deny her. Not when she was giving him those big, brown puppy dog eyes.

"All right. I'll think about it."

Fraser held his breath as he stepped into his childhood home. He was soon reassured when Brook ran up to him in socked feet that slid against the hardwood floors before sending him stumbling into Fraser's arms. "Uncle Fraser!"

He wore orange face paint that was already melting around his eyes. Fraser recognised the work of his mum, who had never quite mastered the art of Halloween makeup, but tried every year nonetheless.

"Hello, mate," Fraser said, lifting him up and squeezing him tightly. "You okay?"

"Mummy says you're looking after us tonight! Are we going trick-or-treating?"

"We'll have to see about that." He tickled Brook's chin. "Are you excited to stay at Uncle Fraser's?"

Brook nodded, displaying a gummy grin. Unlike his two siblings, he shared his father's ash-brown hair and green eyes, but Eiley's beauty still freckled his skin and shaped his smile.

He pointed over Fraser's shoulder to ask, "Who's that lass?"

Harper offered a meek wave. "Hello. I'm Harper, a friend of your uncle's. I've never met a talking pumpkin before!"

Brook giggled. "I'm only a talking human, really."

"Oh! Well, I won't tell anyone."

Fraser's heart warmed. He wondered how she'd come to be so good with kids if she had none in her family. Was it natural for her the way it was for him?

Brook cupped his hand over his mouth and whispered, not very quietly, in Fraser's ear: "Is she a girlfriend?" He rubbed his hands together with glee. Since Fraser didn't have a child-friendly answer to what they were, he set Brook down and freed Bernard from his lead before he dragged it around and scratched the floors he'd put in last year. Bernard ran straight to the kitchen, where Mum's chicken scraps usually waited for him.

Today, though, the house was quiet. He popped his head into the living room, just to check. Sky and Saffron sat on the red rug before the unlit fire, mesmerised by a Halloween special of Peppa Pig. Sky flapped his hands excitedly to the theme song, while Saffron fought sleep in her baby walker.

"Oh, thank goodness you're here." Mum appeared from the kitchen on one crutch, a plate of Sky's favourite mac and cheese in her free hand. Her hair was a mess of brown, red, and silver-streaked waves on top of her head, and her glasses were steamed up from cooking. Out of all of them, Fraser was often told he looked the most like her, which he considered an enviable compliment. He certainly would hate to see his dad every time he looked in the mirror.

"Oh!" She looked taken aback by the sight of Harper, then whispered, "Is this her?" as though Harper could not still hear her in the echoey hallway. Her eyes glimmered with excitement.

"Mum, this is Harper," Fraser said through a sigh.

Mum squealed, shoving the plate of food into Fraser's hand so that she could shuffle to Harper. She yanked Harper into a tight one-armed hug, squashing her face against her fluffy rainbow cardigan.

Fraser mouthed, *Sorry.*

"Oh, I've heard so much about you!" Mum cast Fraser a stony glance, her swollen hand rising to her hip. "Not from our Fraser, of course. He's quiet as a mouse about these sorts of things. Luckily, my daughters have been singing your praises!"

"Thank you. It's nice to meet you," Harper said, releasing a breath when she was finally freed. "I hope it's okay that I came. I thought maybe Eiley could use the company, or at the very least, you might want me to watch the kids."

"Oh, you're too kind, my dear!" Mum put her face in her palm as though she was smitten. "You can call me Myra, by the way."

Fraser couldn't help but feel amused. If Cam and Sorcha were here too, the house would officially be more overpowered by wonderful women than it ever had been before. Harper would fit right in.

Not that he wanted her to, of course. She didn't plan to. He couldn't expect her to.

"You're rather upbeat for someone who texted me ten poop emojis today, Mum," he pointed out, inching his way down the hallway slowly. He could hear sniffling from the kitchen and almost didn't want to go in. He was tired of seeing his sister in pain.

As predicted, Mum glared. Talk of Finlay always made her frosty. Though they were all grown up now, she was still protective over his sisters. Him, too, sometimes, so he made sure never to give her reasons to worry. "Aye, well, go and talk to your sister. You'll understand why."

Mum snatched the plate back from Fraser and disappeared into the living room to give Sky his dinner.

Fraser exchanged a wary glance with Harper. She took his hand without question, and they walked down the hallway. When they got to the kitchen, she pulled away, nudging him forwards.

He walked in first.

Eiley was sitting at the kitchen table, looking more than ever like the ancient porcelain dolls Mum liked to display in the living room. Scrunched tissues surrounded her, her face red and blotchy and her eyes swollen from tears, as she planted a kiss on Brook's forehead before fussing over Bernard.

"I told Mum not to call you," she muttered, then said to her son: "Brook, go and help Sky with his dinner, please."

"When is *our* dinner?" Brook groused, rubbing his stomach.

"Soon." He left still grumbling, but not before Fraser ruffled his long brown hair. It was his job, after all, to annoy his nephew.

As Eiley lifted her head, she blew her nose and squeezed her eyes closed. "Harper. Sorry. I didn't know you'd be here."

"I thought you might like a friend," Harper said quietly. She brushed past Fraser to sit at the table with his sister, taking her hand. "I know we don't know each other very well, but I *am* your friend. I have decided, and you're not allowed to disagree. Besides, I've always been told I have exceptionally good shoulders to cry on. Feel them. They're very soft."

Eiley laughed through more tears, which squeezed Fraser's heart. For a better reason this time. How was it that Harper always knew what to say?

"I haven't had a friend in a long time, really. I wouldn't dare disagree."

Harper smiled, first at her, and then at Fraser when he sat down opposite. For such a full household, it was only a small table, and his thighs brushed with hers underneath it.

"What happened?" he asked. "What did the prick do this time?"

Eiley shuddered. "I hate him, Frase. I've never hated anyone as much as I hate him."

"Are you sure I can't get out the chainsaw?"

"I'm starting to seriously consider it."

"I'm quite dangerous with a hammer, too, it turns out. If you're looking for a hitwoman," Harper added, nudging Fraser's knee.

Eiley let out a sad chuckle, but it only triggered more tears.

"Come on, Eiley. What did he do?" Fraser prodded.

Part of him was afraid to know, but he had to.

Eiley's chin wobbled, and she dabbed her cheeks with a crumpled tissue. "He came around to see the kids completely out of the blue, and I was thick enough to let him through the door. I thought maybe he'd seen sense, but he…" Her voice cracked, and Fraser darted to the other side of the table, pulling her to his chest.

"It's okay," he soothed, as Harper squeezed Eiley's hand tighter.

"He said," Eiley continued, "that he only wanted to take Brook. He said Sky is too difficult, and Saffron won't remember these things anyway. As though he isn't their father! Like he's just some glorified babysitter!" She was shouting now. "I don't get to choose which child I get to take care of every day. I don't get to choose whether I want to wake up with my seven-month-old five times a night, or watch Sky struggle with things beyond my control, or go to every school play Brook signs up for even when I'm exhausted – and even if I did, I *wouldn't* choose between them because I'm their mother! Because I love them! But he… He doesn't love any of us unless it's easy."

"I'm so sorry, Eiley," Harper said. "It just isn't fair, and you all deserve better."

Fraser gave a painful wince, kissing Eiley's forehead. "He's unbelievable."

"He's a wee shitebag," Harper said fiercely. "Isn't that what you call it?"

"Aye, that's one way of putting it." Eiley crumpled all over again. "I just don't get it. I'll never get it. He's just like our dad."

"Then you know you and the kids are better off without him," he offered gently, "just like we were." After Dad had left and the dust had settled, Fraser had found himself strangely relieved. He wouldn't have to stand on his tiptoes anymore to search for a face that wasn't there, during school nativities and junior rugby matches. He wouldn't have to ask Mum *Is Dad coming?*, knowing that the answer would be *Not this time, love*, ever again.

He saw Harper process it. Understand. She leaned back, still gripping Eiley's hand, her features soft and receptive. She wasn't even a little afraid of big emotions, and fuck, he admired that about her.

"What did you say to him after that?" Harper asked.

"I told him to get fucked," Eiley admitted.

Fraser let out a noise of surprise. His littlest sister never swore. Cam had the mouth of a sailor, but he hadn't heard Eiley curse once in her life, not even the three times she'd been in labour.

"I don't want him here anymore. I don't need him, and neither do the kids," she decided. "I told him that if he only wanted to be a part-time dad, he wasn't welcome. I was silly enough to expect a fight from him... but he just walked away like it was nothing."

"It's his loss," Fraser said.

Harper nodded in agreement. "Your kids have more love here than he could ever give them. I know it hurts now. You'll always want him to be worth the love you once gave him. You'll always want him to change. But some people just aren't right. Some people just need to go and digest a cactus."

They both laughed at that, Eiley far harder than Fraser. Hysterical peals fell from her until she was gripping her stomach. "Digest a cactus!" she repeated incredulously, tears streaming down her face.

It was hard to tell whose laughter was whose in the end, as they sat there around the table and thought up ways to make a shitty man suffer. Fraser was so full of love in that moment that he might have been bursting with it.

Love. Shite. Was that true? Did he *love* Harper?

All he knew was that Eiley usually ended nights like these crying. That night, there was no room for sobs in her chest.

Because of her.

23

Harper was still half-asleep when she plonked down in the cabin's front room the following Monday morning, at her brand-new writing desk. She rested her half-drained mug of tea on one of Fraser's wooden coasters, blinking groggily at her laptop screen. Her inbox had been empty for weeks, which was both a blessing and a curse. A blessing, because she hated replying to emails and had always worried that she used too many exclamation points with clients and co-workers. A curse, because now that her days were no longer structured for her by whatever lay in her inbox, she was floundering in freedom. She could – in theory – write as much as she wanted to, with nobody to tell her when or what or why. If she could – in practice – stop procrastinating.

So why on earth was her former boss's name appearing in bold at the top of her screen now?

Anxiety trickled through her, unpleasant but not unfamiliar. Her stomach cramped with the same dread, and it was like she was sitting in that stuffy office again, with co-workers who gossiped quietly in break rooms, and tasks she had to miserably slog through until the day finally ended when she was too exhausted to do anything for herself.

She considered not opening it – even switched tabs back to her open manuscript. She'd churned out fifty-thousand words of her novel now. With Fraser busy babysitting yesterday, she'd curled up in bed, the rain her soundtrack, and typed until her wrists ached. It was becoming an instinct, something she didn't even have to think about before she started.

She rubbed her eyes, eager to dive back into the fantastical world she'd been living in. Yesterday, she'd been certain of what would come next in the story.

Today, she stared at the last line she'd written and found her brain completely devoid of any words that weren't in the subject line of that email.

New job opening?

She couldn't ignore it. It would press into her mind like a bruise until she found out what her ex-employer wanted.

Drawing herself up, she closed her manuscript and returned to her inbox. Her fingers shook as she clicked on the new message.

Subject: New job opening?
From: Chris Bailey
To: Harper Clegg

Harper,
I hope this email finds you well.

"All the better now I don't read *that* soulless line twenty times a day," she muttered.

While I am sure you have probably already found a new position following your regretful departure from Brentworth Furnishings, there has been an unexpected opening for the role of Marketing Director that I believe would suit your skillset well. If you would be interested in rejoining us, I would like to invite you to interview for the position. Naturally, the managerial role offers a higher salary and greater responsibility than your previous title, but after working with you for several years, I am confident that you have the potential to perform well under pressure.

"Oh, that's very nice of you to say – after *already letting me go*," she quipped sourly.

I would be interested to hear your thoughts. If you would like to book a meeting, please do let me know. My schedule is open for interviews the week beginning November 18th.

Many thanks,
Chris

She should have been happy. Chris clearly regretted his choice to make her redundant, and waltzing back into that office would show everybody at Brentworth that she was worth more. Chris would see she wasn't just a worker ant to swat away, but a person who was needed to help the company thrive. She could even make him grovel.

Then there was the fact that, should she take the job, she would be Kenzie's senior. The entire marketing department's senior. What better way to prove that her ex had made a mistake than Harper working as her boss and earning more money than Kenzie in the process? Kenzie would *weep*. She would regret. She would *pine*.

Harper had always wanted to make someone pine.

But did she want *this*?

Of course, she wanted stability. She missed knowing that she had money coming in. She missed feeling satisfied by her work not just when she hit a word count milestone or had a breakthrough in plotting, but when a campaign she'd led succeeded, or when somebody gave positive feedback on her attention to detail or her great advice on copywriting. In such a fast-paced company, she'd been fuelled by everyday accomplishments, and not having them had made her feel unsteady. Unsure of herself. Nobody was here to praise her.

Nobody was here to demean her, either.

She sank lower into her chair, resting her head on the keyboard until her reply box was filled with long lines of Xs and Vs, accompanied by the jolting noise warning her that she was typing utter nonsense. She ignored it.

"This is bad. This is really, really bad." Just the thought of heading back to Manchester and stepping back into that office, wearing something far less comfortable than her current thermal leggings and cosy jumpers, made her mouth dry as sandpaper. At least before, she'd been able to work from home when the pressure got to her. The last marketing and sales director, Debra, had practically lived in the office, always rushing from meeting to meeting while trying to supervise Harper and her colleagues, too. Over coffee, she'd confessed that the work was piling up and it was causing problems with her wife and kids at home. Harper didn't have a partner or kids, but she wanted them. One day. And in the meantime, she wanted at least six hours a night to watch reality TV in her pyjamas, or catch up with friends, or read, or perhaps even keep her newfound connection to nature intact. She didn't want to feel like she was just trying to survive each day, each week, each month.

And she wanted time to finish her book. She still had a long way to go. If she went to this meeting, she'd have to cut her trip short. And if she got the job, what if it left her with no time to write?

She'd come too far to abandon the novel.

And…

Fraser. She didn't want to leave Fraser.

"Bollocks." She whined into her hands, tearing apart at the seams. She couldn't just turn down an opportunity like this when she was painfully unemployed, could she? Maybe the increased salary would mean she could save up, take a gap year to continue writing in the future.

"Morning, sunshine." She slammed her laptop shut when the door swung open and Fraser appeared. Bernard jumped straight onto her lap, licking her cheek in greeting.

"Good morning." Her voice came out loud and squeaky, not hers, but he was too busy striding towards the kettle to notice.

"Sleep well?"

"Uh-huh."

"Enjoying your new desk?"

Harper stared out at the woods. *Her* woods. She'd grown accustomed to this view. Fraser's chopping block, the saplings slowly rising from the soil, the carpet of fallen leaves and pine needles surrounding tall trees that were gradually turning bare. November had come too quickly, and the proof was written in the cool fog blanketing the golden forest. At Brentworth, the only view was a big yellow crane across the street, hovering over a new apartment build that never seemed to be finished. When she was lucky, the eternal scaffolding was blurred out by the rain.

Was she willing to give this – *him* – up?

She couldn't even look at him, couldn't even think about saying goodbye. She buried her face into Bernard's musky fur and sighed.

"Harp?" Fraser whirled around before the kettle, concern tugging down the corners of his mouth. "You all right?"

She couldn't tell him. Not until she'd had a proper chance to think about it.

So she nodded with feigned enthusiasm. "Yep, I'm good. How was babysitting? Is Eiley feeling any better? Did she hear anything from Finlay? What did Cam say?"

"Steady on." He ducked his head as though her words were flying right at him. "That's a lot of questions in a very short amount of time." He rested on the arm of his sofa so there was nothing between them but Bernard. He reached out, brushed his knuckles across the back of her hand before petting Bernard between the ears. "Eiley is surprisingly okay, for now, but I'm going to keep checking in between work. Babysitting was good. We ate too many sweets on Saturday, and yesterday I took them along the Fairy Trail with Cam and Sorcha to tire them out. Sky was a little upset, but Isla soon cheered him up, and... what were the other questions?"

Harper shook her head. Her brain couldn't focus on anything other than that email. It felt like a shadow peering over her back. Like somehow, Fraser might be able to see through the closed lid of her laptop to what lay beneath. Their impending farewell. "I can't remember, honestly."

His cheek dimpled as he bent forwards, the pad of his thumb tracing her cupid's bow. "What's on the agenda for today? I feel like I didn't see you nearly enough this weekend. Forty-eight hours feels like a lifetime without you."

He might as well have ripped her heart open, the way he tore apart pieces of kindling outside. She would love nothing more than to sink into him and forget, but what if that only made the inevitable more painful? What if she should already be preparing herself to say goodbye?

It would be the sensible thing to do. She would need a job eventually, and it would be nice to line her pockets with extra money before Christmas.

She frowned, taking his hand and kissing his palm, because it was about all she could muster. "I think… I don't know, honestly. I haven't thought about it."

"You're supposed to say you missed me, too," he pointed out, nudging her shin with the steel-cap toe of his boot.

"I did miss you," she said. It was the truth. She'd felt lonely without him here yesterday. She'd even gone for a walk to ease her restlessness, before knuckling down to her writing.

"I wanted to thank you for the way you looked out for Eiley," he said. "You really helped her on Saturday."

Harper shrugged. "If she needs anything, I'm here." Which reminded her. She was due back at the preschool tomorrow morning. Another thing she would have to give up soon if she agreed to the interview. Sixteen days was all she had, and before then, she had to make a decision. "I'll ask her if she fancies a coffee or something after playgroup tomorrow. If you think she'd like it."

"I think she'd love it."

He sighed, seeming not to notice when the kettle came to a boil. "I was thinking a lot about what you said. About my woodwork."

At this, she finally jumped back into her own body, eyes widening eagerly. "Oh? Have you finally realised I am right about everything all the time?"

Fraser offered her a deadpan stare, but he struggled to keep a straight face, so maybe he really had changed his mind. She twisted just to admire her fairy figurine, placed proudly on the shelf of her beautiful desk.

"It's the autumn festival in the village this weekend," he said instead of admitting that she was, in fact, right about everything all the time.

"Do you think there will be PSLs?" she enquired. One thing she had not yet grown used to was the lack of seasonal drinks on Belbarrow's café and tearoom menus. Her last decent beverage had been from the coffee truck next to the Fairy Trail, and she didn't know how to get there on foot.

"What the hell is a PSL?" asked Fraser.

"Pumpkin spice latte. It's not autumn without them. There's a café near my house called Coco Cups, and *oof*!" She licked her lips for emphasis. "So good. I sometimes worked from home just to set up camp at one of their tables. I need pumpkin spice set up in an IV, I think. With whipped cream. Although, then I'd miss the taste, and maybe the whipped cream would clog the IV—"

"There was a point to my earlier sentence. When you're ready to hear it." He crossed his arms patiently, eyes glittering with amusement. "Take your time."

Of course she was babbling. Because she was nervous. And because she thought that maybe if she was too quiet, he'd sense something was wrong, and then she'd have to tell him.

"Apologies. Go on."

"Thank you." He cleared the gravel from his throat. "The autumn festival is this weekend, and I signed up for a stall to sell my figurines."

"Oh my god!"

"I'm not sure I'm ready to go all out with my furniture, yet. It takes a lot more work and resources. But… you were right about the fairies. The kids loved the trail so much yesterday. Sky wanted to take the fairy house home with him. And after our conversations last week, in the shed and with Eiley… I've realised that I would never, ever want Brook, Sky, and Archie to grow up the way I did. Thinking they're not good enough, or that they can't make art because they're boys. I want to surprise them all. Tell them that Uncle Fraser made them."

"That's really lovely, Fraser," Harper said softly. "They're going to love it – but it shouldn't just be for them. I hope you're doing this for you, too."

He gave a small nod, mouth dimpling at the corners. "I am."

"Oh, I can't wait!"

"Don't get too excited. I might back out before then. I'm still nervous."

"Understandably, but this could be so special!" She clapped her hands together. "I'm *so* excited! We can make posters and I can help bring people to your table!"

"I don't want to make a big deal out of—"

"Oh my goodness, what if we made a huge sign? 'Fraser's Fairies'—"

"Now that just sounds weird."

"— And I can find decorations. It will be like autumn sneezed all over your stall!"

"Gross."

"Wait there!" She pushed him onto the couch, leaving him sprawled on his back in surprise. "I have so much planned already!"

When she hadn't been writing yesterday, she'd been planning. For Andy's reopening, but mostly for Fraser, in the event he changed his mind.

She'd had a feeling he would.

Maybe marketing was still in her blood, after all.

24

Fraser sat with Bernard on the middle step of his porch, shaking his head slowly from side to side at Harper. She was struggling to hold up a gigantic cork board in front of her face, nose squished against the back of the frame. "Where did you even get a cork board that big?"

Harper propped said board against his chopping block, ready to present him with her marketing strategy. The board was almost as tall as her, rising from the soil to her chest, and was covered in magazine clippings and note cards dense with scrawled and highlighted ideas. She'd even made a mood board of what his shop might look like, if he chose to open one.

At his question, Harper twirled a strand of hair around her finger, the picture of innocence, before she dropped the ruse and crouched guiltily behind the board. "Alice and Cam weren't using it at the café."

"You *stole* it?" His voice rose in… well, he didn't know what. If stealing was bad, why did she look so terribly cute, with that hopeful smile dazzling him like sunlight? Besides, he couldn't imagine she was a very subtle thief, if his experience of her trespassing was any indication.

"I borrowed it. Secretly. Without asking." She scratched her head with the lid of the black Sharpie she held, then quickly brushed past her confession. "*Anyway*—"

He couldn't help but chuckle, scraping a hand over his face. "You're ridiculous."

There was a loud whoosh as an Unidentified Blurry Object flew towards him before the pen promptly bounced off his head. Bernard sniffed it when it fell to the ground, disappointed to find it wasn't ball-shaped.

"Ridiculously amazing?" she said.

"That was implied." He picked the pen up and threw it back at her feet.

Harper hummed, unconvinced, but her focus returned to the board. She pointed to the top corner, where Flockhart's B&B was written in blue bubble letters, along with a wonky smiley face. "First, as we discussed – and I know your answer was no, but I am persistent in a non-annoying, adorable way – I think it would be good to get your furniture in the B&B and in other local establishments. When you're ready, of course. No pressure. But picture this: a cheeky set of shelves in the bookstore, a nice little armchair in the tearoom… The entire town could have Fraser Originals!"

"We're not calling them that, either," he groused.

She ignored him, of course. "Just imagine. A tourist walks into Andy's lobby and Fraser's handcrafted cabinet in the corner catches their eye. They ask where it's from so they can get one, too, and then they hear all about your portfolio!"

The idea wasn't half-bad, but would he have the time and energy to focus on dozens of pieces to fill Andy's B&B? Not to mention, Andy's interior design taste was very... *particular.* Hence Andy's tendency to enter dragon mode every time he helped with the renovation. Andy might not even *want* Fraser's stuff. It was far more elaborate than their usual quirky, modern style.

He opened his mouth to say just that, but Harper stopped him with a raised index finger. "I know you're not keen yet. But eventually you might be. One day, I hope you will be. Until then, I've designed business cards that can be left around town. We could order them in time for Saturday. Look." She scooped up her laptop from the porch bench, then sidled beside him on the step until all he felt was her warmth. Until he couldn't quite remember what he was supposed to be looking at.

Her scent was so pleasingly familiar. Like morning tea and that fruity perfume he didn't know the name of. And, now, the woodsy aroma of his cabin, as though the forest was entwining with her DNA. As though *he* was entwining with her DNA.

"Fraser."

"Hmm?"

"Focus." She shoved the laptop in his face so that he had no choice but to stop ogling her.

When he saw her design, he drew in a small gasp, genuinely surprised. She had put real effort into this, from the swirling wood grain-patterned background to the neat, whimsical font reading *Handmade by Fraser* at the top. *Handmade by Fraser.* He liked that; it was simple, like him. Didn't promise too much or too little. In the corners, silvery, gossamer-like wings and illustrated toadstools paid homage to his pieces on the Fairy Trail, not enough to make the card too busy, but enough to add a magical charm to the aesthetic.

How long had she spent making this? How much time out of her own busy day had she taken to come up with this plan?

He couldn't believe her. Couldn't believe how willing she was to encourage him.

When she saw that he was stunned to silence, she wrinkled her nose. "This is just a rough draft. It's okay if you don't like it. I have lots of other ideas for the brand name besides *Handmade by Fraser*. And graphic design is *not* my passion."

"Are you mad? I love it, Harp. And the name is perfect." He took her hand, squeezing as a chasm opened up inside him. This was becoming real. His work could become a living, breathing thing that people knew about. That people *cared* about.

She'd made all that possible.

"You could even make key rings – from wood, of course," she said. "Maybe offer some out to potential customers, as free incentives to keep people coming back. I know it would cost a lot to set up, but I have a full plan in place that would hopefully ensure a profit in the long run. Plus, you said my rent is helping with your extra expenses. Couldn't you put some aside for this?"

He did have a nice little stash of money saved from her weekly payments. Enough to at least print business cards and maybe carve the free gifts. Besides, most of his stuff was upcycled. He sought out fabrics from charity shops and flea markets, used scrap materials from his carpentry work, and there was no shortage of wood in the forest, as long as he kept planting new trees to replace the ones he'd felled.

He took a deep, jagged breath as he pushed the laptop into Harper's lap. "This is a lot."

"I know," she replied gently. "And there's no pressure. I just want you to know that your work deserves to be seen. I know what it looks like to hold yourself back. It took me years to work up enough confidence to write, even though there have always been stories in my brain. It's scary, to want something so badly, but to be afraid that people might take it away or ruin it. I get it. I really do."

He swallowed, finding his throat parched. She was right, and not just about his woodworking. He felt that way about her, too. He wanted her in every possible way, yet he knew one wrong move, one step too far, could leave him hurt. Ruined.

But she was here now, and she was doing anything but ruining him.

She was uprooting him. Planting him in new soil. And whether he liked it or not, he was growing.

He kissed her because he didn't know what to say, what else to do. He felt her tense under him in surprise, then melt quickly after, abandoning the laptop beside her on the step. "You know me better than I know myself sometimes," he whispered against her jaw, fingers tracing the knots of her spine through thick wool and soft skin.

"I am good like that, aren't I?" she teased, brushing the overhanging hair from his brow. "Now, the website. How terrified will you get if I start talking about pay-per-click search campaigns and TikTok promotion?"

"Extremely terrified, but go on. I'm listening."

"And what's this here?" asked Fraser, jabbing at a cut-out photo of colourful, glittery balloons, pinned beneath a sticky note that read: *Launch Party*. "I don't like the word 'party'."

They had moved from the step over to the busy cork board, Harper perched on his chopping block while she adjusted her plans in red marker.

"Don't worry, old man." She grinned. "It won't go on until the wee hours. We can make sure you're home by ten."

"Still past my bedtime." He was unable to keep his touch from trailing over her curves, from the side of her hip, into the small dip of her waist, to her ribs. He wanted her. Badly. He'd never thought the words "closed-loop marketing" or "native advertising" would sound so sexy, but watching Harper shine in a universe she'd clearly grown comfortable in was…

It was inspiring, but it was also really fucking hot. More so because she'd done it for him. She'd said marketing wasn't her passion anymore, but she'd imagined a world where Fraser's work mattered – "art", she was calling it, which he'd never considered it as before.

At his touch, she edged closer, finally abandoning her Sharpie to stand and press her back against his stomach. "Andy liked the idea of a grand reopening for Flockhart's. You could make it a joint event. There's lots of space in the B&B's dining room, and I think it's important in a community this close that you collaborate. I said the same thing to Andy."

"It's not a bad idea. Not at all." He hooked his hand around the nape of her neck, desperate to feel her mouth on his but unwilling to stop her in the middle of a conversation that might just change the rest of his life.

"You could partner with the nature reserve in charge of the Fairy Trail, too," she pointed out. "Imagine if you could have your own little stall to sell the figurines along the walk on sunny days?"

"Don't you think we're getting ahead of ourselves? People might not even want my tat."

"Don't call it tat," she warned. "You have a gift. People will love it. This town is all about supporting different, unique, one-of-a-kind things."

"I suppose that's why I'm so obsessed with you," he muttered against her lobe.

She shivered, more so when he pressed his body against hers and let his lips trace the space behind her ear, then the beauty mark by her jaw. Her cold, gold hoop earrings grazed his skin, teasing him. They hadn't touched like this since she'd stayed at his house, and fuck, he'd missed her. Dreamed about her. Had woken up this morning hard and desperate to be inside her again. He'd even blurted her name when he'd used his hand to climax in the shower this morning.

His cock hardened. She turned her head and grinned up at him, shimmying her hips so her full ass rutted against it. *God, help me*, he thought. It was all he could do not to fall to his knees and take a bite.

"Are you trying to use sex to get me to stop talking about you?" she whispered.

"Maybe a little bit." He swept her hair from her face so he could see her better, so he could memorise the way she looked in this moment, hold onto it once it had passed. Eyes the colour of the serene forest around them. Freckles uncovered on her cheeks. She was even more beautiful without makeup, all rosy patches and little blemishes, some scars left behind by stories he hadn't yet heard. He traced the one that ran into her hairline, then moved his thumb to press against her lush bottom lip. "Maybe because I've been thinking about you. Constantly. I missed the way you feel against me. Around me."

She blushed, but a wicked glint shone in her eye. The next second, he felt her palming his length through his jeans. His hips bucked, his self-control hopeless and weak when it came to her. "Maybe I've been thinking about you, too."

"Oh, aye?" He cocked his head. "What have you been thinking?"

"I've been thinking about this." She traced the leather edges of his belt, pressing when she reached the skin above it. Electricity bolted through him, from his belly button down to his cock. He felt like he might combust if she didn't touch him properly soon. "And I've been thinking about how sexy you are. How strong and gentle, all at once. How good you make me feel when your hands are on me."

"My ego can't handle so many compliments."

She turned and began unbuttoning his shirt at a devastatingly unhurried pace. When the cold autumn air kissed his bare chest, she traced the rim of his nipple until he was certain his skin was throbbing. Everything was throbbing. His entire being cried for her.

"I was thinking about how this time, I don't want you to be gentle with me," she whispered. "Maybe I want you to bend me over this chopping block and slam into me until we both come."

"Fuck, Harper." His fingers coiled into his palms at the image. Not even he could conjure something so sexual, so raw and primal. He'd never had a reason to until he'd met her. Now, it felt like they were in a race only she could ever win. He wasn't used to being rough.

But for her, he might try.

He grabbed her hips, firmly enough that she gasped, and turned her back around so she was facing his block. She kicked the cork board away, bracing against him as he kissed her throat until the skin turned pink.

"Do you want that now?" He squeezed her full breasts through her clothes. He'd never been gladder for the six-foot fence surrounding them, nor the seclusion his cabin brought. In this corner of the world, nobody would stumble across them. They were free.

Her head bobbed against his shoulder, a nod. "Yes." She gulped. "I'm on the pill, and I was tested a couple of months ago. You don't need a condom if you're safe, too."

"I am. Got tested after the last time I was with someone. But if it gets uncomfortable…"

"Then I'll tell you," she assured, placing a gentle kiss on his chin.

Then, she guided his hand down, over her stomach, under the waistband of her leggings.

"You'll be the death of me." He slid his hand quickly between her legs, finding her perfectly wet and ready. When he stroked her, she jolted against him, and he held her steady as he dipped his finger inside, curling towards her G-spot. "Will you be a good lass and tell me something?"

She moaned, fingers lacing through his hair. "Fuck, Fraser."

"Have you been using your little toy this weekend?" he asked, voice hoarse with desire. Imagining her, spread wide on *his* bed, in *his* cabin, as she pleasured herself. "Have you been thinking of me while you play with it?"

She nodded, rocking against him now. "Yes."

"I've been thinking of you, too." The confession made him feel vulnerable, but powerful at the same time. "In the middle of the night, I imagine your pretty mouth around my cock. In the shower, I shout out your fucking name." He thrust another finger inside her, moving quicker now.

"Oh, god." She turned her face away from him, moaning, but he needed to see her. He tipped her chin back, swallowing more pleas from her mouth with a frenzied kiss.

Her impatient ruts brushed his cock, each harder than the last, and it was an effort to keep going, to not throw her over the block now and have done with it.

But he wanted this first. He wanted her to come around his fingers so that the next orgasm would feel even better for her.

He got his wish, her walls clenching around him all at once as her erratic breaths ripped through the clearing. She buckled against him, trembling when he brushed her clit with the lightest of touches.

When she'd steadied herself, he wrapped her hair around his fist with his free hand and tasted her on his soaked fingers with the other. She didn't need to be told what came next. Together, they grappled to undo his belt and roll down her leggings. She didn't bother to step out of them, nor him from his jeans, too rushed, too needy, to waste any time.

Harper bent over the chopping block finally, her bare ass dimpled and perfect in front of him. He swore again. Gulped. Traced his fingers over her swollen pussy until she was panting.

"Are you sure?" he asked gently.

"Do I *look* unsure?" She wiggled to prove her point, and a rich, belly-deep laugh erupted from him.

"You look like a fucking Aphrodite sculpture," he said, lining himself up. When his tip brushed her, she whined. He wanted that sound recorded, wanted to hear it night and day. "You talk about my art? Your body is art, Harp, and you can't even imagine all the ways I want to worship it."

He entered her before she could reply, mouth opening in a silent, stolen shout of pleasure as she stretched around him. Feeling her wetness, her heat, without barriers felt so intensely good that he had to bite his lip to keep from groaning.

Her knuckles turned white at the edge of the block, back arching as he sank deeper, deeper, until she was taking all of his length.

"Go hard. Fast," she begged.

His fingers dug into her hips, and he obeyed. The sound of their skin slapping together filled his ears as he thrust into her again and again. He would never get tired, would give her everything she needed for as long as she needed it. He felt like he was floating somewhere outside his body, like bliss had been given a physical form in the shape of Harper, and it carried him now somewhere higher, where nothing else could touch him but her.

"Good?" he asked, panting. "Tell me it feels good."

"*So* good."

He clamped her hips against his, burying himself until it felt as though they were merging together completely. When he found her clit, running dogged circles over it, she let out a hoarse cry.

"Fraser!" she sobbed. She chased her orgasm wildly and hurriedly, and then that knot in his stomach was unravelling, his seed spilling into her until they were slippery and spent. Until he wasn't sure he was even still here. His body felt too weightless, too exhilarated, to be real.

He caught her before she could collapse against the chopping block, his arms folding around her stomach as he steadied his breath against her shoulder.

"I'm not done with you yet," he said.

"Oh?"

He was already fingering her swollen, slippery clit again, and her thighs clenched around his hand as though unsure whether she wanted to keep him there or push him out.

"Where's that toy of yours, hmm? I think it's time we played with it together."

Slowly, she rolled her body so they were facing one another, her hair a wild tangle around his hands and jaw reddened from his rough kisses. Still, she smiled hazily and led him into the cabin.

25

Harper was so overwhelmed by pleasure that she could barely breathe. The space between her legs throbbed with the ghost of Fraser's cock as she hopped onto the bed. They'd shut the door, leaving Bernard to curl up on the couch with their abandoned clothes in the front room.

She could have told Fraser where her vibrator was, tucked into the drawer in the nightstand beside her, but it was much more fun to watch him tear through her suitcase like a man possessed, half-naked, tattoos flexing around freckled sinew and muscle.

When the remaining contents of her suitcase were strewn about the floor, he growled in frustration. "Where is it?"

"Oh, you mean this?" Harper slid open the drawer and pulled out the rose-shaped toy, eagerness plunging through her like a stone into a lake. She shivered when he glanced sharply at her, eyes darkening as he licked his lips.

"Evil woman."

She grinned. Opened her legs wide to bear herself to him as she reclined against the pillows.

"I want to watch you," he confessed gruffly. "Will you show me how you use it, love?"

She gulped. She'd never touched herself in front of someone before, never wanted to. But the hunger in his eyes devoured her own self-consciousness, and she realised, with her hand curled around her favourite toy, that perhaps she would give him anything he asked for if it meant he kept looking at her like that.

She inched a lazy finger between her slick folds. When she reached her clit, she whimpered and bit down roughly on her bottom lip, half-expecting to taste blood. "I'm already so sensitive," she admitted. "I don't know if I can."

But Fraser's hand was already wrapped around his length, which was hardening again. She felt like she might have come then and there just from the sight of him and what it meant: that he wanted her, badly.

Half of her wanted to crawl over to him, tear him back to bed with her and close this gaping distance. Half of her never wanted to move. She found that she wanted to watch him, too. When he'd been behind her, she'd hated not being able to see him come inside of her. Now, she had the perfect view.

"If you need to stop, we'll stop," he said.

"I never want to stop with you," she admitted – then flicked the button on her toy. It came to life with a faint buzz – she'd been embarrassed to order anything louder – and she suddenly regretted choosing something so quiet, so subtle.

Before she started, she pinched her nipples, rolling them between her thumbs and forefingers. Fraser swore, pumping his dick again. Urging her on.

She pressed the toy to her overstimulated clit, gently at first, to make sure she could handle it.

She could. Just.

Her head tipped back without her permission, and it was an effort to keep her eyes open, to watch him as the silicone lapped at her. It wasn't nearly as warm or satisfying as his tongue, but it was quicker, harsher, and it didn't take long for a knot to build.

"Good lass," he breathed. "Just like that."

"Aren't you going to help?"

Fraser steeled himself, barely able to tear his hands from his length for long enough to crawl onto the bed. He took the toy from her trembling fingers, planting heavy, hot kisses against her mouth. "You are so fucking sexy."

She thanked him by tracing the outline of his tip, relishing in his sharp intake of breath when she followed the thick vein down his shaft. He responded in kind, finally pressing the toy back where she needed it until her legs were quaking and she was crying out. He watched her with a feverish, ravenous expression as she grew closer to her third climax. Just when she thought she couldn't take anymore, he plunged his finger inside her, the friction audible.

"Oh, god." A tear rolled down her cheek. She could barely hold herself up, but she kept her momentum as she worked him, too, revelling in his groans until her core tightened and she knew she was done for.

"I'm coming, Fraser," she let out shakily, and then couldn't contain her cries as both he and the toy left her unravelled. Her orgasm ripped through her, reducing her words to incoherent panting, and then she was pushing away the toy, his hands, without meaning to, afraid that any more would leave her shattered in pieces on the bed.

"Fucking *hell*, Harp." He grunted, thrusting harder into her hand once, twice. It was all it took for him to climax with her, a shuddering weight on top of her spent, bliss-flooded body. He muttered her name, over and over. Not the one her parents had given her, but the shortened version only he used: *Harp, Harp, Harp*. Like she was a song he wanted to sing on repeat. Like she was his.

When her body settled back into the mattress, she sucked in a ragged breath and clamped her legs around his body. As fun as their game had been, she needed to feel him again, needed him to cling to her like a second skin. She felt safest only when he was that close.

He turned the toy off, pushed it aside. Left kisses on her jaw, her shoulder, her collarbone, until there was no part of her skin left unmarred by him. Until she might as well have been ashes in his hands.

I never want to lose this.

The thought lanced through her pleasure like a serrated knife, leaving her stinging.

But I am going to lose this. Sooner or later.

His stubble scraped against her cheek, bringing her back if only for a moment. Exhaustion warred with the weightlessness she felt. She met his eyes, tangling her legs around his hips as he rolled just far enough onto the mattress that she wasn't bearing all of his weight.

Gently, he pushed her matted hair from her eyes. "Have to clean up."

"In a minute," she muttered, voice thick with fatigue. "Stay just a minute longer."

"I have to work, sweetheart."

"A minute longer," she pleaded again, kissing his throat until he succumbed. He sidled further down the bed, kissing her body again, as though he still hadn't learned all he wanted despite journeying her skin for days. He took her nipple in his mouth, tenderly this time – not to initiate more, but just because he could. Because he wanted to.

It felt a lot like being worshipped.

Harper followed the curvature of his ear with her finger, then his harsh jaw and just slightly crooked nose. He looked up at her, resting his chin on her chest. His gaze swam with…

Adoration, she would have said if it wasn't directed at her. She couldn't quite believe it, or maybe she didn't want to, so she pushed it down, pretended it was just plain fondness. An expression any short-term lover would wear.

But then he laced his fingers into hers and kissed each of her knuckles, and it was getting harder to lie to herself. Getting harder to convince herself that surely he couldn't like her as much as she liked him. That would be too perfect, and perfect didn't exist for her. Something was always off, wrong, ruined.

Feeling too vulnerable, she turned her face away, pretending to be interested in the moss-faded view of the woods outside. How quickly they had become her home, her safety net.

"What are you thinking?" he asked.

She shrugged, forcing herself to look back at him. She ran her hands through his coppery hair, trying to smooth down the tousled waves she'd ruined earlier. "Nothing interesting."

"That's a lie. Everything you think is interesting. Bizarre, but interesting."

She tugged playfully on a tuft above his forehead. "I've never done any of this before," she finally admitted. "Sex felt scary. I followed their lead. Not the other way around. Like if I let myself go, if I felt too free, the other person wouldn't want me anymore."

"I want you more and more every fucking day."

She scoffed, but he tilted her chin to force her to look at him.

"I haven't, either. I've never been that eager to have sex before, or to let someone in. My walls have well and truly crumbled – for you."

Cool fear flooded Harper's veins when her eyes began to prickle. What did it mean? It was like the universe had thrown them together just to spite them. They couldn't take this any further, couldn't think about long-term, but they were…

Well, they were perfect for each other. So it felt like, anyway, in moments like this.

She wanted to tell him then, about the email from Chris, but she couldn't bear to spoil such a peaceful, golden moment.

The end was coming. Did it matter if she told him now or later? It would hurt all the same.

"Are you okay?" he asked tenderly.

"Just sleepy."

He left a final kiss on her cheek, then pushed himself up from the bed. "I'll clean us up. You stay put." He booped her nose. "Just don't fall asleep yet."

"No promises." She shifted onto her side to watch him go, his naked form as familiar to her as her own now.

Once he'd left, everything flooded back. The knowledge that she would have to make her decision soon stifled her. She groaned into her pillow. Again, she felt like she'd been thrown off a cliff and he held the rope keeping her from falling.

How long before it snapped?

Harper couldn't tell him. Not when her week had continued with more of the most mind-blowing sex she'd ever had. While Fraser remained busy with work, coming home to her in the evenings, she spent her days staring at her manuscript. By Friday morning, she'd managed to add less than four thousand words, which she would have been proud of a month ago. But that had been her daily word count last week, and now even the sentences she managed barely made sense.

What if the novel had just been a silly dream, a passing fancy? What if she really did belong in the corporate world, and she should just respond to Chris to tell him she would be happy to attend the interview?

Come Friday afternoon, she felt... flat. Not herself, or maybe just the version of her she'd been before coming to Belbarrow. Luckily, she'd kept busy at the preschool two mornings this week, and was now busy preparing for the autumn festival. It was simple, easy work, putting together stalls and decorating the streets with garlands. Eiley was there to help her.

If nothing else, she'd at least found connections she'd always remember here.

"Are you all right, Harper?" asked Eiley now. She was stringing a trail of fake autumn leaves around the stall table beside her, while Harper did...

Nothing.

She couldn't remember what she was even *supposed* to be doing. There were twigs in her hand, rich red and orange paints on the table, and preschool children gathered around her still covered in their lunchtime spaghetti, so she was fairly certain she was supposed to be crafting with them.

Sky took one of the faux sunflowers lying on the crafting table without warning, enjoying the texture of the petals with an excited sound. The other children were growing restless, some of them calling out to the other preschool carers.

Luckily, Alice appeared next to them and offered her hand out. "I'll show them how to do that, hen. Wreath-making took me years of practice."

With an appreciative smile, Harper offered over the crafting materials, aware that Eiley still hadn't received an answer. Aware that Harper still didn't have one.

As soon as Alice had ambled away with the children, Eiley said, "Okay. Is that a no, then?"

"I'm just... out of my element. I'm not used to all this." Harper motioned around her. Bridge Walk was busier than she'd ever seen the street before. Wooden cabins had been lined up on either side of the road, not yet filled with wares but still reminding her, with a faint twinge of homesickness and a pang of something quite the opposite, of Manchester's Christmas Markets. Orange and yellow lights had been strung from one lamppost to the next, adding colour to the brick walls and faded awnings. Barrels spilling with bright sunflowers, marigolds, and fluffy purple pampas grass were set out between each table, with straw-stuffed scarecrows guarding the bridge on both sides.

It really was lovely. Harper of the past would have been impatient to capture it all for Instagram. Harper of the present just felt… lost. What if this festival was her last weekend in Belbarrow? If she accepted the interview, she'd have to go home as soon as possible to get her head on straight. Her mum had suggested as much, reminding Harper of how wonderful a higher salary would be for her future plans to raise a family, not to mention *those expensive clothes* she liked.

She was right. Those were things Harper wanted, and they required money.

But this place…

Her book…

Fraser.

"Harper." Eiley sidled closer, brushing Harper's arm lightly. "You were there for me last week. If something is wrong…"

Thankfully, Harper didn't have to answer. One of the children, Asha, barrelled over with orange paint all over her hands. Harper began searching for some paper towels, then changed her mind.

"I have an idea!" she said to Asha, squatting down to her eye level. "Do you trust me?"

Asha nodded, scratching her nose and leaving it amber. Harper took a large white sheet of card from the table and lightly took Asha's wrist, guiding her hand down. She left a perfect handprint in the corner. A few more, and they'd have a lovely border. "One more for each corner?"

Asha enjoyed lathering more paint onto her hands. By the end, her prints resembled abstract autumn leaves in vivid orange, gold, red, and green. Harper helped her clean up, then returned to her crafting table in the hopes of enlisting some more children who liked getting paint on their hands.

"You're great with them," Eiley praised. "And so creative!"

"Thank you. I figured paint is better on paper than on clothes." Harper chuckled. "How are things with you? Have you heard from Finlay again?"

Eiley shook her head, expression turning as glum as the grey day. She ran her hand over the strawberry blonde crown of Saffron's head, and the baby gurgled against her mother's chest, snug in the carrier strapped to Eiley's slim torso.

"I've decided not to give him any more chances," she said, voice wobbling with sadness. "I've blocked his number from my phone. If he wants to see his kids, he can work for it this time."

"You should be proud of yourself for that," Harper said gently. "I know it isn't easy to let go, but you deserve better, and you can't be the best mum you can be if he's getting in your head all the time, upsetting you with every phone call and text."

Eiley nodded resolutely, looking just like her stoic brother in that moment, with her chin set and eyes narrowed. "Exactly. I just wish it hadn't taken me so long to realise that. Thank you, Harper."

"Of course."

She elbowed Harper playfully. "But I *did* notice that you were trying to distract me. Not very subtly, either."

Harper grimaced.

"It's okay. I'm here when you're ready. Just as long as it isn't something Fraser's done?"

"No. Your brother is aggravatingly wonderful." Harper could no longer pretend that she wasn't falling for him – in an all-consuming, devastating way that would make it all the harder to leave. But also all the easier, if she was sensible enough. At least if she headed back to Manchester early, she wouldn't be delaying the inevitable. Like pulling off a waxing strip, it would be quick and… not at all painless. But quick. Maybe that was the best she could hope for.

Eiley beamed. "He is *infuriatingly* fab, isn't he? I don't know what we'd all do without him."

That much was clear. The entire town relied on him in some way or other. He was everything to them…

But Harper wasn't anyone's *everything*. She wasn't special like him. She didn't even have much luck on Instagram at the minute. Since she'd stopped posting so often, the algorithm had turned against her, and her engagement was slowly teetering into oblivion.

"But you're fab, too," Eiley said, giving Harper a gentle nudge. "That's why you're so magnetic together."

Harper wanted to believe her. But as more children flocked their way to paint their hands the colours of autumn, she couldn't stop thinking of the email.

The interview.

The looming end.

26

The next morning, Fraser froze in the middle of Bridge Walk. He carried a crate full of fairy figurines and handcrafted miniature houses, having cleared his table in the shed of every single one, including a few he'd only finished this week. He'd thought it wishful thinking to expect to sell so many, but now...

Harper and the preschool team had worked hard to make this festival a special one. Welcome signs with the kids' handprints were hung on the bridge. His stall was draped with vibrant bouquets, a handmade seasonal wreath, and a small sign that Harper had printed off at the library yesterday. Like the business cards she'd designed, it read *Handmade by Fraser* and featured whimsical woodland motifs on a wood grain background. A tagline read: *Beautiful unique ornaments and furniture, upcycled and sustainably crafted from Highland wood*.

Without warning, Harper popped up behind the table, arms brimming with more flowers. "Boo!"

"Ah!" He stepped back, putting a hand to his chest. "Jesus, Harp! You nearly gave me a heart attack."

Judging by the glint in her eye, that had clearly been the goal. She looked like one of his woodland fairies today, with a crown of sunflowers on her head and her lips stained a rich burgundy. She wore a burnt orange and brown plaid skirt that accentuated the curves of her hips, matched with a turtleneck and her new suede jacket. He grinned, remembering how she'd bounced into the cabin yesterday afternoon with the shopping bag in her hands, rejoicing that she'd found a French Connection piece for five pounds – "Five Great British Pounds, Fraser! That's the same price as a posh coffee!" – among the racks.

Stepping forwards again, he motioned to the elaborate display. "Are you kidding with all this?"

She glanced around as though she'd only just noticed it herself. "You don't like it?"

"Of course I bloody like it, you mad woman." He placed his crate of wares on the table and rested his hands over it. "You just shouldn't have gone to so much effort. You're busy enough as it is."

Harper's smile faltered as she tied a handful of marigold stems with a neat twine bow. "Not *that* busy at the moment."

"Busy enough. You're writing a future Nobel Prize winner. Or whatever awards exist for books." He rounded the stall, unable to stand all the obstacles between them. When he entered the side door, though, he didn't like what he found. Harper's mouth drooping at the corners unhappily.

Something was wrong. Had been all week. She'd claimed otherwise, but he'd still noticed a difference. It had been harder to coax laughs from her when they walked Bernard before he started work. Easier to get her to hush up in the evenings when he was trying to focus on *The X-Files*, which she'd insisted they watch together, only to chatter all the way through, mostly about how she couldn't decide whether she was more in love with Mulder or Scully. Secretly, he liked hearing her voice over those of the actors. But whenever he'd asked if she was okay, she'd brushed him off.

He was pretty sure it was nothing to do with him. They'd been intimate more and more each day, getting lost in one another's bodies every spare hour they had. She'd stayed over at his house the night before last and they'd taken advantage of his bathtub, which had fitted them both. He'd worried briefly that she might want to end things with him, but she didn't act like that was the case when they were together.

She was just… different.

He poked her in the soft flesh between her ribs. "You okay?"

Harper nodded swiftly. "I've not been writing much this week. That's all."

He felt a pang of guilt. Was it because of him? She'd put so much work into the festival, into the business he'd been hellbent on not starting until she encouraged him, and then there'd been helping Andy out at the B&B and working on Flockhart's marketing plans, too. And the preschool. And checking up on Eiley. Had Fraser's overwhelming community burned her out?

"How come?" He took her hand, pulling her closer so she would stop using the flower arrangements as a distraction.

"Just writer's block." She shivered as though dispelling an unwelcome thought, before brightening so quickly he felt whiplashed. "No time for that today, anyway! Let's get your fairies on display! Are you nervous?"

He was, actually, but less so with her here. Before he could even think about setting up the stall, he locked his arms around her waist, his nose grazing hers before he kissed her. "Thank you for doing this for me. You're pretty amazing."

"I *am* pretty amazing," she agreed. "But you're welcome. Thank you for letting me be part of it all. And for letting me be the first person you trusted with this."

He kissed the crease between her brows gently. "Who else would have forced me into this?"

She slapped his arm lightly, feigning offence. "I did no such thing! I just… nudged."

"Aggressively."

"Attentively," she corrected.

"Annoyingly."

"*Adorably*."

They paused for a beat, exchanging soft expressions of amusement. He felt energised, as he often did with her, but something more, too. Today felt like a new beginning. Of course, he was terrified of showing his work to the town, his mum, and his sisters, but he was excited, too. He'd been hiding this part of himself for too long.

"I'm just beginning to think maybe you miss your career," he said, opening the lid on his crate and beginning to unload his figurines from their protective paper. "You came here for a holiday, but you're still using your expertise to help the rest of us. That boss of yours must have been a wee shitebag to let you go."

He waited for a witty response, or at least something to acknowledge she'd heard him.

But she offered nothing. When he turned around, she was focused intently on readjusting the pile of business cards on the side, though they'd already been stacked neatly.

He frowned. "Harp?"

"*What*?!" shrieked a voice outside the stall. Fraser held his breath. He didn't need to look to know who it belonged to. "*No. Way!*"

When he turned, Cam was already dashing over to them, gasping at the rows of figurines. She wore her blue Raindrop Café apron, having complained the evening before over dinner at her house that Alice was putting her "out on the street" to man their coffee stand. Afterwards, Fraser had babysat while she and Sorcha ventured out on their first date since Archie's arrival. If he hadn't forced her to hand the baby over, she never would have gone, but he knew how important it was that they step away. After Sorcha had birthed Isla, Fraser had watched a disconnect grow in their marriage that had almost devastated Cam beyond words, and he didn't want that again.

"Morning, Cam." He sighed now, rubbing his eyes. He loved her. He really did. But out of everyone in his family, she was the loudest, and he hadn't even had breakfast yet. She was also the most unpredictable, so he had no idea what she'd be loudly saying next.

"I can't believe this!" she shouted shrilly. "It was *you*! You made the ornaments on the Fairy Trail!"

"Surprise." He waggled his fingers unenthusiastically, nerves drawing tight beneath his skin.

"How could you not say something sooner? The kids would have lost their shit if they knew!" She picked up the fairy closest to her, inspecting the wings of the boy he'd chiselled. He'd used Sky as inspiration for that one, with the red tones in his floppy hair – Sky hated haircuts, so Eiley let him grow it as long as he wanted – and loose green clothes to match his nephew's favourite Peter Pan pyjamas. Cam shifted her keen gaze from the figurine to Harper. "Did *you* know?"

Harper seesawed her hand. "A little bit. Not when he took me to the trail, though."

"Sneaky, sneaky bastard," Cam uttered. "My brother is a liar!"

"A very talented liar," said Harper.

Fraser winced. He didn't want to be branded as that.

"Look. This one's for you." Nervously, he grabbed the auburn-haired fairy with tattoos and forced it into Cam's hands. "And Sorcha." The one with brown skin and dark clothes came next. He'd also made one each for the kids – and almost one for everybody in the village, he'd realised only after he'd finished carving them. All of his inspiration came from the faces he saw every day, and not only that, but he'd wanted to make sure that even strangers found themselves in the collection. Some were seated in moss-covered wheelchairs, or used crutches like his mum. Some were plus-size like

Harper, and some were androgynous like Andy. He'd fashioned hijabs from recycled fabric and included stretch marks and scars like the ones he loved to explore on Harper's body. After seeing how happy the bisexual colours on her writing desk had made Harper, he even hoped to create a Pride collection in time for Belbarrow's small parade the coming summer.

As predicted, Cam softened as she faced the fairy version of herself, tracing the outline of her miniature fringe and pierced button nose, as well as the roundness of her stomach. She sniffed when she picked up Sorcha's piece. If he knew his sister, she was probably trying to force her tears to crawl back deep, deep inside. Cam wasn't a crier. "Can't you let me be mad at you for a minute?"

"No." Relief washed over Fraser, and he pinched his mouth between his fingers to keep from grinning.

"Does Mum know?"

"No. I'd like to surprise her and Eiley when they come later."

Cam set the figures down and reached across the table, grabbing Fraser's head between her heavy hands so she could squeeze his cheeks together. He groaned, ignoring Harper's laughs at his expense. "She's going to be ever so proud of little Frasy Baby," she cooed like he was ten years old.

"Get off me, you daft sod." He slapped her off finally, but not before she pinched his nose.

Then, she turned to Harper. "Are you sure you have to leave Belbarrow? You've only been here a month, and my brother's already spilling his deepest, darkest secrets."

Harper's mouth opened, then closed. For once, she didn't seem to have anything to say.

Cam pocketed her new figurines and rocked on her heels, apparently oblivious. "Well, make sure you come to Raindrop's stall later. Alice made cheesecake, and I'll be bored shitless standing there alone in the cold."

Cam ruffled his hair, then shook her head to show her disapproval a final time. Then, she kissed Sorcha's figurine. So many emotions in such a short space of time. He could barely keep up.

When she left, he let out a relieved breath.

One down, two more to go.

Harper took his hand and squeezed. "I think that was Cam language for *Your work is wonderful. Thank you.*"

He chuckled at that, and he knew Harper was right. Still, he doubted Cam would let him live his secret down anytime soon.

27

"You, my friend, are a fucking superstar." Andy appeared seemingly out of nowhere, emerging from the bustling crowd like an apparition with a broad grin on their face. Harper assumed they were talking about Fraser and his work until Andy pointed right at her. "I showed my parents everything you came up with the other day. They were so excited about the plans that they barely even noticed the reno!"

Harper felt Fraser's arm snake around her waist and give her a congratulatory squeeze. She loved that feeling, the way he always seemed to want her close, but today it felt... *tainted*. Would he still want to touch her when she told him about the job interview, or would this be the end of them? He'd already pulled away from her once. He could easily do it again.

She swallowed the trepidation rising in her throat. "That's great news, Andy. I'm so glad."

"So, your crisis was for nothing?" Fraser joshed.

Andy put their hands on their hips and glared, revealing a blue and pink striped T-shirt printed with the words, *sisterhood, not cisterhood* beneath their denim jacket. Harper wanted it immediately. "Not for nothing. My mother would like to know how long it will take to finish renovating her beloved B&B. I told her it would depend on whether you plan to show your face at work or skive off again."

Fraser's body tensed against Harper's, and she looked up to see his face darkening, despite the clear sarcasm in Andy's tone. She placed a steadying hand on his chest, wondering if perhaps Andy had finally gone a step too far. Fraser was no skiver, and to keep throwing that absent afternoon in his face, which he'd made up for on a bloody weekend, wasn't fair – even if it was a joke.

Andy noticed Fraser's change in mood and tutted, standing on their tiptoes to ruffle his hair across the table. "I'm kidding, pal. What are all these?"

They picked up one of the figurines, a beautiful pink-haired trans fairy with top scars whom Harper had already asked to feature in her novel.

"Fairies," Fraser said bluntly.

"Sick! Who made them?" Andy traced the top scars, reverence glistening in their eyes. Harper's heart warmed. "I've seen some on the Fairy Trail, but never ones like this."

Since Fraser still seemed frozen, Harper cleared her throat and picked out the fairy resembling Andy, with silver wings and dungarees, a perfect balance of realistic and whimsical.

Andy blinked as though none of it made sense, then twirled their own lip ring as though pondering the shared characteristic. "Wait… Is that me?" They slowly lifted their head to Fraser. "Who…" Realisation settled like daylight on their elfin face: hazy at first, and then bright all at once. "*You!*"

Fraser nodded once, tersely. "You're not the only one Harper has worked her marketing magic on."

"Shut up!" Andy punched him in the arm, hard enough that he winced. "Fucking hell, Fraser. These are amazing. Can you make me some more for the B&B?" They gasped. "My mum loves sentimental shite."

"Not that these are *shite*," Harper was quick to cut in.

"No, no." They shook their head, wide-eyed. "These are…" They licked their lips, seemingly lost for words as they took in the other figurines. "These are something else."

"We were thinking that maybe you could share your grand reopening with Fraser's launch party," Harper said before Fraser could stop her. "Have a little celebration for the businesses of Belbarrow and kill two birds with one stone. What do you think?"

"That's not a bad idea, actually. I was planning for the twenty-third of November. Will you still be here then?"

Harper tensed. That was the week of her interview, should she choose to go. Still, she refused to miss the party either way, even if the train fares would cost a fortune. One last weekend in Belbarrow… "Yes. Of course!"

"Let's do it, then." Andy shook their head again. "Why didn't you tell us?"

"That's a good question." Eiley sidled up beside Andy, stationing her pram. She didn't even look at Fraser, instead going straight to the figurines.

Beside her, his mum put a hand over her mouth. "Fraser Thomas Milligan. What on earth are you like?"

Fraser took a deep breath, rearing back on his heels. Harper offered him a supportive smile, but she couldn't help but mouth *Thomas* mischievously, and he rolled his eyes in response.

Fraser swallowed. "What do you think, Mum? Eiley?"

"I can't believe this," Myra said, shaking her head, and he stiffened until Eiley cut in.

"They're amazing, Fraser." Eiley's face was shining with pride.

"They're wondrous," breathed Myra, eyes glistening. "My boy, an artist!"

Finally, Fraser broke into a smile. He blinked rapidly then cleared his throat. "I know I should have said something to you sooner." He turned his gaze to Harper. "But I'm glad somebody convinced me they deserved to be shown off."

"Aye, that they do!" Myra exclaimed, leaning heavily on her crutch as though he'd truly swept her off her feet. "I remember you used to bring home all sorts of beautiful work when you were at high school. I always hoped you'd stick with something creative."

"*Creativity doesn't pay the bills* is actually what you said," Fraser replied pointedly. Another pang shot through Harper. Unfortunately, that was true. Her unfinished novel wouldn't be garnering an income any time soon, even if she aimed for a bestseller.

Returning to Brentworth would.

"Well, you might just prove me wrong." Myra slipped between the stalls to take Fraser's face in her hands. Her cheeks were swollen with pride, eyes glittering with the same ocean-blue clarity as his. "You make me so proud."

Fraser slipped out of the stall and pulled his mother into a hug. Eiley joined, along with Brook, and Harper was content to stand back and watch the sweet moment unfold. It must be the best feeling in the world, she thought, to have a big family like that, full of love and support. Her own parents were wonderful, but she'd always longed for funny aunts and gruff uncles, kind-hearted grandmas and softly spoken grandpas. Cousins. Nieces, nephews. A full circle of people she *belonged* with, not just at Christmas and birthdays, but all year round.

Andy, on the other hand, mimicked poking their finger down their throat and gagging. "That's my cue to leave. Cheers though, pal. And you, Harper. Come and stop by the B&B this week, won't you? I promise I won't force you to paint again."

Harper laughed. "I'll try," was all she could promise.

While Fraser and his mum continued chatting, a few of the locals joining in, Eiley tugged Harper's sleeve gently. "Shall we grab a coffee?" Her gaze was soft. Knowing.

Harper nodded. Eiley asked Myra to watch Brook, then Harper followed Eiley past the sunflower barrels and face-painting stand. She wheeled Saffron and Sky expertly across the cobbles, all the way to the Raindrop Café's minute stall. A few tables and chairs had been set up around it, and Cam was offering out tasters of scones and flavoured lattes to those interested. *Still no pumpkin spice*, Harper lamented sadly.

"We'll have whatever drinks have the most calories," Eiley said as they greeted Cam, perching on the chair closest.

"I like your style." Harper took a deep breath as she joined her at the table. Her feet throbbed from standing up for most of the day in her heeled boots, but she found she quite liked the ache. It was proof she'd made a change, done something different and important with someone she…

She bit down on the inside of her cheek, a small punishment for being so silly. *Loved*, she'd wanted to think. Suddenly, she wished she could pause time. Wanted to stay frozen here at this table, so that she would never have to tell Fraser about the job, and so that she would never have to get on the train back to Manchester.

Eiley glanced at her as she rocked the pram back and forth. Behind her, Cam steamed the milk with a raucous sputter from the machine.

"You've done so much for my brother," Eiley began finally. "He never would have shown us his work without you."

Harper shrugged. "I'm sure he would have eventually. He just needed a bit of prodding."

"He needed more than that." Eiley leaned forwards, playing with the laminated menu on the table. "I've always tried to give him the same support that he gives me, but he usually likes to keep quiet when he's struggling. He's always so… hyper-focused on work, or whatever else needs to be done. It's like he's put up a barrier between us."

"I think he likes to take care of you," Harper said tenderly. But she knew exactly what Eiley meant about the barrier. She wasn't entirely convinced she'd passed over it yet, either.

"It's more than that. He *needs* to take care of us, or at least, he thinks he does."

Harper frowned, so Eiley continued. "I barely remember our dad, but I know Fraser saw a lot of the hurt Mum was put through when he left. I think maybe he thinks he has to be our father as well as our brother, to make up for it. All that 'man of the house' crap. I don't believe in it, but Dad did. Fraser does."

"He does take on too much," she agreed, thinking of Fraser's reaction to Andy and their pointed remarks. He didn't like to fall short. Liked to be on top of everything all the time. Even down to the feelings he had for Harper, and hers for him – he'd been so reluctant to give in to them.

Harper understood. She'd lived most of her life trying to be perfect, whether it was on social media, at work, in her relationships. Every setback felt like the end of the world, a personal failure, proof she was just not good enough.

She hated to think of Fraser with that same mindset, especially when it came to family. Wasn't that supposed to be the one thing in life that was simple, easy? One thing you didn't have to work for?

"But he's got better since he met you," said Eiley. She sat back as Cam placed down their drinks, two large mugs towering with whipped cream, caramel sauce, and chocolate sprinkles.

Harper looked up at Cam. "My sweet tooth and I love you."

Cam patted her shoulder. "I love you both, too. What are we talking about?" She peeked over her shoulder, found no customers waiting at the counter, and straddled the back of a chair from the next table over to face them.

"Fraser, and how good Harper is for him." Eiley beamed.

"Oh, aye. This I can attest to."

Harper sank deeper into her chair. She wasn't sure she wanted to hear the two most important people in his life sing her praises, not when she might never see them again. Or him. Whether she was good for him or not, she was leaving. It didn't matter whether it was now or later. This thing couldn't last.

"But something is wrong," Eiley whispered, placing her hand over Harper's on the table.

Tears sprang to Harper's eyes. She couldn't deny it anymore.

"Oh, shite. Now look what you've done, Eiley. Usually, I'm the one who makes people cry." Cam pulled a wad of napkins out of her apron and set them before Harper. Harper took one, dabbing her eyes, but it was no use. One tear was wiped, and two more took its place. Before she knew it, streams were rolling down her cheeks.

Eiley tutted and shifted her chair closer, metal legs scraping against stone as she placed her arm around Harper's shuddering shoulders. "I knew something was up. I'm sorry, Harper."

Harper shook her head, covering her face to hide her twisted expression of pain. "I just don't know what to do."

"About what?" asked Cam.

"I got an invitation from my old boss to interview for a new position, a promotion. He would want me back in Manchester to meet him the week after next."

"That's so soon," Eiley breathed nervously. "Have you told Fraser?"

Harper studied her hands. "I don't know how! Part of me doesn't want to. Part of me doesn't want to leave at all. But I can't just stay here forever. I won't get an opportunity like this again. It took me years to find a decent job in the first place."

"Shite," Cam murmured again. "This is really fucking shite."

Harper was inclined to agree. "It's my own fault. We promised each other this would be casual. Easy."

"I'm going to tell you a secret, babe. Our brother is rarely casual or easy."

Eiley nodded, mouth set into a solemn line. "I haven't seen him like this with somebody for years. He always calls things off the minute it gets too intense."

"Not helping!" Harper whined and hit her head against the table.

Cam ran soothing circles between her shoulder blades. "If you did tell him, what would be the ideal outcome? What would you want him to say? Would you want to try long distance?"

Harper had been wondering the same thing all week. What *would* he say? Part of her dreamed he might ask her to stay, like he was some knight in a fairy tale willing to sweep her off her feet, keep her here where things were quiet and peaceful and good. But that was too *Hallmark movie*, even for her. She couldn't just… stay. She'd always been used to the big city, to a steady job. What would she do here when the novelty of it all wore off? Who would she be without her family nearby and her old job long gone?

Writing in the cabin all day was a nice dream, but was it hers, or just the escape she'd needed after a rough few months?

And long distance… She could already feel those two words ripping a hole in her heart, making it hard to breathe. Face-Time calls and rushed text messages wouldn't be enough for her. Not with him. She would miss him more than she'd see him, and she was not prepared to become a full-time yearner.

It just wasn't fair. It wasn't fair that her new favourite person lived three hundred miles north of her. It wasn't fair that she'd finally found a place where she felt true belonging and acceptance, but it wasn't permanent.

"I don't know. I really don't know," she admitted finally. "We both know this is coming to an end sooner or later. I can't expect anything from him."

Eiley sighed. "I think you can. If you want to, you can."

"And *if* you want to," Cam said, "maybe it's a sign that this was never supposed to be just casual. You're allowed to want more, Harper. Things aren't usually so simple. Fuck, it took me many pep talks in front of the mirror to ask Sorcha out. Months to ask her if she wanted to make things serious. I was scared shitless the whole time."

"Cam's right." Eiley spooned some whipped cream into her mouth. "You might have agreed that this would end, but feelings change. Look at Finlay. We decided to have three kids together, and then he decided to leave us."

Harper appreciated Cam and Eiley immensely, but none of these things were helping. If there were no rules here that she could follow to avoid getting hurt, how was she supposed to survive? What if she was foolish enough to turn down the job interview only to find out in another few weeks, months, years, that she and Fraser were never meant to be? What if she *did* attend the interview but Brentworth didn't hire her? What if she *was* hired and she hated every moment of it, and working with Kenzie again left her broken, and her novel was never written, and she had to push down this new version of herself until she was dead on the inside?

What if she felt like she was always making the wrong decisions because there were no right ones? What if she would always feel just a little bit wrong, a little bit too vulnerable?

"I don't want my decision to depend on him," she admitted. "I don't want to be that girl who turns down a job because she fancies someone."

"I think it's more than just a case of fancying him." Cam lifted her brows. "And you're not 'that girl', Harper. 'That girl' doesn't exist. It's just a bullshit stereotype to make women who want love and peace over independence and work feel bad. You're a strong woman with a lot to offer the world. Your decision would never change that. There's nothing wrong with choosing a connection over a career, if that's what you want. It's only an issue if you feel like you're being forced to sacrifice one for the other, and he would never put you in that position."

"The best thing you can do is talk to him," Eiley added. "You're driving yourself mad, but he's a good man. He'll help you figure it out. He would *want* to figure it out. I know he would."

Harper looked down, playing with the wooden button on her coat sleeve. Her fingers were cold. Her coffee would be, too. "It's more than just choosing him or my job. It's the writing, too. For once in my life, I've been doing something

I really love, something I'm learning not to need immediate validation for, all on my own."

"It sounds like maybe you've already made your decision, then," Cam replied.

Harper took a deep breath and closed her eyes. She wished it was that simple.

28

Half of Fraser's stock was gone by the end of the day, and almost all of his business cards. Fairies that had spent years in his shed now belonged to people who would hopefully care for them a little better. A warmth settled in his chest as he packed up his stall. Thank goodness Harper had pushed him to do this. Being praised for his work all day had left him overwhelmed with pride. He hadn't quite realised how great an impact the fairies had made on the locals, how much they'd been enjoyed on the trail.

His gaze fell to Harper. She'd been quiet this afternoon, but he hadn't had time to ask why. She looked gorgeous in the amber light of the setting sun, her nose pink from the cold as she carefully wrapped up his unsold pieces and placed each one back in the crate. Her teeth chattered, lips pale.

Without thinking, he pulled off his red tartan scarf and wound it around her neck, causing her to startle. "I know it doesn't match your outfit, but…"

She soon melted into a smile, burying her chin into the wool. "Thanks."

"Fancy a drink after this?" He nodded across the road to the Turloch Corner Tavern, which was already piled full of people. Despite the chill in the air, patrons were eating and drinking outside, the atmosphere loud and bubbly after such a cheerful day. "I think Mum's already inside with Cam."

Harper hesitated. Just for a second, but he saw it. Something in her eyes was dark and lifeless, like he was looking at her through tinted windows. "Sure. Sounds good."

"We don't have to, if you're tired," he said. Maybe he'd relied on her too much today. Drained her. The thought made him uneasy.

She shook her head. Went back to tidying. "I'm sure I can manage a pint."

Whatever it was, she was trying to hide it, and some part of him didn't want to push – afraid if he did, it might break the spell of the day's festivities.

"Thank you for everything today, Harp." His voice was delicate, barely concealing a plea – for what, he didn't quite know. Perhaps he just wanted her to look at him. Perhaps he just wanted to be sure that everything was okay.

"Of course. It was good fun."

He placed the lid on the box of figurines then slapped his hands together. "All done."

Harper said nothing, still searching for more things to clean or put away. But there was nothing left on the table, and the silence between them was laid bare too.

He couldn't not ask. "Is something wrong, sunshine?"

She shook her head, playing with the frayed tassels of his scarf nervously.

So something *was* wrong, then, and she was doing a terrible job of denying it.

Anxiety bounced like springs inside him. He took her hand carefully and waited.

She traced the rough callouses on his fingers. "I don't want to do this. I don't want to ruin the day."

Oh, god. She was going to break it off with him. A lump built in his throat, and he worked hard to gulp it down, but that only served to make it worse. "Do what?" he croaked.

"I…" She sighed, finally meeting his eyes. Hers were glossy, and her lip quivered. His insecurity quickly turned to concern. Was it something else? "I got an email from my old boss the other day. He wants me to interview with him again."

Fraser narrowed his eyes. "The same boss who made you redundant?"

A nod. "But not the same role, otherwise I wouldn't even be considering it, trust me. He wants me to step in as the director of the marketing team."

"Wow…" He dropped her hand without realising it, trying to comprehend what that meant. *Director.*

It was a good opportunity. One she was "considering".

She'd proven herself to be a skilled marketer, not just to him, but to Andy and everybody else who had benefitted from her ideas.

He wanted to say so many things. Wanted to point out that, not too long ago, she'd claimed to be unhappy at that company.

But it wouldn't be right to do that. She'd supported *him* enough, encouraged him into the spotlight with his work. Wasn't it his responsibility to do the same?

He'd always known she would have to go home. Why couldn't he just... let her?

His face stung, and something far deeper within him, too, when he realised what all of this truly meant.

She was leaving.

"When is the interview?"

"The week after next." Her voice was hollow. So was his chest.

He slid his hands into his pockets, fixing his stare on a sunflower petal on the ground because he couldn't bear to look at her. Couldn't bear to remind himself of what he was in the process of losing. Knowing that this moment had always been inevitable didn't make it any easier.

This, he realised, was why he'd held back in the beginning. This was why he hadn't wanted to get too attached. Because now the goodbye was coming, sooner than he'd expected, and it felt like...

He didn't even know what it felt like. His ears were ringing, heart thudding, and every nerve in his body jangled.

He squeezed his eyes closed quickly. *Don't be so fucking selfish, Fraser. Support her the way she's supported you. Tell her you're bloody happy for her, for Christ's sake.*

He inhaled shakily, scratching his locked jaw. "You should go for it."

The silence teetered like a glass on the brink of shattering between them. She tilted her head, throat bobbing. "You think?"

"Aye. Of course. You're great at what you do. It's about time people started recognising that." His words sounded stiff even to his own ears.

Harper took a step back. "Oh. Okay."

He didn't understand. Had she been expecting something else? What could he possibly say? He couldn't tell her how to live her life. Couldn't ask her to stay. She could be successful in Manchester. What could he possibly offer her that trumped that?

"I would have to leave soon," she said quietly. "Next week."

"I could drive you into Glasgow, if it makes it easier. You know, to plan travel stuff."

What was he *doing*? Another version of himself stood behind him, screaming at him to *stop*. Shut up. He didn't *want* to drive her into Glasgow. He didn't want to drive her anywhere that wasn't home – his house, or his cabin.

Harper blinked as though his words surprised her. "Okay. Thank you." She paused. "I would come back for the launch party, if you wanted me to. I wouldn't want to miss it."

"That would be nice, but you wouldn't have to." He didn't even want a launch party if she wasn't going to be here anymore. He didn't want *anything* that wasn't complete and utter numbness. He certainly didn't want any more of this sharp stabbing in his chest, which was penetrating deeper with every word she said.

"Whatever you want, Fraser." She sighed, wrapping her arms around herself. "You know, I think I'll save that drink for tomorrow. I'm tired." She unwound his scarf from her neck quickly, pressing it into his chest.

Why was she giving it back?

He frowned, fingers loose around it. "I'll drive you, then."

"No. Your mum is waiting for you inside. Go. I'll walk."

"It's cold," he pointed out.

"The walk will warm me up." And then she was brushing past him. Walking towards the bridge. Fraser's heart rang out like alarm bells in his ears, in perfect unison with the ones drifting from St. Margaret's to signal the new hour.

He wanted to call out, bring her back to him, but what was the point?

She was leaving, whether he liked it or not. Maybe it was better not to pretend otherwise.

They never should have done it in the first place, but he'd let himself fall despite wanting so badly not to.

He'd brought this pain on himself by being reckless and impulsive and *addicted* – to her laugh, her taste, her warmth. To *her*.

Fraser felt like the life had been leached from him as he crossed the road. He forced his legs to walk into the tavern, only to distract himself from the truth stirring like cement in his chest.

She was already gone.

"Where's Harper?" was the first question his Mum asked when he walked into the Turloch Corner Tavern alone. He huffed and slumped onto the chair opposite her and his sister, shaking his head.

"Oh, crap," Cam said quietly. "She told you."

He snapped his head up, ire burning inside him. "You *knew*?"

Harper had told his bloody meddling sister before she'd told *him*? They might not have been in a serious relationship, but he sort of thought he'd earned the right to know that the woman he'd been making love to just two nights ago was leaving.

Cam lifted her hands in surrender. "She only told me and Eiley today! She was upset, that was all. We helped talk her—" She paused. "Hang on. Why aren't you with her instead of us?"

"What do you mean she was upset?" Fraser asked. *Why* was she upset? She'd made the choice to leave. She was getting the promotion she'd clearly wanted. She'd been the one to keep this casual, convince him to make the most of each other while they could.

Cam jabbed a thumb into her shoulder. "I asked first. What have you gone and done, you big tube?"

"I didn't do anything. I said she should go for it because she deserves the success she wants. Then she said she was tired and she wanted to walk home."

"You utter nincompoop!" She flicked him on the forehead. Hard.

"*Ow*!" he complained, rubbing away the sharp sting.

"Oh, deary me," said Mum, shaking her head. "Deary, deary me, Fraser."

"*What*? I did the right thing!" His voice rose to a shrill, defensive crescendo. Why were they looking at him like he was the child at preschool who kept licking the fingerpaints?

"You absolutely did," said Cam.

"Thank you."

"*Not!*" she bellowed, slamming her elbows on the table so hard that her pint sloshed in its glass. A sea of eyes turned to their table in surprise, but Cam didn't seem to care. "You were supposed to ask her how she was feeling, not pack up her suitcase and send her on her merry way!"

Fraser rubbed a hand over his face roughly. He really didn't need this tonight. "I didn't *need* to ask how she feels," he spoke through gritted teeth. "We both knew this would come to an end."

"Oh, Fraser, I despair." Mum huffed out a long breath and glugged down her white wine. "You were supposed to ask her to stay!"

"Yes!" agreed Cam, but then her brows knitted together. "Wait, no. That wasn't what he was supposed to do, Mum. You can't be asking a strong, independent woman to sacrifice her career."

"Exactly. So I didn't," he retorted.

"Oh, that's very true. So what was he supposed to do?" asked Mum.

"He was *supposed* to ask her what *she* wanted," she answered pointedly. "If he had, he might have realised that Harper does not *want* to go back to Manchester yet, because she's obsessed with him and her heart is in writing."

"*Obsessed*?" Fraser cut in. "She said that?"

"She didn't have to, you dolt," said Cam, "because it's patently obvious that you are both mad for each other. Now, as I was saying: if you had asked her, you could have figured out a way where you can both get what you want."

"Oh, yes. That sounds reasonable." Mum nodded, wiping the wine from her mouth. "You should have done that, Fraser."

He scoffed, casting his eyes to the heavens. "It must be nice to live in a fantasy world where everything is all butterflies and rainbows! We agreed that there would come a time when Harper would have to leave. This was inevitable. I'm not going to fight for something we already knew we'd have to lose and make things complicated!"

"Yes, because god forbid things get complicated, Fraser." Cam's tone verged on something beyond her usual sarcasm. Something cutting.

Fraser flinched. "What's that supposed to mean?"

"Look at you. Every day, you live the same life. You get up, go to work, help a friend or one of us, go to bed."

"There's nothing wrong with a routine. You get up and go to work, too. And you're welcome, for the helping thing, by the way!"

"I didn't get a wife and two children by *only* going to work, or by avoiding change!" Cam said. "I worked hard for it. I put time and effort into it. I took a chance, even when I was fucking terrified."

He leaned back in his chair impatiently, unable to hold back his sneer. "And that makes you a love guru? Come off it, Cam."

"It makes me not alone!"

He recoiled; the insult felt like a slap. *Alone?*

"Okay, now that's enough," Mum interjected with a cautious arm between them. "Your brother isn't alone, and there's nothing wrong with choosing not to be in love."

"No, there isn't. But he isn't choosing that, Mum, because he's already *in* love. What he's choosing is to let it pass him by because he's scared."

"Scared!" He let out a hollow laugh, but it only made his ribs ache more.

Scared. Was that what he was? What he'd always been?

The colour drained from his face as he realised that perhaps he was. He'd been holding back on Harper since the beginning. He'd avoided dating and had swiftly put an end to past relationships before the other party could do it first.

No. No, he refused to live in a world where his harsh, know-it-all sister actually *did* know it all. "I'm not in love with Harper," he said. "We haven't even known each other that long."

"Like that has anything to do with it." Cam blew her thick fringe from her eyes.

Mum looked sadly between them. She hated when they fought. She'd never told them, but Fraser suspected it was because their house had once been an echo chamber of fighting, and his dad, with the loudest voice and the sharpest tongue, always won.

Fraser would rather live the rest of his life in the same routine than ever risk being dragged into something so volatile. So what if things with Harper had been good? They wouldn't be forever. People fought and they broke up. They hurt each other. They left. It was better to end on a high note than risk a sour one.

"Fraser… I think your sister is trying to say that, if you like this woman as much as you seem to, maybe you shouldn't just let her go," Mum said.

He opened his mouth to argue, but she cut in quickly. "You thought you were doing right by her. I know, love. But she might have wanted more. She might have wanted to at least know if you wanted her to stay, even if you couldn't ask her to. She might have wanted to figure out a way to keep you both: the job and you. It sounds like you didn't offer her that."

A dull ache pounded behind his eyes. Was she right? Had he been so quick to support her that he hadn't even noticed perhaps she'd needed more? *Deserved* more?

It didn't matter, not really. He couldn't give Harper an answer. He wanted her to stay, but the world didn't work that way. Things changed. Fraser just wanted to maintain enough stability to carry on. To survive. It was easier to do that without her, even if it meant more suffering in the short run.

"There isn't a way to do that. She has her life and I have mine." He sounded hoarse. Close to tears. Felt it, too, like somebody had scrubbed him down with sandpaper, leaving his skin shredded and raw.

"No. That was how it was before, when you didn't know her," Mum said. "That girl helped you chase a dream we didn't even know you had. Your lives aren't separate at all." She shifted and pursed her lips. "And they probably never will be again, no matter what you do. You don't just untangle yourself from the people you love. Even if you want to."

She was talking about Dad. It still lingered with her. *He* still lingered. Fraser felt it, when they were sitting down at the table and one of the chairs was empty, or when he went into the attic and found a box of Dad's things he'd never come back to collect.

Even now, he could smell Harper on his scarf. Her perfume, her skin, that fruity lip gloss she wore and the caramel coffee she'd been drinking earlier that day.

What if he couldn't wash it away?

What if he would be stuck here, thinking of her, forever?

When he thought of his future, it suddenly felt like a black hole – or perhaps it had for a while. He'd never dared imagine a partner or a family of his own, though he'd always wanted it. His life revolved around the same work he did every day. Like that old redwood tree by the loch that never seemed to change, not even in punishing winds and rain. It had been there for far longer than he'd been alive. The landscape wouldn't be the same without it.

He'd thought he was meant to be like that: stationary, evergreen.

Harper had changed that.

"I can see common sense creeping back into his eyes," Cam whispered. "Well done, Mum."

It wasn't common sense. It was panic: that he'd done the wrong thing, that everything had changed. That he was in love with a woman who wouldn't be easy to keep.

Would he forgive himself if he didn't at least try?

29

Subject: New job opening?
From: Harper Clegg
To: Chris Bailey

  Chris,
  I would certainly be interested in inter-
viewing for the new position. Thank you for
thinking of me. Let me know what date/time
suits you.

  Best,
  Harper

Harper closed her laptop before she could regret sending the email. She was doing this. Fraser had made it quite clear that there was no reason to stay – not that she'd expected one.

Not even for a minute.

All right, perhaps a part of her had been hoping he would at least show a little bit of sadness. An "I'll miss you, Harp," or "Is this *really* what you want?" Instead, he'd seemed painfully eager to cart her off to the train station.

Tears rolled down her face as she sat back in her chair, tracing the neat, curved corners of her desk. Had she misread him? Fine, they'd agreed that this was only a holiday fling, but he'd made her a bloody writing corner with her name on it. He'd carved a fairy from wood for her. She'd thought maybe that meant something.

She'd got her silly hopes up, like a naive little girl who still believed in fairy tales. This was her problem. It would always be her problem. She wanted more than anybody else could give her. She expected happy endings where they didn't exist. She saw kindness and mistook it for love because she was too desperate to have it.

Choking on a sob, Harper pushed herself away from the desk. She couldn't remember the cabin ever being this quiet before. Not even the owl kept her company tonight.

It was early. Almost five o'clock in the morning. She hadn't been able to sleep, so she'd hammered nonsensical words into her manuscript all night, desperate to finish at least something properly before she left. She'd wanted to prove to herself that she could be more than one thing. That if Fraser didn't want her, it didn't mean she wasn't still worth something.

Of course, she'd done a terrible job and would likely delete it all when she was in the right headspace.

Huffing, she decided to calm her noisy brain down with some fresh air. Outside, the moon was a silver smudge in the cloudy indigo sky. The earth smelled fresh and clean, but relief lasted only seconds. After that, her eyes caught on the chopping block. The memories they'd made there resurfaced, from the first time she'd seen Fraser cutting wood, to the feeling of him inside her, making her feel fuller, more wanted than she ever had before.

"Fuck off," she snapped at the block, marching away from the cabin. She couldn't be here, not when he was so engrained in everything around her. It was his fault she was in this mess. If she hadn't fallen for him, her decision would have been simple. Easy. She would have gone back to Manchester as planned, and that would be that.

Leaves crunched underfoot as she trudged through the woods in her slipper boots. She didn't know where she was going. The café wouldn't be open for hours, and the loch carried just as many memories of him.

But then his words echoed in her head.

I'm just saying, when I want to sort my head out, the loch does the trick. It's like a natural reset button for the body.

A reset was exactly what Harper needed, especially for her body, which was still all... achy and Fraser-obsessed. She didn't want her skin to feel like his anymore. She needed to wash him away, wash away all the things holding her back from just getting on with her life.

A fine, chilly mist lingered over the water's surface. The café was nothing more than a silhouette ahead of her, and she could vaguely make out the black dot of Captain Angus's docked boat beyond the reflected moonlight. She let out a deep breath, already feeling better for being out in the open. Free. She pushed away memories of Fraser daring her to dip her toe in. This wasn't about him.

"*I'm* the main character!" she shouted into the air defiantly. It didn't feel true, but it was nice to hear the words bouncing off the trees. "Or at least, I'm supposed to be!"

One day, she thought, she might be. She'd thought Belbarrow had been important because it was where she'd found Fraser, but there were other things she'd discovered here. The ability to hike up a small mountain without passing out. Confirmation that she was good with kids, and mums, and demanding B&B owners. A story that might not be finished yet, but had still been fun to write.

She'd found out here that she wasn't just one thing. She wasn't just a heartbroken, pathetic woman running away from her problems. She was a writer, a creative, a helper, a friend. She was sexy and silly and shy and confident. *He* hadn't made her those things. He'd just brought them out in her.

Roughly, she slid off her clothes. The cold pinched her skin instantly, like claws. She shivered. Thought about going back. But she wasn't that person anymore, either. She didn't back down from difficult things.

She peeled off her leggings and stepped into the water.

Fraser knocked on the door of the cabin, his jaw tender from grinding his teeth all night. He wasn't willing to leave things with Harper like this, so much so that as soon as dawn had showed signs of breaking, he'd rushed to his car, unable to wait a moment longer. He wasn't even sure what to say. That he cared for her? She surely already knew that. That he was sad she was leaving? That wouldn't make the leaving part any easier for either of them.

The cabin remained silent. He considered turning around. Going home. Cam would kill him, though, and probably Mum, too. He wasn't sure what they expected from him, but it wasn't this.

So he pulled out his keys, thinking Harper was probably still asleep. The least he could do was make her a cup of tea and be sure the heater was running hot enough. The temperature had dropped overnight, coating the fallen leaves in frost. She would need more layers than she'd been surviving in from now on, and she could say goodbye to cold showers unless she wanted to come down with pneumonia.

However, when he slipped the key in, he found it already unlocked. Thank god they were in the middle of nowhere, otherwise he'd have to lecture her on how dangerous that could be. He stepped in as quietly as his heavy boots and creaky floorboards would allow, wincing as the door clicked shut.

He froze when he saw a heap of shadows on the couch. Had she fallen asleep here?

"Harp?" he whispered gently, his blood pounding in his ears. Just her presence made him regret everything he'd said yesterday. Made him regret not just begging her to stay because he—

No. She was shivering, her face pale enough to stand out in the shadow of her blanket. Her lips were a frightening shade of blue, teeth chattering uncontrollably, and her hair…

Damp.

"*Harper?*" Fraser dropped to his knees, brushing the tangled hair from her face. He gasped when his knuckle brushed her cheek.

"You're freezing. Why the fuck are you so freezing?" Instinct drove him up, seeking another blanket. In his panic, he couldn't find one, eventually tearing off his coat to press over her in the hopes it would transfer his warmth. "Harper, love, talk to me, please."

Though her lids remained shut, she mumbled something raspy and unintelligible under her breath. He leaned in, cupping her quivering jaw in his hands. A waxy sheen coated her face, terrifying him, but he tried to keep his voice even. "What? What did you say, sweetheart?"

"Went for a swim." Her words slurred together like sludge in her mouth. Dread tore through him like somebody had buried his axe right down his middle.

She'd gone for a swim. Before dawn. In freezing cold weather.

"We need to get you to a hospital. Now." He wasn't even sure if he should move her. She looked so small, so breakable, hidden under the pile of blankets, which was clearly doing nothing to warm her up.

"I'll b' fine," she said, a confused wrinkle burrowing between her brows. "Jus' cold."

"You're not just cold," he whispered. "You're hypothermic. What were you thinking?"

"'m the main character."

He frowned. She was talking nonsense.

Any hope that this looked worse than it was dissipated, especially when her lids drooped closed again. Fraser swore, pressing his forehead against hers and wincing when that icy cold frosted his own skin. He should call an ambulance, but this cabin was miles from anywhere. There was no street number, no street, only a dirt track leading up to his gate. Who knew how long it would take for the paramedics to find them?

No. He would have to take her himself. He could go to Fort William. It was only forty minutes away. Thirty if he was lucky enough to avoid the traffic, which he should be so early.

"Hold on, sweetheart." He stood up, trying to find where she ended and the blankets began. When he found her knees, he scooped her up, whispering soothing words he wasn't sure she could even hear.

She mumbled again, something he couldn't make out, and his throat clogged with a fear he'd only ever felt for his family before. This was so much worse than the day Harper climbed Macaskill Ridge. He wasn't even sure if he'd been this scared when Cam had her emergency C-section, when Mum's knee gave out, or when Eiley didn't pick up her phone.

"I've got you. Stay with me, Harp. Please," he begged. He held her to him with one arm while he wrestled with the car door, swearing until it finally came free. Carefully, he placed her into the passenger seat, his hands fumbling and trembling as he wrapped the blankets around her tightly and tried to fasten the seatbelt over them.

"Fuck!"

All this time he'd spent trying to control everything. To make everyone's lives easier. To be the one immovable oak in everybody else's hurricane. And now he couldn't help the woman he loved. He couldn't make her open her eyes, couldn't get her to talk to him, couldn't chase away this cold.

"Please don't do this." The plea cracked through his voice. "Please be okay."

He wasn't sure what he would do if she wasn't.

He shut the door, climbed in beside her, and immediately put the heat on the highest setting before starting the car.

How he would manage to drive in a straight line with this much terror surging through him, he didn't know.

30

Fraser felt like he was floating in a dream – or, rather, a night-mare – as he watched the nurses care for Harper. The fluorescent lights and white walls were too bright after driving in the near-dark, and he soon found there was nothing he could do but stand back and watch. In no time, she was hooked up to oxygen and warm IV fluids, which were bringing colour back into her cheeks. The doctor had confirmed it was hypothermia, and everything beyond that had been nothing more than muffled, underwater speech he didn't understand.

Hypothermia.

He should have been there earlier. He should have made sure she was safe.

"You did the right thing by bringing her in, pet," one of the nurses said once Harper's condition improved, squeezing his shoulder. "You should grab a coffee and sit down. Your wife needs to rest now, and so should you."

He swallowed thickly, not quite able to choke out that she wasn't his wife. She wasn't his anything.

Except that wasn't true. The cavern in his chest wouldn't be quite so deep if she wasn't *anything*. For just a flicker in time, she had felt like everything, and he wasn't sure what to do with that.

He sank down into the chair beside her bed, refusing to cry even when his eyes seared.

This was his fault. He'd let her walk away last night. If he hadn't pulled his head out of his ass for long enough to go and talk to her this morning, he wouldn't have even known that she was in grave danger.

Groggily, Harper's lids prised open. She was still pale, veins dark under translucent skin, but clarity was returning to her eyes.

Fraser wanted to reach for her hand, buried beneath layers of blankets. He didn't. Instead, his fists remained firmly in his lap, nails digging into his palms.

Her focus landed on him finally and relief flickered across her face.

"Hi," she croaked.

He gulped, unable to say anything.

"What? Do I look like a corpse?" Mirth danced in her sleepy voice.

He was in no mood to humour her.

"What were you doing, Harper?" he asked slowly, his voice fracturing as if his throat was filled with sharp, shattered glass. "Why the hell were you swimming at night, on your own, in the freezing cold?"

She shrugged. "I needed to clear my head."

He fought not to recoil, his own words hitting him like a boomerang. He had told her that he went swimming in the loch when he needed to sort his head out. To reset.

She'd done it because he'd planted that idea, not thinking about the cold. Not thinking she would end up here. Not thinking that if she was seriously hurt, he'd have to carry that unbearable guilt forever. Why had she done that? He was just barely juggling his other responsibilities. He couldn't bear this burden too.

He scrubbed a hand over his quivering jaw. "You brainless bloody numbskull."

She flinched at this tone. "I didn't think…" As she trailed off, se glanced around the hospital room as though only just noticing where she was. "I thought it would be fine."

"You could have *died*," he snapped. "If I hadn't found you—"

If he hadn't found her, he couldn't even finish that sentence. Whatever happened to her, it would have destroyed him.

This was why, he realised. Why he'd run away, why he'd pushed Harper back, why he'd told her to go for the job in England. He wasn't capable of taking care of another person. He already had an entire army to work for and protect.

"Fraser…" Harper swallowed, with some difficulty. He sighed, standing up to roughly pour her some water from the bedside table. He handed her the plastic cup without meeting her eye, then sat back down as she sipped.

"I can call your parents," he said tersely. "They'd probably want to know…"

"No. God, no. I'll never live it down." She shook her head, damp layers of hair coiling at the ends and framing her face.

He wanted to call them. He wanted somebody else to take care of her so he wouldn't have to. So he wouldn't have to keep worrying too much, keep *feeling* too much.

Pursing his lips, he steepled his fingers together, glaring at his bitten-down nails.

"Why are you angry?" she asked quietly.

"I'm not."

"Well then why won't you look at me?"

He huffed out a long breath. "I can't."

"*Why*?" she pressed, exasperated now.

"I just can't, Harper." He didn't know what more to say. His heart thudded, lungs tight. He was drowning, because even though she was okay, that worry wouldn't just abate. He was still trapped in that moment when he'd found her, barely conscious. Almost gone. Every muscle in his body was still helplessly trying to figure out how to save her, how to stop the worst from happening.

"Fraser… It was an accident."

"I know."

She rubbed her face wearily. "I'm sorry if I worried you."

He said nothing, only clenched his fingers around the arms of his chair. *You did worry me*, he wanted to say. *You worried me so much I can't fucking breathe.*

"Maybe it's good that I'm leaving," she whispered finally. "I won't keep getting myself into trouble. Won't keep causing you problems."

"Aye, maybe." His words were harsh, unfairly so, and he knew he would regret them later. Now, he could only think about getting through this moment.

Harper's chin wobbled. She looked down at the thick blankets encasing her. "You don't have to stay."

He did, actually. If she thought he was going to leave her here alone, she was mad. "The nurses say you'll be discharged once your temperature is back to normal. You should be home by tonight. I may as well wait."

"Well, if you may as well…" Sarcasm laced her voice, but she slumped into the pillow as though she was already defeated. "Why were you even at the cabin?"

He closed his eyes. He couldn't tell her now that he'd wanted to make amends. What was the point when their separation was more inevitable than ever? The best thing he could do was leave things as they were. Distant. "Work."

"It's a Sunday," she pointed out, because of course he could never fool her. She was too sharp to believe his excuses even after this.

"I wanted to spend some quiet time in the shed," he lied. What he wouldn't give to lock himself away now – but even in there, he wouldn't be free of her. She'd tainted that, too, by needling into his most personal hobby and thrusting it out of the shadows. She'd refused to leave his simple little life the same way she had found it.

She nodded just once. "Then I'm sorry I stopped you."

Silence engulfed them after that. There was nothing left to say, and even if there was, he was too tired, too trapped inside his own mind to articulate it. She rolled over, turning her back to him, and stayed that way until the nurses came in to check on her later that morning.

Fraser barely spoke on the drive home, except to ask if she was warm enough. The answer was yes, she was fairly sweltering against the heat blasting through his truck vent, thank you very much. He bid her farewell inside the car, not bothering to escort her into the cabin, despite having tried to convince her to use a wheelchair on their way out of the hospital. On that short walk from the truck to the door, it dawned on her: it was really over. No more kissing. No more falling asleep in one another's arms.

What had happened? One moment, he'd been the closest person in her life. But on that hospital ward, he'd been a stranger. Talking to her like he blamed her for getting hypothermia. Unable to so much as look at her. What had she done to deserve that? Fine, bathing in an icy loch in November hadn't been her smartest move, but she hadn't meant to make herself ill.

She hadn't meant to make him hate her.

She collapsed onto the couch, bone-tired and raw. The emptiness of the cabin crawled across her skin, and she knew she couldn't stay here if this was how it would be. Tomorrow, she would leave. She didn't want to feel like a burden to him anymore, and he clearly didn't want that either.

Had she been silly to even wonder if she should stay? Had Fraser really fooled her with charm and kindness and dry humour, weaselling his way into her heart and her body until she hadn't been able to see sense? Well, she saw it now. He was just like everybody else in her life. He'd grown bored of her. Annoyed by her.

She wasn't good enough for him.

More than anything else in the world, she just wanted to go home. She stood on stiff legs, grabbing her laptop from her writing desk. Her manuscript remained open on the screen, the one she'd rushed to finish. Badly. So much of Fraser and her experiences with him had bled through into the story and characters, and he didn't deserve to take up that space if he could wipe her away so easily.

She left the tab open and opened a new one to search for train tickets. It would mean a long and exhausting day of travelling while inhabiting a body that still felt strange and not hers, but anything would be better than sitting in a cabin where things had once felt magical.

So, she booked a train for ten a.m. the next morning, shoved her laptop under the couch cushion where the sight of it wouldn't haunt her, and began packing.

Fraser had been right. Wild swimming *had* provided a reset, just not in the way she'd predicted.

31

Fraser couldn't avoid the cabin forever. He did, after all, have wood to chop and furniture to craft if he was going to make a go of his new business. His fingers trembled on the steering wheel as he parked outside his gate, and after pulling his keys from the ignition, he urged Bernard onto his lap to bury his head in his fur.

"What am I going to do, Bern?" he whispered, scratching his pointy ears.

Bernard put his paw on the window as though pointing to the cabin and saying, *Just go inside and ask her how she is, you plonker.*

"I can't do that. I have to let go of all this now," Fraser argued, resting his temple on the cool windowpane. Rain pattered down, adding loud white noise to his conflicted brain chatter. "She's going. Any day now. And she's not good for me. Everybody else needs me, too!"

Bernard whined.

"I know, but it was my fault she got hurt, so I'm clearly no good for her either. And we just… we can't keep giving each other so much when it can't lead to anything. All it does is hurt. I don't have time to be hurt."

Closing his eyes, Fraser shook his head. *I'm monologuing to my bloody dog now. That's how ridiculous this woman has made me.*

Clearly, his sad little speech had bored Bernard, because he placed his paw on the door handle, swung it open and rushed out. He pushed the unlocked gate open and sprinted straight to the cabin, where his new favourite person resided.

A rock buried in Fraser's chest. Even his dog wanted to keep her here. He would be furious if Bernard started showing signs of separation anxiety once Harper returned to Manchester.

When Bernard barked at the door impatiently, Fraser forced himself out of the truck. The soil squelched against his boots as icy rain ran down his face. He marched up the porch steps and knocked on the door. Like yesterday, there was no reply, and that same panic returned like a gale-force wind.

"Harper. Answer the door, please," he called.

She didn't. Probably still angry at him, which she had every right to be. Maybe she'd already headed out to write, but he'd hoped she might be tucked up in bed, recovering properly, so that he wouldn't have to fret about her health for another day and night.

Impatiently, Bernard hopped up on his hind legs, lowering the door handle. It creaked open to reveal an empty cabin.

Her things were gone. The blanket she'd kept on his couch. The collection of coats she'd hung on his door.

His stomach dropped. He strode in on shaking knees, going straight to the bedroom.

The sheets were made neatly, pillows plumped in place. No suitcase, no clothes, no her.

She was gone.

Fraser opened his mouth to swear, but no sound came out. If he had felt broken yesterday, he felt ruined now. He went back into the living room, convinced that if he just looked again, he'd find proof that she was still there. That she hadn't just left without saying goodbye.

All he found instead was an envelope on the coffee table. He sank onto the couch and grabbed it, tracing the letters on the back.

Thank you for everything.

Her curly handwriting had become as familiar to him as his own after so many weeks of watching her plan in that little notebook, fluffy pen in hand. The envelope was heavy: bank notes, he realised, filled it. Her week's rent, and surely extra, along with the key to his cabin.

Gone. She was really gone.

He dug his palms into his eyes, trying to force his breathing to remain steady, but it was hard when he felt like something had been ripped from him. He'd known it would hurt, but not this much. This, he'd never be able to protect himself from. No amount of caution could have prevented it.

Bernard whimpered quietly, nuzzling beneath Fraser's hands to lick his chin.

"She's gone, bud," he rasped. "Sorry. It's my fault."

He couldn't blame her for it, either. He'd been a bawbag yesterday, and had spent the night feeling sick as he replayed his own stiff responses in his head. And for what? He was still on the brink of tears. Pushing her away hadn't saved him from feeling pain or abandonment.

If anything, it made it worse. She didn't know what she meant to him. She didn't know how badly he'd miss her.

Leaning back on the couch, Fraser wrapped his arms around his torso as though he could contain the hurt. It spilled out anyway, making it hard to catch a full breath. What now? Would he just have to carry on with his day, even though he was heartbroken?

A sharp corner jutted into his hip. He sighed, reaching under the cushion to yank it away — and froze when he felt cool metal.

He recognised the smooth matte rose-gold instantly. Her laptop. She'd left her laptop.

Though he knew it was wrong, a kernel of hope grew inside him. This gave her a reason to come back. Besides, she'd said she would be here for Flockhart's reopening and Fraser's launch. Surely, even if she didn't want to see him, she'd return for the sake of the friends she'd made. To say goodbye.

His hands shook as he pulled out his phone and snapped a picture of the laptop, opening their short text thread. They hadn't needed to message one another much, seeing as they were usually together.

You left something, he typed quickly.

He sent the picture, laying his hand atop the lid as though it was a living, breathing thing. A tangible piece of her he could hold onto until she came back.

The three dots indicating that she was typing appeared. Stopped. Started.

Stopped.

He waited like a fool for minutes, expecting them to return, but they didn't.

In the end, the reply never came.

"You're late. Again," Andy said, offering a reproachful glance as Fraser walked into Flockhart's. Andy stood behind the brand-new front desk, which Jack and Fraser had built together but not yet painted. To Andy's left, Jack hammered away at the frame of the new arched doorway to the dining room. The reception area might not have been finished quite yet, but it already felt much brighter and airier, drawing light from the dining room windows and giving a view of the old tree swing in the garden.

"Slacker," Jack muttered, winking at Fraser before stepping down the ladder.

"Got caught up with something." Fraser's jaw ticked with a tension he couldn't dissolve. He unfastened Bernard's lead so the dog could roam freely, then set down his toolbox on the desk. On top of it lay Harper's laptop. He hadn't been able to just leave it. She didn't have a key to the cabin, and what if she was on her way back for it now?

Deep down, he knew this was unlikely. Knew that he was just grasping for hope where it didn't exist. He didn't even know what he'd say to her if she did come back. "Sorry that your near-death experience sent me spiralling into a pit of self-loathing"? "Sorry that I care so much that I'm too afraid to be with you, too afraid to get my heart broken"? "Sorry I'm a fucking prick who doesn't know what to do with all the things you make me feel"?

Nothing he said would change the truth: that he was a coward.

"Something, or some*one*?" Andy asked, their hazel eyes sparkling.

He ignored them. "Where do you want me?"

"Uh oh. He's cocked up. I can tell." Jack rubbed his hands together as though he quite enjoyed the idea. "First fight already? That must be a record."

Fraser's nostrils flared as he tried to keep his breathing even. He didn't need this today. He just wanted to work so he wouldn't spend hours, days, weeks thinking about her. He just wanted this weight on his chest to be lifted.

"Oh, shite," Andy whispered, ducking their head to look up at him properly. "What happened?"

"I don't want to talk about it."

"Fraser—"

"I *don't* want to talk about it," he uttered sharply, cutting them off.

Jack raised his brows in surprise. Andy stepped back, surrendering.

The uncomfortable silence soon grew stifling, and Fraser almost wanted to shout it out then and there. *She's gone. She's left me. It's all my fault.*

Instead, he gripped his tape measure, snapping it open to figure out how long the skirting boards would need to be across the newly constructed staircase.

Working didn't help any. In no time, he was reimagining that last interaction they'd shared. He'd dropped her off outside the cabin, hospital band still wrapped around her wrist. They'd barely spoken — because of him. Because he'd pulled away.

"Goodbye, Fraser," she'd murmured.

He'd only grunted out a "See you", relieved when she'd disappeared inside. He'd wondered what was wrong with him to react so drastically to what he knew was an accident. Why couldn't he just suck it up, take the good with the bad the way most people did? Why was he so unbearably afraid of what he felt?

"Fuck!" A searing pain bit into his finger. In his distraction, he'd placed his hand too close to the bloody saw, and now blood gushed from the tip. "Fucking eejit. *Stupid* fucking eejit!" Anger rushed through him without warning, and he kicked the closest thing he could find: Jack's box of tools.

Clutching his hand to his chest, he let out a guttural shout, no longer knowing if it was the pain in his finger driving him, or the one in his chest. He was just tired of this day. Tired of himself. Tired of everything. A week ago, he'd been happier than he'd ever known possible. Now, he was broken.

"Jesus, Fraser, stay still." Andy rushed to him, grabbing his wrist firmly. "Let me look." Their brows knitted in worry as they prised his hand away from his shirt, where already rusty blood stained the fabric. It trickled down his knuckles, and he stared at it without really seeing it, his breaths reduced to shallow gasps.

"Jack, get us a cloth or something," Andy demanded.

A moment later, a towel was thrown their way. With shaking fingers, Andy wrapped his hand up. "Fraser, just breathe," they said softly. "You're all right, pal. I don't think it's that deep."

But it was. It was so deep that he didn't know where to go next. It was so deep that he saw her everywhere he looked: painting the wall by the staircase, tapping on her keyboard in the dining room, crouched lovingly beside Bernard.

"*Fraser*," Andy repeated.

He was sweating. When had he started sweating?

Andy sighed, turning to Jack again. "There's a first aid kit in the kitchen cupboard. Could you get it, please?"

"Aye, of course." Jack left the room.

Gently, Andy guided Fraser backwards. "Sit down on the stairs. You look like you're going to pass out on me."

He felt like it, growing dizzy. Together, they lowered onto the third step, knees bumping as Andy edged closer to inspect his finger. He worked up the courage to look at it, glad to find the blood flow was already slowing.

Andy breathed a sigh of relief. "It isn't as deep as it looked. You just caught the tip." Pressure squeezed around his shoulder, and it took him a moment to realise it was Andy's hand soothing him. "Fraser, what the fuck is going on with you? You don't make mistakes."

"I do, actually." His voice cracked. "Big ones."

Rattles emerged from the kitchen, echoing down the empty hallway. Clearly, Jack was having trouble finding the first aid kit.

Fraser was glad. Andy seeing him like this was one thing, but Jack… He wouldn't get it.

He wasn't sure anybody would.

"What've you done? Where is Harper?" Andy asked, face creased with concern.

He shook his head. "Gone. She's gone home."

"*Why*?"

"I told her to. She had a job interview back in Manchester."

"But she didn't say anything to me," Andy said. "We were planning the reopening!"

"Because she wasn't going to leave so soon until I drove her away." Bitterness seeped into his tone, burning his tongue like acid. "I freaked out."

Andy blinked. "That much is clear."

"I started caring too much."

"Is that a bad thing?" They cocked their head. "You've always cared too much. About everyone. You're the first person anybody in this town calls when they need help."

"Exactly. I feel like I'm always worrying about something. Mum, or my sisters, you and this place. If I care this much about someone else, about someone who isn't family, how am I supposed to keep the rest of my life together?" He pressed his lips into a fine, miserable line, the corner of his mouth trembling. "My family needs me, and I can't…" He sniffed, wiping his cheek with the back of his uninjured hand. It came away damp. "I can just about hold it together for them, but for her?" A sad chuckle. "For her, I'm already fucking ruined."

"Oh, you silly, silly boy." Andy shook their head slowly, placing his bloody hand in theirs. "You silly, silly, silly boy."

"I'm really glad I chose you to confide in. You always know the right thing to say," he groused.

They tutted, though their expression was laced with sympathy. "Fraser. Why do you think I stay far, far away from relationships?"

"Because you have a cold, cold heart?"

"Yes, but no. Because I have a B&B to run, and it's sort of hard work." They lowered their gaze to his hand, applying more pressure with the towel. "If somebody made me feel the way she makes you feel, mad enough to cut my bloody finger off, I would be terrified, too. I wouldn't be brave enough to let them all the way in, not even into this place, even if it would be better run with a partner like my parents did it. But this is my home, and it's all I've ever known, and why would I risk someone hurting not just me, but this, too?"

"Here it is!" Jack startled both of them, emerging from the kitchen with the green first aid kit in his hand. He placed it beside them on the step, scratching his rough beard. "Should I call an ambulance, or what?"

"No. Sit down. We're having an intervention," Andy demanded.

Fraser groaned.

Jack obeyed.

As Andy opened the kit and produced a packet of bandages, they continued, "Fraser has chased off the woman he loves because he is scared."

"Uh oh. That's a very bloke-ish thing to do, mate."

That was an insult, as far as he was concerned. Fraser prided himself on *not* being a bloke, or at least not a typical one. Not like Jack and his series of unfortunate escapades featuring too much beer, and too many lasses whose names he couldn't remember.

He winced as Andy wiped down his wound, revealing the gash beneath the blood. It wasn't deep enough to warrant stitches – or so he told himself. Two hospital trips in as many days would be excessive. He was sure Sorcha would help him out later, not before reprimanding him for being an incompetent tube.

"He thinks that he has too many people to take care of, and being with Harper would be too much," Andy informed as though he wasn't there at all. "Of course, this is an absolutely bonkers assessment."

"Absolutely," Jack agreed solemnly. Then frowned. "Why?"

"*Because*," Andy locked their gaze on Fraser's, "his family and friends are quite capable of looking after themselves, even if he is a very kind, supportive individual skilled at taking care of people and places."

He rolled his eyes. "My sister is barely holding it together."

"Well, that's not true. Your sister went out on Saturday and had a nice wee day with her kids and her new friend, Harper. I saw her smiling with my own eyes."

"My mum raised us all on her own!" he reminded Andy. "She needs help, too!"

"She *needed* help when you were kids. Now, she lives with her daughter and three grandchildren. I reckon when she needs an extra set of hands, she'll ask for it. Don't you?" Andy said sternly.

He glowered, hating that they made it sound so simple. So easy. "She has her own health issues. Living with arthritis isn't easy for her."

"Good thing a team of doctors and support workers, as well as all *three* of her children, are helping her with that," Andy retorted. "Please, do continue with the excuses."

He was having trouble finding any more, honestly. He looked to Jack for help, but he only shrugged. "You're on your own, mate."

"There's work," Fraser decided. "I'm always working."

"Oh, yeah, with that business that Harper herself *helped you set up*."

His friend was impossible. He was quite sick of their rationality, honestly. Usually, it was Andy's job to be unreasonable, and his job to talk them down.

"*And*," Andy cut in before he could say more, "don't you dare use this place as an excuse, either. I know I've been hard on you, but most of it was either in jest or a 'me' problem, and I suppose I didn't actually realise how much of a nitwit you are. By that, I mean how much you choose to put on your plate, beyond what we ask of you."

They bit through some tape, wrapping it around Fraser's bandages. Then, they softened. "I'm sorry for that. You've done more for me than I know how to thank you for, and I never meant to make it seem otherwise."

"Now I know something's wrong. Andy is apologising," he murmured.

"Honestly, I'm getting a wee bit uncomfortable." Jack tugged at the collar of his shirt with a grimace. "We're not going to start singing around a campfire, are we?"

"Grow up. This is how adults talk," Andy snapped. "By the way, I hate it when you make me act emotionally intelligent. I'm supposed to be the moody eejit, not you." They poked Fraser in the shoulder. "So do me a favour. Put your big girl pants on and tell the bloody woman you love her. Yes, it is scary, and yes, I too would shite myself, but she made you happy. More importantly, she made *me* happy. Her paintwork was actually very good!" They motioned to the walls behind them, now a smooth, creamy shade of orchid white.

Fraser rolled his eyes. "It isn't that simple. She lives in Manchester."

"Oh, no. Not that terribly far away city inaccessible by public transport!" mocked Andy.

Jack snorted. "They have a point, Fraser. It isn't that far in the grand scheme of things."

This intervention was starting to feel an awful lot like a press gang. He scowled at both of them. "It's far away enough to disrupt my old life!"

"Love is disruptive. She's been gone a few hours and you've already chopped off your finger. You can't expect things to be easy, Fraser. That isn't how life works. Except for me. I refuse to suffer through anything remotely difficult." They slapped his shoulder and stood up. "Anyway, now that you've clearly decided to sort out your shite and live happily ever after, we need to go back to my problems. Is Harper still going to be here for the big party or not?"

Fraser breathed out hard and leaned against the wall, the smell of fresh paint making him dizzy. At least the throbbing in his finger was already fading. All that drama, and it was only a wee gash. He would have been embarrassed if he wasn't so rattled. "Probably not. By then, she'll have a job. Her old life back."

"By then, you will have made amends."

"Andy," he deadpanned. "I'm not going to do that to her. She deserves something uncomplicated, and right now, I can't give her that."

"So the intervention didn't work at all." Andy leaned against the desk glumly. "*Men*. It's all right. I'll write her a strongly worded email."

Fraser had given up trying to have a normal conversation. He tipped his head back, lids drooping shut.

"Fraser, have you been writing fairy smut?"

"Fairy *what*?" Jack asked.

Fraser snapped his head up in bewilderment, finding Andy staring wide-eyed at their laptop screen.

No, not theirs. Harper's.

"I know you're into fairies and all, but this is extreme…"

He jumped up quickly, which only set his finger throbbing again. "That isn't mine. It's Harper's!"

"Oh, cool! I've been wondering what she's working on." Andy began scanning over what must have been her manuscript.

Jack peered over Andy's shoulder. "Is this what lasses are into nowadays?"

"Yep. That's why you're not having any luck recently. You don't have wings."

Jack rolled his shoulders back as though mildly insulted.

An uncomfortable feeling writhed in Fraser, and he went to bat them both away, but Andy tore the laptop off the desk and stepped away to keep reading. "This is actually really good. It's a wee bit self-inserty if you ask me, though. A princess in an enchanted forest? Let's see if we get an appearance from a handsome lumberjack, eh?"

"Andy, stop it!" he scolded. "That's personal. She wouldn't want you reading it. She wouldn't even let *me* read it."

"That's because it's very obviously a love story about the two of *you*!" Andy scrolled further, pulling a face. "Ick, that's some smutty smut." But they kept going until Fraser would have risked losing another finger to stop them. "Oh my god."

"Andy—"

"Okay, what I can glean from this is that she wants to stay here after all. This is one big 'fuck big city dreams, I want to live in the woods' story."

He faltered at that, heart pounding. "Really?"

"Yup. The princess is trying to find her way back to the place where she was born." Andy narrowed their eyes. "The goal is to live there again with her family after getting taken from them as a kid. But… when she gets there, she isn't happy, because it means she has to leave the handsome fella who helped her on her way."

"That doesn't mean anything," he muttered, though his heart pitter-pattered as though maybe it did.

"It means something. Trust me." Andy looked up at him. "Either she's going to realise it first, or you're going to have to get on your horse and go to save her yourself."

Jack frowned. "You have a horse?"

Fraser ignored him, pinching the bridge of his nose as it began to sting again.

This wasn't a fairy tale. He couldn't let himself believe that it was.

But he wanted to. God, he wanted to.

32

Harper strutted into the pristine lobby with her head held high, but it didn't stop her knees from wobbling like they were made of jelly. After four weeks immersed in nature, the return to Manchester had taken some getting used to. Had trams always been that loud, or had she just grown too used to gentle birdsong?

One thing she hadn't missed was the pigeons of Piccadilly Gardens. She tried to wipe the white patch of poo from the shoulder of her blazer as subtly as possible while checking in at reception, then made her way up to Brentworth's floor in the shiny elevator. Anxiety was cold and heavy as clotted cream in her throat, but not nearly as delicious. Here, nothing had changed. Even *she* looked the same in the pristine mirror, her eyes tired and her hair slicked back into a neat ponytail that would make her head ache soon enough. And if that didn't, the artificial lighting would. Being here only made her long for her pyjamas, which she'd lived in since coming home.

She took a deep breath and eyed the stain on the charcoal fabric, then decided there would be no scrubbing it off. Pulling her hair down, she arranged her blonde curls over the ruined shoulder just in time for the doors to ding open. Nobody looked up from their desks as she headed into the office, the quiet broken only by the sound of tapping keyboards and mouse clicks. It made her want to shudder. She had always felt... muted here. Like she was anonymous. No one.

But surely the promotion would change that. She would be a director, would decide how people should or shouldn't work. She would dissolve the silence with orders and chitchat – with people who would probably dislike her, as everyone disliked their bosses, but what did that matter?

Pulling her CV and portfolio from her purse, Harper knocked on Chris's door before she could second guess herself. Her palms were clammy, fingers shaking.

"Come in," he called from the other side of the door, so she did.

Chris's office was large and open, with a perfect view of the uneven skyline behind him. It was a sunny, frosty day in Manchester, but somehow the cold didn't touch her the way it had in Scotland. Perhaps her hypothermia had affected her internal thermometer, or perhaps it was something to do with the glumness she'd been drowning in ever since getting home.

The older man gave her a clipped smile and gestured to the chair opposite. Chris was as plain as ever, with his blue collar askew, shirtsleeves rolled to his elbows, and his greying hair combed to one side. "Take a seat, Harper."

"Thank you." She sat, picking nervously at the corner of her leather-bound portfolio.

"It's good to have you back. Thank you again for agreeing to the interview."

"Of course. Thank you for inviting me." Her words were wooden. The air around her thickened with her palpable discomfort, and she found it difficult to draw a full breath, just like the night she'd swum alone in the loch. For a moment, she wondered if the doctors had been wrong and she was still unwell. Then she realised that the problem didn't start in her lungs, but with that same tightness around her chest that she used to wake up with daily.

Anxiety she'd never really acknowledged until it hadn't been there anymore.

"How have you been spending your time off?" Chris asked through a sip of coffee, light bouncing off his shiny temple.

Time off? Is that what they were calling it?

"I went away for a few weeks," she said. "To Scotland."

"Oh, very nice. I suppose you're welcome, then, for the bit of free time!"

Her fingernails dug into her palms. "Hmm, yes. Thank you ever so much for putting me out of a job, Chris," she blurted without thinking.

His laughter ebbed, and he shifted awkwardly.

Oops.

A year ago, she would have panicked, but she found that voicing her truth made her feel freer.

"Anyway, let's get down to it, shall we?" He sat back in his swivel chair, crossing his hands over his belly. His shirt strained at the buttons, displaying stomach hair she'd rather not see. He'd always commented on her appearance before, noting when her skirt was a bit too short for the office or her hair looked unprofessional, and yet the man had the nerve to wear his tie askew and his clothes two sizes too small. "As you probably guessed, Debra has left us for a swanky new company around the corner, completely without warning, so I need to fill this position quite quickly."

As he explained the expectations of the role, Harper found herself zoning out, fixating on the tall clocktower hotel bathing in the low sunlight behind him. She used to imagine working for a nice hotel like that, where she would get more creative freedom and perhaps market something more rewarding than the furnishings she promoted here.

In Belbarrow, she hadn't had to imagine. She'd had a hand in helping the only B&B in town. She'd encouraged Fraser to be proud of his art. She'd been part of something.

What was she part of here? Nothing she really cared about.

Her throat went dry as she pretended to listen, while he piled on duty after duty. More work than even Debra had complained about. More work than she wanted to do.

She managed to get through the interview section by the skin of her teeth, pulling out clichés such as "I thrive in a fast-paced environment" and "I certainly have lots of ideas on how to deliver brand new results while appealing to our existing customers", both of which were lies. When he saw her out, she felt numb. She rubbed her chest roughly to chase it away, but it stayed.

"You'll be hearing from me shortly. Cheers again, Harper. I'm so glad we can count on you."

Harper nodded without conviction, closing her eyes when the door closed and she was left alone.

Until she heard heels clicking down the hallway towards her. She stepped back to let the person pass—

And wished she could dissolve into the wall when she saw the cortado-wielding woman in front of her.

"Kenzie."

"Harper." Kenzie's mouth hung upon for a moment. She looked as beautiful as ever, her black hair slicked into a braided bun and her dark eyes bright. She wore a khaki-green turtleneck and a brown pleated skirt. Harper had picked up a similar one on their last shopping trip, then been encouraged to put it down because Kenzie worried it might make her look a bit "frumpy".

Harper waited for her heart to break, or at least stumble over itself, but it didn't. Kenzie stood in front of her, and nothing changed.

"What are you doing here?" Kenzie asked finally, an incredulous look on her face. "I didn't think I'd ever see you in this office again!"

Harper's fingers tightened around her purse strap. "I'm here for a job interview."

Kenzie's plump red lips parted again in surprise. "Oh, really? Why?"

If she was aware of her bluntness, she didn't show it, her gaze as intense and unwavering as ever.

Harper wanted to shrink, but she didn't. Wouldn't. She'd been made to feel small enough by the people in this office, and if she did come back here, she wouldn't let it happen again. For the first time in her life, she felt worthy of better.

Living in a place where she'd been appreciated for who she was, she realised only now, had revived and reinvented her. All that shame and insecurity had never been her burden to bear. She'd just been carrying it around because it had been thrust upon her when she'd been too young to know any better.

She'd thought that it was normal to be treated as less than. Thought she was just a person people tolerated, and that she was lucky to have relationships at all.

It wasn't true.

Tears pricked her eyes. She was so sad for the past version of her. The Harper who would have stood here and forced kindness, meekness, just to keep Kenzie happy.

But now, what was she even doing here? She'd outgrown this place. It wasn't her home, and she knew it.

She took a deep breath. "Chris asked me to come back. He invited me to apply for Debra's position."

Kenzie's surprise merged into disbelief. The corner of her mouth twitched with something akin to amusement. Like she knew something Harper didn't. It made her feel oily.

"No way. Me, too."

Of course. Of course she hadn't been the only person in the office considered. Of course, even now, she'd been forced into a race she'd never win. Did Chris even believe she was right for the job, or did he just like to keep his staff, past and present, on short strings for a bit of fun?

"How did it go?" Kenzie tipped her head towards Chris's door.

"It was fine. It went well."

"Good!" Kenzie's tone was forced. Harper knew the sound well; she'd often used it among friends she didn't truly like, colleagues she'd later complain about having to spend time with. "Hey, if you get the job, perhaps we could sit down for coffee or something? We've lots to catch up on. I saw you took a trip down to Devon. How nice!"

"It was up to Scotland, actually." And then Harper frowned, focus zooming in on Kenzie's earlier words. "*Only* if I get the job?"

"Well, yeah…" Kenzie chewed on her bottom lip. "It would be a bit inappropriate otherwise. I'm in a new relationship—"

"I know." But it wasn't lost on Harper that her job status was the only reason Kenzie might want to talk. For two years, she'd thought they'd been in love, and this was what it had whittled down to? A chat over coffee, but only if Harper got the job Kenzie was also vying for? Only on her terms?

It was bullshit, all of it. She'd done the same with Debra. They'd been the best of friends, heading out to lunches together so that Kenzie would always be the front runner for the best projects and the new training courses. She'd bet that, now Debra was gone, Kenzie wouldn't even bother with her – or maybe she would, if her new job was as fancy as Chris had bitterly made out.

Either way, it was fake. It depended only on what Kenzie could gain from it. Harper found herself wondering how she hadn't seen it all sooner. She'd been so in love with the strong, successful woman in front of her, outspoken and full of ambition and drive, that she hadn't realised the cost of those qualities. The thorns adorning the roses.

"Things with Michelle are actually quite wonderful," Kenzie continued in a chirpy tone. "She's so great. She runs one of the most successful real estate businesses in the northwest, you know!"

"I don't think I asked," Harper stated bluntly.

Kenzie blinked, stunned. "Well, there's no need to be so rude. I just thought you'd like to know."

Harper shook her head. She didn't want this. She didn't want to work with, for, or above Kenzie. She didn't want to sit in this office. She didn't want to spend her entire day promoting fixtures and fittings that were, quite frankly, only meant for colourblind grandmas.

She wanted to go home and cry, and then she wanted to figure out what the hell she was going to do with her life. She wanted to get back her laptop that she'd stupidly forgotten in Scotland, and finish her story. She wanted to say a proper goodbye to the friends she'd quickly learned to love: Eiley, Cam, Andy, Dot, Sorcha, Alice, Bernard.

Fraser.

Even if he didn't want to hear it, she needed the closure.

She deserved it.

"Good luck with the job, Kenzie. I truly hope you get everything you want." It wasn't a lie. There was still a tender part of Harper that would always love Kenzie. She was so many of her firsts, and she wouldn't forget the way they'd laughed and grown together.

But that was over now, and she was ready to be somebody new.

Before Kenzie had time to respond, she walked out of the office and didn't look back.

"Harper, darling! What on earth—?" Harper's mother gasped, bewildered, as Harper stepped into the house. She was sopping wet from a surprise rainfall that had caught her just as she'd alighted the train, and had followed her all the way to the little cul-de-sac she'd grown up on.

"I'll make us a brew," Mum decided after her eyes drifted from Harper's waterlogged loafers to her no doubt dripping mascara.

Harper kicked off her shoes. She left a trail of water as she followed Mum into the kitchen, but she would worry about mopping it later. "I need you to tell me that I'm not making a complete and utter mess of my life," she blurted, collapsing against the kitchen countertop.

With raised brows, Mum flicked on the kettle. Her round face, so much like the one Harper saw in the mirror every day, was a comfort she hadn't known she'd needed. She'd been avoiding coming home, knowing that if she did, she might curl up in her childhood single bed, with its sheets smelling of lavender, and never emerge. Or she'd spill everything that had happened in Scotland, including the parts her parents were better off not knowing.

In truth, she'd wanted to avoid speaking about it at all, so she'd holed up in her flat until the interview, watching regency romances that did nothing to prevent her from thinking about Fraser and his annoying, beautiful face.

"Here." Mum took a fluffy lilac bath towel from the clothes airer standing by the radiator, her face soft with sympathy. Harper already felt better, especially when she buried her face in the freshly laundered fabric.

Smoothing Harper's hair with gentle fingers, Mum stood over her. "Why don't you tell me what's to do? I've been worried about you. So has your dad."

"Is he at work?"

She nodded, rubbing warmth back into Harper's damp clothes. "Tell you what. Go and get your jamas on, and I'll grab the biscuit tin."

Harper released a sigh into her mother's scratchy cardigan. She'd missed her terribly, and only really realised it now.

Pyjamas sounded perfect, so she ran upstairs. Her old room was kept the way she'd left it when she'd moved out at twenty-two, from posters of a baby-faced One Direction ripped from *We Love Pop* magazine, to the shelf of young adult fantasy books she'd devoured during her summer holidays – the ones that had made her want to write in the first place. In her teenage years, everything had felt simple in this room, and yet she remembered the harder times too. Crying after school because people were just so mean, and why couldn't she be pretty and skinny like the other girls? Discovering that, actually, she quite wanted to kiss her best friend, who happened to be an aggressively heterosexual girl. Chloe had never spoken to Harper again after she'd confessed as much. Then there had been studying to the brink of exhaustion during exam season until she'd wanted to erupt with rage from the slightest noise outside her window.

She'd grown so much since then. She liked her body, most of the time. She was proud to be bisexual, even if she still fell for *all* the wrong people. The only thing she wasn't sure of now was whether she could confidently choose to pursue happiness over success. To remain unemployed for long enough to finish her book. To submit it to agents and publishers, even if she was only met with rejection. She didn't want to fail. She'd worked her entire life not to fail, because her top grades and creativity were all she'd had to fall back on.

But that was why she was here. To figure it out. Maybe she would have to fail before she could move forwards.

She changed into pyjamas that were too small for her and unironically featured the words *Dare to Dream*. Maybe it was time to replace her nightwear with clothes she hadn't picked out as a seventeen-year-old.

When she headed back downstairs, Mum was on her way into the living room with two mugs. "Better?" she asked.

"Better," Harper agreed. They sat down, Mum draping a thick blanket over them both and pulling a plate of chocolate digestives closer from the coffee table. Not much had changed since Harper's youth. Her school pictures littered the walls, one for every year, so that her passage from a buck-toothed six-year-old to a spotty adolescent was here for any visitors to see. At least she looked nice in her graduation picture, beaming as she held her degree and threw up her cap.

"Go on, then. Tell me everything." Mum patted her thigh.

Harper sighed, and began. She told her about all the things she'd discovered in Belbarrow, from her love of volunteering at the preschool to the way she'd helped local businesses with their marketing plans. She told her about the book, leaving out the detail about it being quite spicy, and how she was most inspired when she was out doing things. Living her life. And then she told her about Fraser – again, leaving out the spicy parts. How they had been so good, and then so bad. She recounted the interview, and Kenzie, and how she really didn't want to go back to Brentworth. How she might have to return to Belbarrow if only to claim her laptop, and the closure she hadn't allowed herself before.

Mum was misty-eyed by the end. "You've had quite a journey, darling."

Harper's own throat was thick with tears. "I don't know what's wrong with me. I was okay before. I was managing. I dealt with the fact that my job lacked passion, and that I always felt on the outside of everything, even in my own relationships. But now it's like that's not enough for me."

"Because you know you deserve better, you silly sausage." Mum squeezed her hand. "Harper, I have always been proud of you."

"I know. Because I've always worked so hard. But what if I stop?"

"You would never stop. Even if you never set foot in an office again. Even if you have to move back home to chase your dreams as an author, you'd still be working hard. And if you decided it wasn't for you? If you fancied lying around in your PJs all day with me? Well, as long as you did the hoovering, I'm sure we'd make it work."

Harper laughed through her sob, pressing her head against Mum's shoulder. She smelled like home: like milky tea and lemony soap. "I don't want that. I want to be important. I want to be really good at something." She squeezed her eyes closed, tasting her own tears. "I always feel like I have to chase something. I want to feel productive, like my life is worth something, because then maybe other people will see it, too."

"But your life is *already* worth something simply because you're kind and creative. It has nothing to do with your work or how you spend your time, or even how other people see you." Mum kissed her hair lightly. "You don't have to earn love or respect. You're worthy of it just because you're you. I've always known that, chicken. Why don't you?"

She burned with grief for all the times she hadn't understood such a simple notion. That she didn't have anything to prove, especially not here.

She didn't have an answer, but naturally, Mum did.

"You are a dope," she decided. "You can accomplish all the things in the world, but it won't mean anything if it doesn't make you happy. It sounds like perhaps you were starting to see that in Scotland."

"But he doesn't love me, Mum. Not the way I love him." And Harper did. She loved him. It was a rock-solid certainty, one that wouldn't budge no matter how hard she willed it.

He wouldn't leave her alone. He hadn't since the moment they'd met.

"So blooming what?" Mum burst out. "It sounds like you made lots of friends there. It sounds like everybody else saw just how lovely you are. If he doesn't love you, it's his loss."

"And it wouldn't make me look pathetic if I went back there?"

Mum shook her head. "It would make you look as strong as I know you are. If it's what you need, then do it. Don't think about anybody else. For once, Harper, just do it for yourself – because you want to, not because you feel like you should." She sniffed. "Besides, that laptop cost a fortune. If you don't go and get it, your dad will march there himself just to make sure he doesn't have to buy you a new one."

She choked on her tea. That was true. Dad hated frivolous spending.

"Thank you, Mum. I love you."

"I love you, too, darling. More than anything." Mum nudged her gently. "Now go and show him what a fool he is for letting you go."

33

After two weeks of consecutive ten-hour shifts, Flockhart's B&B looked like something out of a storybook. Fraser hadn't been certain they would fix it up in time for the launch party, but somehow, they'd managed. It helped that he'd been burying his head in work to avoid thoughts of Harper, but mostly, he'd wanted this. For Andy, of course, but also for himself. He was excited to launch his new business tonight. In ten minutes or so, the town would arrive for Andy's reopening.

He placed the last of his carved fairies on one of his hand-made tables. Andy had convinced him to "soft launch" his furniture, and the gilded vines etched on the oak legs matched the fairy figurines perfectly.

Flockhart's dining room had been entirely designed to reflect the community's love of Belbarrow's greenery, with leafy garlands and string lights twisting over almost every surface. The dining tables were lit with softly scented candles and dotted with seasonal foliage: berries, holly, and a few dahlias saved from the garden out back. A local photographer had provided prints of the woods and loch, bringing life to walls that had once been covered in ancient paper and faded memories. In place of the old worn couch, a pair of armchairs that Fraser had created with recycled tartan and oak now looked over the brand-new brick fireplace, ready to warm guests through the coming winter months.

He couldn't help but imagine said guests were Harper. He could see her so clearly, socked feet curled underneath her as she balanced her laptop on the arm of the chair, face aglow in the firelight.

Shaking his head, he tore his gaze away. Better not to think of things that would never happen. He hadn't heard from her once, though he'd lugged that laptop with him everywhere. Just in case. Did she really hate him so much that she wouldn't come back for it?

Rubbing the ache in his chest, he stood back and tried to admire his handiwork instead of torturing himself. He'd done enough of that recently.

"Not bad, eh?" Andy asked, eyes sparkling. They were happy in a way Fraser hadn't seen in a while as they scanned the space proudly.

"Not bad at all." That was an understatement.

Despite it only being ten minutes to six, the place was filling with locals who looked around approvingly at the new decor. But as Eiley, Cam, Mum, and Sorcha entered, Fraser tamped down a wave of nerves.

Andy nudged him now. "Have you heard from her?"

He shook his head, working hard to keep his features neutral. He couldn't imagine it worked. "Let's just not talk about that tonight, eh? We're celebrating."

They gave him a placating pat on the back. "Fine, but only because I owe you one. You've really helped me out, Fraser, even when I was an absolute stress demon about it. Thank you so much. I hope you know I'd do the same. If you need someone to stand in the pouring rain for your wee craft markets and whatnot, I'll be there."

Gratitude welled inside him. Since their little heart-to-heart, the stress demon had retired... Mostly. Andy was learning the art of patience, or trying to at least, and he appreciated how careful they'd been not to take out their own problems on him and Jack. "Cheers. It means a lot."

He'd learned this week that Andy's advice had been right, though he would never admit it for fear of their ego ballooning to intolerable proportions. His role in life wasn't just to support everybody. And since his revelation at the autumn festival, they'd all rallied to support him, too – both his friends and the local community. Some of his figurines already decorated the tavern's bar, and after discovering his hidden talent, the forest reservation team had set up a donations box on the Fairy Trail so that children could take some figurines home and the money could go back towards him making more. Eiley had also taken him out for a beer to get him to open up about Harper, which had ended with him slightly tipsy and very, very sad – but he didn't like to think about that.

"Here he is. The man of the hour." Cam rushed over and suffocated Fraser in a tight hug. "Proud of you."

"Me, too!" said Sorcha, wrapping her arms around them both.

"Me three." Eiley joined in, then Mum.

He chuckled despite the ever-present, Harper-shaped hole in his chest. "Thank you. I'm glad I decided to take the plunge, in the end."

Cam gasped, eyeing the drinks and food table. "Are those pigs in blankets?" She dashed away quickly, dragging Sorcha with her.

Fraser rolled his eyes fondly. "How could I compete with party food?"

"You can't." Mum poked his chest. "But you come close. It's their first night without the kids for a while, so you'll cut them some slack."

"Aye, I suppose I will."

"Good lad."

Mum was soon called away by one of her many friends, and then it was just him and Eiley. Her gaze was overbearing as she folded her arms, waiting. She knew him better than to believe he really was okay, and she clearly wasn't afraid to make that clear. "Liar."

"Shut up." It was almost a plea.

"Say it. You miss her."

He scratched the back of his neck, which prickled with heat.

This was a celebration she'd planned. Of course he'd wanted her here. Wanted to thank her properly for all she'd given him. Wanted to show her how much he appreciated her unwavering belief in him.

Most of all, he'd just wanted the pleasure of her company. There was none like it, no one else who made him feel so... *at home*. Like he wasn't just surviving, but wonderfully, effortlessly alive.

No. He'd just fooled himself into feeling that way. All because he'd wanted to know what rest, belonging, and happiness felt like, after years of trying to run from them.

He brushed a hand across his stinging ribs absently, dipping his head.

"Don't want to," he said stubbornly, sounding like a petulant child.

She tutted. "Well, when you stop being a boy about it, I'm here."

"I know." He wrapped his arms around her, balancing his chin on her head. It wasn't nearly enough thanks, but until the lump in his throat cleared, it would have to do. "How are you? And the kids?"

She let out a long sigh. "You know what? I think I'm okay. It's still hard, but life has been a lot more peaceful since I blocked Finlay's number, and the kids don't seem to miss him much. Brook asks about him sometimes, but he's soon distracted."

"Good." He was relieved to find she looked better, too, her complexion rosy and her hair a little glossier with the haircut Cam had given her a few nights ago. She'd even put on makeup, something she rarely had the time or energy for, and he hoped that meant she might be ready for new beginnings, too. She certainly deserved them.

"I think I'm going to take some driving lessons," she admitted. "It isn't fair that you're always running around after us all. I want to be the one to take Mum to her hospital appointments sometimes, or take the kids out on day trips."

He frowned. Did she think he'd had enough of taking care of them? That could never be true. "You know I don't mind doing all that stuff."

"I know, but *I* would like to, too." She licked her lips, eyes turning damp. "Fraser, you were never allowed to just be our brother. You had to be our dad, too. I think you're still holding onto that, and I think it's part of why you let Harper go."

He opened his mouth to argue, but she placed a finger over his lips quickly.

"You need to stop, now. I love you so much for caring, but it's time for you to just be our brother again. Put yourself first. Okay?"

He sagged in defeat. Maybe she was right. Maybe it was time he stopped treating his mum and sisters like they were made of glass. He'd seen them go through hell and back in so many ways, and it wasn't him that had kept them going. It was their own resilience, and the love they shared with Sorcha and the kids.

His gaze fell to his shoes. He'd thought his busy schedule, juggling all the responsibilities he thrust upon himself every day, stopped him being capable of love, but nothing had stopped him from thinking about Harper this week. Not even when Andy had shouted loud enough to shake the new staircase because Jack had scratched the paintwork.

He'd even opened a bloody TikTok account to start promoting his business after all Harper's social media advice, and it was gaining momentum quickly. He'd done all the things he'd thought would replace the gap in his heart where she'd been... and they hadn't. It didn't matter how many responsibilities he had, how busy he was, how many people he tried to support. He still wanted her here. She *should* have been here. He never should have pushed her away, never should have treated his own love for her like a burden. So what if he didn't want to be casual? So what if falling was terrifying?

She was worth it. She'd given him a new zest for life, renewed hope, and losing her hadn't saved him. It had broken him.

"Call her," Eiley whispered. She picked up one of the figurines from the table: the blonde fairy he'd carved for Harper. She'd left it on her writing desk, and it was just another part of her he'd wanted to bring with him tonight. It didn't have a price sticker like all the others. He wouldn't dare let it go. "Better yet, go to Manchester and *be* with her. If not for you, then for me. I want my friend back."

He had no response to that, so he didn't try to come up with one. He couldn't just go off to Manchester. He didn't even know where he'd find her.

He *could* call her, though.

He could tell her, at the very least, how sorry he was.

34

Harper stepped out of the cab, turning her face to the golden glow of Flockhart's. Inside, silhouettes danced and weaved, and she allowed herself a smile. The party was going well, then.

She drew a shaky breath, smoothing the creases from her burgundy wrap dress, which she'd hurriedly changed into in the bathroom of Glasgow train station. She was tired and afraid, and still felt like she was walking around in a dream state after such a full, confusing few weeks, but...

She also felt like she was home.

Her heels clicked against the cobblestones as she approached the B&B, heart pounding harder with each step. She paused when a shadow emerged from the arched doorway, tall and broad and instantly recognisable.

Fraser.

Instinct made her stop still as he turned his back to her, in a restless pace back and forth. Before she could even contemplate how she might greet him, he said her name.

"Harper." Her knees went weak. She had missed that gruff brogue, the way her name sounded new and remade but still so familiar on his tongue. "Hi. I, er… I was thinking about you."

A glint against his ear caught her eye. His phone. The realisation that he hadn't seen her, that he was *calling* her, ricocheted through her. She wasn't sure whether to be glad that her phone had died forty minutes ago and now sat buried and useless in her purse. This was certainly a conversation she wanted to hear in person, but listening to him leave her a voicemail felt like she was spying, somehow.

Clenching the handle of her suitcase, she couldn't bring herself to interrupt. What if he realised she was here and no longer had anything to say?

She was too curious to stop him.

He cleared his throat, pressing his head against the wall as though he was too exhausted to hold himself up any longer. "I wanted to tell you… that I miss you."

Harper held her breath.

"And I'm sorry," he continued, voice growing gravelly with emotion. "I don't like how we left things. I was a *wrongun*, to put it like a Mancunian, and I just wish you were still here so I could thank you. The launch is going well, and everybody is missing you, and… Fuck, Harp. I haven't been able to *breathe* properly since you left."

Tears blurred her vision, turning the street into strobes of watery light. The outline of his solid figure was the only thing she could see clearly.

She tasted copper and realised she'd been biting down on her tongue. Hard.

Here he was, saying everything she'd wanted to hear, and he didn't even know she was just a few yards away.

Fraser bowed his head, running a hand over his wavy red hair. "I don't know what happened between us. Whether I was the only one who fell too deep. But I want you to know that I only pushed you away because I was terrified. What I feel for you is terrifying. I've realised, though, that you not being here is worse. So if you could just maybe... I don't know, I can't ask you to come back, can I? What if I came to you, and we talked, and—"

"I'm already here." Her voice wavered into fragments on the breeze.

Slowly, Fraser turned around, lowering his phone to his chest. His mouth parted with shock as his eyes locked on hers.

"Harper."

She shuddered, feeling the intensity of his voice from the arches of her feet to the hinges of her jaw and all the parts in between. Her body seemed to wake all at once, like she'd been plunged into cold water in her sleep. Like she was back in that loch, seeking respite, only it was really here this time.

"Hi," she said quietly, not quite sure what to do now. She wanted to kiss him. She wanted to hear more about how he couldn't breathe, and about how he wanted to talk to her, and about how he would be willing to be the one to travel to do it.

She wanted to forget they'd ever separated at all.

"I didn't think you'd come," he admitted finally, taking a step towards her. "How much of that did you hear?"

"All of it, actually."

"That's, er, embarrassing." He bit down on his lower lip, then sucked in a sharp breath. "Actually, no it's not. It's just true. It's very, very true."

"That's two verys," she pointed out, and felt silly for it. Her mind couldn't seem to focus fully, with all the electricity surging through her. "Very, squared."

His laugh fell out of him mangled and hoarse. "Fucking hell, I've missed you." He frowned. "But why are you here?"

"I left my laptop," she said. "And I have a book to finish." Disappointment pulled at his features. "Oh."

"And I like it here," she continued. "And I wanted to support Andy. And maybe volunteer at the preschool some more. And get that B&B discount I was promised."

"Well, I'm sure they'll be happy to check you in right away."

She traced the satin belt of her dress absently. "And before you left me an in-person voicemail, I thought maybe I deserved closure."

"Okay. Yeah." And then he cocked his head and asked, "And *after* the in-person voicemail? Did it… change anything?"

"Well, I don't know. I wasn't really expecting it."

"Harper." He squeezed his eyes closed, lashes damp. When he reached for her hands, she didn't pull away, although they were clammy. Her body fluttered with his coarse touch, her palms warming against his. "I'm sorry. I'm so sorry."

"For what?" She lifted her chin stubbornly.

"For everything. For freaking out and pushing you away. For not telling you that I didn't want you to go, or at least, that I didn't want to end things between us if you had to."

She couldn't remember closing the gap between them, but then his back was against the wall and his chest was heaving, brushing hers with every rasp, and it felt the same as it had before all of the bad things happened. Better, even. It felt like she was falling all over again.

She'd come back here to gain control of her own life, but as long as he was here, that was impossible. He left her too wild, too desperate.

"I didn't want things to end," he confessed, swallowing. "I never did. You make me feel – *everything*. You jumped over that bloody fence, and my heart wouldn't let you go. It couldn't. And I wouldn't want it to, because fuck, Harper, I was just getting by before I met you. I was just trying to keep myself upright. But now I know what it's like to fall into someone and know that they'll catch me, and I can't go back." He cupped her face, eyes burning with desperation. "I'm in love with you. I'm in love with the way you laugh, the way you see the world, the way you *are*. And when I thought I might lose you that night, I felt like I was dying, too. I've never felt a fear that unbearable before. It shut me down. I'm sorry."

She pulled his hands away when a strange, smooth texture brushed her cheek. A plaster was wrapped around his index finger. "What's that?"

He choked on another laugh. "Your fault. I nearly cut my bloody finger off for thinking about you."

Harper trapped down a sob. She believed him, every word, and she felt the same. The only word she could summon was, "*Eejit.*"

He softened. "Only for you."

"Debatable."

He rolled his eyes. "Did you take in anything I just said, or are you only here to insult me?"

She pretended to ponder for a moment. "Something about how you love me and you'd die without me."

"That was the general gist, yeah. Any thoughts about that?"

She traced the jut of his stubbled chin. He was so beautiful, and he was hers, and if she ever had to let him go again, she might just die too. Or at the very least, cry about it for a long time, since she was a new and improved version of herself who allowed herself to wallow *and then* move on.

She laced her fingers through his coyly. "Well, if I was writing a confession of love in my book, I would have included a gift, just to win her over."

He bowed his head so their noses grazed. She could see his breath, and hear it falling from him, as loud as falling trees and twice as dangerous. She had missed feeling like his. She had missed feeling like herself even more. "I believe I've given you several gifts."

"Something shiny would be nice," she teased. "I like hammers, as we established last time we were here together. I would settle for flowers, though."

He let out an irreverent grunt and searched the pocket of his jeans, producing something silver a moment later. A key. "Is this shiny enough?"

"The key to your cabin. That's forward." She waggled her brows.

Another roll of his eyes. "Harper. You're killing me. Please."

357

She sighed, deliberately drawing it out for long enough to make him squirm with impatience. Finally, she pulled on his shirt, tugging him closer, then whispered into his mouth, "Obviously, I love you, too, Fraser. You're the home I've been looking for all my life."

"So that's why they say you should fall in love with a writer."

"You might have outdone me with your monologue, though." She plucked the key from his palm happily, then felt one final shiver of wariness. "Are you sure?"

His features were fixed with intimate resoluteness. "The cabin was yours as soon as you walked through the door, sunshine. So was I."

Their lips met before she could respond, and she smiled into his kiss until his tongue found hers.

She was right. He felt exactly like home, his strong arms holding her steady, never willing to let her fall.

Already, a new ending for her story began to write itself in her mind.

Flockhart's teemed with lively chatter as Harper stepped in, Fraser's hand a warm, steadying pressure on her lower back. He planted a final kiss on her forehead before closing the door to keep out the cold.

"YES!" screamed someone among the sea of familiar faces. Harper should have guessed it would be Cam, who almost knocked over a bewildered elderly man with a walking stick in an effort to reach them. "You came!"

Harper barely had time to take a breath before Cam enveloped her into an aggressively tight squeeze. She felt the weight of many eyes on her as she giggled into Cam's shoulder. "I wouldn't miss it for the world."

"Fuck, yeah!" a broad voice exclaimed from nearby. Andy, Harper saw when she pulled away. They beamed, and Harper wondered if they'd been possessed. Andy had never *beamed* before. Not since she'd met them, at least.

Tears filled her eyes as she hugged them. "This place looks amazing, Andy. Congratulations. It's hard to believe this place was chaos a few weeks ago."

"Aye, well, your boyfriend works hard when he's pining after you. You should leave him more often."

Fraser shot Andy a glare, and they held up two hands shimmering with a dozen rings quickly. "Kidding! Don't ever leave again. He's a nightmare when he's heartsick."

"So I heard," Harper said gently, leaning into him again.

Eiley appeared then, sniffling as she took Harper's hand. "Oh, thank goodness you're here. I was worried we'd never see you again!"

Harper dipped her head timidly. "I'm sorry I left so suddenly. I meant to say goodbye, I just…"

"You just needed to be dramatic. We get it." Andy ruffled her hair fondly. "I knew you'd be back, anyway. Saved you a room if you get bored of that dusty old cabin in the woods." And then they pointed at Fraser. "*You're* not allowed to stay, though. I don't need to hear you making up tonight."

"Let's not talk about that in front of his sisters, please." Cam faked gagging.

Harper only smiled warmly up at Fraser. "I may not need that room after all. I think the cabin is waiting."

Cam's gagging intensified.

Eiley laughed. "So, how long are you back? Did you go to the interview, in the end?"

Harper took a deep breath. "I did. And I got the job." Against her, Fraser tensed up, and she poked him in the ribs. "Don't worry. I didn't take it."

"You *didn't*?" he repeated incredulously. "But you're brilliant at it! It's what you wanted!"

"I didn't ever want it. You just assumed that." She wrapped her arms around him, meeting his heated gaze. "What I wanted was to be here. I wanted to finish my book and help you all out and discover more things about myself."

"Aye? Like what?" Fraser's voice was so soft, she barely heard it. He tucked her hair behind her ear, face full of a love she didn't quite know what to do with – because she'd never had it before. Not like this.

"Well, that having a cushy job and lots of jealous Instagram followers isn't the only version of success. That people can be good and kind and quickly become family." She smiled coyly at the faces around her. "And that I'm far too fabulous for office life."

"I could have told you that for free," said Cam.

"So could I," agreed Fraser. "You deserve all that and more. I'm sorry I didn't tell you that before you left."

She shrugged. "It was good for me to go back home. It made me realise that I'd outgrown things that used to mean the world to me." Wistfully, she thought of Kenzie and the office, and her flat back in Manchester. She'd been mulling over the idea of moving out – to where, she didn't know yet. She wouldn't mind moving in with her parents again, even if it felt like a step backward. Nor would she mind if the cabin key in her pocket became a little more permanent until she figured out what was next. If the hot water was fixed, that is.

"I'm ready for a gentler life," she admitted, "with people who really care about me."

"Good, because I really need your help with the website," Andy said, elbowing her wickedly. "And I have something for you in return."

"Oh, yeah?" Harper leaned forwards, curious.

"I got a new coffee machine," they said, "and I've been learning to brew those pumpkin spice lattes you keep going on about."

Harper gasped. "You really will do anything to keep me here!"

"Aye, apparently so, because they taste like crap." Andy wrinkled their nose. "Now if you'll excuse me, I'm going to make this a proper party." They disappeared behind the front desk, connecting their phone to a pair of speakers beside their computer.

Eiley hugged Harper whispering, "I'm so happy for you."

A tear dripped down Harper's cheek. She was happy, too. Happier than she'd allowed herself to be for far too long.

Fraser tugged her closer as the music started, and she looped her arms around his neck as they began to sway gently. "You should be tending to your new business." The locals were admiring his wares nonstop, just as they had at the autumn festival. "Your customers are waiting."

"They can wait a bit longer. I've got some making up for lost time to do." He drew light circles on her lower back as they moved, sending another shiver through her. As happy as she was to be in a room full of people she admired, people who admired her, she couldn't wait until they were alone.

He must have had the same thought, because his eyes darkened to a blazing night-sky blue.

Right on cue, an acoustic cover of "I Wanna Dance With Somebody" began to play from the speakers. Andy cleared their throat and clapped their hands together to announce, "For the record, this is *not* my playlist. It's Cam's. But tonight is for celebrating, so have a boogie if you fancy it. I won't judge. Much."

The little makeshift dance floor of twinkle lights and glossy floorboards was soon bustling. Myra passed them, placing a kiss on the side of Harper's temple, and then her son's. "Welcome to the family, love."

And then it was just the two of them again, and Harper couldn't remember a time when she'd ever been so happy. He twirled her under his arm suddenly, drawing a loud laugh from her that made him sparkle, too.

His lips grazed her ear lobe as he leaned in close. "How long do you think they expect us to stay?"

She scoffed. "It's your launch party. I think you're sort of expected all night."

He feigned dismay, a soft groan vibrating from his throat. "I want to take you home."

She wanted that, too. For now, she could only kiss him lightly: a promise, one she hoped they would both keep.

"Take me soon."

Epilogue

"So, Princess Callie ran back into the forest – to her friends, to home. And there, she lived happily ever after." Harper placed down the printed pages of her new story, swallowing against her parched throat. It was the first time in weeks that most of the children were quiet. As Christmas approached at the preschool, the excitement had risen to a constant, audible buzz, and Harper had soon discovered that taking care of three-year-olds wasn't always fun and games. Sometimes, it was tired temper tantrums and melted reindeer biscuits in every crevice of the room.

It was worth it for moments like this. While she was still editing her adult novel, she had adapted a simpler, child-friendly version for the playgroup after discovering they liked her often improvised tales of fairy folk and found family. In this one, all the characters were inspired by Harper's loved ones here in Belbarrow. The biggest focus, though, was self-acceptance. She hoped that if she explored this theme with the beautiful little minds that surrounded her, they might not grow up as she did, searching for validation in all the wrong places.

The children and parents clapped as she drew her reading to a close. She was certain Eiley even wiped a tear from her eye before encouraging little Saffron to clap, too.

"And there we have it," said Dot, climbing into the circle of children with a warm smile. "What a lovely story to finish with on our very last session before Christmas. I hope you all have a fab festive period. We'll be open again in the New Year — hopefully with some more stories from Miss Harper! Parents, don't forget to grab a mince pie on your way out."

Harper had already eaten two for breakfast, but she itched for more all the same. It was Christmas, after all. She planned to celebrate early with Fraser and his family tomorrow, and then would risk the mayhem of Christmas Day traffic to take him home to meet her parents. Fraser had dithered at first, worried his family would need him here — but Cam had practically packed his bags for him and told him, in no uncertain terms, to "Fuck off to Manchester."

Harper couldn't wait to see Myra open her present from Fraser. He'd decided to give her his beloved birdhouse — his very first childhood passion project. While Fraser's dad had never appreciated it, Harper knew his mum would be overjoyed to display it in her garden, sharing it with the birds as her young son had once so earnestly hoped.

But already, Harper felt anxious to return to Scotland in the New Year. Fraser wanted to focus more on his crafts, something he was able to do now her rent was a steady income, so they'd scheduled market events around Scotland, planning themselves a little road trip to breathe life back into

January. Though it felt odd to be working at her own pace for once, taking time away from her usual productivity, she was slowly settling in and letting herself be grateful. She even planned to freelance as a marketing specialist focused on small businesses on a budget, while she fixed up her novel and searched for beta readers.

She couldn't rush a bestseller, after all.

As the children and parents began to disperse, many of them wearing merry and bright Christmas jumpers, Harper joined Eiley and Sorcha by the table of "eggnog", which was actually just banana-flavoured milk for the kids. Isla jumped straight into her arms, the blue tinsel she'd used to decorate her hair tickling Harper's face. "Princess Callie is my new favourite princess," she decided matter-of-factly.

Harper squeezed her tight. "Well, I'm glad. She reminds me a lot of you."

"You did an amazing job," Eiley said. "I wish they listened to me half as intently as they do you. You have a magic touch."

Harper shrugged off the compliment, though her chest swelled. Being accepted by Fraser's family was special, but there was something about being welcomed with open arms by children that really made her feel accomplished in a way an office job never could. These tiny, little people trusted her to entertain them, to teach them love through words and stories.

"Are you all ready for your trip home?" Sorcha asked while rocking Archie from side to side.

"I am. Fraser, on the other hand..."

Eiley rolled her eyes. "I don't know how many times we have to tell him that we can manage without him."

In truth, Fraser was doing better recently. With Eiley learning to drive, Flockhart's up and running smoothly, and everybody in high spirits, he was trying harder than ever to make time for himself. To take care of his own wellbeing as well as everyone else's.

And when he didn't, Harper had many ways to take care of him on his behalf.

"His heart is too big for his own good," Harper said softly, "but I wouldn't have it any other way."

Fondness creased Eiley's cheeks. "I'm just so happy for you both."

"I'm happy for all of us," said Sorcha, bumping Eiley's hip. "It's been a tough year, but we all found our way." She blew a raspberry on Archie's face, forcing a gorgeous belly laugh and a gummy grin from him. "And with even more than we had before."

Eiley looked lovingly down at Saffron and Sky, who were enjoying their sensory play, rolling around with fabrics and toys on the mat at the adults' feet. "If I've learned anything this year, it's that even a loss can be a win." She met Harper's eye. "Except in your case. Don't you ever leave us again."

"I don't plan on it. Promise."

Sorcha let out a loud yawn as she placed Archie down in his pram. "Anyway, I need to get some Christmas shopping done before Cam kills me for leaving it so late. Anyone want to join?"

Both Harper and Eiley were quick to say yes.

Fraser slapped his hands together, then swept the sweat from his brow with the sleeve of his shirt. It felt like this piece had taken eons to come together, but finally, it resembled the fairy tale-inspired double bed he'd been striving for, from the floral motif etched into the wooden legs and frame, to the sheer chiffon canopy cascading across all four posters. The mattress had been delivered not an hour ago, so he'd rushed to remove the packaging and make sure the jade-green bedsheets matched the vision he'd had in his head.

Right on time, a knock rattled his shed door. He turned around, excitement fizzing in his belly. "Come in, sunshine."

Harper crept in as if she still believed she was forbidden, though they'd done far more than admire his work in here over the last month. Some of his figurines hadn't survived their antics – not that he was complaining.

She gasped when she saw the new bed. Fraser cleared her path as he wiped his clammy hands on a rag. She dashed straight over to it, fingering the pleats of the shimmering curtains gently. With Jack and Andy's help, he'd extended his shed for this project alone – and for others he hoped to do in the future. He wanted to make her a thousand different things, each of them with some special meaning, some memory behind it.

This one had come from—

"The bed in my book," she whispered. "It's exactly how I described it." She traced the sun and moon carved into the elm headboard.

He nodded, elated that she'd noticed so quickly. "Aye, it is, isn't it? Almost like it was intentional."

She whipped around, dewy-eyed. She'd only gained the confidence to show him her novel-in-progress a few weeks ago. He hadn't pushed her, but he'd loved diving deeper into her mind when she'd finally trusted him. Even if she couldn't look at him for several days afterwards, no doubt feeling vulnerable that somebody over the age of four was finally reading her words.

He didn't know much about literature, but it was gorgeous. Magical. Something that deserved to be on shelves – and would be. Even if it only made it onto his, he'd make sure of it.

"This isn't fair. Somebody is going to buy it. I mean, it's beautiful, and I'm proud of you and all that, but..." She pouted like a child, tracing the chiselled patterns around the head-board. "*I* want it."

"You complete and utter eejit," he remarked lovingly.

"Oi!" She glared. "Why?"

"It's already yours." And then he changed his mind. "Well, actually, it's *ours*."

She gasped again. "*No!*"

"Yes."

"You made it for me?"

"That part is obvious. For a writer, you take quite a lot of time to connect the dots."

"Stop it!" She rushed over, slapping him on the chest lightly. "Do you mean it? It's really ours?"

"It's supposed to be your Christmas present, but it wouldn't fit under the tree." He smirked, lacing his hands around her

369

back so that she was pressed against his torso. She gazed up at him, eyes round with awe as she traced the shape of his mouth.

"I only got you a new shirt," she admitted dryly.

He softened as he tilted her chin up to kiss her. "You got me much more than that, sweetheart."

She let out a content sigh, turning around in his arms to admire the bed again. "Where will it even go?"

Stroking the top of her head, he answered, "In your cabin."

"*Our* cabin," she corrected.

A scoff. "Please. It's been yours since the day you set foot in it and demanded Wi-Fi. It wasn't a home before you."

He'd even made sure to sort out the boiler as soon as she'd returned to Belbarrow, just so she wasn't tempted to leave again. Of course, she also stayed at his house plenty, but he'd seen how much she loved nestling into the cabin's small space, gazing out into the woods between furiously typed paragraphs. He loved stepping out onto the porch to spend frosty mornings together, swaddled in blankets and sipping tea, their breaths visible in the hazy air. Soaking in the quiet before the day began. He didn't want her to feel like she didn't have her own place here, too. She was his home, but he knew better than to try to be hers, at least completely. She was too wild. She deserved everything he could give her.

Her eyes fluttered shut as she folded her hands atop his. "I love you a ridiculous amount, Fraser Thomas Milligan."

"I love you, too." He placed a kiss in her hair, and then another for good measure. He'd never get tired of soaking her in like soil with rain, roots growing and growing and growing until she was all he could see, hear, think about. He traced the side of her abdomen, letting his fingers fall just close enough to her breast that she shuddered. "Do you think maybe we should test it out?"

Her eyes sparked as she turned, and already he was hardening against her. "It would be the practical thing to do, wouldn't it? We want to make sure your furniture is… sturdy."

She was falling on the bed in moments, laughter and then later moans filling the workshop as he showed her just how much he loved her. Just how sturdy he could make things as long as she was here.

This shed had once been full of shadows, things he'd thought better off hidden. She'd shown him he deserved more, casting light into all that darkness like a bonfire in a clearing.

He'd never let that blaze burn out.

Acknowledgements

Writing Harper and Fraser's electric love story has been a pleasure I couldn't have dreamed of this time last year. Being chronically ill and neurodivergent means my world can often feel very small; writing is the thing that keeps me tethered to the life around me, and I will never take it for granted. Whether you helped me tell the story, published it, supported me along the way, or you're just here to read it, thank you for helping my world grow a little bit bigger.

As always, I would like to thank the wonderful Clare Coombes at Liverpool Literary Agency, who has supported me not just as an agent, but also as a friend. I'm so glad this book meant we could meet in person for the first time. I'm in constant awe of your work, and so glad northern authors have a champion like you behind us.

This book wouldn't exist without the talented Daisy Watt. Thank you for trusting me to write something coherent, and for editing it when it was *in*coherent! Also to the rest of the team at HarperNorth, who made me feel right at home. You are the most enthusiastic, hard-working group I've ever worked with, and your passion and excitement for this book means the world!

To my best friends, Ivy and Leah, who keep me sane when the imposter syndrome kicks in: I'm so grateful to have you as my safe place the way Harper has Belbarrow. You will forever be my first readers. I write for you before anyone else. To Mill, who was as excited as I was – especially about the spicy scenes – thank you for always being there to celebrate the little and big things.

To the Swords & Sapphics Discord, for letting me bounce ideas and worries off you, and for being the kind community I always dreamed of building – Merlina, Ames, Lillian, Nikki (who provided advice re: Scottish slang), and many more. To author and reader friends who have supported me from being a little-known indie author to now: Rebecca Crunden, AKA Indie Book Spotlight; Jane, who is too supportive for words; Hayley Anderton, a generous and bright light in the indie community; and Bethany, AKA beths_bookblog, for the same reason. To Abbie, for sharing my books with anyone who will listen, including your students (though probably not this one!) Authors couldn't exist without support like yours, and I appreciate you endlessly.

To my family – no, you are still not allowed to read this book – and to Enzo the dog, who is thankfully not as mischievous as Bernard but who sat on my feet, snoring, while I wrote most of the story.

Finally, I would like to thank my readers, not just of this book, but the ones that came before, especially *Honeymoon for One*. It was my dream to have my words highlighted, copied, read, felt, and you made it a reality. It never gets any less magical. To queer readers, plus-size readers, and/or northern readers; readers who struggle or readers who feel alone; readers who have ever seen themselves in my characters: you deserve your happily ever after, too, and my books are here to remind you of that.

For more unmissable reads,
sign up to the HarperNorth newsletter at
www.harpernorth.co.uk

or find us on Twitter at
@HarperNorthUK

Harper
North